"PLEASE, SUH, DON' HURT ME...."

"Cap'n, I don' know *how* to pleasure a man!"

He reached out, under the water, and put a hand around her waist to draw her closer. Sheba flinched at his touch, but she was as afraid to defy a white man as she was of what she knew was coming.

"Please, Suh, don' hurt me!"

He soothed her with soft words devoid of meaning as he picked her up and started wading toward the shallows.

"Please, Cap'n. I'll do anythin' you say, but please don' hurt me!"

"I won't make you do this if you don't want to. . . ." And then he grinned and forced her knees apart. . . .

D1136100

CHAINS

JUSTIN ADAMS

A DELL BOOK

Published by
Dell Publishing Co., Inc.
1 Dag Hammarskjold Plaza
New York, New York 10017

Dell ® TM 681510, Dell Publishing Co., Inc.

ISBN: 0-440-13993-7

Printed in the United States of America

First printing—November 1977

BOOK ONE

THE
BUILDING
OF
INDIGO HALL

ONE

On a raw, wet, September afternoon in 1746 two slave ships were sheltering in the broad estuary of the Savannah River. Both vessels flew the red ensign of the British merchant marine. One was the brig *Prudence*, two hundred eighteen days out of Boston under Captain Caleb Lodge, Master. In her hold, the *Prudence* carried just over a hundred West African tribesmen taken in battle by His Majesty, the King of Dahomey.

The other slaver was the lugger *Thistlegorm*, thirty-four days out of Glasgow under Tackman Ian MacGregor Campbell, Master and Owner. In the *Thistlegorm*'s hold lay two score of West Highland tribesmen taken in battle by His Highness, the Duke of Cumberland.

The two slavers lay at hailing distance with gunports open and lookouts aloft. This was not prompted by mutual distrust. The infant Colony of Georgia lay in a disputed buffer zone between Spanish Florida to the south and the flourishing, older British colonies to the north. There was supposed to be an English garrison a few miles upstream, but no pilot boat had made an appearance, and who could say when some cutthroat Spanish privateer might slip up between the Sea Islands to pounce on honest British merchantmen?

As the sky began to darken with never a sign of life from the low, brushcovered riverbanks upstream, the master of the *Thistlegorm* had himself rowed over in his gig to the larger vessel.

The New Englanders lining the lee rail of the *Prudence* watched and listened with undisguised amusement as the Scottish master's boat approached. As tackman to his laird—His Grace, the Duke of Argyll—Ian Campbell rated his own piper; and piper he had, playing "Gang Wary Loch Lomond" as his gillies rowed him across the pewter water. The laughter died as the gig approached, for the tall red-faced man scowling up at them from the bow of his tiny gig was armed to the teeth, and the recent troubles north of the English border had given all Scotsmen a renewed reputation for truculence.

Caleb Lodge met his guest at the ladder's head and held out a hand to help him aboard, but the big redhead ignored the offer and leaped over the rail with a swish of kilt and a clatter of cutlery. He stared for a long moment at the leaner, shorter captain, then smiled thinly and said, "I approve a man who wears his own hair. I powder my own when attending on Himself at Inveraray, but, och, it's a fool I feel, aping the English and their Frenchy ways."

He patted the hilt of his basket-hilted broadsword with one hand, gripped the hilt of his murderous-looking Highland dirk with the other, and added, "Amongst my own, I dress in the proper auld way."

The Bostonian waited until his visitor had finished delivering his opinion, nodded at his nearby bos'n, who put a whistle to his lips and gave the captain's boarding call. Campbell nodded and said, "It's good to know I've fallen amongst gentlemen, then. Now, on *my* ship, it's the custom to break out the Creature when friends are piped aboard!"

Captain Lodge permitted himself a frosty smile and said, "If you'll follow me to my quarters, you'll find it tolerable dry, and I do mind we've a few bottles of Madeira left."

Campbell frowned, went back to the rail, and yelled down to his boat crew in Gaelic. One of them tossed up a silver-trimmed black leather bottle, and, as he caught it with a sweep of his massive arm, the Scotsman turned back to his host with a grin and explained, "It's a cruel wet day for wine, ye ken, but dinna frush ye. I'll just sip at me wee blackjack whilst we visit."

"At least the cabin's dry." The New Englander shrugged and led his guest aft. On the way to the cabins under the quarterdeck, they passed an open hatch and Campbell grimaced, noting, "I see ye've had a few dee on ye."

Caleb Lodge shrugged again and explained, "We had a bad middle passage. We threw them over the side as fast as we discovered a litch down there, but the contrary niggers hid a few until they started to stink."

His voice was self-righteous as he added, "Lord knows I try to run a taut ship, but those damned Ibos—they're just as wrong-headed as a dog that's been at the sheep. You can't do anything with Ibo once they take a notion in their stubborn heads!"

Campbell nodded. "I've a few lads like that aboard yon *Thistlegorm*. These Ibos of yours—would they be some African clan?"

By this time they had reached the cabin bulkhead. Lodge opened the sliding hatch as he explained, "I've Ibo, Fan, Mandingo, and Ashanti this voyage. Picked them up at a bargain, I thought, until the rations began to run low in the middle passage. Those damned Portugee I bought this gaggle off of said they'd all been salted, but I lost damn near a third of 'em on the way—after paying good Liverpool trade goods for every man Jack of 'em! And those Ibos! Had it been up to me, I'd have thrown every Ibo to the sharks, along with the dead."

He ushered his guest into a small, tidy cabin, waved him to a seat on the folded-down bunk, and muttered, "Next voyage, I'll know better," as he took his own seat on an upturned powder keg.

Tackman Campbell uncorked his blackjack, held it out to his host, and, when the New Englander declined, took a healthy swig of malt liquor. He lowered the bottle with a sigh and said, "Och, it's few can abide our Scots whiskey, but that leaves all the more for our ainsel's, ye ken. The reason I wanted this talk wi' ye, Captain Lodge, is to study our next move on this rum coast. I dinna like the looks of my falling glass, and the way these waters are charted by some blind Sassunach in yon Admiralty—"

"I am not exactly a stranger to American waters, Captain Campbell," said Lodge dryly, adding, "Winds from nor'east—three days at least. The prevailing southerlies won't pick up again for at least three days, and that's being optimistic. I have seen a nor'easter lay on this coast for a week."

"Och, I canna waste so much time! I've gaol fever aboard yon *Thistlegorm,* and dinna I unship some of yon Jacobite lads, I'll haul into Charleston Roads with muckle a cargo of litches!"

"It's the crowding breeds gaol fever," Lodge agreed. "How many of those damned Scotch rebels do you have over there, anyway?"

Campbell frowned and said, "Bite yer tongue, Sassunach! I'll not have yon prisoners referred to as *Scots,* Goddamn yer eyes!"

Lodge blinked in surprise. "What have I said to offend you? You *are* transporting Scotsmen captured in the Rebellion of '45, aren't you?"

"Ay, but I'll noo have it that *Scotland* rose against the Hoose of Hanover, damn it!" He patted the dark green kilt above his rawboned red knee as he insisted, "I'm a Scot and a Highlander and proud of it. Ay, and I fought at Culloden Moor, as did many another brave Highland lad. Your English wouldna *won*, had noo Clan Campbell hit the Jacobites on the flank and turned 'em!"

He took another swig of whiskey, gasped, and raised his voice to roar, "The Chisholms breached the redcoats' line. Lochiel was doon, but the Sons of the Hound kept coming, ay, and the Children of the Cat, led by their ain bra' *Bantigherna*, Lady Mackintosh! The Frasers fought well, as did muckle a lad in the red tartans of the Catholic Clans. The Laird of the Islands was coming to Charlie's aid, with a regiment of Clan Donald, and, had noo it been for Argyll— Och, ye should ha' *seen* us, mon! Over a stain dyke and into their flank we charged, wi' pipes skirling and the black plaids flying and Colin the Red Fox shouting, 'Loch Lomond and King Georgie forever!'"

Caleb Lodge made a wry face, reached into a sea chest for a flask, and uncorked it while he tried to think of a polite way to change the subject. As a Whig, Lodge, like Campbell, supported the House of Hanover. The crushing of the recent uprisings in the north of England, however, seemed needlessly theatrical, and his guest belonged in some Italian opera with his garish costume, bellowing voice, and clanging weaponry. Lodge glanced down at the deck between them as he finished a polite sip of Madeira and discovered—good Lord—the big ruffian had *another* dagger tucked in his gartered stocking!

As if enchanted with his own oratory, Campbell was saying, "A thousand of them we left there, stark in the trampled heather wi' the rain to fall on them and the corgie crows to pick the eyes from their pale white faces. Och, ye say a thousand and it's noo that much, but had ye *been* there, mon—"

"You sound as if you feel sorry for the rebels, Captain."

"Och, little pity have we shown them. As little pity as *they'd* ha' shown, had that wee fool Charlie Darling won. But I'll noo be called a captain. It's a *tackman* I am. Sent over the water with yon captives to raise money for Himself, the Duke of Argyll."

Relieved to be on more familiar ground, Caleb Lodge smiled and said, "You'll want to deliver them in Charleston, then. The going price on a slave these days is nearly thirty guineas. Those Carolina rice planters can't harvest all that cheap swampland up there with the hands they've already bought."

"Ay, they told me as much in Glasgow. I've been wondering, though, about *this* colony. Yon port of Savannah's only a wee sweep upstream."

Lodge pursed his lips and said, "Georgia? Forget it! Didn't they tell you about Praying Jamie Oglethorpe, the royal governor here?"

"Och, would that be the same James Oglethorpe wha' led a regiment at Culloden Moor?"

"I think he did fight for the king, back in the old country. Do you know him?"

"Och, only to bow to, passin' by. I saw him riding in the van wi' the Duke of Cumberland one time. Cumberland's a wee fat thing wi' a nasty curl to his lip, for a' that he's a bonny fighter and the king's ain son. Colonel Oglethorpe was taller and older. His men took off their hats and cheered as Himself and the duke rode by. The duke knew it was noo for him they cheered, and his lip curled all the more. I ken noo more than that about Jamie Oglethorpe."

"He started this colony in '33," said Caleb Lodge, adding, "They say he'd served as a soldier for a time before running for Parliament. I don't know what sort of soldier he was, but he was a calf-eyed mealymouth as an M.P. Why, do you know he went up on some hill with the Indians, after England took this land from the Dons, and paid out good money for this swamp you see around us?"

"He treated with yon Indians? As if they were Christians?"

"That's not the half of it! He'd been on some committee, investigating the debtors' prisons in the old country, see? So once he'd pushed the Spanish south, got a royal grant, and then made a treaty with the damned Indians, what in tarnation do you s'pose he done?"

"He went back to England to fight the Jacobites?"

"Nope. That come after. What the fool did on *this* side of the water was to bring a hundred-odd debtors out of the gaol, after paying off their just debts, and setting them free. Then, as if that wasn't enough, the damned fool laid out a town, all square and Frenchified like Penn's Philadelphia, and then, you'll never believe it, he *gave land* to those worthless paupers! Georgia's not a colony, as we understand the word in Boston and the *other* colonies. Georgia is some sort of hare-brained scheme dreamed up by Oglethorpe and his circle of Utopian fops. England is losing at least a thousand pounds a year on the scheme. Praying Jamie has his misfits trying to grow silkworms, wine grapes, olives, and other fool crops anyone in the Carolinas could tell him won't grow in this climate. Meanwhile the Wesley Brothers have come over to start one of their damned Methodist churches, and another evangelist crackpot named George Whitefield is trying to build an orphan asylum and a hospital!"

Campbell shrugged. "It seems to me, then, they could use some bra' strong lads upstream, to help them build yon U— What did ye call that toon?"

"Utopia. It's a notion some rich fools with nothing better to do got from reading Thomas More. You know, of course, that Thomas More was a *Papist!*" Lodge sniffed and added, "It wouldn't surprise me a bit to learn Praying Jamie Oglethorpe's a secret Catholic!"

"Och, fair is fair, mon. He fought the Papist clans at Culloden!"

"Well, he's still got Papist notions. They say he runs Georgia like a military camp. When his settlers aren't trying to grow silkworms and such, he's got them drilling as a trained band of militia."

"Ay, but getting back to serious matters, ye'll ken we must unship some of our slaves, even at a wee loss. It wouldna hurt to take on vittles and water, or, for aw that, a wee butt of rum!"

Lodge shook his head. "You'll get no rum in Georgia. The laws of the praying governor forbid strong drink."

"Och, well, I'll just sell them a few troublemakers and—"

"You haven't been listening, damn it! Oglethorpe's against strong drink, absentee landholding, *and* chattel slavery."

The big Scot stared blankly as the other's words sank in. Then he laughed and said, "No slavery? The mon *must* be daft! Our whole civilization was built on slavery. Didna Solomon and Davie keep slaves in the Good Book?"

"Ayep, but try telling that to Praying Jamie. He says he's bound and determined to build a Utopian society on the North American continent with free labor and Christian charity, or, in other words, he's out to lift himself and his flock to heaven by the boot straps!"

Campbell took another swig of whiskey, wiped his mouth, and said, "It canna be doon. No mon's ever been willing to work as hard for his ainsel' as he has for a bra' laird! Yon fools in yon wee toon upstream will starve—if the red Indians don't slaughter them first!"

"I agree, but in the meantime there's nothing we can do but wait out this storm and beat our way up the coast to civilization."

The other slaver nodded and rose to return to his own vessel, saying, "A'weel, I'll sell Argyll's captives in Charleston, then."

Caleb Lodge was of the same mind, and, in truth, it should have worked out that way, but despite the dreams and the more pragmatic plans of Georgia's royal governor, a fateful change was in the air.

James Oglethorpe's friends in Parliament still backed him to the tune of eight thousand pounds a year. He enjoyed the tolerance if not the enthusiasm of the German-speaking king, George II. Chief Toma-Chi-Chi of the Muskogee nation still smiled on his White-Brother-Who-Spoke-Straight. Most of the resettled English debtors, German Lutheran refugees, imported Swiss and Italian artisans, and the desperately grateful Sephardic Jews whom Oglethorpe had rescued from a Portuguese pogrom were as anxious as their governor to make the experiment succeed. But, though neither of the slavers knew it as they waited out the nor'easter, intent on weighing anchor for the Carolinas at the first opportunity, things had been happening ten miles up the river.

After fruitless experiments with exotic crops, a few of Oglethorpe's yeoman farmers had planted crops more suited to the Georgia tidewater. Corn, tobacco, and indigo had sprung up like weeds on freshly cleared virgin soil. Other settlers had discovered that rice grew lushly in hitherto worthless wetlands near the river. The warehouses of tiny Savannah were bursting with cash crops, but twice that amount stood unharvested in the fields for lack of unskilled labor. Other rich farmlands were there for the taking, waiting only to be cleared or drained. The few hundred Georgia settlers were working themselves into the ground in the subtropical heat, yet somehow there was always more to be done, and if Georgia was to grow even another square mile, they would need help. All the help they could get.

There was another, more serious problem. Governor

Oglethorpe was not at his post that autumn as the bumper crops rotted, standing in the fields. He'd been called back to England to face a military court martial—charged, by the jealous young Duke of Cumberland, with laxity in following up on their victory at Culloden Moor. Oglethorpe, in the end, would be acquitted of the ridiculous accusation that his merciful treatment of captured Highlanders had been occasioned by secret Jacobite leanings, but meanwhile he'd been forced to appoint trusted friends to govern Georgia in his absence.

James Edward Oglethorpe was about to go down in history as a good Christian gentleman who trusted, perhaps, a bit too freely.

"There's no question about the Negroes," the rather dandy young man said as he stood on the deck of *Thistlegorm* with Tackman Campbell. The Englishman had come downstream from Savannah with the dawn, paddled by two Indians in a big dugout canoe and wearing a silly white wig under his lace-trimmed tricorn hat. The wig and everything else the young man wore had been soaked in the rain, and Campbell thought he smelled like a wet perfumed sheep. He'd said he was the harbormaster's clerk, and so the burly Scot had tried not to laugh at him when, with a horrified sniff, he'd refused the offer of a drink.

Tackman Campbell repeated his question about the prisoners in the reeking hold below, and the clerk insisted, "Governor Oglethorpe was quite clear about Negro slaves. That other ship I visited is welcome to take on food and water, but we simply can't allow Captain Lodge to unload those African slaves."

Campbell spit over the rail and said, "Yon *Prudence* is noo a ship, she's a brig, and my lads below are noo African slaves—they're a' Scotsmen. Once ye give 'em a wash, they'll be as white as yer ainsel'."

"Yes, but they're still slaves, aren't they? I mean, the governor was most specific on that point."

Campbell shot the younger man a shrewd look and said, "A'weel, there's points and then there's points, if ye take me meaning, lad."

"I'm not quite sure I follow you, Captain."

Campbell ignored the chance to correct a Sassunach and contented himself with, "The sticking point is the word *slave*, ye ken. Ye've agreed the lads I ha' to sell are *white*, so let's see wha' we can do wi' that one wicked word. I mean, ye *do* ha' indentured men up in yon bonny settlement, do ye nicht?"

"Oh, you mean those chaps who signed a labor contract to pay for their passage across the sea? Some of the Italian glassblowers sent home for relatives and, yes, I do seem to recall that they agreed to work out their passage money that way. I think some Irish and French Huguenots came over as indentured servants, too."

"Och, then what's frushin' ye, lad? I'll just be selling ye the indentures for some likely lads wi' a taste for adventure in the New World and—"

"Are you certain that would be legal, Captain? I mean, it was my understanding that those men down there were transported convicts, to be sold on the block as chattel, uh, laborers."

"Och, have ye noo heard of the apprentice system, lad?"

"Of course—I was apprenticed as a clerk myself. I was fourteen at the time and—"

"Och, there ye are, then! What if I was to apprentice some of my lads to them as needs a bra' strong working mon?"

"I'm not sure. According to law, an apprentice should be signed on under his own free will—or the free will of his legal guardian, at any rate."

"A'weel, there ye are then. These rebel lads has been given into my hands by His Grace, the Duke of Argyll. Doesna that make myself their legal guardian?"

He saw the hesitation in the other's face and pressed on. "I'll tell ye the truth, lad. I'm crowded doon below and I'll let ye have 'em cheap. Twenty poonds apiece, wi' seven years' indenture on e'ry one I sell ye."

The harbormaster's clerk grimaced and said, "I wish you wouldn't say *sell* them, Captain. You can sell a man's indenture, you can sell the papers of an apprentice with time left on his contract, but to sell a *man*, you have to put it down as chattel slavery, and in this colony, the law distinctly states that—"

"Foosh! Away wi' yer Frenchified English law! Gae back and talk wi' yer betters. Then let me know wha' they decide. Mind ye come back soon, though, for I'm off for the Carolinas as soon as yon wind should shift."

The clerk nodded and said he'd carry Campbell's message to the Board of Proprietors up the river. He started for the rail, then turned with a malicious little smile to ask, "Speaking of English law, Captain Campbell, are you aware of the Disarmament Act just passed by Parliament?"

"Och, of course I am. The act doesna apply to Clan Campbell."

"I'm afraid it does, you know. Highland dress has been forbidden anywhere in the British Empire. I fear those kilts and bonnet could see you into gaol if some Frenchified English lawyer wished to take it to law."

Ian Campbell placed a casual palm on the steel grip of the Highland pistol tucked in his sword belt and asked, in a dangerously polite tone, "Do ye ken such a mon, lad?"

The Englishman laughed, shook his head, and climbed over the rail to the bobbing dugout moored alongside.

Campbell waited until the clerk was out of range before he shrugged, called to his bos'n in Gaelic, and, free once more of the hated Doric English that twisted so in a man's mouth, said, "I do think the Strangers will be ridding us of some of our troubles, though I doubt we'll be treated fairly here."

The bos'n asked, in the same language, "Are not we selling them in the Carolinas, then, Ian Roy?"

Campbell started for his cabin, explaining, "Most of them will be sold on the Charleston quay, but I'd as soon be rid of the sick and the troublemakers. What call you that wild young Lochaber man with the straw-colored hair and dangerous eyes?"

"That would be Rory MacMartin from the Great Glen, Ian Roy. He's the ringleader of those wild young whelps who tried to break out of Sterling Gaol."

"I remember him now. He's one of the Sons of the Hound. His friends are that damned MacMillan, that small, dark MacPhie, and—what's his name?—from Clan Chattan."

"MacQueen. Angus Mohr MacQueen. He has the English and it's said they issued him a musket, too. It's passing strange to see an upper-class Child of the Cat consorting with barefoot gillies of the Hound, but they do say war has a way of leveling men."

"I'll have MacMartin and the others up on deck. Make certain you pour a bucket or two of seawater over them before you bring them into my cabin. War has a way of making men stink, too."

The bos'n laughed. "Do you want us to strike their chains, Ian Roy?"

"Are you mad, man? I'll want them chained and with a musket trained on each and every one until we're rid of them! You'd best bring up that MacUlrich and the young MacGillonie while you're about it. The two of them are clansmen of MacMartin, and I'm wary of the Sons of the Hound."

The bos'n tugged his forelock and said, "I'll see to it, then." But the tackman called him back and snapped, "What do you mean by that Saxon salute, Cullen Mac-Dermid?"

The bos'n looked abashed and stammered, "You know I served on a royal ship of the line, Ian Roy."

"Well, and this is the lugger of a clansman, unless you've lied about your name. I'll have none of that two-faced Saxon bowing and scraping from a man of my clan or any bearing a sept-name of it. Do you understand me, Cullen MacDermid of the Strangers' ways?"

The bos'n grinned, clasped a hand to his dirk as a freeborn man should, and went to get the prisoners.

Ian Campbell continued on to his cabin, where he rummaged about in a sea chest for some paper, a quill, and an ink horn. He closed the chest and upended it near his narrow bunk, spreading the writing materials out on it. The quill was blunted, so he drew the *sgian dubh* from his stocking and started to sharpen the quill, grimacing in distaste as he thought about the legalistic young stranger who had come aboard to tell a man it was forbidden by law to wear the clothes of a human being.

"You try your Strangers' laws on Clan Campbell," he muttered to himself, "and you'll see a rising that will make the '15 and the '45 *together* look like one of your Saxon tea parties!"

He started writing, forcing his Gaelic mind to form the proper Saxon words. Their language was even harder to spell than it was to pronounce. The first indenture form was difficult, but, after that, he merely had to copy. His mind tended to wander from the text as his stubby fingers wrote the English words, and he wondered, once again, if his chief, the Duke of Argyll, had made the right choice in siding with German Georgie against Prince Charles.

"It was Hanover or Stuart!" he told himself for perhaps

the hundredth time. "The Stuarts have been worthless since
Contrary Mary started the feud by blowing her husband up
in his own bed and running off to live in sin with the mad
Bothwell. That fool, Prince Charlie, was no better than the
others, with his Italian mother and French Catholic ways."

But what was this about German Georgie wanting to
turn the Children of the Mist into Saxons in wigs and
breeches? Surely Argyll had fought to preserve his people
in their ancient ways? Surely the Saxons would be grateful
to the Highlanders who had fought at their sides against the
Young Pretender? . . .

Out on deck, Rory MacMartin blinked in the compara-
tive glare of a gray overcast morning; he'd been in the fetid
darkness of the hold so long that his eyes had grown accustomed to it—though, in truth, there was little worth
seeing in the hold of any slave ship.

One of the crewmen sloshed seawater over his head and
his naked shoulders and MacMartin snarled like an animal,
fighting the chains that bound his manacled hands to the
leg irons around his raw ankles. The crewman flinched,
startled by the blazing hatred in the captive's wide-set hazel
eyes. Then he laughed and sloshed more water over the
nearly naked youth, saying, in Gaelic, "You've no Lochaber axe in your hands, now, gillie, and you'll only reopen
your scabs if you fight those chains."

The captive shrugged in silence as another crew member
murmured, "Will everyone here look at the shoulders on
this one! Was it your mother or your father as was the ox,
gillie?"

"If you're speaking to your betters," said Rory MacMartin dryly, "I am called Rory of the Broad Axe, and it's no
gillie I was, but a free crofter under the Gentle Lochiel!"

The crewman with the bucket sloshed him again and
jeered, "For a beardless child who smells so bad, you do
take on airs, don't you?"

Rory ignored the thrust. He had no need to put on airs;
he knew his genealogy all the way back to the Norman
knight named Martin and a remote ancestor who'd fought
the Danish Vikings under Somerled of the Islands. There
were other great kinsmen he could have mentioned—in
friendlier surroundings—but for now there was little a man
could do but take their insults as he waited for a chance to
get his hands on a bit of steel.

Little Gavin MacPhie was being subjected to the same rough cleaning nearby; as always, MacPhie was silent, his dark feline face a perfect blank. Nicol MacMillan was somewhere behind them, his chains clanking as he fought them in sullen silence. Rory had warned him to let the festering chain sores heal, but MacMillan had been driven mad by the indignities they'd suffered, and there was little use in talking to him now.

The bos'n, MacDermid, came over to say, "That's enough of the water. The tackman wants the six of them to sign some papers in his cabin."

"I'll sign no papers," Rory said flatly, not adding that he didn't know how to read or write in any language.

MacDermid drew a pistol, hefted it thoughtfully, and said, "You'll do as you're told. The tackman will see you first, MacMartin."

Rory stared unblinkingly into the gun barrel as he thought about that. Behind him, someone whispered, "We're with you, Axeman!"

That would be young MacUlrich, Rory thought, deciding, with regret, that the time had not yet arrived. He turned in his chains to face his followers, smiling thinly as he murmured, "We'll wait a bit before we feed the Hound."

A tall hatchet-faced prisoner in tattered shreds of Highland finery said soberly, "Don't forget the Cat!" and Rory laughed.

"I'll save you a bite, Angus Mohr, but first I'd best see what the False Argyll's gillie wants of us."

A cable length away, aboard the *Prudence*, Captain Lodge was just finishing his own sheaf of apprentice contracts as the mate came in with a tall tribesman. The mate said, "This one speaks a bit of English, Cap'n. I still don't see what you want him for, though. They've told us we can't land any niggers here in Georgia."

Caleb Lodge looked up frostily and replied, "They said we can't land *slaves*."

"Slaves or niggers, sir."

"We'll see about that. Meanwhile, it only takes a few minutes to write up the proper forms." He let his eyes drift over the sullen eyes and tribal scars of the chained man before he asked, "What's your name, boy?"

The slave didn't answer.

The mate nudged him and said, "Don't pull that dumb

nigger story on us, boy. I heard you asking the bos'n for water that time."

The slave shrugged and said, "I am called Kofi. My father sat on a stool and I led a regiment against Dahomey."

Lodge wrote "Coffee" on the paper in front of him and said, "You *lost*, too. What do those scars mean? They're not regular Ibo scars."

"I am not an Ibo. My people are Ashanti, and my father sat on a stool."

The slaver frowned up at Kofi. "Ashanti, you say? How come you've been so thick with those damned Ibo troublemakers since you came aboard? I thought you Ashantis and Ibos hated each other's guts."

Kofi's face was passive as he replied, "In Africa, we do."

"Are you funning me, boy?"

"You asked a question. I have answered it. Your friend here asked me if I was a dumb nigger. I did not know I was a nigger until the Slattee raiders marched us to the sea and sold us to you. If I was truly stupid, the Ibos I have been chained among would still be my enemies."

"I see. You and the others made up during the middle passage. Is that it?"

"That is it. All of us have new enemies now."

Caleb Lodge frowned as the mate said, "I told you he was one of the troublemakers, Cap'n. I don't know where he learned English, but he's purely got a sassy mouth."

Kofi said, "Before the war with Dahomey, my father traded with the English and Portuguese. I can read and write English, too."

"Goddamnit!" snapped Lodge. "Nobody asked you how you learned it. You'd best learn to keep a civil tongue in your woolly head, and that's a fact!"

He suddenly brightened, held out his quill to the slave, and said, "Here, if you're so damned smart, let's see you sign your name to this paper."

The Ashanti picked up the form and started to read it. The mate gasped, "Well, of all the sassy black bastards!" but the captain silenced him with a glance. He knew what he'd written and, if this arrogant slave was really a natural leader, it might not hurt to let him have his head a bit. Caleb Lodge was a man who rode a horse with a gentle hand on the reins, and the big buck was worth more if he could be sold intact.

Kofi frowned as he went over the contract, not quite understanding its seemingly generous terms. Then he asked, "Is this part true, about freedom after seven years of good behavior?"

"It's a standard apprentice contract, Coffee. It's the same as the one young white men sign to learn a trade."

"And, after I learn this trade, will I be allowed to go back to my homeland?"

"If you want to. But there's lots of opportunity in this new world for a smart young fellow like yourself."

Kofi hesitated as he thought of what it would be like to be back with his people. The people he'd thought never to see again in this life. Seven years was not that long. He already knew the language of these strange people and, though their smell and fishbelly skins revolted him, there were things one could learn from the English.

He remembered the trade guns of the King of Dahomey with bitterness, and his eyes narrowed thoughtfully as he considered returning to his confederation with the white man's secret of making them. Like most West African nations, the Ashanti were skilled iron workers. If he were to return to the Court of the Golden Stool with plans for the muskets and pistols in the English pattern . . .

"I'll sign," said Kofi, reaching for the pen in Lodge's hand.

The slaver grinned as he watched the Ashanti write his name in block letters on the apprentice contract. Kofi was smiling too. It seemed a small price to pay for a certain chance to return in triumph to the green hills of Kumasi. His father, Karikari, was already a subchief of the Ashanti Confederacy. With the white man's secret recipe for making guns, there was no way of telling how far his clan might rise among the stooled ones.

Caleb Lodge took the pen back and beamed approvingly at the tall man he supposed to be his pupil. Then he asked, "Could you get some of those Ibo you're so friendly with to sign these other papers, son?"

"Would I be able to promise them their freedom in seven years too?"

"Why, of course you would, son. That's what the contracts all say, don't they?"

"Yes, but I do not understand this business of the writing of names. In my country, when a man is made a slave, he remains a slave until he escapes, or until his master frees him."

"Well, you just get those other boys to sign and let us worry about the law. English law can be a mite tricky, even for an Englishman."

The Ashanti held out his manacled hands and said, "Since I have given my word to serve you willingly, I would like to have these chains taken from me."

The mate snorted, but Caleb Lodge studied his captive for a time before he said quietly, "You want those chains off, boy, you'll have to ask the right way."

"What way is that?"

"Well, you start by calling me Master. You call all white men Master unless one of us tells you different."

Kofi stared down at the smaller white man, trying to control his revulsion, forcing himself not to remind him that he, Kofi, was a regimental commander of the Ashanti Confederacy. Then he licked his lips and softly asked, "May I have these chains off, Master?"

"Why, sure, boy. You just go back out on deck and talk to those Ibo for me like I told you to. Then, directly they've all agreed to sign these contracts, we'll just set you apart from the others and strike your shackles."

He pointed at the door with his chin and told the mate to let Kofi out on deck. The mate went with him to pass along to the bos'n the skipper's strange new orders. When he returned to the cabin he said, "I suspicion we're taking a chance on them niggers, Cap'n. Have you forgotten Coffee is the ringleader of the meanest bucks we have aboard?"

"I haven't forgotten. I just want to get rid of them at any profit I can make, damn those Portugee."

"But Cap'n, do you strike their chains, with the passle of 'em up on deck—"

"I know, but how in tarnation do we sell them to the settlers as *apprentices* if they're in *chains,* damnit?" He held up the contract Kofi had signed. "Those pettifogging Utopians are going to raise a fuss about 'em being niggers, even if we call 'em apprentice farm hands. We'll just have to take a chance on old Coffee and his friends."

"What if they make a break for it?"

"Where in tarnation can they break to? Besides, I don't 'spect they will. I'll allow old Coffee's too smart to chance a ball between the shoulder blades when all he has to do is mind his manners and, in a little while, walk off in one piece."

"You reckon them lawyer-loving settlers will really take them rascals off our hands in spite of their governor?"

"Ayep. They'll hem and haw a mite first. But you know how lawyers are for twisting words until they fit the way folks want them to. I'm offering them a good buy on a dozen husky niggers and, like it or not, they know it."

"Well, maybe the fancy paperwork will get us 'round these fool Georgia laws, Cap'n. But ain't it likely to make trouble, later on?"

"What sort of trouble? We'll be long gone before Praying Jamie gets back."

"I'm not talking about *us*, Cap'n. I was thinking about what them settlers can do about them contracts, once they expire."

"Well, don't fret about 'em. They don't expire for seven years."

"I know, but Cap'n, you know blame well them lawyers ain't about to turn loose thirty guineas' worth of nigger just because the terms of some contract runs out!"

Caleb Lodge shrugged. "That's *their* problem. Likely they'll work something out when the time comes."

TWO

It took them nearly three days to work the problem out, for the men James Oglethorpe had left in charge were cautious twisters of the Common Law and more than a little frightened at their own audacity.

The first meeting of the Proprietors dismissed the notion out of hand. A rice planter named Scruggs pointed out that Oglethorpe would probably be convicted back in England at the court martial demanded by the Duke of Cumberland, and the meeting ended in a prayer for his safe return.

The second session reconsidered the governor's chances at the court martial and, when someone pointed out that the duke was the younger son of George II, another member made a motion that they at least read the suggested contracts. This led to a few hours of nit-picking as those members who had read for law decided the slavers' efforts were not only poorly drafted, but transparently fraudulent.

Planter Scruggs suggested that the legal committee might reword the terms of the labor contracts to make them legally binding while protecting the rights of all concerned. Everyone agreed that the Highlanders and the Negroes had certain rights. A colony that offered refuge to Jews and Salzburgers, and treated with the Muskogee and Cherokee nations as equal members of the human race, had certain standards to uphold.

A new contract was cautiously drafted, providing for the new colonists (as they were to be called) to pay for their passage and room and board, with seven years of indentured labor to those planters, artisans, or mechanics who might purchase their contracts and their just debts to the owners of the *Thistlegorm* and the *Prudence*. The Highlanders were to be granted religious liberty, with Sabbaths and certain Papist feast days set aside for them to pray on. The Africans, of course, would be expected to observe the Christian holidays and abstain from heathen rites; they would of course be converted to more conventional religious expression. A member named Margolis raised the question of possible African Judaism and was ruled out of order. It was well known that Africans filed their teeth, prayed to abominable idols, and ate people unless closely watched. Their apprenticeships under decent, God-fearing masters would doubtless improve and instruct them a great deal.

The first rough drafts were amended, rewritten, and amended again until everyone was confused, bored, and satisfied that legality had been observed. By the time the Proprietors were satisfied, the storm had lifted and both slavers expressed a willingness to forget the whole thing. A series of visits back and forth ensued as the final terms were worked out. In the end, both sides agreed that the landing of a dozen indentured servants, six from each vessel, would be allowed as an experiment in what was, after all, an experimental colony.

By this time, everyone in Savannah knew of the scheme, but the captive tribesmen, white and black, were unloaded discreetly and each man sent alone to the colonist who'd bought his contract.

Kofi, the Ashanti, was sent, unchained, to a Sephardic Jewish planter named Pardus, who seemed both surprised and delighted to learn that his new helper spoke English better than anyone in the family and had never, to his knowledge, partaken of human flesh. Kofi, in turn, was pleasantly surprised at the luxury of his quarters in the original log hut the Pardus family had occupied while they'd built the larger cabin they now lived in. It was connected to the original by a common wall of mud-chinked logs.

The Pardus family consisted of Isaac, Kofi's short, dark master; Rebecca, his plump wife; and two children named Aaron and Sarah. After some discussion, it was decided that Coffee, as they insisted on calling him, would eat with the family in the modest kitchen. Kofi was amused at being made to wear a skullcap to his first meal in America, but the food, while strange, was delicious. After the watery beans and rice of the middle passage, it was all Kofi could do to keep from bolting his food like a half-starved animal. Rebecca Pardus complimented him on his table manners after she had noted the way he imitated the children. The children, in turn, were enchanted with the exotic servant Papa had brought home to them. When it developed that neither Kofi nor his Sephardic employers felt any great

love for Portugal, the big Ashanti decided it was all right if
they called him Coffee, after all.

Later, Isaac showed him around the modest farm and
explained that when the earth dried a bit, he would try to
teach him the rudiments of cultivating corn and tobacco.
Kofi bent over, pulled a clump of bindweed from between
two corn stalks, and said, "I know these plants from my
country. You have let the weeds grow too close and your
rows should be farther apart."

The white man blinked. "You have corn and tobacco in
Africa, Coffee?"

"Of course. White traders introduced them to us long
ago, in the days of my grandparents. Some of the men I
came here with have seeds in little fetish bags. The Ibo
carry seeds as a charm. If you wish, I shall try and obtain
some from them, but we may have to give them something
of value in return."

"I'm willing to trade, but what do I need with more corn
and tobacco seeds, Coffee?"

"I do not speak of the crops you have. I speak of African
crops. Your woman is a good cook, but has she ever made
an okra gumbo for you? Have your children tasted yams in
butter? There are beans you may find interesting, too. If
you are not afraid I'll run away, I'll find out where the
others are. I know a man named Quaco who says he kept
some fine okra seed when the Slattee raided his village."

Pardus laughed. "I don't know what you're talking
about, but I'm willing to learn. As for your running
away—if you run, you run. If we intend to work these
fields together, Coffee, we're going to have to learn to trust
each other."

He held out a hand. The Ashanti stared down blankly at
it. Then, remembering the white traders who had come to
his father's court, he gingerly shook hands with the farmer,
and smiled.

As they were walking back to the house, Pardus said, "I
owe you an apology, Coffee. You know more about farming than I expected. Are there any other skills you're keeping from me?"

"I do not keep secrets, uh, Master. I have some skill
with the working of iron. I am even better as a wood
carver. If you wish, I can make better stools for you than
the ones you have. There are many trees on your land. If
you wish, I will build you a bigger house."

Pardus laughed again. "Not tonight, Coffee. First we'll sleep. Later, we can talk about rebuilding the whole farm!"

Kofi failed to grasp the jest, but no matter. These people had good hearts, despite their savage looks. He would make their miserable little farm over for them. Then he would obtain a gun, somehow, and dissect it until he knew how the damned thing worked. There were books in the white man's cabin, too. Some of them had funny letters he'd never seen before, but he would master them and read them when the white people were not looking. Truly, this new land held many opportunities for a man who kept his wits about him.

Meanwhile, Rory MacMartin and Angus MacQueen had been sent together to another planter. Angus Mohr had the English, and the man who'd bought their contracts didn't see how he was going to get any work out of husky young MacMartin unless there was someone to pass his orders on.

Thatcher was a bitter middle-aged bachelor—though, as they soon discovered, their master did not live alone. His housekeeper was a darkly pretty indentured maid called Rose, and though Rory thought she looked like one of the fey darklings of the Western Isles, MacQueen decided she was Welsh. The two men's conversation took place in Gaelic as Rose fed them in the lean-to attached to the farmer's cabin. Their speculations ended when Yeoman Thatcher came out to snap, "Talk English, damn it! Has the wench shown you where you're to sleep?"

Angus Mohr smiled thinly and said, "Yes, and a fine hayloft it is, too. Would you mind telling us when we're to get some clothes to wear? You may well have overlooked it, but my friend's near naked, and I could do with a change myself."

Thatcher shrugged. "We'll see about it in the morning. I have some old clothes as may fit the two of you."

MacQueen stared at the Englishman's bony frame and asked, "Fit the two of *us*? I'm sure you were too busy finding us the cold mush we've just been after eating, Master dear, but the next time you take note of us, please consider that you come about to me belt buckle, and my Lochaber friend is broader across the shoulders than both of us together!"

Thatcher made a wry face. "I'm not a rich man."

In Gaelic, MacQueen translated for Rory and added,

"He's grown poor from buying himself two men and a girl. I wonder what he had to pay for a woman with such a grand behind!"

Rory flushed and murmured, "Hush, that's no way to speak of a woman who's just fed you!"

"Och, neither of them has the Gaelic, you fool. We can say anything we like about the Stranger and his wench."

Angus MacQueen suddenly laughed as his advantage sank in, and, keeping an innocent expression, he smiled at the yeoman and said softly, "After I steal all your silver, you old fool, I'm going to run off with your serving wench and have her till she begs for mercy."

Neither of the Strangers gave any sign of understanding, but Rory's face was flushed as he pleaded, "Stop it, you fool."

When Thatcher uneasily ordered MacQueen to speak English, Angus Mohr smiled sweetly and explained, "I was only telling young Rory to help dear Rose with the dishes. You piled so many of them before us it's a shame to ask the lass to wash them all herself."

"Rose can do the housework," Thatcher grumbled. "The two of you are to help me in the fields. It's too wet to cultivate the indigo, but I've five acres of timber to clear, and the ground's not too soft for felling pine. Have either of you ever handled an axe?"

MacQueen gasped with pleasure and insisted on translating to Rory, who, this time, laughed out loud himself. The yeoman frowned and asked what the joke was. MacQueen pointed at Rory with his chin and explained, "He's a Lochaber man, you see."

"What's that supposed to mean? What in thunder is a Lochaber man?"

"Well, now, 'tis a place in the old country, and the name of the great broad axe they hammer out in a dozen Highland smithies. Yon Rory's trained from infancy with an axe no Sassunach would be man enough to swing."

"He knows how to chop wood, then?"

"Ay, and anything else as needs chopping down to size. Him and his kind are sent into battle barefoot and stripped to the waist, armed only with those great terrible Lochabers. The Highland broad axe has its limitations against cannon fire, as we found out one day on Culloden Moor, but against anything made of blood and bone—"

"You've made your point. I'll want him to start clearing timber in the morning. We rise with the sun on this plantation. If the two of you expect to be fed before you start to work, you'll be well advised to get up when the cocks start to crow."

Thatcher turned sharply and went back inside the cabin. The girl, Rose, murmured, "I've the butt of a ham in the smokehouse, if either of you are still hungry."

Angus said, "Och, we're so full of that grand corn mush it seems another bite would burst us, but, if you don't want the ham to go to waste . . ."

"I'll fetch it," said the girl, ducking out the open side of the lean-to. As soon as they were alone, Angus Mohr said, in Gaelic, "I'm off, Rory of the Broad Axe. I'll not be after staying the night under that miserly Stranger's roof. Is any man here going with me?"

"You're mad, man! It's almost pitch black out there, and we've no idea of the lay of this land!"

"Och, the Carolinas are somewheres to the north, are they not? If we were to get a good start on the Strangers, run a bit through the night, you understand—"

"From what I've seen of it, Georgia's mostly bog, you fool," Rory said. "And, should we get to the Carolinas, what then? We're still transported prisoners. Every man's hand will be raised against us no matter where we go in this land!"

Angus Mohr looked away. "Well, I've got the English, you see, and since I learned it as a strange tongue, after I was fair grown, I don't speak it with the burr of the Lowlands. Most of the Saxons take me for some sort of Frenchman or Welshman or—"

"In other words, you can pass yourself off in the Carolinas."

"Well, I wasn't thinking of having myself skirled through the streets by a piper. As for yourself, I can teach it to you along the way. I figure it will take us nearly a month to reach the next settled country, and by then I'll have you speaking like the Strangers—or, at least, like some damned Dutchman or other. Do you see what the plan is, Rory?"

Rory saw. He saw, all too clearly, that his skills as a crofter used to living off the land were intended to see MacQueen through until the softer man could reach civilization, where *he*, but not a Highland crofter, could pass as Saxon. He shook his head wearily and said, "I always wondered why we fought the Children of the Cat for three hundred years. Now I'm beginning to understand it all."

"Och, it was the Hound's idea to have the feud in the first place, and in the second, didn't we fight side by side against the German Georges?"

The girl came back with the mildewed butt of ham and Angus smiled up at her and said, "We're talking about our master's lovely indigo. My friend here keeps saying it's naught but a weed in the old country."

He tore off a chunk of ham, stuffed it into his mouth, and, continuing in Gaelic, said, "Forget the Battle of Invernahavan, damn it. Are you with me in this or not?"

"I'm not. We've only been ashore a few hours. In a few days, when we know where we are, it might be worth talking about. If either of us were to run for it now, we wouldn't stand a chance."

"Och, we'd have a whole night before anyone missed us." Angus shot a thoughtful look at the girl, hovering in the triangular opening of the lean-to, and added, "We'd have an even better chance if we were to finish off the two of them before we left."

Rory shot a glance at the girl, saw that her expression was still one of mild puzzlement, and said, "The old man, maybe. The girl, no. And, if we do it at all, I'll need some time to make plans of my own. We have to get some decent clothes. I need shoes and a gun, or at least a good axe!"

"Och, you're stalling for time, man. There's all we'd need in the Stranger's cabin. I'll tell you what I'll do. I'll go in and finish off the man. You can do as you like with the girl."

"Now, what's that supposed to mean?"

"What do you think it means, man? I can see you've the hunger for her. Not that I blame you. I've been cooped up all these months without a woman too, but if she's that important to you, I'll leave you here to have your way with her while I do the old man and loot the cabin."

Rory's voice was ominously calm as he said, "You'll do no such thing, Angus MacQueen. I'm staying here at least until I get my bearings, and while I'm under their roof, no harm will come to either of them."

Angus shook his head in disgust. "Och, what's the use of talking? I might have known you'd want to stay here to moon over yon woman. What's the matter with you, man? Don't you know who gets to bed her? It's Himself in yon cabin owns her, ass, tits, and all!"

Rory half rose as he said, "I told you not to talk that way in front of her."

"What does it matter? She doesn't understand my Gaelic."

"No, but I do. And I don't intend to say it again, Child of the Cat!"

MacQueen laughed incredulously and said, "It's the clans we're after evoking, is it?"

"If you want it that way, Cat."

"Och, you've been playing with yourself too long, man! Defending a maiden's honor when she's got none left and doesn't understand a word of your gallantry besides!"

He looked over at Rose, smiled, and said in English, "We're still talking about indigo, darling. You can see how upset poor Rory is to be after cultivating what he takes for a common roadside weed."

Rose said, "He certainly looks upset. Have you been teasing him?"

Angus turned back to Rory and said, in Gaelic, "She likes you too. Are you sure you haven't been feeling her bottom while I wasn't looking?"

Rory got to his feet, stooping slightly under the low slanted rafters of the lean-to, and said flatly, "One more remark like that, Child of the Cat, and I promise you the Hound will be fed!"

"Good God! Are we going to have a duel? With *what*, you fool? They took your axe away from you at Culloden, remember?"

"I remember. They didn't take my hands, though."

"Do you really think you could, with your bare hands?"

"Do you want to try me, Cat?"

Angus Mohr MacQueen sat very quietly, staring up at the younger man as he made up his mind. MacQueen was a vicious swordsman who, with a blade in his hand, was not afraid to face man or devil. A bare-handed fight with a man as strong as Rory MacMartin, however, was not the sort of thing into which one entered lightly. He shook his head and said, "My apologies to both of you, then. I'm just a bit insane, you know, from the way my life turned out."

The girl, seemingly fed up with the endless conversation in a barbarous toungue, said, "I have to get back to my chores. I'll see if I can make a better breakfast."

The two nodded her away and neither said anything for

a time. Then Rory ducked out the triangular opening and said, "I'm going to see if I can sleep. Are you coming?"

"You go ahead," said Angus, adding, "I'm nervous as a cat—no jest intended. I think I'll just walk up and down a bit until I feel a few cobwebs in my eyes."

He waited until Rory had vanished into the shadows of the log barn across the yard. Then he stared at the single window of the Thatcher cabin, weighing his next move.

He took a few steps toward the cabin, considering both sets of odds. "The devil with it," he finally decided. "I'd sooner have a hundred Saxons trailing me than one angry Hound named MacMartin."

The yeoman had no horse, he knew, and besides, Rory was in the barn. Angus Mohr strolled out to the clam-shell road that the Thatcher holdings fronted on. The white shell shards led northward, gleaming ghostly in the starlight. The shell shards gritted under his feet as he walked slowly away from the cluster of darkened log buildings. Somewhere in the night a dog was barking, but there were no other buildings near Thatcher's place, and MacQueen's pace quickened as he began to sing softly,

> "Och, Charlie is me darling, me darling, me darling,
> Charlie is me darling, the only lad for me!"

And then he was running. Running in the mile-eating lope of a Highland-bred raider as he laughed wildly and shouted to the stars, "Touch not the Cat but *agloved*, you Sassunach bastards!"

He would still be running, hours later, when the Indians caught him.

After months in chains, Rory's sleeping wrists and ankles seemed to miss the weight of the iron. He thrashed about in the damp hay of Thatcher's barn, his body refusing to relax in rhythm with his sleeping brain, and the restless motions added panic to his dream—the dream he'd had so many times since that awful day on Culloden Moor.

The cannonballs were coming at him, bouncing like Dutchmen's nine-pins balls across the knee-high heather. The Strangers' lines were far across the moor, hidden in the smoke of their own gunfire as Rory and the others waited, waited, waited, and why didn't the prince give the God-damned order?

Some of the kilted Highlanders were cursing as they stood there, taking the Strangers' fire like a long, ragged line of stationary targets. The cannonballs lost speed as they bounced across the moor, and some of the lads laughed as they easily sidestepped those that reached the Highland line. A freckled youngster in the tartan of Clan Fraser, becoming overconfident, stepped out of ranks to try to stop a rolling ball with one foot, and, as if he'd seen what was to happen a hundred times before, Rory yelled, "Don't do it!" But the Fraser didn't listen, and he was smiling like the boy he was when the heavy cast-iron ball connected with his foot, tore it off, and left him, still standing, still with that silly grin on his face, the life draining out of him into the flattened heather.

A man on a prancing bay gelding rode down along their line, shouting at them in French. That would be General Sullivan, Prince Charlie's aide-de-camp and a fool when it came to fighting—or anything else for that matter. Another officer rode down the other way, shouting, "Stand your ground!" in Gaelic, and, while this time the men understood the words, they didn't understand the orders. What were they waiting for? What sort of battle was this?

Lochiel and Murray had tried to tell Charles Edward and his mad French staff officers that Highlanders didn't fight this way, but the prince had been to some school in France during the long exile of the Stuarts, and for a lad who didn't have the Gaelic, he thought he knew a lot.

A man nearby went down in a blur of MacPherson tartan and blood. Another bounding ball took a man from the divided Clan MacNab, and still the stupid order was passed down the line: "Hold fast, lads! Stand your ground!"

But they'd not be standing it long, he knew—wondering, even as he tensed to charge, *how* he knew what was coming next. The Chisholms would break first, he seemed to remember. Later, they would argue over who had disregarded the order and charged, a dozen clans claiming the honor. But from where he was standing near the banner of Lochiel, it seemed to Rory that the Chisholms were suddenly running at the Strangers' guns. Then Lochiel was charging with them on his stallion, and someone shouted, "Come, Sons of the Hound, and taste this fresh meat!"

Then Rory was running, the wet heather lashing his bare legs as he carried the heavy axe on one shoulder through the blue-gray gunsmoke. Lochiel was down, his horse shot out from under him and the bone showing through the flesh of one leg. Rory ran to the aid of his chief, but the Gentle Lochiel waved him past, shouting, "Meat! Fresh meat!" and then someone was before him in the smoke and the great axe swung, taking off the head in one blow and leaving him to wonder, as he ran on, which side the man he'd killed had been on. The MacBean was just ahead of him, a giant of a man with a great claymore brandished like a banner. Major MacBean would reach the Strangers' lines, he knew, and hack twelve men and a Saxon laird to death with his claymore before he fell. But the heather gripped Rory's legs and he somehow couldn't run as fast as he knew he should be able to. The legs moved slowly, as if through water, and the harder he tried to run, the slower he seemed to move. The Strangers were visible now, their dull red coats far behind the solid line of winking bayonets, and his eyes locked on those of a pale-faced lad of perhaps fifteen. He fought the thickening air to reach his chosen foeman, but he couldn't seem to close the distance, and somewhere a voice was crooning, "There, there, it's all right, Rory of the Great Axe!"

He was falling. This time he hadn't felt the musket ball that had creased his skull, but he knew somehow what had happened, and he had to stay on his feet, but he wasn't on his feet, he was stretched flat on his back in the . . . heather? No, it didn't feel like heather.

The soft voice said, "You've been dreaming, Rory my heart," and the bewildered youth flinched away from the touch of smooth fingers on his naked shoulder. He opened his eyes, stared up at the dark outline of a woman, and asked, "Who are you? What do you want?"

Still in Gaelic, Rose answered, "I brought you a blanket from the cabin. Himself is fast asleep. He drinks a bit, you see."

Rory shook himself more fully awake and marveled, "You have the Gaelic, then? Why didn't you say so before?"

"Och, sometimes it pays to keep a few things to oneself, you see."

"You heard, before, when we were talking about you?"

"Of course I heard, and understood each word you said in my defense. Your friend was a fool, and that's the truth of it. We're well rid of Angus Mohr, if you want my opinion."

Rory sat up suddenly. "Has he run away, then?"

"He has that, and the Indians are welcome to him if the serpents don't get him first. I thought you were wise for your years when you warned him of the bog hereabouts. I've seen the serpents that grow in this land, Rory my heart. They grow dragons here too. Great gray-green dragons the Strangers call 'gators."

"The devil take that Child of the Cat. Where did you learn the Gaelic? I *said* you were from the Western Isles, but Angus thought you might be Welsh."

Rose laughed and replied, "I'm *Irish*, you fool. My people's name was Donovan, and I came from County Limerick, at the mouth of Silver Shannon. We still hold to the old ways in the West Country, you see, though the Strangers have forbidden it and the nuns made me learn the Saxon before I was half grown."

"What are you doing in Georgia, then, Rose Donovan of the Secrets?"

"Och, first I'll thank you not to call me a Donovan, for it was my own people as sold me, during a hungry harvest. As to what I'd be doing here, I'm doing the same as yourself. Indentured servants go where they're told. The papers my father signed were for seven years. I've been a servant, and worse, for nine. Each time they sell my time, you see, they make up new papers on me."

He became aware of the rough blanket she was pulling up over his bare legs as she observed, "Silas Thatcher's not the worst master I've had. His bark is worse than his bite, and, as you see, he sleeps like a log." She chuckled and added roguishly, "A lot of rum and a little pleasuring will do that to a man his age."

Rory stiffened as her meaning sank in. Rose sidled down into the hay at his side, drew the blanket over both of them, and soothed, "Now, now, it's not as if he'd bought a blushing virgin with my papers. How old are you, Rory my heart?"

"I'll be twenty this winter," he replied in a defensive tone.

"Really? I thought you were much older. I fear I've a few years on you, Rory of the Shoulders. I suppose that's why I shock you by speaking so freely of country matters."

"You didn't shock me. I didn't think that old goat who owns our time was in the habit of sleeping with his *hand*."

"I know. I heard the way the two of you spoke about me

when you thought I was a Stranger. You were very kind, Rory. There are times when any woman longs to hear a few kind words."

Her hand was creeping over his stomach and he felt the breath catch in his throat as he asked, "What are you doing?"

"What does it feel like I'm doing, you darling fool? Your mad friend said neither of you had had a woman for over a year. Will you tell me something, as one lonely exile to another?"

"What's that? What do you want to know?"

"Have you *ever* been with a woman, Rory of the Many Battles?"

He started to brazen it out. Then he shrugged and said, "I grew up on a lonely croft. There were no women about but my kinswomen. I remember a time when some of my cousins were doing strange things to a sheep, but I was, well . . ."

"Afraid? Even of a sheep? Or was it the laughter of the others you were afraid of, Rory of the Highland Pride?"

"Och, for God's sake, what sort of a man would have it with a sheep? Do you take me for a Goddamned Campbell?"

She let her fingers linger just below his navel as she purred, "Come now, confess it like a man. Are you sure there's never been a time when you wished you'd done it with that sheep?"

"Christ, no!" he lied, even as his groin tingled to the memory of the lost opportunity. His cousin, Dugall, had sworn the vagina of a sheep was exactly the same as a woman's, and he'd often wondered if it was really true about the half-human monsters that shepherds had been accused of producing.

"I did it with a dog one time," said Rose, adding, "It wasn't very good. We were just trying to get back at the nuns, and none of us was experienced enough to know what we were doing."

Rory grimaced and allowed his voice to grow cruel as he asked lightly, "Is it better with that skinny old man whose bed you just came from?"

"Och, it's jealous you are! And here I was, just trying to be friendly. Would you like to be inside me, Rory of the Many Conquests?"

He started to say no, but her hand had reached his groin and he knew his turgid flesh had betrayed him. He put a hand over hers, helping her to stroke him as he sighed and said, "You're shameless!"

"That's not what I asked," she insisted. "Would you like me to teach you how, my darling virgin boy?"

"I'd rather have someone teach me the Saxon's tongue," he groaned, totally confused by his mingled desire and revulsion. She took her hand away, sat up, and pulled her shift over her head, saying, "I'll teach you the Saxon later. Do you want me to get on top?"

"I don't know. I suppose you think I am a frightened child at that. You see, there was so much work on my father's croft, and such free time as I had was spent in the study of war—"

"Hush, my heart. I was a virgin once myself. Just lie still and let me show you the way."

He froze, his heart pounding. A part of him wanted her to vanish in a puff of smoke even as another sobbed silently with desire. Rose threw the blanket down around his feet as she slid her naked thigh across his shivering legs. A voice in his inner mind shouted, "No, she's a shameless slut with the juices of another man still in her!" even as his pelvis rose to meet her descending vulva. He gasped as her wet warmth enclosed his throbbing penis, and then her naked breasts were dancing on his bare chest as she moved up and down in wild gyrations, crooning, "Och, you've such a lovely body, Rory of the Mighty Shaft!"

He wrapped his arms around her, pumping his flesh up into hers as he felt his orgasm exploding inside her. He groaned and let his arms fall out to either side of his body as she planted her pelvis firmly in place and said, "There's more where that came from. Just relax and let it soak until your breath comes back."

"I think we'd better stop," he said, as sanity began to creep back into his excited brain. She remained as she was, saying, "Just one more time, before I have to go back to the cabin."

He pushed her off with a snarl as his former distaste returned. She lay there at his side, barely visible in the dim light, and he couldn't see her face as she whispered, "Was it so terrible, then? I didn't think I was that old, but—"

"Damnit, you know what's wrong with it!"

"You mean the old man in the cabin? I told you his demands were modest, and it's not as if I were some camp follower with the seed of a hundred men running down my legs, or even your darling sheep after the others had had their way with her."

"All right, it's probably something wrong with me, then. I was with some other Blue Bonnets when we crossed the border into a Saxon town with friendly whores. There was one I found as bonny as a queen, and I had the silver, too, but somehow . . ."

"Somehow you'd rather bash men's heads in with a battleaxe? There's nothing wrong with what we've just done, Rory of the Purity. It was friendly and warm and you know we both enjoyed it, though in God's own truth I'd have enjoyed it more if you'd lasted a little longer."

"Is it friendly and warm when you're like that with other men?"

"Would you have me lie and say it's never been as grand with any other?"

"I don't know what I want. The truth, I suppose."

"Well, if you must know, it was better tonight with Silas in yon cabin. We don't do it as often as you might think, which is one reason I'm here. I've had many men since first a man I'd rather not speak of raped me as a lass of ten. Since then I've been raped, I've been sold, and I've sold myself to eat. Some of it's been good, some of it's been bad, and most, I fear, has hardly been worth the effort."

"You're a slut! A shameless, brazen slut!"

"I know, but wouldn't you like to have me again?"

"We're going to get into trouble. What if the master catches us? What if . . . one of us should get you in a family way?"

"The first man who bought me taught me how to avoid that. And, by the way, I did wash myself before I climbed up here with you. Would you like to be the one on top this time? Or, if you like, I can get on my hands and knees and pretend I'm your long-lost sheep!"

This time he laughed, and Rose laughed with him, rolling closer to caress his flank and to purr, "It's much better the second time."

She was right, too. This time he knew what was expected of him, and they climaxed at the same moment. When she demanded a third attempt, he gave in without much argument.

THREE

The escape of Angus Mohr caused excitement enough, but when it was learned that a Negro called Jeaco had run away that same first night, the little town of Savannah was in an uproar. Some men came to question Rory, of course, but their examination of the witness left something to be desired. Neither Silas Thatcher nor the investigators for the Board of Proprietors spoke a word of the Gaelic. Rose Donovan had neglected to inform their master of her own fluency in the tongue, and while Rory had picked up from Rose a few English expressions dealing with the more intimate parts of their two bodies, he hardly thought the white-wigged gentlemen who came out to the plantation wanted to hear them.

He had risen at dawn as if nothing had happened, and, finding an axe in the tool shed, had gone to work in the woodlot as Angus had instructed him to the night before.

They found him there, surrounded by chips and fallen pine logs. He saluted them in Gaelic, shot them a puzzled, innocent look, and went back to work on the tree he had been felling.

The Englishmen watched morosely as Rory swung the axe. He was still naked to the waist, but Rose had found him a pair of Thatcher's loose linen pantaloons to wear. That is, the pantaloons had been loose on Silas Thatcher. The muscular young Scot's body filled them to skin-tightness, and as he worked, one of the Englishmen observed, "He's a beautiful animal, isn't he? Pity so few of them have any brains." He reached for his snuff box as he added, casually, "Did you hear what the Duke of Cumberland said about them after he subdued the Highlands last year? He said the average Scot was far inferior, as game, to the common red fox. He said it's much more difficult to run the more intelligent animal to earth."

Silas Thatcher complained, "I haven't seen anyone catch that rascal, MacQueen, as yet. Who's going to stand my loss if the bastard gets away with his contract unserved?"

One of the visitors shrugged and answered, "We really

can't say. This one here seems to be a good worker, though."

A younger man with a malicious twist to his grin added, "I daresay you're getting good service from the Irish wench, too. You wouldn't like to sell *her* indenture, would you, Friend Silas?"

The others chuckled as Silas Thatcher flushed and looked away, muttering, "I'm more worried about the servant that ran away than I am about either of the ones I have. Do you suppose I could add the seven years I have coming from MacQueen to this one here?"

The only lawyer in the delegation stared thoughtfully at the young man swinging the axe and said, "I daresay it would be legal, if you think that big lout would stand for it. I mean, dash it all, Silas, fourteen years does seem a bit thick!"

"He rebelled against his king, didn't he? I mean, he's lucky they didn't have him drawn and quartered like Simon Fraser and those other Highland chiefs."

An older member of the delegation warned, "I don't think we should be talking like this in front of him. Some of them do know a spot of English, you know."

Thatcher shook his head and said, "He's completely savage. My wench and I have both tried talking to him in the king's English. He doesn't understand a word of it. You have to point him at a chore until he gets the idea. Once he starts a task, as you see, he's tolerable for unskilled labor."

The older man nodded slowly. "He's deadly with that axe, that's plain enough. He doesn't just swing that thing— he puts the blade where it will chip out the most wood with the least effort. I daresay he could hit a fly with that blade, and I'd hate to be the one to tell him he'd just had seven years tacked onto his indenture."

"He's stupid, I tell you," Thatcher said. "He'd never know the difference. All any of them want is a roof over their heads and three square meals a day."

"They're a lot like children," agreed the man who'd spoken of the Duke of Cumberland's latest hobby. "I understand they'll dance and sing all night, given half the chance. I saw some Jacobite prisoners when I was in England last year. One of them had one of those bagpipe things, and the others kept leaping around in circles till one would think even a monkey would get bored with the silly business. I suppose, when one has had nothing in the way of books or plays to improve the mind, the simple, childish pleasures suffice."

Silas Thatcher said, "Hell, they wouldn't read a book if you gave them a dozen. How long has it been since *our* people were civilized—a thousand years or so?"

"More like two thousand, if one counts the Roman occupation and ignores a dark age, more or less."

"Well, that's what I mean. We English have been right across the border from the Scotch for all these years, and they still haven't learned to wear pantaloons or speak like human beings. It's in their brains, I suspect. You take those thick Scotch skulls of theirs and figure out how many brains you could pack in such a little space, and, well, they just can't think as well as we can."

The lawyer nodded but said, "We'd best put off tinkering with his papers, though. We still don't know how the governor's going to take the indentures we just had them put their marks to. Meanwhile, gentlemen, I suggest we all go over to Isaac Pardus' homestead and see if his boy, Coffee, can tell us anything about that other runaway."

There was a murmur of agreement and someone said, "I understand this Coffee speaks English. You can't beat a Jew when it comes to making a good buy."

The lawyer made an uncomfortable noise in his throat and said, "Excuse me, sir, but I happen to be of the Hebrew faith."

The man who had spoken out of turn brightened and said, "Oh, are you, Rubin? I assure you no slur was intended against my good friend, Pardus."

Rubin Margolis nodded coldly and replied, "In that case, none was taken, Friend Warren."

To change the subject, another man asked Thatcher, "Where do you keep the Scotchman, Silas? That cabin of yours is barely big enough for three."

"I keep him in the barn," said Thatcher, adding, "When and if I can afford a team, I suppose I'll have to let him build a shack for himself." The yeoman shot a tolerant look at his bondservant as he mused, "He might rate better quarters if I can work it so's to keep him past his first seven years."

When the same delegation called on Isaac Pardus, they found the owner of the small plantation working with his new servant in the barnyard. Both men were chopping at the hand-packed earth with hoes, and when one of the visitors asked what they were doing, Pardus straightened and said, "Building a smithy, I hope. Coffee here seems to think he can fix things, given a hot enough fire and a place to work."

"Are you taking orders from your blackamoor, then?" the man with the snuff box sniffed.

"Not orders, suggestions," Pardus said. "Coffee knows how to work with iron. I don't. It's as simple as that."

Lawyer Margolis nodded and, turning to the Ashanti, asked, "Do you speak English, my good man?"

Kofi stopped what he was doing and came to attention, saying, "Yes, Master. Have you come about that boy, Jeaco?"

"I'll ask the questions, Coffee. What do you know about Jeaco?"

"He ran away. He is very young, very frightened, and not very smart."

"Did he tell any of you, um, blackamoors of his intentions?"

"No, Master. If he had told us, we would have urged him to stay. I understand he ran away as soon as he saw the chance. None of us knew he was such a fool."

"You agree it's foolish to run away from a kind master, then?"

Kofi shrugged. "Where would any of us go, even if he had a cruel master? I do not know how wide the great sea is, but it must be much too wide to swim. We were many days on the black ship. The stars in this part of the world are different too. I think if Jeaco does not get lost in the great forest beyond the last fields, he will come back when he gets hungry. Jeaco is not a boy who thinks deep thoughts."

One of the others strolled over to the hole in the ground, scuffed at the rim with the toe of his boot, and asked, "You call this hole a forge, boy?"

Kofi said, "No. I call it a hole in the ground. When it is big enough, we shall line it with bricks. There are no stones in this country."

"Damned few bricks to spare, either," laughed the curious man. He turned to Pardus to ask, "Can you really afford so many bricks, Friend Isaac? I know they come in as ship's ballast, but; dash it all, we need every brick we can get from England for housing!"

Pardus looked uncomfortable and said, "Ah, Coffee here thinks he can make us all the bricks we'll need."

Another man laughed and asked, "Bricks, from an African? They live in grass huts over there, Isaac!"

Kofi said, "In Africa, not far north of where my people live, there is a city called Timbuktu. Two hundred thousand people live there. They are black. The city is built of bricks."

This time Margolis, who considered himself a well-traveled man, said flatly, "Two hundred thousand? That's preposterous. There aren't that many people in Philadelphia!"

Kofi said, "I have never been to your Philadelphia. I have been to Timbuktu. You row up the Niger from Kanoo, many many days, until there are no trees. When you come to Timbuktu, the houses are made of brick because there is no wood. I have heard of another city, far to the east of my homeland. It has no name. The people who lived there are all dead. The city is made of stone."

"All right, but *your* tribe lives in grass huts, damnit!"

"The Ashanti build their cities of wattle and daub because they move every few years. After a field has been cleared for some time in Kumasi, the soil dies. A new field must be burned out of the forest. I think my people would be fools if they built brick houses when they must move every few years."

He bent down to scoop a handful of soil from the pit. He held it out on his wide pink palm and explained, "There is clay in this earth. My people make few bricks, but they are skilled potters. I do not think it can be much harder to make a brick than it is to make a man-sized water jar. If I am wrong, I shall fill in the hole and smooth the dirt back the way it was."

He saw that none of the white men had any further objections, and he went back to his digging. Margolis took Pardus by the elbow and steered the group toward the house, observing, "You're letting that nigger get a little out of hand, Isaac. *They're* not supposed to give the orders. *We* are!"

Pardus shrugged and said, "Look, you want to build me a smithy, I'll let you build me a smithy. Face it, Rubin, our people haven't farmed for centuries. This is the first land anyone in my family has ever been allowed to own since the dispersal. The boy is clever. Is that a thing I should curse him for? I paid good money for his papers. Shall I pray to God to make him stupid?"

The lawyer shook his head but insisted, "You'd better keep an eye on him, just the same. I understand that last night you let him sit at table with you and your family?"

Pardus swore in Ladino and said, "You live in a small town, and small news gets around, eh? Where do you *want* us to feed him, out in the yard with the chickens?"

"You've got to remember the man's a savage, Isaac!"

"So? My people were a thousand years in Spain and Portugal. You think living with savages should be a new experience?"

"Damn it, it's not the same thing!"

"You're right. In Spain and Portugal the savages were the masters. Here, *Pardus* is the master. You worry too much, Rubin. Coffee told us already he doesn't eat people."

"Yes, but what about your wife?"

"You think Coffee will eat my wife?"

"Damnit, Isaac, you know what I'm talking about!"

Pardus sobered and said, "I know what you're talking about, and I don't like it. My Becky is a good wife and mother. Also, she's a religious woman who left a stained sheet on our wedding night. You think, after all these years, I'm afraid to trust her?"

"I know you can trust your *wife*, damnit. It's the *nigger* you have to keep an eye on. It's simply not safe to take a stranger under your own roof, black or white—not until you know him better."

Isaac Pardus shook his head wearily. "I thought we were of the same faith, Rubin. In *my* scriptures we're told to treat our servants like human beings. Where in *your* Talmud does it say we should feed a man like a dog?"

The others of the delegation had held back a few paces, bemused by the conversation between their Jewish fellow colonists, but the man with the snuff box could not contain himself any longer. He stepped up on Pardus' other side and said, "What Lawyer Margolis is saying makes sense, you know. We were just over at Thatcher's, and you don't see *him* sitting at table with a bondservant."

Pardus laughed and, remembering the gossip about the old man and his Irish wench, asked, "Rose Donovan is eating with the chickens, then?"

"Dash it all, I'm talking about his Scotchman. He keeps the rebel in the barn, like the livestock he is."

"Thatcher is a Christian. I suppose we have to make allowances," Pardus said dryly.

The English Protestant did not think that was funny. He asked, "All right, what would you do if that nigger back there attacked your wife or daughter?"

"I'd kill him, I suppose," Pardus said. "But in the meantime, he *hasn't* attacked my wife or daughter, and until he does, we treat him as the scriptures say a servant should be treated." He smiled and added, "So if he doesn't attack my family or murder me in my bed he'll probably show me how to make bricks. Our people have always had trouble making bricks, you know."

It was nearly a week later that Muskeecola came to town with a message from his people. Few of the English colonists noticed him as he walked stiffly down the main street, for Indians were a familiar sight in Savannah, and Muskeecola came unarmed. He was a small, wiry man in his middle years; his face was blank as he ignored the few settlers who glanced his way. He had left his weapons and dugout hidden in a reed bank up the river, but his face was streaked with red from eye to chin, for this was a somber occasion.

He stared straight ahead as he made for the governor's mansion near the center of town. Muskeecola was familiar with the monotonous layout of Savannah's rectilinear streets, some of them paved with ballast rock near the central area. The houses were all the same, too. The English lived in boxes with silly waist-high stockades around them. The picket fences were a mystery to Muskeecola's people, who understood a fortified camp but failed to see the sense in a palisade any man could jump over. Many of the things the white men did were silly. That was why he was on his way to see the governor.

He spotted two Cherokee from far upstream standing near a public square, their gazes fixed on the green lawn. Muskeecola risked a glance and saw that the English were drilling on the field with muskets—another futile habit of the white man.

Muskeecola ignored the Cherokee as he passed them. They pretended not to see him. It was well. The Cherokee did not belong in the tidewater. Their homeland lay above the fall-line in the Piedmont country, but many young men of many nations were attracted to the busy, mysterious streets of Savannah these days. The English paid well for small errands, and sometimes they gave presents for no reason at all. It almost seemed as if the white people found the native population as exotic as the Indians found the English.

A trio of small white boys jeered at Muskeecola from behind the fancied safety of a ridiculous picket fence. The Indian ignored them. Small boys were the same no matter where one went.

Another militia band was marching toward Muskeecola on the other side of the street. Their clothes were motley, and some of them were out of step. The Indian knew they were following the orders of his friend, Oglethorpe. Each household in the colony was required to keep one musket and supply one family member for periodic training as a member of the Georgia militia. Of late, it was said, many colonists were shirking their duties with the trained bands. This, too, was a good thing, for Muskeecola's message was an ultimatum.

The man called Oglethorpe had a good heart, but some of his people were evil, or perhaps simply foolish. There were fools among his own people, too. Many of the young men had wanted to fight before Oglethorpe had spoken.

Muskeecola reached the small square in front of the governor's modest mansion. He walked up the brick steps, opened the front door without knocking, and stepped into the vestibule to shout, in the English that had earned him his position as a herald, "Heya! Where is Oglethorpe?"

He shouted twice more before a door down the corridor opened and a worried-looking young man in a white wig came out, asking, "Who the devil are you? What's the meaning of this uproar?"

"Heya, I want Oglethorpe! I am Muskeecola! Oglethorpe knows my heart. I am not a bad man."

The young man ushered Muskeecola into a side parlor, saying, "I'm afraid the governor is not here, uh, sir. Won't you have a seat?"

Muskeecola squatted on the floor near the fireplace and said firmly, "I bring the words of my people. Someone here had better listen!"

The young man went out and returned a few moments later with two older men. One of them offered the Indian a plug of trade tobacco and said he was the lieutenant governor. Muskeecola ignored the offer and complained, "Fif-

teen summers ago I stood on Yamacraw Bluff with Oglethorpe and Toma-Chi-Chi. They spoke long, as brothers,
and our people have not been bad with one another. Is this
not true?"

The white who said he spoke for Oglethorpe smiled
down at the Indian and agreed, "The Creeks have always
been our friends, sir."

"We are not Creeks. We are Muskogee. Many summers
ago the Spanish came to our lands and taught us to hate
them. They raped our women, burned our chi-chis, and
even dug open the graves of long dead chiefs for the pearls
buried with them. When the English came to fight the
Spanish, we welcomed them as brothers. When Oglethorpe
fought the Spanish at Frederica, our warriors fought at his
side. Our bones lie mingled with the bones of Englishmen
killed by the Spanish from this place to St. Augustine.
Heya, everyone knows these things to be true."

"We know all this, sir. What do you want of us, another
gift like those muskets we sent you last year?"

The Indian frowned and said, "Those muskets were paid
for in many skins and freshwater pearls. I seek no gift. I
come to *offer* two—with a warning."

"You, ah, have something you wish to donate to our colony?"

"We have two of your people. One is a black man; the
other is white, and very tall. He told us he was an enemy of
the English. Then, when he saw we meant to kill him, he
said he was one of your captives who'd run away from this
place."

One of the other men in the room gasped. "By God,
they've recaptured those two runaways—MacQueen and
the nigger, Jeaco!"

"Those were the names they gave us," agreed the Indian,
adding, "If you want them back, my people will send them
down to you in a day or so. They offer these men as a gift.
We want nothing for them."

The lieutenant governor grinned and said, "By George,
sir, I'm sure the men they ran away from will offer a reward."

But Muskeecola raised a hand for silence and said,
"Heya, I have not finished. My message has two blades.
You have heard the good side. The bad side is the warning
to some of your people."

"What warning, sir? What have they done?"

"Heya, they have been bad in as many ways as I have fingers on my hands, but I will speak only of those things that must stop now!" He held up a finger and said, "Ogle-thorpe said the English wanted only a bit of our land, and Toma-Chi-Chi gave it, as a brother. Now, some of your people are pressing beyond the grants of our chief." He held up another finger and said, "Some of your people are hunting on our lands—not for food, but to gather skins. The animals they kill are left to rot, and when we tell them not to do this thing, they laugh at us." He raised another finger and said, "Traders coming to our chi-chis cheat us and abuse our women. Heya, this must stop."

Another finger went up as the Indian said, "The pearls in our creeks belong to us. This has always been the law. Not even the Cherokee dredge for pearls in our creeks. If you want pearls, we will sell them to you. If you take them from our creeks, we will kill you as we did the Spanish in the days of our fathers."

The white man who said he spoke for Oglethorpe nod-ded and said, "All of your complaints are justified and against the laws of this colony. If you bring such men be-fore us, we shall punish them."

The Indian said, "Your words are good, if you mean them. I will tell my people not to tighten the heads on the war drums. There is one more thing. Some of your traders are selling rum to our young men. It makes them crazy, and Oglethorpe promised not to let such things happen."

"The importation of rum is forbidden in Georgia. The traders you complain about must be from the Carolinas. They are not our responsibility!"

The Indian frowned and said, "I do not know this word. What do you mean by responsibility?"

"I mean we have no authority over traders from the other colonies. There's nothing we can do about them."

"You mean they are not English?"

"Um, well, some of them may be English, but there's nothing we can do to stop them from, ah, bothering you."

The Indian got to his feet and said, "Heya, I do not like your words about this thing, responsibility."

Then, having said what he had come to say, Muskeecola turned without another word and strode from the room.

There was a moment of silence. Then one of the English-men muttered, "Arrogant bastard, don't you think?"

The lieutenant governor sighed and said, "At least we're

getting those runaway rascals back. It's only a net gain of one, however. That one Scotchman died on Carruthers after all."

"That would be the one called MacMillan, wouldn't it, sir?"

"Yes, Nicol MacMillan. He was sick when he came ashore, but Carruthers took a chance on his gaol fever and, um, lost. I don't want the other Scotchmen to know about it until they've settled in a bit."

"What about this Indian business, sir?"

"I rather imagine they simply want a greater annuity, don't you? We'll throw in some extra pigs of bullet-lead for the bucks and a few more scarlet ribbons for the squaws and that should suffice for now."

"Don't you think we should look into that business about the rum trade, sir? I mean, I'm dead certain none of the Savannah traders are working the creeks with contraband rum. Such little as they can smuggle in finds many a buyer within a block of Factor's Wharf!"

The older man sniffed and said, "I daresay. The chaps who've been trifling with the Creeks are probably more of those damned Ulstermen they brought into Philadelphia a few years back. That was one idea of Penn's that went awry."

"What on earth would Pennsylvania frontiersmen be doing so far south, sir?"

"What, indeed? Those damned Scotch-Irish from Ulster are a wandering breed. I don't know where Cromwell recruited them from in the first place. The North Country and Scottish Lowlands is the story they give out, but they must have had some gypsy blood in them. Cromwell planted them on the lands he'd seized from Irish rebels in Ulster, but the beggars simply wouldn't stay put. They run to size and they're natural bullies, so they simply started moving in on the smaller Irish Catholics whether they were rebels or not. By the time Penn was ready to expand his colony to the west, the damned north of Ireland was a bloody cock-pit, so Penn suggested, and the Crown agreed, that transporting the excess Protestant population of Ulster to the Pennsylvania frontier might afford the big bastards an outlet for their aggressive tendencies."

"I can see the sense in that, sir. Big, tough men are an asset on any frontier. But we're a long way from Pennsylvania, and—"

"Thats the point I was trying to make, damnit! The Ulstermen took to pioneering as ducks to water, but if you want my opinion, they tend to overdo it. They've cowed the Indians whenever they could, killed them if they couldn't, and simply turned to a new breed of savage along the whole British frontier. Today you'll find them anywhere from the Green Mountains to the south end of the Appalachians. Why, some have even been rumored to have crossed over into the French claims and God knows where else. There's simply no controlling them. They dress in Indian buckskins, live with a rifle in one hand and a dagger or a tomahawk in the other, and obey no rules of God or Crown. They don't pay rent or taxes. They laugh at regulations, and, all in all, I think we were better off when there were only *Indians* up there along the ridge lines."

"Then you think this hunting and pearl-dredging business might be the work of those renegade Scotch-Irish, sir?"

"It's probably that new lot who've settled the Carolina Piedmont. I'll dispatch a complaint to Charleston, of course, but I doubt me it will do much for the Creeks."

"Perhaps if we told the Creeks it was all right to defend themselves against these trespassers, sir—"

"Don't be a fool! You know the Crown would never allow us to sanction Indian violence against any white man. Let them get the idea it's permissible to kill *one* of us, and what do you get? You get another Massacre of Virginia! No, we'll just have to muddle through as best we can until the colonies grow enough to insist on law and order—and make it stick!"

The two younger men in the room exchanged glances. Then one of them asked, "What say you to a show of force, sir? Many of the settlers have been shirking their duties with the trained bands. If we were to impose a few fines, insist on each household's minuteman showing up for drill, we'd have a more impressive showing on the muster days."

The lieutenant governor shrugged and said, "I like the idea of fines. Our treasury could use the extra funds. I doubt me it would impress the Carolinians, however."

"I'm thinking of the Indians, sir. You know they're always mucking about in town, selling their freshwater pearls and basketry and such. If we let it get back to the chi-chis that we have at least a regiment under arms, and coupled that with a generous annuity—"

"I'd leave the bullet-lead out, however," the other man cut in.

The man who had been speaking nodded and said, "Quite. We'd better make the extra presents Venetian beads. At any rate, what I'm suggesting is the carrot in one hand and the stick in the other."

The lieutenant governor nodded impatiently. "You gentlemen work it out as you see fit. I've an appointment for afternoon tea, and I fear I'm already late." He went to the door, turned, and bowed slightly as he said, "Good day to you, gentlemen."

The older of the two Proprietors left in the room sighed and said, "At least he didn't say no this time. You'll see to the proclamation about the next muster day, won't you?"

"Yes sir. I'll get the clerks right on it. Um, is there any news of Governor Oglethorpe's trial, sir?"

"If I knew a thing I'd have told you. I'd have held off, just now, if I knew he was coming back for certain. I don't like this business of making decisions for the colony in his absence. The governor has a certain flair for making the oddest ideas work. I fear our esteemed lieutenant governor, while a decent enough sort—"

"Dash it all," snapped the younger Proprietor. "The man's a fool and we all know it!"

The older and more level-headed Proprietor frowned at his colleague's political naïveté and said, "I'd rather you said that to the man's face, if you insist on passing judgment on your superiors. The man means well, as do we all. It's just that none of us quite understands Governor Oglethorpe's methods. I, for one, have tried to carry out his orders in the most practical manner, but with him in England, the situation's getting out of hand. You know how the rum laws have been flouted. The minutemen refuse to train, and I don't know *what* Oglethorpe will say when he finds out about those bondservants we just allowed in."

"I see no problem with that, sir," the younger man soothed. "We already have a good number of indentured servants in the colony. Many of the new colonists arrive with one or two paupers or orphans bound over to them on the other side."

"Yes, damnit, but none of those lot have been Negroes."

"A lot have been Irish, sir, and you know what they say about an Irishman just being a nigger turned inside out."

"I beg your pardon?"

The younger man, who was new to politics indeed, smirked as he explained, "A nigger is pink on the inside, black on the outside. An Irishman is pink on the outside, black on the—"

"Young sir! I *happen* to be a *Fitzgerald* on my mother's side!"

The other man paled, recovered, and quickly added, "I was refering to the Irish *peasantry*, sir! I assure you I have nothing but the greatest respect for the noble house of the Geraldines!"

"Accepted, then," said the older man, who really did not feel up to an affair of honor in this beastly heat. To hasten the healing process on his own part, he said, "Getting back to proverbs less distasteful, I'm reminded of one that Governor Oglethorpe was fond of. You know he fought the Turks at Belgrade, didn't you? At any rate, he picked up a Turkish proverb there that he was fond of quoting when someone at a meeting suggested, say, choosing a lesser evil. He said that accepting the smallest evil was like letting a camel get its nose inside one's tent."

"I'm afraid I fail to understand that, sir."

"Oh? Pity. I don't think many people do."

FOUR

Rory walked into the wide doorway of the warehouse near the Factor's Wharf with the heavy peeled pine log on his shoulder and gazed around for a place to put it. The cavernous interior was filled with barrels of tar, coils of hemp rope, and other material needed for the ships putting in to Savannah. Rose had explained that the log was to be delivered to the ship's chandler, Efram Starr & Sons, before she had given him the new burlap smock, clubbed his blonde hair with a black ribbon, and sent him the three miles into town with the eighty-pound log on his shoulder.

The log belonged, of course, to Silas Thatcher, who, lacking other livestock, delivered his lumber the best way he knew how—on Rory's broad shoulders and strong legs.

Rory found a space on the tamped earthen floor and let the log fall with a mighty thud. A side door leading to the chandler's office opened, and a young woman stuck her head in with a puzzled smile.

Rory felt his breath catch in his throat at the sight of her chestnut curls and delicate features. Then he pointed at the log and stammered, "*Seo caber bith . . .*" Then, noting the blank look his words were producing on the bonny Saxon woman's face, he reached inside the rough smock, took out Thatcher's bill, and held the slip out to her, muttering, "*An lach nan Thatcher.*"

The English girl nodded in sudden understanding and stepped over the threshold into the storage area, accepting the bill and tucking it into the top of her low-cut taffeta bodice as she said, "You must be one of those poor Scotch lads. Did you carry that big timber all the way from Thatcher's? I'm afraid it will never do where you dropped it."

She saw that the bondservant did not understand and stepped over to the log, bending to pat it with one hand as she pointed to a spot nearer the wall with the other. "Over there, do you see?"

Rory's face reddened as he stared at the soft roundness of her buttocks under the summer-weight taffeta skirts. The past few nights in the hayloft had taught him a new appreciation for feminine curves, and he could picture the chestnut hair lining the slit between those firm young hemispheres just under the smooth cloth.

Grasping the girl's meaning as well as the beauty of her figure, Rory quickly went over to her and squatted to grip one end of the log. The girl remained bent over for a moment as she faced him, repeating her order, and Rory could smell her clean breath as he stared into her warm brown eyes.

A voice from the doorway gasped, "Gloria, I say!" and the two of them turned to see a pink-faced young man in shirt sleeves and a powdered periwig moving quickly to join them. The lovely girl the Strangers apparently called Gloria straightened up, saying, "This boy just brought us more timber from Thatcher. I've been trying to show him where I want it, but he doesn't speak English."

The bewigged young man frowned at Rory and pointed to a different spot, saying, "Over there, my good fellow."

Rory lifted the end of the log, walked it up on his shoulder with his hands, and, balancing it for a moment, tossed it into the spot the girl had first indicated.

"Idiot!" snapped the Englishman, but the girl called Gloria laughed and said, "It's all right, Nathan. I told him to put it there."

"Hmm, quite! He seems to be a bit too aware of you, for a servant!"

"Oh, Nathan, don't be silly. He's a poor Scotch bumpkin who's confused by our English ways."

She smiled at Rory and said, "That will be all, my good man. Thank you and good day." But, as she turned to walk back to the office, Rory stammered, "*Na lach, Te og An uair diol Thu mas e do thoil?*"

The girl turned, smiled in confusion, and said, "I beg your pardon?"

Rory reached out and snatched Thatcher's bill from between her breasts, making a signing motion with his free hand as Nathan Starr gasped, "I *say!*" and reached for a nearby length of cooperage.

Gloria laughed and said, "It's all right, Nathan! I understand. He wants us to sign for the log!"

"He, he *touched* you!" gagged the Englishman, swinging the length of live-oak barrel stave through the space Rory's head had just occupied. Rory moved back with surprising grace for such a big man, and thrust out a hand to grip the

Englishman's wrist as he prepared to aim another blow. Gloria stepped forward, putting a hand on each man's shoulder as she tried to push them apart, shouting, "Stop it, you two! There's no need for this nonsense! It's a simple and innocent mistake!"

Nathan Starr's face was red as he tried to pull the hand that held the stave from Rory's steel grip. The hand was rapidly growing numb as the big Highlander held him, helpless as a babe, and watched with curious detachment as his white fingers slowly lost their hold on the curved length of wood. The girl had wedged herself between them now and her face was toward Rory as she pleaded, "Let him go like a good lad, won't you?"

The barrel stave dropped to the earthen floor. Rory nodded as her meaning sank in and stepped back, releasing the Englishman's tingling hand as he waited, balanced on the balls of his bare feet, for the little Saxon's next mad move.

"I'll have the bailiff on this maniac!" Nathan swore, rubbing his wrist while stepping back out of the Scot's reach. The girl took two steps backward, for there was something oddly disturbing about this big blonde barbarian, although she knew somehow that she was perfectly safe with him. She smiled at Nathan Starr and soothed, "Oh, it's hardly a thing to take to law, Nathan. He didn't know we have an account with his master, and he merely asked for a signed receipt, like any good servant should."

"He laid hands on both of us! That's a lashing offense and you know it, Gloria! Why, damnit, we're gentlefolk!"

"Well, *I* know that, Nathan. I'm afraid we have to make allowances for inferiors who don't speak English, though. I'm sure he's unaware of English customs, and, finding us working like tradespeople, and me in my own hair . . . well, I think we'd best forgive and forget this one time."

She was right that Rory was ignorant of the vicious pecking order of eightheenth-century English society. The "macaroni" lace and white periwigs of the upper classes were more than simple vanity.

Georgia was perhaps the most democratic colony in North America, save for Quaker Pennsylvania, but the complicated English caste system, almost as complex as that of Calcutta, had made its way across the sea despite Oglethorpe's democratic dreams. Englishmen of the era were divided roughly into "gentlefolk" and "simple folk," but that was only the beginning of it.

The simple folk were yeomen, who owned land; freemen, who did not; and servants, who were at the bottom of the pecking order.

Exactly what constituted a gentleman was a bit vague, but it had to do with landed wealth, family connections, and education. The lace, wigs, powdered faces, and French rapiers worn by English gentlemen served much the same function as the bright feathers of a game cock: they identified a stranger at a glance, and told a man entitled to a sword whether a man who had annoyed him was owed a formal challenge or was simply a lout who could be horse-whipped or, if the boor persisted, executed in cold blood.

If a gentleman of the time was too busy to attend the matter at hand with a riding crop or sword, the sheriff's bailiff would take care of the matter after a summary trial. Even a yeoman striking a landed gentleman with his fist could expect to be hanged or transported for the crime of petty treason, while merely insulting gentlefolk was punishable by no fewer than five hundred lashes, to be administered fifty at a time over a ten-day period at the nearest gaol.

Rory, raised in the Highlands where every member of the armed peasantry was considered a blood relative, however distant, of his chief, was unaware of his danger as he watched the Strangers argue and tried to understand their outlandish words. He knew the woman was speaking for him, although he failed to see the need of it. He did not want to hurt the little Saxon, but if the idiot persisted, Rory knew he could break him over one knee like the wee twig of a man he was.

Gloria was firm but gentle as she reminded the irate Nathan Starr of a few persuasive facts. The Starrs, while gentleborn, had been sent to Georgia from a debtors' prison after failing in business in Liverpool. In any colony but this one, Nathan's pretensions could cause a lot of trouble for a macaroni young man who was, after all, in trade. In Oglethorpe's Utopia, even a non-Christian like Lawyer Margolis might affect a periwig without being twitted into a deadly contest on the dueling field, but insisting on punctilio over a fancied insult at the expense of another property-owner's bondservant—that could well backfire, and they had *not* paid Yeoman Thatcher for a goodly time.

Nathan Starr finally shrugged and said, "I say, it's hardly worth so much bother in all this heat. I'll let your pet off this once, but I mean to have a word with Thatcher about the oaf's manners!"

Gloria smiled at Rory and asked for the bill. He gave it to her wordlessly, and she stepped over to a nearby barrel, taking a clerk's lead from where it had been hidden in her thick hair. She signed the bill and gave it back to Rory, saying, "There, good fellow. You'd best be off now."

Rory bowed and murmured, "*Slan leat, an diugh,*" as he left the two of them to discuss his strange tongue and even stranger manners.

Out on the dirt road, he encountered young MacGillonie, who had been bound to a master in this neighborhood. He waved a greeting and said, "I just had a bit of a set-to with a silly Saxon in an even sillier little wig. He works in the chandler's back there. Do you know him?"

MacGillonie, a short, broad-featured youth with bushy brows that met in the middle, said, "He's a nasty one, even for a Stranger. His name is Nathan Starr, and he has a short temper for such a little man."

"I know. He just was after hitting me with a barrel stave."

"Ah, you want me to help you get back at him, then?" His distant clansman grinned and broke into the old ditty that went:

"On a windy night, in snow or rain
With neither stars nor moon agleam
Foes of the Hound, beware thy bane!"

Rory laughed and said, "Och, it's not that serious. I took the stick away from him before he brought it to a killing matter. I was just wondering who he was, is all."

Rory's voice was desperately casual as he added, "You wouldn't know of the lass he has working for him, would you? She has bonny brown hair and he called her Gloria."

MacGillonie nodded. "That would be his wife, then. A waste of good woman-flesh on a wee thing like Starr, if you ask me."

Rory had not asked him, but, as he walked the three miles back to Thatcher's, he concluded that he more than agreed. His new-won carnal knowledge tortured him with pictures of that foppish little Stranger rutting with Herself who was born to be queen, and later that night Rose was pleasantly surprised by the savagery of his lovemaking.

A week later, Kofi the Ashanti was reassembling Isaac Pardus' musket on the deal table in his own quarters. The mechanism was simpler than he had imagined. The thing that looked like a bird's head with a bit of stone in its beak snapped down along a strip of serrated fire-steel, shooting sparks into a little pan of the magic powder on the weapon's side. The burning powder went through a little hole and ignited the larger charge behind the lead ball. This made the ball fly out with a loud bang, and, as he knew from the Battle of Lake Bintihene, men fell down as far as three spear-casts away.

He had the parts memorized. The workmanship was no better than his people's spearsmiths were capable of, but without the secret of the magic powder, the weapon was simply a toy. The white man's civilization was more complicated that he had imagined. As soon as you learned one secret, it seemed to open the lid to another further inside.

There were sounds of movement from behind the wall that his small cabin shared with the bigger house where the white people lived. Kofi willed himself to ignore them as he threaded a retaining screw into place. The white man and his wife made love every chance they had. The children were over at a neighboring cabin for the morning, and now the white woman, Rebecca, was making a lot of noise as she pleasured her man. Kofi felt a slight tingle in his groin as a picture flashed before his mind. He had seen the white woman with her clothes off for just an instant as he'd brought in the hot water for her bath.

Her back had been to the door, and she had not seen him in the split second it had taken him to grasp the situation and fade quietly back from the door that the foolish woman had left slightly ajar. The white people had a custom of knocking on their thick wooden doors before entering. It was a good custom. If people made love in broad daylight and allowed their women to moan out loud with pleasure, it was no wonder they needed thick doors.

A stray tendril of evil thinking had crept, unbidden, from somewhere deep in the Ashanti's mind. He had been without a woman for a long time, and the great pink buttocks of the white woman had been interesting in an oddly repellent way. That night, as he had relieved his sexual tension with his hand, he had started to allow himself to fantasize about his master's wife. He had quickly bitten off the evil thoughts by picturing that night in Kumasi with the two dancing girls his host had lent him while he was away from home—the elders had impressed on him early that a man was not a man unless he had control of his own mind. Adultery was almost unknown among his nation, although many wives were to be prized, and sodomy among friends was condoned, if not approved, when warriors were in enemy country and no enemy women were on hand to rape and kill in the customary manner. The taking of a friend's wife, with her consent or against it, was punished by a long and lingering death. The white men did not seem to have a Leopard Society to mete out punishment to evil men, but doubtless they had some sort of punishment worked out for men who violated other men's women.

The vision of the pink, curvaceous white woman had gone away—for now. Kofi screwed the butt-plate of the musket back in place. There had been no secrets hidden under it. The butt-plate appeared to be there simply to keep the wood from scraping on the ground. Kofi wiped the musket down with an oily rag and held it up to the light, nodding his approval at the well-worked steel.

There was a polite tap on the door, and it opened to reveal Isaac Pardus in his militia costume—a blue, frogged coat and a tricorn hat—thrown on over his regular work clothes. He smiled and asked, "Have you finished with the gun, Coffee?"

Kofi got to his feet, holding the musket out to his master as he smiled back, and said, "Yes. This time, I do not think your sergeant will be cross with you for having a rusty weapon."

Pardus took it from him sheepishly, saying, "Listen, I have a lot to do on this place. What do I know about guns? I'll tell you what I know about guns—they're a damned nuisance to keep clean. Thanks for taking care of it for me, Coffee."

Kofi saw that Pardus was about to leave for the drill field and asked, "May I go with you, Master? I'll carry the musket for you, if you like."

"I'd better carry it myself, but you're welcome to come along. Do you like watching us marching up and down, making asses of ourselves in the hot sun?"

"It is interesting, Master. My people fight in formation, too. I have seen that you form your lines differently when you have guns."

"Let's go, then. Frankly, I've never understood the point in all this dress right, dress left, keep in step. You think it makes a big difference in a war if a man should be out of step?"

Kofi followed him outside, saying, "Yes. You white people march close together. If one man is out of step, he kicks the heel of the man in front of him. With those boxes you wear on your feet, a kick in the heel must hurt!"

Pardus laughed and said, "You should be the soldier, then."

"In my country, I was."

The cabin door opened as they passed, and Rebecca came out to kiss her husband goodbye. Pardus patted her fondly on the rump and said, "Farewell, my queen. I'm off to the wars for king and country!"

"Isaac, you be careful," his wife warned, letting go of him with some reluctance.

The two men walked out to the road, Kofi nursing a small pang in his heart. He knew they were on their way to a mock drill in the middle of town, but his own wives had acted much the same as he had left them to fight the King of Dahomey. He had never seen them again. They would have new husbands when and if he ever got back to Kumasi. A man taken in battle was considered dead by the Ashanti.

It was a short walk from the Pardus holding to the trained band's drill field near the governor's mansion. Other minutemen had preceded them and stood about in groups, waiting for the whole band and the drill sergeant to arrive. Kofi stopped as his master went over to join some men he knew. A cannon sat in the middle of the field, where the sun was hottest. It had not been there last muster day. Neither had the two men tied to its big wooden wheels, back to back.

Kofi recognized the Negro lashed to one of the wheels. It was the runaway, Jeaco. He had heard that the Indians had brought the man back to Savannah tied like an animal. He had been wondering what the white men did to runaways. This business with the cannon wheel seemed mild enough in comparison to the African punishments for a runaway slave unlucky enough to be recaptured. The man on the other wheel was white. This was encouraging. It meant that, in Georgia, white men and black men would be treated the same way.

Kofi strolled over to the cannon, raised a hand, and said, "*Jambo*, Jeaco. How long do you have to stay like that?"

The slender youth tied to the wheel raised his head and grinned. He said, "I know you from the ship. You are the Ashanti the mate kept hitting for asking too often for water. Where did you get those white man's pants?"

"My master's wife made them for me out of a torn sheet. When she has time, she says she will make me a shirt. Where is your loin cloth? You're as naked as a boy."

"The Indians took it from me. They played with my penis and laughed at me a lot. Some of the children prodded me with sticks until a woman made them stop. I do not like Indians. They are almost as cruel as Portuguese."

"Did the Indians use you as a woman? I remember, on the ship, you were quite good at taking the woman's part."

Jeaco shook his head and said, "I offered, if they would let me stay with them, but they didn't understand my words. And when I tried to pleasure the leader of the Indians, to show him my meaning, he slapped me. Then they all laughed. They have plenty of women, so I had nothing to offer them. Their women are ugly, but you know how most men are, given their choice."

An idea sprang into Kofi's mind. This was not an evil thought, and so he allowed it to grow. He said, "I asked you how long you had to be tied up like that."

"I don't know. It's very uncomfortable. Do you see the white man behind me? We can't talk to each other because he is ignorant of human speech, but he keeps groaning like a baby. They took away his shirt and the sun is baking him red. I see, now, why white men wear so many clothes. They can't take even a day in sunlight. There's something wrong with their skins."

Kofi walked around the muzzle of the cannon and stared at the white man lashed to the other side. The white man was bigger than Jeaco and his eyes were green. His flesh, from the waist up, was lobster red, save for where his face and neck had grown accustomed to sunlight. The white man frowned at Kofi and asked, "What are you looking at, you black bastard?"

In English, Kofi said, "I am Kofi, of the Ashanti nation. My mother was the principal wife of my father, so I am black, but I am not a bastard."

Relieved to have any distraction, Angus Mohr smiled thinly and said, "I stand corrected. What were you and that other nigger just after jabbering about? You sounded like a pair of monkeys."

"I was asking him how he felt. He said he was uncomfortable. Once, my people tied a Portuguese slaver in the hot sun, waiting for the cool of night before they got down to the pleasures of his death. The Portuguese died before he could be tortured. One of the elders said it was the sun that killed him."

"Jesus, you're a cheerful sonofabitch. Why don't you tell me a story I don't already know?"

"My master allows me to roam freely. If you like, I will go and tell your master that this punishment is the wrong one for a white man. You are badly burned, and the day is still young."

"The damned Indians did most of this to me. They took my shirt away when they captured me. It's a cruel sun they have in this place, and that's a fact."

"I could point that out to your master. Tell me who he is and I shall talk to him for you."

Angus Mohr shook his head. "I don't have a master now. The Sassunach who owned my papers sold them back to the government. He says I'm too wild for him to handle." Angus Mohr laughed harshly and added, "The old bastard's right."

Another white man was approaching the cannon, and Kofi stepped to one side, turning to face him. The white man was big, with straw-colored hair, and was dressed in soiled white linen. There were no shoes on his big feet. The white man tied to the cannon shouted, "*Slàinte*, Rory *nan Con*!" and the white man joined them, asking, "*Seasgair*, Angus?" in a sarcastic tone.

Kofi was puzzled by the exchange. The tongue was neither English nor Portuguese. He turned to the newcomer and said, in English, "This man is badly burned by the sun. If we don't help him, he will die."

Rory frowned at the Negro and said, "Sassunach *bruidhinn me bochd*." Then he licked his lips and stammered, "No speak English."

In Gaelic, Angus asked, "What do you mean you speak it poorly? You don't speak it at all, you great ox!"

Rory shrugged and answered, "I have a few words of it now. Did they tell you how long you're to be tied to that great gun?"

Kofi, still puzzled by the exchange, walked away, leaving them to their own barbarous gibberish.

Angus grinned and said, "Until I die of sunstroke, I suppose. Who's been teaching you the Saxon, that dark-haired wench of the old man? What's she like with her legs apart?"

"I don't hit people when they're tied to cannons, so I'll pretend I didn't hear that." Rory felt the blood rush to his tanned cheeks. In truth, the Irish girl had taught him much in the past few days—or, rather, nights.

The advantages of her superior sexual experience were only part of it. Rory had managed to repress his continued revulsion at the thought of his grotesque competitor for Rose's favors by telling himself that bedding Rose was the quickest way to learn English. He was as helpless in this land as a fish out of water without a knowledge of the hated tongue. Rose seemed more interested in the carnal side of their relationship, but he had been forcing her to give him more of the Strangers' words each time they found themselves alone.

The old man had not guessed that his bondsmaid spoke Gaelic, and Rose seemed to derive much amusement from Thatcher's remarks that the young Scot was learning fast. The jest was lost on Rory, who preferred to oppose an enemy in the open. That time they had raided the Campbells for cattle, he had left a strip of tartan on a fence rail for the hated enemies to find. Deviousness, like sex, was new to Rory of the Broad Axe.

Angus Mohr was asking, "If I'm still here, and alive, at sunset, will you slip back and untie me, Rory?"

Rory frowned and said, "I don't know. If they catch you again, and you should tell them who set you free—"

"What do you take me for? Did I tell them you helped me escape from Thatcher's place?"

"It would have been a lie if you had."

"Just the same, I kept my mouth shut and told them you'd known nothing about my plan. One of them doubted me and slapped my face. I told him that you'd have come along if you'd known I was off for the open road. I saved you from a beating, Rory. You owe me a favor."

Rory mulled that over as he wondered how much of it was true. Rose might give him an alibi if he slipped back by starlight to untie his fellow Highlander. He asked, "What about the black behind you?"

"What about him? Leave him for the Sassunach to find there in the dawn!"

"I wasn't thinking about whether we should untie him or not. I was thinking he'd tell them how you got loose."

"I see what you mean. We'll have to cut his throat, then."

Rory kept his face blank, his mind made up. Angus Mohr was completely mad. Running away was one thing. Cold-blooded murder was a hanging offense.

"I'll be back if I can slip away," Rory lied. "The old man keeps a watch on me."

Before they could argue further, Kofi the Ashanti and Pardus came to join them. Kofi pointed to Angus Mohr and said, "See, Master? The white man is burned, as I told you."

Isaac Pardus nodded, took off his militia greatcoat, and draped it backwards over the Highlander's chest, buttoning the collar around the back of Angus Mohr's neck as he soothed, "I'm going over to the mansion and have a talk with the Proprietors about this, Scottie."

Angus Mohr blinked in surprise. Then he asked, "Do you have a name, Sassunach?"

"I'm Issac Pardus. Is that important, now?"

"It is if I live and you ever need a favor. They call me Angus Mohr and my people are the children of Rod Dhu Revan Sweyn—or, as we're called for short, MacQueen."

Pardus stepped back and said, "Pleased to meet you, Mister MacQueen."

Rory said something in the Gaelic, and Angus Mohr said, "My friend says he'll remember you, too. We've had little kindness from your people, so such as we receive is easy to remember."

Pardus said, "Wait right here," and then flushed and stammered, "I didn't mean that as a joke. I'll be back to tell you what they say."

Pardus and his servant walked away toward the governor's mansion and MacQueen started to explain. Rory cut in with, "I got the drift of it. Their tongue is easier to understand than it is to speak."

"Let's get back to getting me out of this fix, damnit."

"Why don't we wait and see what the Saxon can do?"

"I'm going to be lashed, at the very least of it. Remember how they lashed us both that time we tried to break out of Sterling?"

Rory laughed. "Och, those were the good old days, weren't they? If you'd only learn to keep a cool head, Angus, you'd spend less time being beaten."

"Och, what's a rebel for if he gives in?"

"He's dead, most likely. There's nothing left to fight for, Angus. Our chiefs are all dead, in exile with the Stuarts, or licking the boots of German Georgie. The risings are all over and done with."

"That's not true. The Highlands will rise again and again till our own are on the throne again. Why, we only lost a thousand or so at Culloden. If the chiefs should ever burn the crosses on the beacon hills again to assemble the clans—"

"The days for burning crosses are over, Angus. Half the clans who were out in the '15 turned their backs on us in '45. The Campbells, MacLeods, and half the MacBeans fought *against* us! Clan Donald held back and never really got into it this last time. Like it or not, the old ways are finished."

"What are you going to do, drop the Mac from the front of your name and become a damned Sassunach named Martin?"

"That's not a bad idea for the future. Right now, I have to stay alive, learn the Strangers' tongue, and work off my indenture."

Pardus and his Negro returned with two militiamen and a plump man in white wig and too-tight pink satin breeches. Pardus removed his coat from Angus Mohr's chest and said, "See? What did I tell you?"

The official from the Proprietors' office made a silent whistle and said, "By George, he is a bit well done." He addressed his next remarks to Angus, saying, "Through the good offices of Private Pardus and the gramercy of the Georgia governing body, young man, I intend to end your punishment—subject to your word that you'll stop this foolish mucking about in the swamps with the Indians."

"I've had my fill of Creeks, Gov'nor," MacQueen said cautiously.

"I should hope so. You'll be bound over to Master Carruthers, to take the place of that chap who died over there. I understand he's draining more rice lands, and you'll have more than enough to keep you out of mischief. Do we understand one another, young man?"

Angus nodded and the plump man signaled the militia-men to untie him. As soon as he was free of the wheel, Angus Mohr attempted a few steps and fell, unconscious, to the grass.

"I told you this sun was too much for him," Pardus said.

The bewigged official said, "Quite. We'll wet him down and carry him to Carruthers. What was that you were say-ing about the nigger on the other wheel?"

"*You* were saying his master feels he's incorrigible," Par-dus said.

"Quite. The Palmers need a house servant, not a nigger who thinks he's a damned racehorse."

"I understand, but my man Coffee here tells me he thinks he can handle the boy. Coffee's a good worker, but there's just too much at my place for the two of us to han-dle. If the price was right, I might take the boy off the Palmers' hands."

"Mmm, I think that might be arranged. What do you mean by the right price?"

"Half," said Pardus flatly. He saw the undecided look in the fat man's eyes and quickly added, "Listen, he's a run-away and can't understand orders in English, right? I have Coffee to pass my orders on to him, but he's a skinny little thing and we know he's not too bright. I'll give Palmer ten shillings on the pound and take my chances with, uh, what's his name?"

"Jeaco."

"Right, Jacob it is, then. What do you say?"

"You'll have to work it out with Palmer."

"So I'll work it out. Meanwhile, let us untie him. He's been on that wheel as long as the white boy, and you can see what being left there overnight did to *him*."

The fat man sniffed and said, "Don't be ridiculous—he's a nigger. Everyone knows they don't feel pain as we do. We'll just leave him out here to think things over until you've bought his papers—if you do."

Rose Donovan lay spreadeagled on the rumpled bed staring at the rough-hewn rafters of Thatcher's cabin as the old man licked her groin between her generous thighs. It felt pleasant, but, in truth, Rose was sated with her double ration of nightly sex and getting a bit bored with the two of them. Silas was a skilled lover, but unsightly. Rory, waiting in the barn for what they had come to call his English lessons, was handsome but clumsy, and unwilling to experiment with oral sex. Neither of them, she knew, respected her. To both men, she was merely an object.

Rose was tired of being an object. She had been no more than that since that awful day her father had sold her, crying and pleading, to the people in the Great House. The landlord's son had said he loved her as he'd bruised her with his brutal and unnatural desires, but when Herself of the house had caught them on the back stair and ordered her indenture sold, the lord's son had gone riding and never said a word in her defense.

Silas put two fingers in her. Now he was getting excited. Rose moved her pelvis skillfully as her mind drifted back to the Great House on the hill and how enchanted she had been by it after her father's wee stone shanty with the pigsty in one corner and the chickens scratching on the dirt floor.

"Art coming, lass?" Silas mumbled, his lips moving in her pubic hair, and Rose murmured, "Oh, do it some more!" and went back to dreaming of the Great House on the hill.

She knew just how she'd have it, if ever her fortunes should turn. She knew, as well, that she was probably doomed to the life she was leading now, for she was sterile from that brutal abortion and nearly thirty besides. But it was a pleasure to dream when dreams were all one had to live for. If *she* had been the mistress of the Great House, there would have been more color in the rooms. Once she had seen red velvet drapes, and they had been made a part of her dream house. Another time, taken to a rich man's apartments for the night, she had been delighted by the rainbow facets of a cut-glass chandelier. Some day she would have an even bigger one made for her bedroom. There was an Italian glassmaker down by the docks who made trade beads for the Creeks. He would know how to make that glass that the rainbows danced in.

Silas was caressing her more urgently now, and she made her muscles tighten around his thrusting fingers. He slid his lips up her body, groping at her flesh as he got into position and thrust his poor little thing into her. She bit his collarbone and murmured, "Och, *do* it to me, darling!" as she wondered just how much the Italian would charge for a modest chandelier. She had six Spanish dollars and an English shilling held back from the household expenses. The mean old man was tight-fisted with his money, even though he couldn't seem to get enough of slobbering love words up her cunt. . . .

He was slobbering them in her ear at the moment, so Rose wrapped her legs around his waist, raked his heaving back with her nails to excite him, and murmured huskily, "Now! I want it all now!"

She waited until his thrusting had subsided and whispered, "That was lovely. Can't we do it again?"

She knew he couldn't, but it pleased him so to have her ask. Silas rolled off her, sighing, "I'd like to, lass, but it's late and the lad and I have more timber to clear tomorrow."

He reached out a hand for the tumbler of rum she'd placed on a box near the bed and mused, "The Scotchman's a good worker. It's all I can do to keep up with him."

Rose laughed and said, "Garn, he hasn't half your staying strength, old man. I'll bet he's fast asleep right now. He looked tired when I fed him in the lean-to before."

"Well, he's not used to long hours like an honest English farmer is. Them Highland rascals are only good for bursts of raiding and cow thievery. Steady toil weakens them."

He took another sip as Rose cuddled against him, stroking his bony chest. She knew the stroking and the rum would have him fast asleep in no time, and Rory was waiting for her in the barn.

Over at the Pardus holdings, young Jeaco was learning about life in the New World. He had behaved well enough at the supper table in front of the master and his wife, but in the quarters he was to share with Kofi, he had just made his first mistake.

Kofi had indicated the pallet in one corner where Jeaco was to sleep and had mentioned casually that they would be up early the next morning to put the finishing touches on the shed he had built over the new forge in the yard. Jeaco had said, "I don't take orders from you, boy. If the white man wants his old shed built, he can tell me himself."

Kofi turned from the bunk he had been about to climb into, kicked off his pantaloons, and walked slowly over to the youth in the corner. Jeaco tried to brazen it out by stammering, "Well, you and I are both slaves, aren't we?"

Kofi hit him.

Kofi hit him hard, and Jeaco's head slammed into the chinked logs behind him as another big fist slammed into his midsection. He doubled over. Kofi grabbed Jeaco's hair with one hand, his penis with the other, and threw him bodily across the cabin. Jeaco landed on Kofi's bunk, whimpering with pain and fear. The bigger man walked slowly over to him as Jeaco sobbed, "Enough! Don't hurt me any more!"

"Keep your voice down. The white people can hear us through that wall. You were saying something about masters and slaves. I know who the *slave* is here. Do you know who the *master* is?"

"I know, I know! It's the white man, Pardus."

Kofi smiled, slapped the youth with an open palm, and said, "Try a little harder. I swear, you're stupid, even for an Ibo!"

"You want to be my master, too?"

"I *am* your master, you half-witted little *fisi*! I told the white man I'd make you behave if he bought you. Do you mean to make a liar of me, boy?"

"No! Don't hit me! I'll do anything you say! You say we build the shack in the morning, we build the shack in the morning. We build it right now, if you say so!"

"That's better. Turn over and get on your hands and knees."

Jeaco hesitated, staring in dawning understanding at the bigger man's rising penis. He grinned and said, "You didn't have to hit me if that's all you wanted. I'll be the woman first, then you can take care of me, and—"

"I don't take the woman's part. Turn over, damn you! I've been too long without a woman or even a boy!"

Muttering half-formed protests, Jeaco bent into a doglike position on the bunk, his upthrust buttocks facing the standing Ashanti and his face near the log wall.

Kofi took a buttock in each big palm and thrust his glans hard against the substitute flesh. Jeaco was experienced at this, and he relaxed his sphincter muscles to accept his brutal lover's shaft. Kofi gritted his teeth in pleasure and drove in hard. The thrust banged Jeaco's forehead against the logs and the boy suddenly noticed that some of the chinking had fallen away. A shaft of candlelight was coming through from the other side.

This was interesting enough to occupy him for the time it took him to grow used to the discomfort of the big

Ashanti's selfish pleasure-taking. Jeaco managed to fix an eye to the crack and peeked through. He laughed and whispered, "I can see into the master's bedroom! The white man's pumping away at his fat wife!"

Kofi did not answer; he was enjoying himself so much he barely heard the boy's whispers. Jeaco's hand went to his own penis as he watched Pardus and his wife make love in the next room. The white woman had breasts like big pink melons, and she moved her pelvis rhythmically. Jeaco's imagination divided in a fantasy as he imagined his rectal opening as the white woman's vagina and his own turgid member as the white man's penis. He felt semen running down his scrotum as Kofi muttered, "Again! I want to come at least three times!"

"Go ahead!" gasped Jeaco, stroking himself harder.

On the far side of the wall, Rebecca Pardus stiffened and said, "Darling, I hear whispering."

Isaac said, "Shush, it's only the darkies talking."

Rebecca glanced at the wall and said, "I wish you'd put the candle out. What if there should be a hole in that log wall?"

"Why should there be a hole? I built that wall myself, and I like the candle lit. You have a lovely body, darling. I love to look down between us and watch myself sinking into you. I love to watch your breasts, too. With two children, you still have the breasts of the girl I married!"

"Please put the candle out, just this once? I promise, after I look at the logs from Coffee's side, I'll let you leave it lit all night!"

Pardus rolled half off her plump body and snuffed the candle wick with his work-hardened fingers. On the other side of the wall, Jeaco muttered, "Shit, they put the light out just as I was coming!"

Kofi had not missed Jeaco's complaint. In the morning, he would have to rechink the wall. He knew what peeping through walls could lead to, and, in truth, he was curious himself. He would have to remove the temptation before he found himself doing something wrong.

FIVE

It was nearly a year before the Indian troubles started. By that time, the original Negroes and Highlanders had all become reasonably fluent in English, and others had arrived in a series of small, discreet shipments. Rum and chattel slavery were still officially forbidden in Georgia, but the prohibitions were almost openly flounted. James Oglethorpe remained in England, beset by his political enemies and fighting to keep his seat in Parliament.

The established bondservants instructed the newcomers as the number of contract laborers grew. The legalistic fiction of indenture was preserved with punctilio. Bewildered Africans, after months of brutality on slave ships, were suddenly asked to make their marks on scraps of paper. Those few who refused were ordered back aboard the slavers and sold, with less formality, up the coast in Charleston. The rum from Boston was landed in casks marked "fever medicine" and accepted as such by the harbormaster's understanding clerks.

The flow of Highlanders dried up after a few more ships arrived from Glasgow, but their numbers were made up by orphans, vagabonds, and an occasional innocent apprentice kidnapped by a captain anxious to sail. But strangely, to men accustomed to thinking of Britons as a superior breed, the Negroes were proving much more valuable as workers. There were few skilled farmers among the white indentured servants, and even those few were ignorant of subtropical agriculture. Rory MacMartin and the other Highlanders had grown sheep and cattle on the cool, damp moors, and little but oats on their tiny crofts.

The West Africans, on the other hand, were almost entirely from farming tribes. Their slash-and-burn methods were unscientific and would in time harm the soil of Georgia so severely that their effects would still be visible two hundred years later. But in the beginning, there were bumper crops of tobacco, corn, rice, and indigo.

Indigo was the most profitable of all in those pre-aniline days. The crop required a lot of labor and the preparation of the oxide dye-cake even more, but once the small blue-black cubes were produced, a fortune could be shipped in little space. The Scots and even the English bondsmen recognized indigo as a much larger oriental relative of a common European weed called woad. Once ancient Britons had painted themselves blue with the juice of woad, but their descendants considered cultivating it a waste of effort, and, when forced to, did a poor job of it. The Africans had no idea what the white men wanted with the little blue-black cubes, but they were very good at producing them.

In addition, okra and yams had been introduced by the Africans and now added variety to the planters' tables. An African method of cooking became the basis for the southern style of frying chicken. And so many planters, given their choice, preferred to buy the indenture of a Negro rather than that of some shiftless British vagabond.

Rory MacMartin had cleared all the land Silas Thatcher could legally claim under Oglethorpe's original charter, but, while the timber had been sold at a tidy profit, the homestead was still rundown and the crops poorly tended. Rory was good with an axe, but grubbing with a hoe was not a task to set a Highlander.

The Pardus holdings were now blossoming like a rose. Kofi—or, as he now styled himself, "Coffee Pardus"—had prospered in the land of opportunity. Isaac Pardus had acquired the services of four more Negroes, one of them a woman. The woman was a Fanti, no longer young and very fat, but at least she was a woman. Coffee had appropriated her and kicked Jeaco, now known as Jake, out of his quarters. The boy's services were now rendered to the three new men (renamed Shadrach, Meshach, and Abednego by Pardus in what his wife described as one of her Isaac's silly moods).

The woman's name was Fiba, and, after some argument, she answered to the name of Phoebe. Freed of sexual frustration and his duties in the fields, Coffee tinkered and rebuilt constantly. The small smithy expanded to a sizable workshop, and there Coffee mended or manufactured most of the implements used on the plantation. The "Big House" that the master's family occupied began to be worthy of the name as Coffee added wings and a portico to it. It was he who suggested that they build the row of modest cabins farther back from the big house and the wing that he and Phoebe occupied. He remembered the peeping habits of the unruly Jake, and it had taken a couple of good beatings to cure the boy of his sniggering descriptions of the naked white woman. Shadrach had made the mistake of speculating on the budding breasts of little Sarah, and had been beaten so severely that Pardus had commented on it and had had to be told a lie about a timber falling on his servant's head.

Meanwhile, Coffee was educating himself. His indulgent master encouraged his reading, and one day Coffee came across the secret of gunpowder in an encyclopedia Isaac had loaned him.

It was surprising how many dangerous secrets the white men put in their books for anyone to learn with the small effort of reading them. He had been initiated, and a warrior, before the elders let him have the secret of tempering a spear blade, yet there it was in the book: a pinch of saltpeter, sulfur, and charcoal. Now all he had to know was just what saltpeter was—and, more important, how one made it.

He had grasped alphabetic listings, and, when he had cautiously asked his master for the book marked SA TO TA, Pardus lent it to him with no suspicious questioning.

Saltpeter was a white powder found in urine and barnyard earth, Coffee learned. The process of separating the salts from the other matter was simple. Coffee set up a crude but effective apparatus in his cabin, and when Phoebe asked him what he wanted with jars of stinking soil, he only had to hit her once to curb her curiosity. Phoebe was a good bed partner and she kept his quarters clean, but she had gotten too friendly with the master's wife, and Coffee wasn't sure how Pardus would take it if he learned that his overseer was experimenting with gunpowder in his spare time.

The Hebrew books were beyond him for the moment. Pardus had explained the Hebrew alphabet with some amusement, but the books were written backward, and even when you took this into account, the words made no sense when one formed them on one's lips. Pardus read from the Hebrew books on the Sabbath, so Coffee knew they were worth reading. Truly, the white man's secrets were one basket inside another. Pardus had explained the kosher cooking laws to him and to Phoebe, and the rules were simple enough. The white people ate no pork or shellfish. They never had meat with dairy products on the same

table. That was simple enough. But *why* this should be so
eluded Coffee. Perhaps, when he learned Hebrew, the secret would reveal itself.

Phoebe had not worried about the deeper meaning. Once
Rebecca Pardus had taught her to keep a kosher kitchen,
Phoebe accepted it as simply another custom. Phoebe was
a simple woman who took life as it came. The mistress and
the children never hit her, and Coffee did only on rare occasions when he was having one of his fool notions. He was
nicer to her than her last man had been. Life was good on
the Pardus holdings.

The first man killed by the Creeks was a pearl-dredger
named Collins. After killing him—slowly—they put his
mangled remains in an old canoe and allowed it to float
down the Savannah.

Muskeecola was summoned to the governor's mansion
and made another speech about Oglethorpe and Toma-Chi-
Chi being brothers. He explained that a branch of his nation had broken away, and it was the renegades who had
killed the white man. Muskeecola called the young malcon-
tents Seminoles and explained that the older chiefs had no
control over them. When prodded on this point, Muskeecola reminded the Proprietors that they had claimed to
have no control over the rough long-hunters from the Carolinas. The Proprietors sent him back with trade beads and
a friendly warning.

A week later, the Creeks—or Seminoles—jumped a
party of surveyors and butchered all but one of them. The
survivor, staggering into Savannah with a reed arrow broken off in one arm, said the Creeks had had a Spaniard
with them, urging them on.

A cutter was sent to St. Augustine with a protest. Neither the vessel nor its crew was ever seen again. When His
Majesty's frigate *Medusa* sailed into St. Augustine with its
gunports uncovered, the Spanish governor protested that he
knew nothing of Indians or of a missing cutter from Savannah.

The Proprietors decided it was time to call out the militia.

This was more easily said than done. The military repre-
sentative of each household showed up for muster willingly
enough, but the idea of a punitive expedition into the tidal

swamps and subtropical forests to the south was another matter.

Silas Thatcher came home from the muster badly shaken. He threw his cockaded tricorn on a table and asked Rose to fetch Rory in from the field. When the younger man appeared, Silas waved him to a seat and poured him a stiff drink of rum. Rory sipped it warily as he asked the old man in his new, oddly lilting English, "What is it, Laird? You look like a man who's just met the gray piper in a graveyard."

Silas explained to Rory and Rose about the expedition against the Seminole Creeks. His voice was a whine as he added, "I can't leave with the crops ready to be sold off. I'm not a well man. There's no telling how far we'd have to march, and you know I have a bad leg."

Rory nodded and suggested, "Don't go, then. Tell them you're too old to go for a soldier."

"I'll lose my land and all I've worked for these past ten years! I hold this land on a militia charter, son. You see how it is, don't you?"

Rory shrugged and sipped some more rum. He saw what was coming, but he was enjoying the old goat's agony, and, if he was right about the man, he saw the opportunity he'd been waiting for.

Rose soothed, "You can beg off as a cripple, Silas. If you were to limp a wee bit more when you go to town—"

"That's not the point!" snapped Silas. "I simply have to send an armed militiaman from this plantation or I lose it all!" He smiled suddenly at Rory and said, "You'll do it for me, won't you, lad?"

"I'm an indentured servant, not a soldier."

"Ah, but you used to be a soldier, and a fine one, too, they tell me! If you were to take my place—"

"I'd probably wind up with a Creek arrow in me. I've learned enough English to understand the indenture laws, Laird Silas. If I were to take your place in the trained band, I'd have to volunteer of my own free will."

"Well, now, they'd take you if you *offered*, lad. They know you've been a soldier, and—"

"What's in it for me?" Rory asked flatly.

Silas stammered, "Why, a chance to serve your king and country, of course. Have you no patriotism, lad?"

"My country is Scotland, not Georgia, and my king lies over the water, drinking himself to death in French exile. As for patriotism, I was younger when they burned the assembly crosses on Ben Nevis. I've learned more than the English since then."

Silas Thatcher shook his head, refusing to hear, as he insisted, "You've got to do it, Rory. I worked too hard to lose it all now."

Rory let him sweat a bit more before he said quietly, "I'll take your place on one condition."

Thatcher gasped with relief and answered, "Name it, lad! What is it you want? Silver? I'll give you a shilling a day up to a hundred."

"Keep your silver, old man. It's my *freedom* I want! If I take your place in the trained band, I'll need, oh, fifty Spanish dollars and my indenture papers canceled."

Silas Thatcher blanched. "But, damnit, you owe me six more years, lad!"

"Ay, and you'll have small use for them when you're a lackland, too. We're wasting time in talking of it, Thatcher. I've offered to risk my neck to save yours. Take it or leave it—or would you rather have me get back to the cornfield, dear Master?"

Thatcher started to argue. Then his shoulders sagged and he said, "All right. I'll set you free and get myself a good stout nigger in your place. Does that satisfy you?"

"I'll need the fifty Spanish dollars for decent clothes and a start if ever I get back."

Thatcher, bowing to the inevitable, nodded and said, "Done."

Behind him, Rose had been trying to catch Rory's eye. She finally couldn't restrain herself and blurted, "Rory!"

The Highlander glanced up, met her eyes, and nodded. He took a sip of rum and said, "The lass gets her papers back, too, with ten Spanish dollars and all her clothes."

Thatcher whirled on his stool and gaped at Rose. "She doesn't want to leave me, do you, Rose?"

"I've served nine years on papers for seven," Rose said quietly. "You can keep your silver and the clothes on my back and I'll be content to walk out naked as a jaybird with my freedom!"

Rory said, "She gets ten dollars and her belongings or we both stay put and wait for you to lose us *and* the land!"

Silas jumped to his feet and tried to slap Rose, who

ducked out of range as he shouted, "I see it now! You've been plotting this all along, behind my back!"

"Sit down, you old fool," Rory said. "If you feel like beating someone, try your luck on me."

Thatcher sank to his stool, muttering, "This is petty treason. I could have you both flogged for conspiring against your master."

"Ay, and then you could march off to fight the Creek. Or skulk safe at home like the Sassunach craven you are—until they evict you!"

Silas Thatcher argued, pleaded, and threatened for nearly an hour before he gave in. Then the three of them walked into town and presented themselves at the governor's mansion.

The clerk who received them was surprised by the news of Rose's manumission but delighted to sign one Rory Martin into the trained band. As they stepped outside, Silas looked mournfully at Rose and said, "Well, you're a free woman and I can't lay a finger on you, so will you tell me one thing, Rose?"

"What's that, dear man?"

"You and this damned Scotchman here. Did the two of you . . . you know, behind my back?"

Rose Donovan threw her head back in triumph and jeered, "From the first night he was here—and, since you're so curious, he has a bigger prick!"

Silas Thatcher nodded quietly and walked away, suddenly much older.

Rose laughed and told Rory, "Faith, I expected him to hit me."

"I know, and I'd have let him."

Rory Martin found Isaac Pardus and his Negro, Coffee, working together on a wagon wheel in the Pardus smithy. Pardus stopped to wipe his hands on his leather apron as he took in the figure of a big blonde man in a new linen shirt and buckskin breeches. Pardus smiled and said, "Don't I know you, friend?"

"I'm Rory Martin. The last time we met, I didn't have the English."

"Oh, yes, from that day by the cannon. Tell me, how's your Scotch friend these days?"

"Angus MacQueen has signed up to fight the Creek. His master was a craven, too."

"Too? *You're* going in your master's place?"

"I have no master. I'm a free man now." He held out a piece of paper and said, "This is a drawing of a thing I want made. I understand that your nigger here can make most anything."

Pardus took the sketch, frowned at it, and asked, "What is it, an axe?"

"A Lochaber axe. I've written the dimensions in."

"So I see. What do you intend to cut down with it, a house?"

"Anything that happens to be in the way. Can your nigger make it?"

Isaac handed the sketch to Coffee, who examined it and said, "Too big. No man could hit anything with such a clumsy weapon."

Rory noted a steel plowshare leaning against a post. He picked it up in one hand, hefted it, and said, "Yon oak tree, by the fence," and he indicated a gnarled live oak fifty feet away.

He held the plowshare by one of its two clumsy handles, hefted it again to get the balance, and threw it overhand at the tree. The big awkward plowshare went end over end three times before its dull point thunked solidly into the bole of the tree and stayed there, ringing softly.

Isaac and Coffee stared at the unwieldy plowshare imbedded in solid oak at shoulder height. Finally Pardus laughed in delight and said, "I see it but I don't believe it!"

Coffee grinned and said to Rory, "I can make such an axe for such a man. When do you need it?"

"We march in two days."

Coffee nodded and Rory turned to Pardus, asking, "How much do you want for your nigger's time and the steel?"

"Please, we're comrades in arms. Take it as a gift and promise not to swing it at me!"

"You're marching with the trained band?" Rory frowned down at the smaller man.

Pardus sighed and said, "I know, I'm not even as strong as I look, and my wife is expecting, but what can I do?"

"You could send this nigger here. He looks big enough to go for a soldier."

"Coffee's offered already, but they won't accept darkies. Besides, I don't really mind. This country's been good to me and I knew the terms when I took this land. If only I knew how to shoot a musket, I'd make a fine soldier. Coffee here shoots like an eagle, but——"

"You let your niggers have guns?"

"What guns? I have only the musket they issued me. Coffee uses it to bag game for the table. I know the Torah forbids hunting, but he's not a Jew, and only the darkies eat the venison, so . . ."

He saw the suspicion in the big Scot's eyes and quickly added, "Look, if he wanted to kill somebody, he wouldn't need a gun. He's almost as big as you and as strong as an ox. I'm counting on him to protect my family while we're away. Isn't that right, Coffee?"

Coffee nodded and stared at Rory as he answered, "Yes, Master. Anyone who touches your wife or children while you fight for King George will die. He will die even if his name is King George."

Rory nodded and turned back to Pardus. "Ask the sergeant to put you in the line between Angus MacQueen and me. Angus has said you have his friendship, and the axe you're making for me will keep the gray piper at a distance."

"The gray piper?"

"*Bas*—you English call him Death. The Irish hear a woman keening on the wind when *Bas* comes to visit. My people hear a piper, far off and playing a lament no human piper knows. You stay between Angus Mohr and me in battle, and you'll come back to your wife and bairns, or no man will come back at all."

He nodded to the two of them and turned away, pausing before he left the yard to draw the plowshare out of the oak tree with one hand and return it to the spot where he'd found it.

Isaac Pardus shook his head and asked Coffee, "What do you make of him, Coffee? He's a bit theatrical, don't you think?"

Coffee picked up the wagon wheel he'd been working on and said, "I think you should do as he says and stay between him and his friend. You are strong for your size, Master, but your size is not great. I have been a warrior, and there is a look in the eyes of a man who kills easily. That big man with the yellow hair has that look. I am glad he is your friend instead of your enemy."

"Listen, I did his friend a small favor one time. You

remember. You were there. What did I do for either that
calls for blood oaths and dramatic remarks about fighting
to the death?"

"Forgive me, Master, but you do not understand men
such as that one and his friend. Such promises come easily
to their kind."

"You mean it was all just talk?"

"No, Master. I'm sure they meant every word."

He saw that Pardus still didn't understand and explained, "They are men of war. They *like* to fight. To a
man who enjoys slaughter, it is good to have a reason,
however slight, to keep fighting when their common sense
tells them it's time to stop. I know something of these
Scotchmen. They have no flag to fight under anymore.
They tell each other how much they hate you English—so,
if they intend to fight beside an Englishman, they have to
tell themselves it's to repay a debt. Now do you understand?"

Isaac Pardus shook his head slowly. "I think so. I feel
like David would have felt if he'd been adopted by two
Goliaths!"

The punitive expedition was five days out of Savannah
before they came upon the first Indian village. It would
never be established whether the Indians were nominally
friendly Creek or Spanish-inspired Seminole, but two men
had dropped out of the long hot march and were never
seen again, so it was probable they had reached Seminole
country.

The country was Georgia at its worst. Centuries-old trees
laced with vines barred their way whenever stagnant
swamp water or quicksand didn't. The sixty-odd men of the
column marched in single file with a quartet of friendly
Cherokee scouts to keep them from becoming hopelessly
lost. It was one of the Cherokee, ranging on ahead, who
came upon the stockaded village in a clearing in the marshy
cypress tangle. He reported his find to the ensign in command, a young Englishman named Ashton.

The Georgia militiamen attempted to form a line of battle unobserved, but they were up against some of the best
woodsmen on the North American continent. The Cherokee nearest Ashton heard the cry of an out-of-season robin
and hissed, "They know we come. Better we go back now."

Ensign Ashton shook his head, his white wig wagging its

tail in the forest gloom, and said loudly, "Sergeants, form a line of battle for the charge. We've been spotted and they're behind a palisade. When I give the signal, we'll fire a volley and charge through our own smoke with bayonet and butt-stock!"

There was a murmured consultation as the men fanned out and started marching in line toward the enemy some-where in the trees ahead. Men cursed and stumbled as they tried to keep in skirmish line among the trees, and then they were at the edge of a clearing and drew up, dressing down their line as Ensign Ashton stared thoughtfully at the featureless, drum-shaped wall of vertical logs on a slight rise in the middle of the clearing.

Not sure what the form was in dealing with Indians, Ashton tied his large white kerchief to the blade of his sword and turned to one of the Cherokee. He said, "I'm going to see if I can parley with their chief. I'll need you to translate if he doesn't speak English."

The Cherokee's eyes were impassive under his red tur-ban as he said, "If they are Creek, you will not need me. If they are Seminole, you still won't need me."

"I don't follow you."

"Every band has at least one old man who speaks Eng-lish. How else can they trade?"

"You mean even hostile Seminoles have translators?"

"Maybe yes, maybe no. Seminoles have bad hearts. They do not obey the laws of Toma-Chi-Chi. They obey no laws at all."

"But surely they understand the rules of war. I do have a parley flag here, you know. Let's go see what they have to say about those surveyors, eh?"

"You go. I stay here."

"Are you afraid?"

"Yes. I have been afraid before. That is why I am alive."

Ashton sneered and called out, "Sergeant-major! I'm going to see if they'll parley. Hold the men in line until I get back."

He stepped out into the clearing as his senior non-commissioned officer called out, "Begging the ensign's par-don, sir, but does he think it's wise?"

Young Ashton walked toward the stockaded encamp-ment, waving his parley flag as he called out, "Ahoy, you chaps in there! Do any of you speak English?"

Something glinted through the sunlit air and Ashton

staggered, turning toward his own men with a puzzled expression on his face and a reed arrow in his back.

A Cherokee shouted, "Ambush! *Behind* us!"

Rory too had seen that the arrow was in the officer's back. He snapped at Angus MacQueen, over Isaac Pardus' bewildered head, " 'Ware your rear, Angus! It's the old heather trap!"

Angus hadn't waited to be told. Whirling with sword in hand, he grabbed little Pardus by the belt and snapped, "Come, lad, it's death to stand against the sky like this!" Then the three of them were charging into the forest gloom—or, rather, two of them were charging and Pardus was being half-carried by the belt.

Other arrows were shooting through the trees now as the English milled in confusion and the handful of Highlanders in the band, who had suddenly found themselves in their own element, followed after the trio in the van. A MacAlpine screamed, "*Cumrick Bas Ailpein!*" as a recently arrived MacLean, not to be outdone, shouted, "*Cumrick Killiecrankie agus Sheriffmuir agus Culloden!*"

The forest echoed to the savage war cries of a dozen clans as Angus MacQueen dragged Pardus after Rory of the Battle Axe, who had spotted movement in the leaves ahead and rushed it with his terrible Lochaber, screaming, "Meat! Fresh meat!"

A naked man in warpaint tried to roll aside as Rory crashed through the clump of sea-grape the Indian had been shooting from. The wide steel blade of the Lochaber sang through the air and cut the Indian in two at the waist. Rory tore through the cloud of blood without breaking stride and saw another man rising from a clump beyond with his nocked arrow drawn to his cheek. Rory ran straight until the Indian loosed the long reed arrow; side-stepped; then kept coming as the man fumbled for a second from the quiver at his waist. This time the blow was overhand and the foeman was sliced in two from scalp to crotch. Rory ran between the two halves of the corpse before either had had time to fall. By now his once-white shirt was red.

An Indian he'd overlooked rose behind him with a drawn bow. Angus MacQueen spotted him from behind as Pardus shouted a warning. Angus dragged the frightened Isaac after him, muttering, "Don't yell like that, lad. It spoils the fun of sticking them from the rear!"

"My God, my God, what's happening?" sobbed Pardus as the mad run through bramble and vine continued. His giant captor's glance was turned to the left as, on the right, an Indian leaped to his feet with bow half-drawn. Without thinking, Isaac pointed his musket and fired. The Indian jackknifed and flew backward, screaming. Angus whipped his head around, blood-slicked sword at the ready, and, taking in what had happened, grunted, "That's *two* I owe you, Isaac Pardus!"

"Dear God, I don't believe this!" gasped his unwilling comrade. Isaac Pardus was not a cowardly man. He'd been perfectly willing to fight for king and country in anything resembling a reasonable man's idea of a war—but this was not war, this was madness!

Apparently the Indians felt the same way about it. The Highlanders charged another quarter mile through the forest and then slowed down to a walk when they found no opponents. Behind them gunfire sounded, and Rory turned and said, "Back to the others, lads. That's where the action is."

They returned the way they had come, stepping over broken branches and the mangled bodies of Indians. By the time they reached the clearing, the others were in possession of the village. Only a few men and boys had been left to defend it as the main body slipped around behind the column in a ploy that had often worked quite well for them in the past.

The defenders of the village, while few in number, had fought well to protect their goods and womenfolk. Eight Englishmen had died, in rushing the stockade and battering their way in. Another score were wounded. Of the non-commissioned, one was left in fit condition to command. As for the Highlanders, they had lost only one man in the woods. A kinsman carried him out to lie beside the others in the clearing.

The surviving corporal, now in command, met Rory near the village gate and grinned. "Jesus! You lot did a fine bit of work this day. You're covered with blood, man! Are you wounded?"

"Just a bit soiled with honest toil. What have you got inside?"

"A score of women and children. The others bayoneted all the men and boys before I could stop 'em. I guess we'd better start back to Savannah, eh?"

Rory frowned. "What for?"

"What for? Why, damn it, man, we've got dead and wounded to look after."

"Bury the dead here and send the wounded back with one Cherokee and a few sound men to help them. This must be your first war, eh?"

"Goddamnit, Private Martin, I'll have you know that _I'm_ in command here!"

Others had drifted over to catch the exchange. Rory told the sole surviving officer, "Command me to press on and I'll follow you to Florida. Order me to retreat in the face of the enemy and you've given the one order any soldier is free to disobey."

"We're with you, Martin!" said a dirty, tired militiaman. To Rory's surprise, he was an Englishman.

Rory had been holding his battleaxe at his side, gripping it at a point on the long handle that was close to the heavy blade. Now he let the polished wood slip through his cupped palm until he was gripping it near the handle's end, the broad blade touching the grass tips. He suddenly swung the Lochaber up and let go. The steel flashed in the sunlight as the weapon went end over end to a great height before pausing at the top of Rory's throw and returning to his upthrust hand like some grotesque but well-trained falcon. The corporal flinched back, as Rory had known he would, and the stunt drew the attention of every man in sight—as he'd hoped it would. Holding the Lochaber axe aloft like a banner or a tackman's flaming cross, Rory shouted, "_Cluinn so!_ I am marching for the border! Who goes with me?"

Angus MacQueen yipped, "The Cat and Hound together!" as he drew his rapier and, not to be outdone, sent it flashing end over end three lengths into the air before catching it by the hilt on its return.

Little Gavin MacPhie had been standing in the background, dark and silent as always. He shifted the musket he'd been issued until its bayonet was pointed at the sky. MacPhie had never been a lad for speeches, and the raised blade said it all as far as he was concerned.

Another Englishman, not sure of the form, threw his tricorn hat in the air and shouted, "By God, I say we chase them to Florida!"

Donald MacUlrich drew a kitchen knife he'd tucked in a

stocking from force of habit and held it over his head, saying, "I stand with my clansmen!"

Two militiamen came out of the Indian gate, puzzled by the noise outside. One of them asked, "What's going on?" Another English settler grinned and said, "We're pressing on."

The corporal sputtered, "We are like hell!" but nobody seemed to hear him. One of the Englishmen who'd just joined the group exclaimed, "I like it. Let's drive it into the bastards to the hilt!"

MacGillonie, Rory's clansman of the brows that met in the middle, began to chant, "*Chlanna nan con thigibh a so's . . .*" as other men, including German Lutherans, refugee French Huguenots, a Swiss, two Italians, and most of the English militiamen shouted their agreement.

Isaac Pardus suddenly found himself shouting, "Yes, by God! I say we chase them clean to Florida! I'm with you, Mister Martin!"

Then he lowered his bayonet with a puzzled little smile and muttered, "My God, I just went crazy!"

The English corporal pleaded and threatened, but few of the victory-drunk militiamen could be persuaded by a man they now thought of as a rank coward. In the end he started back for Savannah with the wounded and a handful of men who'd either been impressed by his threat of a mutiny charge or had simply had enough. One of the men who left with the corporal was a Scot. His name was not recorded, or ever again spoken, by the members of what was to go down in Georgia history as Martin's March, for a Highlander who quit after a single battle was hardly worthy of remembrance.

The corporal demanded, then begged for, at least one Cherokee scout, but the Indians flatly refused to leave just as things were getting interesting. The Cherokees had felt a certain amused contempt for the blue-sleeves with his white wig, whereas this new leader who yelled like a wolf and fought like a bear was a man after their own hearts. They had decided to call Rory "Big Tomahawk," and their leader announced that they were with him to the Long Sleep.

When MacQueen suggested a grim solution to the prisoner problem, the Cherokees offered to help MacQueen and two kinsmen of the Highlander who had been killed in the woods by a Creek arrow.

Rory stood in silence, leaning on the handle of his grounded Lochaber, as MacQueen explained the logistics with a lighthearted smile on his flushed face.

"Most of the menfolk were killed in the rush on yon palisade, you ken, but we've muckle women and bairns left to deal with, Rory."

Rory shook his head. "I'll have no Campbell tricks here, Angus."

"Och, who's talking of the Massacre of Glen Coe, lad?" MacQueen quickly protested.

"I thought you were. I see no reason why we can't just leave them to the mercy of the swamp and march on. We've done all the men. Why not leave their squaws to keen over the litches and bury them?"

"Och, Rory, you've a lot to learn of blood and slaughter. The men still thirst for vengeance, ay, and yon Indians will think you've gone soft, for Cherokee take no prisoners."

"Damnit, Angus, I'm not a Cherokee, and we've just agreed the Campbell trick at Glen Coe was a black deed all Scots remember with loathing!"

"Ay, as well they should, for the women and children murdered at Glen Coe were *white*, you see. We're not dealing with Highland croftfolk, here, Rory. A firmer hand is wanted when it comes to savages that even other Indians hate and fear."

"Och, you're daft, man! What can yon squaws and their bairns do, now, to trouble us?"

"Nits grow up to be lice, man. Yon squaws will raise their sons on tales of this day's work, ay, and give birth to other sons to come. Our Cherokee and the others want to do them this day, while the work is still easy. As for myself, I'm of the same mind."

"Damnit, Angus, who's in command here?"

"Now that's a good question, Rory of the Soft-Hearted Lowland Ways. Do you think we should put it to a vote?"

Rory flushed, and for a moment the life of Angus MacQueen was balanced on a finer edge than MacQueen might have thought. Then Rory shrugged and said, "You do as you like with the captives. I'll be after supervising the burial detail over yonder in the meadow."

Hefting his Lochaber, the bigger man walked over to where Gavin MacPhie and some others were digging a slit

trench near the battle casualties stretched out in the trampled grass. He didn't look back as MacQueen shouted
something to one of the Indians. As he stood at the edge of
the mass grave, staring soberly down at the water oozing
up through the black muck as fast as the men could dig, a
high-pitched female scream echoed above the clearing.
Rory cleared his throat and muttered, "You've dug enough,
lads. The water table's high in this swampy ground. We'll
bury them shallow and hope for the best."

The small dark MacPhie stabbed his tool into the semili-
quid spoil pile, shifted the quid of tobacco in his mouth to
one cheek, and asked quietly, "Are we going to bury the
women and bairns when MacQueen's had his way with
them?"

Rory's face was carefully blank as he said, "Angus Mohr
is but carrying out my orders. Do you question them, Wee
Gavin?"

MacPhie shifted his chaw again, spit, and murmured,
"Many years ago my clan was broken by the Laird of the
Isles, as all here ken. Those of us who survived the loss of
Bonny Colonsay and our cows were sheltered by the House
of Lochiel."

"Och, I know that story, Wee Gavin, and I know you
and yours have served my clan faithfully since that day."

"Ay, MacPhie has stood by the Sons of the Hound in
sunshine and in shadow. It was an arrow shot by a Mac-
Phie that killed the Champion of the Cat at Glen Loy. Ay,
and you ken how many of my people died under Lochiel's
red-and-green banner on Culloden Moor."

"Culloden is over and done with. Get to the point,
Gavin."

"I'm asking, as an old and faithful retainer, for a word
in private. It's for you to say if we have it or noo."

Rory nodded. "The rest of you lads start planting the
litches. Let's take a stroll, Gavin of the Puzzled Frowns."

The two Highlanders walked away from the burial detail, their disproportionate shadows on the grass before
them causing Rory to grin and ask, "Is it true that your
clan is related to the Wee Folk, Gavin? I left sisters in the
Great Glen half again as tall as yoursel'."

On other occasions, Gavin had responded to the banter
with teasing jests of his own, but his grim look remained as
he asked, "Why are we murdering the bairns and womenfolk, Rory?"

Rory sighed and said, "*We* do no such thing, Gavin. Angus has his blood lust up and—"

"I thought *you* were in command, Rory."

"A'weel, I am in a way, but have you ever watched cattle stampede, Gavin?"

"Ay, but what have cows to do with the slaughter of prisoners?"

"Forget the damned Indians! I'm trying to teach you a lesson in military strategy."

"Is that what we're after calling murder, then?"

"It is, Goddamn your eyes. What did you think warfare was, a game played by lads with a ball in the grass? I know it's a dark thing I've let MacQueen do, Gavin. Sometimes a leader has little choice. It's like when the cattle stampede. The herd bull can either follow or, if he wants to remain the herd bull, run like the devil and keep his position at the head of the cattle."

MacPhie spat again and said, "Ay, I reckoned as much, but I don't like it. I don't like the change that's come over yoursel', either. You were ever a sober, sensible lad in the old country, fighter though you were. I don't understand this change that's come over you. I don't understand this Cock o' the North swagger, or the new cold heart you seem to have grown."

Rory's voice was bleak as he said, "If my new heart's a cold one, it's because the Strangers broke the one I was born with, Gavin. I know what you're thinking. You think I'm pretending to be something I'm not."

"Well, and aren't you?"

"No, and don't look at me that way. For God's sake, Gavin, less than two weeks ago I was a slave. Today I'm the leader of a royal militia force of a full platoon, counting the Cherokees, and I did it all by simply yelling louder and moving faster than any other man here!"

Somewhere in the balmy sunlit air a baby was crying, and MacPhie said, "Dear God, they're doing the bairns! We have to stop them, Rory!"

The younger man's voice was deliberately cruel as he asked, "How? Would you have me kill Angus and his new-found red-skinned friends?"

"I'd stand by your side if you were of a mind to."

"Och, you're daft, Wee Gavin. It's caught in the tides of war we are this day. All a man with sense can do at times like this is to go with the current and keep his head above water until he sees his way to safe ground."

"It's not right," MacPhie insisted, adding, "For war is a nasty business, as any man named MacPhie should know, but do you remember the day we took Glasgow, and how some of our lads got out of hand with the looting and raping of the city?"

"Och, there was only a wee bit of that, Gavin."

"Ay, because Lochiel went to the prince and told him we'd be no party to the mistreatment of innocents, Lowlanders though they might have been. The Gentle Lochiel spared those redcoats we took near Derby, too. Are you saying your own chief was not a man of war?"

Rory shrugged and answered, "Lochiel is a crippled exile in France this day. The Cluny MacPherson was decent to prisoners, as was Lord Lovat. The Strangers hanged both, pulled out their guts, and cut them in quarters like sides of beef. Lovat's teeth were sent as a trophy to German George."

A child screamed in the distance. MacPhie waited until the frightened wail ended before he observed, "*You* were never born a Sassunach, Rory *nan* Lochaber!"

"Ay, but most of the men I lead this day are. If there's a thing I've learned since I rallied to the cross-burning on Ben Nevis, I've learned that most soldiers are bastards. If any man wants to lead in battle, he has to steel himself to be the biggest bastard in the band!"

"Is it so important, then, to be a leader?"

"It is for a man who's tasted bondage. I came to this land in chains, Gavin. I mean to die a gentleman and be buried on my own land. I'm free this day because I've gritted my teeth hard and accepted much a barefoot crofter would have resisted."

He saw that his follower remained dubious and added savagely, "Listen, damn you, this is my chance. When I saw my chance to gain control of this patrol, I reached out and seized it. I seized it firmly, as a clever man grasps a thistle. That's the trick of grasping a thistle, or any other dangerous prize. It hurts much less if you've the courage to *squeeze*, you see!"

A ghastly scream rent the air, and despite himself Rory blanched. Then he recovered, smiled thinly, and said, "We'd better get back to work. I want to move my patrol out of this clearing before nightfall."

Rory waited until MacPhie had gone back to the burial detail. Then he took himself to a nearby clump of brush, made sure he was unobserved, and vomited into the soft earth. When he had finished, leaning one hand against a tree trunk, he sobbed.

By the time he rejoined his men, Big Tomahawk was smiling, and the prisoners had all been annihilated.

The details of what came to be known as Martin's March were blurred by years of retelling by the men who'd taken part in it. The next few weeks were the stuff legends are made of—but for the militiamen taking part in the expedition, it was sheer hell.

They didn't march straight to the Florida border. Neither the lay of the land nor the objective of their mission would allow it. Rory—or, rather, his Cherokee scouts, who never got the credit—swept in hairpin turns through the tangled green hell of the southern coastal plain. Like a relentless broom, they swept every living thing before them and left little but death behind.

They lived off the country, barbarous as that country seemed to men accustomed to the neat fields and semicultivated forests of Europe. The low-lying ground was dissected by countless creeks of tea-colored water. Most of them were fordable, but sometimes the men rafted across, Rory's axe making short work of such trees as they needed. One man was bitten by a cottonmouth and died, despite the Cherokees' assurances that their rough surgery had always worked before. Another man was nearly taken by a tenfoot alligator, but an Indian scout noticed the strange log that seemed to be drifting against the current and shot the big reptile before it reached the wading militiaman. Its tail made a delicious stew.

They learned to choose between the sour but edible wild plum and the deadly manacheel that looked so much like an apple. The Cherokees introduced the whites to other reptilian fare, and it was generally agreed that diamondback tasted much better than cottonmouth, while the snapping turtle was best of all. They ate 'possum, coon, and venison. They shot colorful birds no white man had a name for and tucked bright feathers in their hats after roasting the birds on sticks. Once the Indians prepared a stew of the big black-and-yellow grasshoppers they'd gathered like berries along the way. Isaac Pardus excused himself by observing that they might not be kosher. The others tasted, gingerly, and then dug in. The thirty-odd men of the expedition fed on whatever they could find—and in turn were fed upon. They were bitten by mosquitoes, tormented by chiggers, and learned to remove ticks with a bit of burning punk. They were covered with insect bites, poison-ivy rash, and festering boils caused by nothing they could see or understand.

But they pressed on, cursing, staggering, and becoming, though they didn't know it, American frontiersmen—the same hard, half-savage breed of men who thirty years in the future would whip a professional British army and, in another century and a half of bitter struggle with nature and the original owners, would seize a continent.

They didn't meet half as many Indians on that march as the survivors would tell their grandchildren they had, but the fights they had were vicious by European or even Indian standards. With Rory leading, advised by his Cherokees, the wearisome rule books and the endless drilling on the muster green were forgotten. Men learned to reload muskets while lying on their sides in the muck behind a fallen log. Isaac Pardus now rammed two or three balls down against a double charge of powder, and when Isaac fired, the roar was awesome. And his aim was improving all the while.

Others preferred cold steel in the brief encounters with such hostiles as they stumbled upon. The skirmishes were short and bloody, and the whites had some advantage in hand-to-hand contests. The American Indian was not a homogeneous race. There was as much difference in size and build between the tall men of the great plains and the men of the southeastern tribes as there was between a Swede and an Arab. Most of the Georgia militiamen ran to size for Europeans. The small-boned Seminole Creeks were quicker, but nearly helpless in a rolling-in-the-mud stabbing contest.

Once Isaac Pardus was pinned for a moment by an Indian larger and heavier than he was, but Angus MacQueen kept a fatherly eye on his friend, and the Indian died before Isaac had fully grasped what he was doing on his back with a painted, naked man on top of him.

They eventually found another fortified village and rushed it under cover of darkness. Rory smashed through the logs with his giant axe and the fight was half over be-

fore the startled Indians knew what had awakened them.
The few survivors fled through the night in panic, pursued
by Cherokee taunts and the horrible sounds of Gaelic war
cries.

Later, they would claim they'd chased the Indians into
Florida. In truth, they were stopped by the swamps of
Okeefenokee. Rory led them a few miles into the trembling
bog while his Cherokees urged him to quit while he was
ahead. They finally convinced him he'd find more fever,
snakes, and quicksand in the Okeefenokee than he would
Indians, and in truth he was glad enough to see the end of
it.

There were more skirmishes on the way back. The noisy,
savage white men hadn't exterminated the Indians or even
driven them out of His Majesty's claims, but they'd taught
the Seminole Creeks to be very wary of proximity to this
new breed of white man.

It took them less than two weeks to march the ninety-
odd miles back to Savannah—they made nine or ten miles
a day while fording creeks, hunting for food, and back-
tracking to cut off Indians sniping at them with long reed
arrows. The last few miles took them through the open,
parklike country that gave the little town of Savannah its
name.

Rory re-formed his men and they marched into town in
step—twenty-two ragged, filthy, mosquito-bitten men in
tattered, blood-stained rags. An outlying planter had seen
them pass and had sent a slave ahead on a fast pony. As
the militiamen reached the center of town, the church bells
were ringing and people were pouring out of their houses
to cheer and ask for news of the casualties. Rory strode at
the side of his column, his Lochaber on his shoulder like a
musket, and as he saw the men in satin and white wigs
ahead, he shouted, "Look sharp and mind your step, Goddamn your eyes!"

The order wasn't really necessary. Encouraged by the
admiring glances and shouted cheers, the ragged men were
marching with a spring in their step and a dress to their
line that the King's Own Regulars might envy. Rory
marched them to the governor's mansion, halted them at
attention, saluted the lieutenant governor with his axe
blade, and snapped, "Martin's Company, Royal Georgia
Militia! Back from the Florida border, sir!"

None of what he said was true. He'd been enlisted as a private and the militia was hardly composed of royal troops, but they believed the part about the Florida border, and the other words didn't matter at the moment. The lieutenant governor and his aides stared at the line of filthy, tattered men for a long moment. Then the man appointed in Oglethorpe's absence asked, "Where are the others, ah, Corporal?"

"Sir, there are no others. But there are damned few Indians left between here and the Spanish claims, either! Didn't Corporal Wooster get back with the wounded, sir?"

"No. You've brought the first news of the fighting we've had. Where is Ensign Ashton?"

"Dead and buried with honors, sir. The Indians killed him under a parley flag. He placed me in command before he died like the hero he was!"

One of the lieutenant governor's aides whispered, "Who the devil is that big chap with the axe?" and another murmured back, "One of the Highlanders, I believe. Pushy bugger, isn't he?"

Someone in the crowd cried out, "Coleman! What happened to Sergeant Coleman?" and Rory said, "Killed in action. I'll put all the details in my official report, and a casualty list can be drawn from it."

The lieutenant governor frowned and asked, "What do you mean by official report, young sir? Just who do you think you are?"

"I'm the leader of Martin's Company, sir. We can discuss my rank in private. If you don't want an official report, I'll just dismiss the company and we'll forget the whole thing. My lads are anxious to rejoin their families and—"

"Hold on, there! Who's the ranking non-com here, Goddamnit?"

A man from the restless line of dirty men shouted, "It's Martin if it's anyone, Gov'nor!" and there was a low rumble of agreement. Another man shouted, "Damnit, Rory, I want to go home!"

Rory grinned at the white-wigged officials, turned to his men, and said, "I've just been told I'm not in command, so what in hell are you all waiting for?"

There was a roar of approval and the battered formation dissolved into men running to greet friends and relations in the surrounding crowd. Isaac Pardus heard his name being called and ran toward the woman standing near Coffee and his children. His steps faltered as he stammered, "Becky, oh, Becky!" and then he'd swept her off her feet and was carrying her to the waiting carriage as young Aaron tugged at his coattail, shouting, "Did you see any Indians, Papa?"

Coffee followed, holding the girl, Sarah, by the hand as he told the boy, "Don't pester your father, Master Aaron. You'll hear all about it many times."

Rory had started to walk away, his axe still on his shoulder, when a young man in face powder and a beribboned wig tugged at his ragged sleeve and said, "They want you over at the mansion, sir."

Rory kept walking, saying, "Och, I'm only a ragged Highland private. What would those grand gentlemen want with the likes of me?"

"They want to discuss plans for our next move against the Spanish Indians, sir."

"Och, do they now? And what rank did they give you to address me by?"

"Would ensign do for now?"

"For the next few minutes, maybe," Rory said, and he turned to follow the dandy young man back to the mansion. Inside, he found a group of officials crowded around the lieutenant governor and two Englishmen in tattered militia blue. The man in charge stood up and held out a hand, saying, "I've a better idea of what you've been up to, uh, Martin. The men you brought back are the only experienced militia we have at the moment. We'll want them reformed into an elite guard."

Rory ignored the hand and lowered his axe to the floorboards with a thunk before saying, "They fought like wildcats and wiped two Spanish Indian villages off the map. A bonus is in order for those lads, if you want my opinion."

"Your opinion is the matter we have under discussion, sir. How long do you think it would take you to get them back in shape to form a guard? We've full dress uniforms in mind, and—"

"They'd fight better in buckskins, and they still have the tomahawks they took from the Spanish Indians. I'd say, with a week's rest, they'd be ready to fight some more." He paused and added, "That is, if you've a man in mind to lead them."

"Um, we were thinking of offering *you* the post, with the

rank of ensign. It's not a full company, you know, and—"

"I can recruit a full company from among the men who know me in this colony, Gov'nor, but my rank would have to be *captain*. I'll need a land grant and some silver, too. I'm standing before you in all I possess, at the moment."

There was a sputter of indignation and then the lieutenant governor held up his hand for silence. "What you ask is out of the question, Martin. Why, damnit, you're not even *English!*"

Rory picked up his axe and said, "I'll be at the Crown and Anchor if you gentlemen should change your minds."

"Damnit, Martin, you're still a militiaman, subject to orders!"

Rory smiled. "I am not. I agreed to take Thatcher's place in the line for the duration of that last campaign. Read my enlistment papers if you doubt my word."

"You're still his substitute. You have to serve in the militia as needed until . . . ummm."

"You do see it, then? Without a land grant, I'm not required to serve as a permanent militiaman. Unless I get a *captain*'s grant, I'm off for the Carolinas as a free man, and you can find some bonny English lad with a beauty mark on his powdered cheek to command those men I whipped into soldiers for you. Whether they'll follow anyone but me is not my problem. I'll be off for the Carolinas long before the Spaniards counterattack."

"Sit down, Martin. Let's not be hasty."

"Och, I've had enough of your gab. I need a bath and some sleep. You can find me where I said when you've finished chewing it over between you."

He turned in the doorway to add, "I'll probably be there until Friday. I've a bit of silver left, but it may take me that long to book passage on a coastal schooner."

He went out to push through the cheering crowd around the steps. A man slapped him on the back and said, "Goddamnit, Martin, they ought to erect a statue to you!"

He shrugged his well-wishers off and made for the waterfront, wondering if he wasn't pushing his luck. Any military rank brought a land grant with it, and . . . then he shook his head. "It's captain I'll have or nothing," he told himself. "When you grab the thistle, you have to *squeeze!*"

SIX

Captain Rory Martin rode out to his grant in a pony cart with little Gavin MacPhie, whose indenture he had bought—along with those of the others in the original band who hadn't been smart enough to press their masters for manumission before taking their places in the campaign against the Spanish Indians. (Angus Mohr MacQueen, of course, had seen and grasped the same opportunity, and the Carruthers felt they were well rid of him.)

Rory was dressed in tight moleskin breeches and a loose linen shirt with a bit of lace at the collar. It was too hot for a waistcoat, but he'd powdered his hair, and a wee macaroni sword dangled at his side, half tripping him as he jumped out of the cart for a better look at his grant.

The block of land they'd given him was covered with sandy loam and perhaps a thousand trees. A solid wall of long-leaf pine faced Rory and Gavin as they studied the grant from the unpaved road.

The new landlord shook his head. "Even with the damned pine cleared away, there's not enough land to get rich on. I can see the soil's thin without testing it, and my captain's grant is not that much larger than Private Thatcher's. Goddamn Praying Jamie and his restrictions on holdings!"

Oglethorpe had made it illegal for any one man in the colony to own more than a "section" of land, or one square English mile. How long this could last was problematical. Savannah was still a mean frontier village compared with Charleston, Newport, and points north, but her merchants were chafing under the restraints of the absent Oglethorpe, and the simple yeoman farmers that the philanthropic governor had dreamed of were barraging Parliament with complaints about the restrictions on land holdings and the unfair competition from the slave-owning planters to the north.

The labor problem seemed to be the bar to further prosperity. Free workmen were able to demand, and get, as much as three shillings a day. In harvest time, they were able to demand four, and there went half the profit on a bumper crop. The trickle of indentured servants had helped a little, but not enough, and even a Negro bondservant had certain protection under English Common Law. A master could punish an unruly apprentice or indentured worker within reason, but he had to answer for a whipping that left scars or such persuasive aids to productivity as the branding iron.

There had to be a better way.

But Rory wasn't thinking about labor problems as he surveyed his new land grant. His Highlanders would work for him willingly enough, at least for now, for little more than food and board and promises. It was paying for the food, the tools they'd need, and the other immediate expenses of getting his first cash crop to the Factor's Wharf that concerned the new master of the unnamed plantation buried in the roots of a thousand or more trees.

Rory glanced back at the pony cart they'd ridden out in and told MacPhie, "I've an axe to cut them with, but pine timber is a glut on the market these days, and with the sailing season growing short—"

"Turpentine," Gavin MacPhie said quietly.

Rory frowned down on the little Island man and said, "Och, by the time we tap yon trees and haul the crude sap to the distillery in Savannah—"

"I can do it," said MacPhie.

"Do what, you fey little man? Why can't you ever come out with what's on your dark wee mind?"

MacPhie shifted his cud of tobacco, spit, and said, "I had a still in the glens, before they burned the crosses on Ben Nevis. It was the Creature we made where the tackmen couldn't see us, but a still is a still, and a man who can boil off malt liquor should be able to produce a wee bit of turpentine. The rosin and tar can be sold at a tidy profit, too, once you have it separated out and kegged."

Rory thought a moment and said, "Isaac Pardus has a nigger who can make anything. Pardus owes me for a Spanish Indian or two I pulled off him down the coast. But tell me, what can I grow on land that's covered by trees, full of turpentine as they are?"

"Why grow anything, Rory? There's no need to break our backs when other men have broken theirs for us!"

"Och, stop your speaking in riddles and have out with it, you wee canny thing! You're as bad as the witch, Gormsuil, when she warned the seventeenth Lochiel in riddles

instead of telling him straight out that the Athol had set a
trap for him by the shores of Lochan a' Chlaidheimh!"

"The warning saved Ewen Lochiel, did it not? You're a
blunt and impatient man, for a Celt. I mind it's the Norman blood in your sept of the clan!"

Rory forgot his English for a moment as he cursed the
little fey man with, "*Marbhphaisg ort*! Get *on* with it,
man!"

MacPhie chuckled and said, "Och, you've a poor mind
for business, I can see, but, taking pity on your great,
shaggy, albeit empty head, I know of a dozen Saxons
who've gone bankrupt in this colony after years of clearing
and draining. It's my thought you'd do better to let these
trees stand and drain them of their treasure till the price of
timber goes up again. Meanwhile, with a wee bit of cash
and the credit on future naval stores from yon grove . . ."

"*Gu dearbh*! You *are* a canny man! With a contract
for turpentine futures, and leaning on my grand new rank a
bit . . ."

"I thought you'd see it if you stopped charging into everything like a great mad bull!"

"We can get Angus, MacUlrich, and the others, and if I
offer them provisions for now and shares in the first shipment of naval stores, we can tap away while we wait for
sailing weather!"

"Angus Mohr's not here. He's up on the fall line with
MacAlpine and Glengarry, dredging for freshwater pearls.
If you want the others to work with a will, you'd best have
some rum out here with the parched corn and bully beef."

"I work as well with a dram myself, but rum is hard to
come by in this praying place, Gavin."

"I know where we can get all we want, and on credit,
too, I'll wager. You mind that Irish wench you were indentured with, Rose Donovan?"

Rory grimaced. "I remember her. Last time I heard of
her she was working in a brothel near the docks."

"Och, she has her own place now, with four bonny Irish
and one French girl to do the harder work. Rose is in free
trade these days."

"Smuggling? That's a hanging offense, man!"

"When the free trader's sleeping with the harbormaster
it's not. If it's true she owes you her freedom, she should be
worth a keg or two of the Creature. God knows she's
bringing in enough of the stuff!"

"I'll see her about it. then. But first I'll have to see Par-dus about the still. There's no sense tapping these trees un-til we know we're in the turpentine trade."

They were walking back to the pony cart when Rory had a sudden idea and asked the smaller man, "These stills you know of, Gavin, could you make *rum* with the right gear, if I got it for you?"

"I could if I had molasses, but there's little sugar grown this far north and we'd be at a disadvantage with the Bos-ton triangular traders. If you want, I can make some drink-able whisky from Indian corn, though."

"Corn liquor? I've never heard of it."

"That's because I haven't made it yet. If the Jew's nigger will build me what I need, I'll see what I can do. Is it to get out of owing Rose Donovan for the rum you're after, Rory?"

"Hell, no. It just came to me that if old Rose is selling Boston rum, we might as well have her selling our Georgia product!"

Rory nodded and said dryly, "Ay, I knew you were pa-triotic."

Despite his son's aristocratic pretensions, Efram Starr of Efram Starr & Sons had no intention of going into debt a second time. A clerk with a fine copperplate hand could be hired for a shilling a day in Liverpool. He'd be damned if he'd pay the three a day they expected on this side of the water for a mere fifteen hours' work! And so, while the heavy work in the chandlery was done by a pair of inden-tured Irish lads, the office work was attended to by old Efram himself—or, when business was slack, by a member of the family.

Rory tied his dappled pony to the rail out front and clumped up the wooden steps, left hand on sword hilt to keep the damned thing from wrapping itself between his ankles. He found a teenaged girl he'd never seen before behind the waist-high counter, and, taking her for a serving wench, he smiled and said, "Be good enough to announce me to your master, lass. It's Captain Martin who's come on business."

The girl flushed, nodded silently, and went to a door to call out, "Gloria, there's a gentleman here to see father!"

As she turned back, Rory removed his tricorn and bowed. "My apologies, mum. I didn't expect to find a highborn lady working here. You'd be Master Starr's daughter, ye say?"

The girl nodded and in a small shy voice said, "I'm Martha Starr, Captain Martin."

"Your servant, mum!" said Martin gallantly. A man had to start somewhere with this tomfoolery if he was to get the hang of playing the macaroon among these Sassunach.

Gloria Starr came out from the back, smiling with a hint of friendly mockery in her warm eyes as she said, "Oh, it's you, then, Rory? Or should I say Captain Martin these days? I was very pleased to learn of your good fortune, ah, Captain."

"It's some improvement over dragging logs, at that, mum, and you can still call me Rory if you've a mind to."

Her young sister-in-law suddenly gasped and asked, "Gloria, is *this* the man you've talked so much about? The Highlander who improved himself fighting the Indians?"

Gloria's cheeks turned a dusky rose as she dropped her mocking eyes and murmured, "Yes, the captain was a prisoner of war when we first met." Then she forced herself to meet his steady gaze as she asked, "What can we do for you, Rory? My husband's off with my father-in-law on business, but if there's anything you need . . ."

"I've been over to the Jew, Pardus."

"Oh, yes, the chap who led the charge against the Indians that time. Has he recovered from the swamp fever he came down with after you all got back?"

"Pardus is well enough. The fever comes and goes. What I went to see him about was a turpentine still. He has a nigger over there who can make most anything, and as you might know, I've a section of pine to be tapped."

"I see. You want to know if we'd be interested? You'll have to discuss terms with my father-in-law, but I know there's a ready market for naval stores. The *Nancy*, out of Bristol, came in last week with daylight showing a third of the way around inside her hold. We sold her a tremendous amount of tar and oakum."

"I intend to produce clear turpentine, clean rosin, and tar as fine as Stockholm can boast of."

"I'm sure you do, but I can't offer you a price until the men get back."

"I'm not worried overmuch about the price. I'm going to need barrels, buckets, and salt pork. I can get all the cornmeal and yams my men will need on credit, but they have to have a bit of meat if they're to work as hard as I mean them to, and—"

"You say you mean to have my father-in-law supply you on credit?" She laughed and added, "You don't know him very well, then, do you?"

Rory shrugged and said, "I've hauled in enough lumber for you people to know a bit about the way you do business, mum. I think I can sweeten the pot with better returns on an investment than most men hereabout."

"Well, if you want to wait a bit, they should be back any minute . . ."

Rory noticed that no mention had been made of his stepping through the counter-leaf to join them over a spot of tea in the back. He knew, from his months of delivering logs on foot, that it was their custom to invite their gentleman customers into the inner office. He felt his jaw muscles tighten and forced a pleasant smile to his lips. "I'll be pleased to do that, mum," he said, thinking, "I'd be pleased to throw you down and have you on the dung-covered floor of your stable, you highborn brown-haired snip!"

Almost as if she'd heard his unspoken thoughts, Gloria licked her lips and said, "I've some papers to attend to in the back, sir. Martha, here, will call me if there's anything else you want."

She turned and left the room, Rory's eyes burning a hole in her back—or, rather, a bit lower down.

The girl called Martha waited until her sister-in-law had left the room before she murmured, "It's my brother, you know."

"Beg pardon, mum?"

"My bother, Nathan. He's terribly jealous of you, Captain Martin. Gloria knew there'd be another scene if she invited you in the back."

Rory shot the young girl a puzzled frown and said, "I don't know what you're thinking, mum, but I assure you there's never been cause for Nathan Starr, or any other man, to be jealous of me where his wife is concerned. I may look the gallant Englishman, but we don't steal anything but cows where I come from!"

Martha laughed, her shyness fading as she realized that the dashing captain was a friendly young man after all. "It's not about Gloria, sir. It's your promotion Nathan can't abide!" she confided.

"Ay, I can see how a man might be galled by having the

gillie who fetched the wood rise a notch above him in yon militia."

"Nathan offered to go, you know. If it hadn't been for his ague, he'd have been with you when you and Ensign Pardus charged the Creeks that time."

"No doubt, mum." Rory smiled thinly.

"Pooh," the girl sighed, "you're jealous too. Is it Gloria or the times my brother twitted you as a transported rebel, Captain Martin?"

He flushed and said, "Och, lass, you don't know what you're talking about."

"I think I do," she insisted. "You men are all such big babies. Sometimes I wish I was big enough to spank the lot of you and make you all behave!"

Rory laughed down at her and said, "You've some growing to do before that day arrives, lass. Excuse me—Mistress Martha."

Before the banter could go further, Nathan Starr and his father came in. Efram Starr was less familiar to Rory than his son, and rather resembled an old woman in his ill-fitting wig and snuff-colored suit with yellowed lace at the collar and cuffs. Rory turned from the counter, bowed curtly, and said, "Good morrow, Chandler Starr. If I may have a word with you—"

The younger man of the family gasped, "God strike me, Rory! Who in blazes do you think you are to swagger in here and talk to your betters in that arrogant tone?"

Rory smiled wolfishly. "It's Captain Martin of Indigo Hall I am, sir. If you find my manner offensive, your seconds may attend on me at the Crown and Anchor any time between sunset and first light."

Nathan Starr blanched and, aware that his father and sister were watching and listening, stammered, " 'Pon my word, sir, you have a hair trigger on that temper of yours, I fear."

"It's been filed down by English insults, sir."

Efram Starr said, "I suggest we drop this macaroni display and find out what Captain Martin wants, Nathan." He turned to Rory with a raised eyebrow and a slight twinkle in his eyes and asked, "Was it for an affair of honor or some ship's stores you came shopping, Captain Martin?"

Rory had an apology or a challenge coming from the pale young Nathan, but he dropped the matter, saying, "I'm starting a turpentine camp in my timber lands, Chandler Starr. I'll need tools, cooperage, and some victuals for my crew."

Efram Starr nodded, lifted the leaf on the end of the counter, and suggested, "Let's go in the back and discuss it, then, Captain."

Rory nodded and stepped through as the chandler held the counter-leaf open for him. Nathan started to follow, but his father said flatly, "Stay out here with your sister. I'm expecting a keg of nails and you'll have to sign for them."

The head of the firm ushered his guest into the rear office and parlor, nodding to Gloria, who was seated at a desk with a quill, and saying, "You know my daughter-in-law, I believe, Captain Martin. Would you leave us a moment, my dear? The captain and I have business matters to discuss."

Gloria got up, looking slightly flustered and more than a little surprised. She said something about ship's biscuits and left by the side door Rory had first seen her in over a year ago.

Had it only been a little over a year? It seemed like a generation since he'd stood out there in the warehouse—a great gawking country lout with devil a word of English to his name. But a lot could happen in a year to a lad who thought on his feet.

Efram Starr waved Rory to the seat Gloria had just vacated and perched on a high clerk's stool that he pulled out from under a ledger stand. The chair Rory leaned back in, crossing his booted legs as he adjusted the infernal little sword, was warm where Gloria's body had been pressed to the polished oak seat.

Efram Starr said, "The first thing we're going to have to get straight is my older son's mouth, Captain. You have to understand that he's never gotten over my bankruptcy in Liverpool. My late wife was related to the Earl of Maclesfield, and I fear Nathan has her pride without the purse we used to have. I'd like your word, as a gentleman, that you don't intend to goad him into anything foolish."

Rory shrugged and said, "I'm after establishing my credit, not my reputation, sir."

"Good. We know you're a fighting man. What do you mean by credit? I'm not in the money-lending trade, you know."

Rory reached into his shirt and took out a folded square of foolscap, saying, "I've written up a list of stores I'll need in the next year, sir. If you'll give me a year from today to pay you—"

"On what terms, Captain?"

"Terms? Why, to pay you in full, of course. I know there's a ready market in naval stores, and—"

"Stop right there. The first thing we have to discuss is your wholesaler. Efram Starr & Sons will take the stores on consignment, agreed?"

"You mean you'll sell my naval stores as best you can and pay me when you collect on them? I suppose that's fair enough, sir."

"All right. What sort of interest are we talking about on the cost of the supplies you want on credit?"

Rory frowned and said, "What sort of interest did you have in mind for the money due *me* while my stores are waiting to be paid for?"

"None. Goods on consignment are paid for at face value or returned after a year—at your expense."

"You mean I get no interest on my investment, while you expect it on yours? That hardly seems fair, sir."

"I never said it was. I paid for my education with eighteen months in debtors' prison. Yours will only cost you twenty-five percent interest, compounded annually."

" 'Pon my word, sir! That's outright usury, if you want my opinion!"

"I don't trade in opinions, young sir. I once found myself in the Manchester Gaol because I extended too much credit to gentlemen whose opinions meant too much to me. I know I have you over a barrel. You dislike my son too much to have thought of coming here if you could get better terms from any of the other chandlers in Savannah, so take them or leave them. Those are my terms."

"I'll take them," Rory said, "but, 'pon my word, I'd rather have dealt with your son over gunsights at that!"

The older man knew he spoke in jest, but there was an edge to the remark he didn't like, so he said, "Nathan is a fool, but he has me, and he has a younger brother back at Oxford reading for law who's neither a craven nor a poor shot. I'd suggest you forego the pleasures of your Highland glens and save your blood feuds for the Spanish Indians. A coastal schooner had a nip-and-tuck race behind the Sea Islands with a Spanish frigate the other day, you know."

"Och, the Indians are quiet, for the now of it, I mind. Angus MacQueen and his lads came back with pearls and beaver pelts from yon fall line, and never an Indian did they meet up there."

"I daresay. I'll have the contracts drawn up for you by this time tomorrow. You do know how to sign your name, don't you?"

Rory's jaw tightened, but he kept his voice light as he replied, "In blood, if you like. I wrote this list I'll be leaving with you. It may not be in a fine copperplate hand, but I've no doubt you've someone here can read it."

The older man chuckled and said, "Forgive me, but you have come a long way since Thatcher had you carrying logs for him, Captain."

Rory stood up and readjusted his dainty sword as he said soberly, "I'll allow I had some English manners to learn, but if you're that concerned with my family tree, it can be traced to 1066 on the MacMartin side, they being newcomers to the Great Glen, and to the noble Scots of Ulster who crossed over with Kenneth MacAlpin to carve his Kingdom of Daridia from the holdings of the Picts in the years of Patrick and Neil of the Nine Hostages. Another ancestor fought as captain of a galley for Somerled of the Islands in—"

"I'm sure that's all very interesting, but—"

"How far back does the noble house of Starr trace its tree? A hundred years, or could it be as many as two?"

"All right, young sir, you've made your point. May a humble Englishman suggest something, though?"

"What's that?"

"Your dress sword is in its harness backward. You're going to find it tripping you with every other step unless you learn to wear it properly."

Rory flushed lobster red, then laughed and said, "Och, we've both been fools, then. I'll come back to sign my name in the morning and I promise to behave if you will."

Efram Starr stood up and shook his hand on it. He said, "You'd best leave by the warehouse, Captain. I'll have a word with my son about his manners before the two of you can get your backs up again."

Rory went out the side door and started walking toward the wide-open front entrance. He fumbled on the way with getting his sword adjusted properly, not noticing Gloria Starr until he nearly collided with her near the entrance, where she'd just finished seeing to the loading of a cart by her warehousemen.

She asked, "Is that your mount out front, Rory? It hardly seems enough horse for a man your size."

He stopped, balanced the macaroni sword with a hand on its wee toy hilt, and said, "It's not a horse, it's a pony, but it gets me about faster than I can walk."

Gloria dropped her eyes, trying to choose her words carefully, and murmured, "My husband didn't mean to be as nasty as he may have sounded."

"You were listening, then? He sounded as nasty as ever to my ownself, mum."

"I know. You have to understand what he's been through, Captain."

"Your father-in-law explained his manners, mum. You can set your mind at ease. I'll not be the one to challenge him, if that's what you meant to ask of me."

"Oh, stop it, Rory Martin. Haven't we always been friendly to you?"

"*You* have, Gloria Starr. My opinion of your husband . . . Och, never mind. I've agreed to bear no grudge against this house."

She followed him out to where he'd tied his pony, teasing him with, "Little Martha seems quite taken by you, Captain. She's just bursting to ask you about the Indian wars."

"That wee young thing? She's not old enough for tales of blood and slaughter."

"She's going on fifteen. That's the age such tales impress us women most."

"Yourself is too old, then, to care for tales of derring-do?"

"I've learned to take them with a grain of salt. When I was Martha's age, I'm afraid I listened overmuch to stories of the New World and of the fortunes to be made there by a young man of a noble house brought down by evil fortune."

Rory nodded and untied his pony, saying, "Ay, there had to be a reason for it." Then he tipped his tricorn, swung up into the saddle, and said, "Good day to you, mum, for I'm off to make me fortune."

She laughed and waved farewell as she stood there, watching his tall form recede from sight on the ridiculous mount. Her face felt warmer than it should have, even in all this heat, and she wondered if she should take some

Jesuit bark in case the fever going 'round had reached this end of town.

Rose Donovan's entrance was down a mean alley near Factor's Wharf. The crooked, narrow walkway had not been paved, and a dead rat lay, bloating, in a puddle the previous night's rain had left undried in the deep shade between the ramshackle buildings.

Rose had no sign over her place of business. Those merchants and young gallants who came to call had their own ways of finding the unpainted plank door. Rory knocked with his riding crop; he'd left his pony tied near the tobacconist's at the alley's entrance.

The door opened and a pair of eyes stared out at him from the gloom inside. He heard a woman's voice inside calling out, "Who is it, Sheba?" and the Negress the eyes belonged to answered, "Hit's a gentleman, Miss Prue!"

"Well, let him in, Goddamn your nigger soul!"

The black girl opened the door wider as the coarse-voiced woman inside called invitingly. "Come in and what's your pleasure, young sir? Art come on rum or country matters?"

Rory stepped inside, ducking his head under the door beam as he saw the plump doxie lounging on an improvised couch made of boxes and corn-husk burlap pillows. She wore a high French wig and little else. Unfurling a black lace Spanish fan, she patted a pillow near her ample rump and said, "Come sit and tell me your pleasure. My name is Prue, and I'm fair lonely this day."

Rory said, "I want to see Rose. Tell her it's Captain Martin, on business."

The near-naked woman shrugged and told the Negress, "Take him back to the Madame, Sheba. Then fetch me some grog, for I'm buring up with the heat!"

The black girl murmured, "This way, sir," and started toward the beaded fly curtain covering another doorway. Rory followed, aware of the low overhead beams and the sickening smell of rum, tobacco, and cheap perfume, and the odor of human sweat and rutting. The Negress was perhaps fourteen, now that he could see her. She was dressed in a thin shift of flour sacking that seemed somehow more revealing than the open nakedness of the slut in the other room.

Rory wondered idly what it would be like to bed a nigger wench, and his groin tingled as he observed the tight roundness of the black girl's oddly outthrust rump. Did she walk that way on purpose, he wondered, or were they built that way?

The girl called Sheba showed him into a hallway beyond the beaded curtain, knocked softly on another door, and, when Rose called out from the other side, opened it for Rory. She vanished as the man passed by with a curt nod of thanks. He smelled of horseflesh and that odd swamp-water scent all white people had, and Sheba was afraid he'd brush against her.

Rose Donovan was lounging on a rope-sprung bed covered with a feather mattress and some shoddy fabric. She wore a silk petticoat below the waist and a strand of blue freshwater pearls around her neck. Her feet and breasts were naked as she sat up, reaching for a robe; then she said, "Och, it's you, Rory. I thought I'd have to dress."

Rory stood in the center of the room, gazing idly around at the log walls. "I need a couple of hogsheads of the Creature, Rose. MacPhie says you're selling it these days."

"I'm selling lots of things." She smiled, leaning back and spreading her knees invitingly as she added, "But there's no charge for old friends."

Rory looked away from the tunnel made by her thighs and the thin silk petticoat. "It's too hot for that," he murmured.

"You're a liar. I can see the bulge in your fine riding breeches from here. What's the matter, Captain Martin? Are we too grand these days for the likes of poor auld Rosie? We've never done it on a fine mattress like this, you know. Ay, and we've no old man to worry about either."

A large square of paper Rose had pinned to the wall caught his eye, and Rory stepped over to it, saying, "What's this, Rose? It looks like a draftsman's elevation of some house."

"That's what it is," said Rose, sitting up again and tucking her feet under her. "A student of the arts gave it to me. It's the façade of a fine Great House in Ireland. I think he said the Earl of Dunraven lived in the original."

Rory studied the spidery brown lines on the fly-specked paper and said, "It's bonny enough for an earl to dwell in. Would you let me have it, Rose?"

"Och, what would you want with an architect's drawing,

Rory *Og*? You were raised in a wee black shanty, the same as myself!"

"I've been planning to build on my grant, once I'm ahead in the game of attracting silver to go with land. A grand house like this one would make the Strangers sit up and take notice, and that's a fact."

Rose pouted and said, "You can't have it, it's mine and it's pretty on yon wall. Besides, it's only the front façade. You'd need architects and craftsmen to build a house half so grand. It reminds me of a house I served in once, and I can tell you the front is only a taste of what belongs behind them doors and windows. They had floors of inlaid maple and oak, and a grand curving staircase made by a French master carver. The fan light was cut Waterford glass and the fireplaces were from Italy and made of marble carved like soap."

"What do you want for it, Rose?"

"It's not for sale. I can get you all the niggers and rum you want, but if anyone builds that grand house on this side of the water, it will be myself, I'm pleased to tell you."

"You?" He laughed incredulously.

"Why not me, you big gillie with the powdered English hair? Do you think you're the only one here who's improved his station? I've more friends in high places than yourself, militia hero though you may be. The likes of you and your guard are worth having when the Spaniards stir the Indians up, but the goods I trade in are wanted all the time. I'll lay you a wager, Captain dear. I'll bet you I'm living in a grand house with red velvet drapes and a crystal chandelier before you've planted your first indigo at your so-called Indigo Hall!" She laughed harshly. "That's a good one! Captain Martin of Indigo Hall, and he's yet to clear the land or put up so much as a log shanty, for all his macaroon ways!"

Rory smiled thinly and said, "It's no bet, for you've negotiable securities between your legs no mortal man's been born with yet. I came to argue about supplies, not architecture. You know about my naval-stores business, don't you, Rose?"

"I do, but what of it? I don't need tar or turpentine."

"I know, but I need rum, and is it true you can get me some niggers?"

"Sure, I'm expecting a gaggle of forty from the West Indies in a few days. I've a friend down there who makes them sign indenture papers before they come aboard. You saw one I bought from Jamaica just now, didn't you?"

"Sheba's from the Indies?"

"You remembered her name, did you? I thought you'd notice the ass on her, Rory *Og*. She's a virgin, if you're interested. These pesky indenture papers limit what we can do to the niggers, and the girl just doesn't see the advantages of learning a good trade."

"I'm not interested in buying women. I need men. Do your West Indies men speak the Sassunach?"

"Most do. That's what makes them more valuable. I've got nearly fifty niggers hired out right now. A free man of any color can't be had on this side for less than two shillings a day, and I rent my bondsmen out for three bob a week. Sheba's the only girl I bought the papers for. As you can see, she's not worth much. My whores could open their own doors and carry their own towels, but—"

"Let's get back to these men you're going to hire out to me. What do you say to five shillings a week with an option to buy their indentures if they work out?"

"I'd say yes—*if* you had the silver to show me, Captain Martin of Indigo Hall."

She saw the embarrassed look on his face and laughed. "You've barely enough to powder your hair and feed the wee pony with, haven't you?"

"I've had a time establishing my credit as a gentleman."

"I know, and a laughingstock you've been making of yourself, too. You're a jumped-up gillie, Rory *Og*. Half the gentlefolk in Savannah are laughing at you. The others don't know you're alive!"

She saw that the thrust had struck home and added, "It's a whorehouse you've come to for help, darling, and you've come to the right place."

"You'll extend me credit on the rum and labor, then?"

"That depends. Take off your clothes. You can hang the gallant sword on the nail behind you."

"Och, Rose, what do you want with my body on a hot sticky day like today? You can't tell me you've been starved for the feel of a man inside you!"

"I've been with, let me see, thirteen men and a boy between last night and this noon. If you'll just fold your clothes over yon chair, yourself will be number fifteen. Does that frush you, Rory *Og*?"

"Goddamnit, you know it does, Rose. It was bad enough when I shared you with one man, and—"

"You shared me, and liked it, because you needed me to give you the English and because I fed you when the old man wasn't looking."

"Och, I paid you back by making him set you free, didn't I?"

"Not enough, Rory. It's dear hard to pay a woman back when a man's called her a slut and a whore."

"Goddamnit, Rose, you *are* a slut and a whore!"

"I know. Take off your clothes."

She saw that he was about to leave and quickly added, "I'll throw in yon drawing of your grand house, Rory. I'll hire out enough niggers to you to clear the space and build it too!"

She saw the hesitation in his eyes and added, "I'll let you have all the rum your turpentine crew can drink until your first cargo's been paid for. I'll give you that girl outside to cook and keep house for you, and you can have her and the other niggers as a free loan until you've silver to buy them. Just think of what I'm offering, as one friend to another—all you'll need to lift yourself another notch by your mad bootstraps, and not one of your fine new friends need know you've been here, Rory, *Caraid na seachad!*"

He stood there for a time, thinking of what her help would mean, as Rose murmured, "A hundred pieces of eight to jingle in your pockets for your fine new friends, as a gift from your *Auld Caileag?*"

Rory started to remove his sword belt, muttering, "Jesus, you must really want to fuck!"

Rose Donovan rolled off her feet, lay back, and spread her legs, pulling the soiled silk up around her waist as she said, "No. This time you're going to *eat* me, gallant captain of the guard!"

She saw the stricken look on his face and said, "Och, you'll argue but you'll do it, Rory MacMartin, for if there's one thing any whore knows, it's another!"

Coffee studied the architectural elevation by the light of an oil lamp on the Pardus' kitchen table. The table had once been the grandest they'd had, but Coffee had made Rebecca an impressive drop-leaf table he'd copied from a Chippendale catalog of furniture design. The lamp, while English in manufacture, was filled with sweet burning oil

Coffee had taught his helpers to press from hemp seed and use in place of the expensive Yankee whale oil most Georgia settlers still used.

Rory stood over the Ashanti as Isaac watched, bemused, from his high-backed chair, a quilt draped across his knees. He'd suffered from periodic chills ever since the Indian fighting, which had left him feeling weak and somewhat detached from reality. His wife kept hounding him to stay in bed, but it was early evening, and there was so much business to attend to these days.

Coffee traced a dark finger along a roof line and said, "This part should come out ten or twelve feet. There will be no shade for the big doors and windows if we build it flat down the front."

Rory said, "I'm facing it southeast, to overlook the tidal creek from the gentle rise I've chosen. The top-story bedrooms will catch the morning sun but be shaded most of the day. The front entrance should be in shade most of the afternoon."

Coffee insisted, "You need the roof out over the veranda. It will offer shade from ten o'clock on, and shelter from the afternoon thunderstorms during summer. If you let me build it *right*, Master Rory, you'll be able to sit out there at ease and watch the boats come up to your landing in fair weather or foul."

"Och, that damned overhanging roof will stick out like a silly hat brim, Coffee! It's an awkward plan you have, practical as it may be."

The Ashanti got up and stepped over to a bookcase, running his finger along the leather bindings until he found what he was looking for. He opened it to the page he wanted and showed it to Rory and Pardus.

"Here. I will put these big white poles under the roof overhang for you. They will keep the big house from looking clumsy."

Rory nodded. "Ay, I *like* the looks of *that*."

Pardus leaned forward, laughed weakly, and said, "A Greek temple you want to build for Captain Martin, Coffee? The wonders never cease in this crazy country!"

Coffee shrugged, as oblivious as Rory to the meaning of the man's sardonic words. "I will let the air reach the bricks so they burn bright red," he said firmly. "With red brick walls and the trim and all else made from whitewashed wood. I shall have them cut bald cypress for the exposed wood. Yes, that will stand up to the weather for as long as any of us or our grandchildren live."

Rory nodded again. "I've an apprentice carpenter, newly arrived and in need of silver, to work out the interior plan, Coffee. If I gave you a dozen niggers to work under you, how long do you think the building of it would take?"

"Less than a year if they are good workers, Master Rory. Longer if I have to beat them."

Pardus sighed and said, "You know you're not allowed to beat anyone, Coffee. You know all about their terms of indenture."

The Ashanti's eyes met Rory's as the servant soothed, "Yes, Master." Then he added, under his breath, "Some niggers don't know how to read indenture papers."

Rory said, "The lads I've hired from Mistress Rose are good workers. I had them build me a cabin out on the grant, and those new turpentine tools you designed have left them with time on their hands. We've got more trees tapped than MacPhie's crew can keep ahead of at the still."

Pardus looked up in sudden interest to ask, "How is MacPhie, and my old friend, the Goliath, MacQueen?"

"Och, MacQueen's enriching himself in the Indian trade these days, Isaac. He's got the Creeks eating out of his hand, between the corn liquor he buys from me and the chasing away of some Carolina long-hunters who'd been pestering our red friends up near the falls. As for MacPhie, there's enough to keep wee Gavin busy. I've made him my overseer since Donald MacUlrich left to start his own weaving business. Donald has two indentured lasses working the wheels to supply his loom, and he's selling sailcloth as fast as he can turn it out."

"You Scotchmen," sighed the Jew. "Sometimes I wonder where you get all the energy."

Rory smiled. "We were born at the lean end of the British hambone, Isaac. A thousand years of scraping a living from granite and a cold gray sea hones a fine edge to a man's ambition."

"But you're never satisfied, Rory. When does a man have enough? When is it time to sit back comfortably and watch your children grow?"

"Och, I've no children and you know it. Your own lad, Aaron, must be nearly old enough to take your place in the trained band, by the way. What was that party we had for him, right after we returned from the swamps—the bar something?"

"Bar mitzvah. Aaron will be fourteen in a few months."

"Well, there you are, then. You've a son old enough to take your place in the line and a daughter old enough to marry off. It's all very well for you to talk of leaning back, but I'm just getting started."

Rory started asking Coffee about a detail on the elevation. Isaac let their voices drone on for a time as his ears rang from the Jesuit bark he'd been taking. Then he suddenly sat up in the chair and asked, "What was that about Aaron and the trained band? He's only a baby, Rory!"

"Och, you said at his bar whatever that he was a *man* that day! But dinna frush ye, it was only talk."

"You're saying I've missed the past few muster days. You're saying my house has to send a musket or we'll lose our holdings! I remember how you gloated when you made Private Thatcher do that extra drill, Goddamn you!"

Rory eased him back gently and soothed, "Hush, you wee fool. You'll lose no land while I'm the captain of your company, whether you come with your ensign's sash or stay home and read your books. It was an idle thought I had and nothing more. You have my word on that."

"You're not going to make my little Aaron shoulder a musket and march out to fight the Creeks? His mother would die if I let him!"

"Och, who's marching on any Creeks? I've had it the Spaniards are having troubles at home in Madrid. They're content to try and hold onto such colonies as they still have. You're frushing yourself for nothing, Isaac. I've given my word your lad will never shoulder a gun while I command our company."

"Lawyer Margolis is worried about me. He said there'd been talk at the mansion about me. He said that as a Jew, it was up to me to prove I was no shirker."

"Och, what does Margolis know in his big fat wig? You leave the Proprietors to me. Besides, there may not *be* a Board of Proprietors much longer, Isaac. It's rumored that Praying Jamie Oglethorpe's sold out his interests to the Crown. In a year or two, Georgia will be just another royal colony, like the Carolinas."

"A year or two? I've got to drag myself down to the muster field each drill day for a year or two?"

Pardus held his hand out to the lamplight, and the three

of them watched it tremble for a time before he dropped it in his lap and sighed. "So why not say a century? The surgeons tell me I'll have this ague for life, Rory. There's no cure. The Jesuit bark helps, but another march through those swamps and—"

"Och, who's marching through any swamps, you wee daft man? You nurse your ague and let me worry about your militia duties. Right now, I want to build my house."

Ignoring Coffee, who, as a Negro, could have nothing to say about money, Rory asked, "What sort of a fee were you thinking of for Coffee's time, Isaac?"

Pardus shrugged. "Look, if he's willing, you work it out. He's got things ticking like a Swiss clock on this plantation. You pay him the same as I do and—"

"You *pay* him?" Rory frowned.

"Of course I've been paying Coffee. Part of it goes to pay me back for his indenture. The rest he spends on . . . what do you buy with the silver I give you, Coffee?"

"Books," said the Ashanti, adding, "Books and other things I need for my studies. Some I give to my woman for small pleasures. The rest I keep, for when the time comes to return to my people."

Rory asked cautiously, "How much do you get, Coffee?"

"One shilling a day. I am not a white man."

"Och, well, I think we can manage that, then." He turned to Pardus and asked, "Does he get the money or do you, Isaac?"

"He gets it, of course. Listen, I've very tired. You two work it out and it's all right with me."

Rory agreed and said he had to get back to Indigo Hall. The Ashanti followed him out to the front veranda and asked, "Will you tell me something, Master Rory?"

"What's that, Coffee?"

"This business of the militia. I, too, have heard bad words about my master not being there much of the time. You are his friend, but you are only a captain. I asked Lawyer Margolis and he said—"

"Do you ever lie to your master, Coffee?"

"Sometimes, when it is for his own good."

Rory nodded and said, "I want to talk with young Master Aaron in private. Is he out back?"

"No. He and his sister went with their mother to welcome the new Jewish family in Savannah. They will not be back for some time."

"All right, have him ride over to my place when he gets the chance. You're right about the pressure they've been putting on me, and the lad is almost as old as I was when—"

"You *promised*!" The Ashanti's face was grave. "You promised his father that Master Aaron would never shoulder a musket while you commanded his company."

"Drummer boy." Rory smiled, starting to explain that a drummer boy was not required to shoulder a gun, but the Ashanti's mind was just as quick and he said, "Yes, that would make your words true and save this place from the bailiff. You twisted your words but you did not lie." Then he grinned and said, "We are not as different as I thought, White Master. You would have made a good Ashanti, had you been born with healthy skin."

SEVEN

It was raining on that Sunday. Rory sat on the plank porch of his small temporary cabin, one booted heel resting against a post. He was smoking a Havana cheroot while he listened to the rain patter on the shakes above his head. The view spread out before him was mostly of tall straight trees bare of branches until two-thirds of the way up and flagged with drooping, long-needled pine boughs the rest of the way to their pointed tops. Many had been cut down near the cabin—both for the building itself and to haul into Savannah as ship's spars—when the tapping had killed them off. The hooked turpentine tools Coffee had made drained an enormous amount of sap from a tree, but there'd been no thought of conservation. Every pole of dead timber meant more land cleared for crops to come.

Usually the smell of MacPhie's distillery drifted through the woods as far as Rory's cabin, but this day was the Sabbath, and his men, under law, could not work on the Lord's Day. Pardus and the other Jewish colonists, unable to work on the Christian holiday, had taken to enjoying a two-day weekend, a slothful habit no sensible man in America hoped would spread beyond the Jews.

Rory was worried about the Pardus family. The boy, Aaron, had seemed pleased enough to step in as his sickly father's replacement in the line on muster days, but his damned mother had found out some way, and the lad was under terrible pressure at home.

A soft voice murmured, "Does you want more tea, Cap'n?" and Rory shook his head, saying, "I'm just fine, Sheba. I'll call you if I need anything."

The girl Rose had loaned him was becoming a bother. He'd only taken her on as housekeeper to spite Rose for the humiliating terms she'd pressed on him that sticky afternoon on the rumpled mattress.

The young Negress was a neat, willing worker, and at least he'd kept Rose from forcing some periwigged young fop on the child. The only trouble was the smallness of this damned cabin. He'd put a sleeping loft up for the girl, and, when his work permitted, he stretched out on the bunk built against the wall below. But the damned girl was a light sleeper, and every time he rolled over or got up to relieve himself, she would call down to ask what he wanted. When he'd shouted, that first night, that he wanted sleep, for God's sake, the fool wench had cried for the better part of an hour, and he'd had to get out of his bunk and comfort her. Some idiot had obviously mistreated the girl, and she was as jumpy as a gunshy hunting hound.

Thunder rolled in the distance, and Rory glanced up at the low scudding clouds, wondering if the weather would clear before dark. He knew it was the Sabbath, but the foundations of his great house lay just beyond that wall of pine over there. The servants had been sent home for the day; not even a bondservant was allowed to work on Sunday. But he was a long way out of town, and if he just went over and laid a few bricks, who'd be the wiser?

The rain kept coming down, cooling the summer air but boring the restless Rory to distraction. He rocked himself on the back legs of his chair, wondering if he had any excuse to ride into town. He had a few things to discuss with Efram Starr, but the shops and businesses were all closed and shuttered, he knew. The only amusements that might be open were the illegal grog shops and the brothels. You couldn't even find a horse race or a cock fight on one of Praying Jamie's effing Sabbaths!

A voice inside him sneered, "Och, it's to moon over a married woman that you'd drench yourself riding into town, and you know it!"

"Not true," he said aloud; then, with a sheepish smile, he added in a whisper, "If you have to talk to your ownself, laddy buck, the least you can be is truthful."

He wanted Gloria Starr, but what of it? Lots of men probably wanted her, for she was a bonny thing with a good mind and a sunny laugh, but she was married and that was that.

The thought of anyone he knew getting a divorce had never crossed his mind, though cold-blooded murder had. Divorce was impossible for an Anglican lady or gentleman, but Rory knew the woman felt something for him. The education he had received from Rose had taught him something of a woman's unspoken feelings; but while her husband lived, Gloria would never allow herself to reconsider the mistake she'd made.

Rory knew he was being a bounder and a fool to consider the matter even for a moment, but there'd been many days when he'd wished untimely death on that Goddamned fop who stood in his way.

Angus Mohr had brought back rumors of another Indian uprising on his last trip in from the chi-chis, but the day would never dawn when Nathan Starr would be anywhere where a reed arrow could reach him. The Starrs owned no farmland. Many other merchants served in the trained bands, but Nathan had a delicate constitution, he said, and there was no way to force him into joining up if they marched out again. The bastard would probably live to be a hundred, and Gloria with him, pleasuring the wee thing he probably sat down to pee with!

Rory's breeches were tight, and he rubbed his free hand over the soft moleskin to ease the discomfort of his groin. He blew a cloud of blue smoke out into the rain and tried to think of something else, but the same vision tortured him—that awful picture of Nathan's head between the creamy thighs of the woman Rory wanted, doing those things Rose had made *him* do before she would back him in his venture.

He closed his eyes, picturing the way Gloria must look with her clothes off. He didn't imagine her in the positions Rose favored, at least not at first, but, remembering that first day in the warehouse, he wondered if, once in a while, Nathan took Gloria on her hands and knees. He suddenly jerked his foot from the post, letting the front legs of the chair slam down as he shouted, "God*damn*it!"

The little Negress, Sheba, hurried out of the cabin with a worried look and gasped, "You called me, sir?"

"No, damnit! Get back to your chores."

"Please, Cap'n, I ain' got no chores. Hit's the Sabbath."

"Och, get back to your praying, then, you fool wee nigger!"

The frightened girl darted back inside like a crayfish hiding from a suddenly looming bass, and Rory chuckled wryly. He was not unaware of the possibilities presented by being alone out here with a reasonably comely virgin. His turpentine crew obviously thought he'd bedded the wench at the first opportunity, and, in truth, the idea had crossed his mind more than once.

But aside from the racial taboos, Rory was still a reasonably decent young man, at least when there was nothing to be gained by outraging the scruples he still had. As a for-

mer bondservant, he felt a certain empathy for the teenaged Negress, and, having heard Rose speak of the men
who had abused her when she was still a servant, he knew
the contempt that Sheba would feel for him should he force
his will on her. He'd be damned if some night, when Sheba
was among her own kind, he'd be jeered at as a man who
had savaged servants because he lacked the wit or charm to
bed a woman with a mind and will of her own!

"God strike me blind!" he muttered. "She'd probably tell
that damned nigger of Isaac's!"

The Ashanti, Coffee, disturbed Rory. It was hard to
know where one stood with a man like Coffee. The nigger
was obviously bright, and there was a dignity in his bearing
that reminded Rory of the people he'd known in the glens:
proud, half-naked barefoot men with ancestral steel spears
or axes hidden in the thatch along with a hobnail-studded
targes and pewter clansmen's badges to buckle around their
left arms if ever they should see the distant gleam of a beacon cross upon the moor.

He'd spoken of the past to Coffee from time to time as
they'd watched the other niggers working on the slowly rising great house beyond the trees. Coffee had seemed surprised that Rory had been able to grasp the meaning of the
Golden Stool that no mortal king was fit to sit on, and of
the dire penalty that awaited an Ashanti spearman who ignored the assembly call of the nation drums as they
throbbed through the hills of Kumasi. As they'd spoken,
Rory had been able to picture the clans gathering around
the Golden Stool, and when Coffee had spoken of the bitterness of defeat, Rory had felt like putting a hand on his
shoulder as he'd said, "Ay, I know the sick hurt of it well,
lad."

Of course, he hadn't made the gesture. A man entitled to
wear a wig and dress sword didn't comfort even a white
servant with a friendly touch. Officers touched loose buttons on enlisted men's coats with the handles of riding
crops. To shake the hand of a member of the simple folk
was a thing no gentleman would dream of, even should
some ignorant yeoman ask such a thing.

Coffee was a servant; ergo, he had no right to hold opinions of his betters, yet somehow Rory didn't want the
Ashanti to have contempt for him. It was mad even to consider the matter, but he knew exactly how the niggers
would talk about him if he behaved in front of them as so

many foppish macaroons had behaved in front of him when *he'd* been bound.

The virgin cowering in the cabin behind him had other considerations protecting her as well. Under Georgia law, Sheba was not a chattel slave, but an indentured maid. Her papers, which Rory didn't even own, bound Sheba to serve her mistress, Rose Donovan, for a term of four more years; then she would get freedom dues of a new dress, ten pounds in silver, and a license to engage as cook or seamstress (to be held in escrow subject to her faithful and obedient service as a maid). Deflowering her against her will could violate the terms of her indenture and quite possibly lead to a fine for Rose, as well as to Sheba's early manumission and the jeers of Savannah's growing black community.

"Och, she's got a pickle-ass and the face of a monkey besides!" he muttered, putting the unbidden carnal thoughts aside for perhaps the hundredth time.

His disturbing train of thought was broken off by the sudden appearance of the Pardus family's covered carriage; it was being driven by the Negro they called Jake.

Rory got to his feet on the porch as he wondered what the devil Isaac Pardus was doing out on a day like this. Jabob drove up, saluted Rory with his whip, and got down to tie the team to the hitching rail in front of the cabin before going around to open the cowhide-curtained side door.

Rebecca Pardus got down from inside, her face pale but for the redness around her eyes.

Rory hurried to offer her his hand, saying, "Your servant, mum. I trust your husband's well?"

Rebecca pulled back and raised a hand as if to strike him. Then she recovered enough to lower the palm as she hissed, "You dirty . . . *goy*! I might have known we were fools to trust you! Under our own roof you planned my child's murder, and after breaking bread with us, too!"

Rory sighed in sudden understanding and said, "Please come inside, mum. I know you're upset about your son, but—"

"Upset? You call a woman with her heart torn out upset?" But she had sense enough to come up onto the porch to get out of the rain, at any rate. Rory opened the door and called, "Sheba, fetch us some tea out here!" as the irate woman snapped, "I don't want tea. I want my baby back!"

"Come inside, then, and we'll talk about your son's enlistment in the trained band."

"Inside? You think I'd be under the roof of such a monster? Let Jake go inside with your blackamoor girl, where it's dry and they can't hear us. Such things I have to say to you, not even a blackamoor should hear!"

Rory motioned with his eyes to Jake, who, trying not to grin, ducked by him into the cabin. Rory threw his cheroot out into the rain and motioned to the single chair, asking, "Won't you sit down, at least, mum?"

"I'll stand, thank you. I'll stand right here until you tell me what you meant by seducing my baby into becoming a drummer boy for your terrible guard company."

Rory dropped his courtly manner and said, "Becky, I did it to save your family. I was hoping to keep it from you and Isaac, but—"

"You call a young boy fighting savages saving his family? Since he followed you into the swamps, my Isaac's been an invalid, and now you want to do as much for my son?"

"It's a hard world we live in, Becky. The rules are not of my making. Your son is a man by the laws of your own faith, and, under the laws of Georgia, a man from your household must serve in the militia or you lose your land grant. It's as simple as that."

"But Aaron's a baby! He's not fourteen yet!"

"The Fencibles have a twelve-year-old drummer boy, Becky. I tried to cover up for Isaac, but he's been missing too many drills. Some new arrivals with no hankering for hard work have been bidding on your military grant."

"Isaac is too sick. You have to understand his condition! I thought you were his friend."

Rory suddenly felt he'd had enough and snapped, "I *am* his friend, you silly great cow! Do you think I had an easy time of it at the mansion, arguing a younger son out of foregoing his claim on a thriving plantation held in tenure by a beardless drummer boy?"

"Listen, Rory, my son is small for his age. They have to understand—"

"No, Goddamnit, it's *you* who has to understand, Rebecca Pardus! You and your people are strangers in a jealous land of property-hungry men! Isaac had the fortune to make a few friends and the reputation of a fighting man before he took sick, but it's damned few friends he has, and not a man of us sits behind a desk in the governor's mansion. I fought them and made a few new enemies in slipping your near-worthless son into an ensign's place in the line. Do you think we *need* another drummer boy, Goddamnit? I did what I had to to save the lot of you from eviction."

Refusing to listen, the frightened mother said, "He's a *baby*, and they say there's trouble with the Indians again. What will become of my Aaron out there in those awful swamps? Isaac told me what it was like out there. He told me about the rolling on the dirt with screaming savages, and my Isaac is a grown man!"

"Isaac had a big mouth," Rory thought, but aloud he said, "Och, there's always talk about Indian trouble, Becky. Young Aaron will meet few Creek on the drilling green, I promise you."

"You have to let him go. He's too young to go for a soldier!"

"If Aaron Pardus asks to quit, I'll press no charge against him. That's my final word on the subject, Becky."

"But you know he won't do that, damn you! You know hc's idiotic enough to *want* to serve in the militia!"

"Ay, he's small, but a lad you and Isaac can be proud of."

"You have to change your mind, Rory. I'll do anything to make you change your mind! I'll give you anything I have if you'll let my baby go!"

Inside the cabin, Jake, after trying to buss Sheba and getting soundly slapped for his effort, was peeking out at them through a chink in the logs. The serving wench sat on an upturned box, rearranging the red calico head kerchief she'd lost for the moment in their short but no-nonsense scuffle.

Jake whispered, "Old white gal's gwine purely fuck your massa 'fore she's done. I seen her fuckin' more'n once, and she purely likes to move her ass!"

Sheba flushed and said, "Come away from there, you fool! You'll get us both in trouble, does my master catch you peerin' out like that."

"They never see me. I'm too smart for them. I've watched old Kofi climb on Fiba lots of times without he knowed it, and Kofi *knows* I likes to watch!"

"Shoot, they ain't doin' nothin' bad out there on no porch!"

"Maybe not, but they figures to. I know Old Missy Becky's been without it long enough with her man too sick to pleasure her right. One time I seen her in the outhouse, playin' with herself with her hand."

"You're a bad nigger, Jake! I don' 'low talk like that in this cabin, so you jest hush, you hear?"

"Shoot, this ain' yo' cabin, girl. You jest a nigger like me. How come you act so proud and sassy? You mind you sumpin special jest 'cause that big white boy put his pink old *uume* in you a couple a' times?"

"That's a *lie*, you bad nigger! Cap'n Martin ain' tried one time to jazz me!"

"With you an' him out here alone at night, girl? Who you funnin'? I mind he's had his corncob up yo' ass, down yo' throat, an', did he want it, in yo' ear!"

Sheba got up, went to the walk-in fireplace, and bent down to pick up a length of pine kindling as Jake, with his eyes glued to his peephole, mused, "Yeah, ol' Mizz Pardus touchin' him now. She purely is the touchin'est white woman I ever seen. She can't talk without she waves her hands and touches folks. Now she's backin' yo' master offen the porch wif her big pink tits!"

Outside, the conversation, heated though it was, was more innocent of carnal desire than the Peeping Tom thought. But it wasn't completely innocent, for Rory was becoming painfully aware of Rebecca's body odor and the feel of her warm flesh as she sobbed and argued.

Rebecca was a virtuous wife and mother who would have been appalled to hear what Rory had made of her desperate promise to do anything to save her son. When Rebecca had said "anything," she'd had suicide, assassination, or grand larceny in mind. The idea that any man but her husband might want her seldom crossed her mind. To a woman raised in the strict Sephardic traditions, by which adultery was punishable by stoning to death, the idea that a man who'd eaten under her husband's roof might entertain a single evil thought about her body was unthinkable. Hence, as she pleaded for her son's release from the militia, the warm-blooded woman argued in the innocent but physical manner that was natural to her. She thrust her face close to Rory's and, as the embarrassed man instinctively drew back to a comfortable distance, Rebecca misinterpreted this as rejection, and hysterically pressed even closer. Without thinking, her fluttering hands grasped his sleeves and she pulled him to her ample bosom, throwing back her head to shout up into his startled face, "I want my baby back! I need him at home with his sister and my poor sick husband!"

Rory tried to disengage himself as he stammered, "I've left it up to the lad, Becky! Calm down and control yourself!"

She wrapped her arms around him, pinning his arms against his sides as she buried her face in his chest and began to sob. Rory took another step backward, found a heel hanging out over the end of the porch, and realized that the mad thing had driven him as far back as they could go without the two of them sprawling into the mud and driving rain like a pair of rutting pigs!

He got his balance, and, using his superior strength and weight, managed to regain a few inches. He tried to pat her back to comfort her as he soothed, "Now, now, it's not as if we were off on another campaign, you know," but his hand came down on her soft warm rump. Because of the heat, Aaron's mother wore nothing but a single petticoat under her outer skirt. Rory moved his hand away as if he'd just put it on a hot stove, but the luxurious feel of her buttocks tingled on his fingers. Her hair was clean and worn piled on her head, and he could smell it as he stammered pointless assurances down at her. His breath was coming in deep gasps, and his heart was pounding too hard for the wee struggle they were having. Was the woman mad, or was she just trying to win the battle with any weapons she had?

There was a sudden loud thud and an anguished howl from inside the cabin, and Rory, anxious for any distraction, shoved the woman away and shouted, "What's going on in there?"

There was no answer for a time. Then the door opened a crack and the girl, Sheba, said, "Please, Cap'n, we was only funnin'."

"Well, stop your foolishness and send that Jake out here. I want him to take his mistress home before the storm gets worse!"

Rebecca tried to wrap herself around him again but Rory grabbed both her wrists, shook her, and said, "No, listen to me, woman! I've told you Aaron is free to leave the service with no charge of desertion pressed any time the lot of you feel like becoming paupers. As to the lad's safety, there's nothing that can happen to him on the drilling green, Goddamnit!"

"But the swamps, the Indians!"

"Stop it, you silly auld woman! I told you he could wait and hold his father's place in the line until we see how things turn out. There's no Indian trouble at the moment and there's talk of a new government. Why not wait and see before you drag the lad away from his safe games on the drill field and lose everything you've worked for? "Meanwhile, there's a few other strings to my bow. I'll have a talk with Aaron and your husband, and it may be possible to hire a substitute from among the new arrivals."

"I'll hire a dozen! I'll give them anything to take my baby's place!"

Rory knew it wasn't that simple. The indentured men arriving would never willingly serve in the militia without manumission, while the free men coming in, able to demand as much as four bob a day for safe work in the shops and fields, would be fools to risk their necks for anything less than land. But he agreed with the frightened woman for the moment, if only to speed her on her way.

Jake came out of the cabin rubbing his hip with a sullen expression, and Rory told him, "Take Ensign Pardus' wife home, Jake."

Rebecca wanted to argue further, but Rory firmly escorted her to the carriage and literally stuffed her inside. He untied the team as Jake climbed up to the rain-soaked driver's seat, gingerly favoring the bruised hip that Sheba had given him with the length of kindling.

The small dapper Negro saluted again with his whip and swung the team around to drive off in the rain. Rory stood there, already soaked to the skin, and shook his head in wonder as the coach dissolved in the silvery curtain of the downpour. The scent of Rebecca Pardus still lingered, mingled with the smell of wet pine needles, and the tall man's knees were still unsteady as he tried to tell himself she'd simply been overwrought. He'd never considered Rebecca Pardus that way before, but damn, she smelled good, and those lush curves under the smooth damp taffeta. . . .

Rory started walking in the rain. He was as wet as he was going to get, and his body ached to be moving. He strode across the cleared yard and through the dripping pines to the spot where Coffee and the others were usually working at this hour.

The site he'd chosen for his Great House occupied a gentle rise. He walked to the waist-high foundation wall around the wet excavation of the cellars and climbed up on the bricks, standing, hands on hips, to gaze down on the tidal creek he'd named Indigo Landing.

He was humorously aware of the empty boast contained in the grand title. There was no hall on the military grant he'd recorded as Indigo Hall Plantation, and no indigo to load aboard such trading schooners as might put in where there was now nothing but a marshy shoreline fenced with tall, feather-topped reeds. It was easy to dream big in this strange new land, but the making of the dreams into reality took silver, and silver was harder to come by than ambition.

The rain was letting up, in the way rain did in a Georgia summer. Up on the Piedmont hills, thunder still rolled and boulders were tumbling over the flooded mussel shoals, but here in the tidewater, the worst was over, and the rest of the afternoon would be steaming hot. Rory's wet clothes were uncomfortable, and he thought of going back to the cabin to change. Then, staring down at the water in the salt creek, he had a better idea.

Removing his clothing and boots, he spread them on the brick wall to dry in the afternoon sun—if ever it appeared. Naked, he walked down toward the water's edge, the gentle drops of warm rain refreshing on his broad shoulders. The encounter with Rebecca had left him with an erection, but a swim in the salt water of the creek would take care of that. It always had.

He parted the reeds at the water's edge and waded out through the mucky shallows until he felt clean sand against his soles. He found the water just right and threw himself forward in a clumsy dive, opening his eyes as he frog-kicked through the shallows.

Like many a self-taught swimmer, Rory found it less tiring to keep his head under most of the time, coming up only for an occasional gasp of air as he explored the fuzzy twilight world below the surface. The brackish water didn't hurt his eyes, but everything was enlarged and blurred by the water. Something dark and ominously large scurried sideways from his path; then Rory realized that it was only a blue crab. Another monster of the deep turned out to be a curious little killifish.

Out of breath, Rory stood up in the shoulder-deep water,

throwing back his head to laugh up into the rain. He didn't know why he was laughing. He'd forgotten what it had been like to be a larking lad in a Highland loch, for he'd been a working crofter since he was eight.

Something moved in the water a hundred yards upstream, and Rory eyed the trailing V of its wake for a tense moment before he saw that it was only a wee turtle swimming with the top of its shell above the surface. He wondered if those tales of great water-horses and other dragons in the lochs of the Great Glen hadn't been inspired by such innocent creatures and a dram too much of the Creature. But it only frushed a man to think of the old country, and, in truth, it was bonny enough here for a man who owned his own land.

A red-wing cried out from a clump of beach-plum at the water's edge, and Rory called out, "Good morrow to you, too, sir, and, 'pon my word, you've an insolent tongue for such a small lad."

The red-wing seemed to answer with another ringing cackle and the man in the water laughed, saying, "My seconds will call on you this evening—unless, of course, you intend to mend your manners."

A human voice answered from the reed-screened shoreline, and Rory realized he was making a fool of himself, larking about out with water beasts and birds. Recognizing the voice, he called out, "What is it, Sheba? Where the devil are you?"

The young Negress parted some reeds, standing gingerly, knee deep in the mucky shallows, as she called, "Please, Cap'n, I was scared."

"Och, what frightened you, lass? Another squirrel on the roof?"

Sheba didn't answer. Everyone laughed at her when they found out she was afraid of thunder. She'd forgotten the reason herself, for the memory of the gunfire when the Slattees had raided her home village near the Bight of Benin had been buried deep under the many other events in her short but terror-filled life.

The white man repeated his question and Sheba stammered, "Please, Cap'n, I wants to stay here with you. When I found yo' clothes on the wall back there, I was scared you'd gone and drownded!"

"Och, it's shallow, and the water's warm despite the rain.

You can come on in if you like. There's no work to be done on the Lord's Day in any case and——"

Sheba grinned and pulled her shift up over her head as Rory muttered, "Och, not *bare*, you wee daft thing!" but his voice didn't carry clearly, and the words caught in his throat as he glimpsed the boyish young figure that the cheap hemp smock had been hiding, albeit poorly.

Sheba draped her smock over some reeds and, still wearing the red kerchief, started wading toward him, unconscious of her own nudity, for she'd only worn clothing for the past few years. The man had told her it was all right, and the thought of swimming other than naked would have struck any of her people as ridiculous. The *Obeah* women had warned her about exposing herself to menfolk after her breasts had budded and she'd been initiated in the secrets of her sex, but the warnings had concerned field hands and uppity bad niggers like that Jake. The captain wasn't like the men they'd warned her about. He was kind and gentle, for an *ofey*, and it only took her a moment to hide her nearly hairless pubis in the tepid water of the tidal creek.

The moment had been enough to arouse Rory's frustrated flesh. He ducked lower in the water, certain she could see his turgid member. She stood in water a little above her waist, her firm little breasts splattered by the gentle rain as she laughed across the water at him. Sheba suddenly ducked under and then resurfaced ten yards away, swimming strongly out into the stream, her wet kerchief wine red as she moved through the water like an otter.

Rory watched in mingled amusement and desire, for, freed from the unsightly sacking, her supple brown body was beautiful to behold. She ducked under the surface, exposing her tight young buttocks in flashes of chocolate flesh. Rory wondered how in God's name he'd get out of the water with the fool girl watching and his erection exposing his forbidden lust.

There was a distant lightning flash and thunder rolled across the treetops from the west. Sheba suddenly swam toward him, whimpering in her own language something about the loud noise. Rory put out his hands to fend her off, aware as never before of their nudity and his embarrassing condition. There was another sullen rumble from

the sky and she clutched at him, sobbing, "*U-vey-vey,*
Cap'n! I'm scared!"

Rory groaned and said, "Och, enough is enough!" and
wrapped his arms around her, pulling her slippery-wet flesh
against his own as he muttered, "The women have all gone
mad this day!" And, taking a deep breath, he kissed the
startled girl full on her pouting lips.

For a moment she returned his kiss; then, eyes wide in
wonder, she tried to draw away, suddenly aware of what
was pressing into her wet belly like the head of rising
cobra. For a moment Rory held her, as confused as she by
his loss of control. Then he released her and said, "Och,
I'm sorry, lass. I don't know what came over us!"

As confused herself, Sheba lowered herself deep into the
water, painfully aware of her own flesh now as she realized
what the white man wanted, but she didn't move away as
she licked her lips and said, "Please, Cap'n, I don' know
how to pleasure a man!"

"Would you like to learn, lass? I'm new at this my ownself, you see, but I'm all right once I've started."

He reached out, under the water, and put a hand around
her waist to draw her closer. Sheba flinched at his touch,
but she was as afraid to defy a white man as she was of
what she knew was coming. She ducked her head, exposing
the top of her kerchief to his lips as she murmured,
"Please, sir, don' *hurt* me!"

He soothed her with soft words devoid of meaning as he
picked her up and started wading toward the shallows, her
lips pressed against his chest as she stammered protestations as futile as his gentle promises. Rory found a spot by
the water's edge where the reeds had been crushed into a
nestlike bower. He placed her on the bed of damp, crushed
green and loomed over her on hands and knees, muttering,
"Och, you're so bonny, and so *clean,* wee Sheba!"

"Please don' hurt me, Cap'n. I'll do anythin' you say, but
please don' hurt me!"

A lingering shred of compassion made the excited man
say, "I won't make you do this if you don't want to, lass. I
mean, if you *really* don't want to. . . ." But then, since she
wasn't fighting him tooth and nail, he grinned and forced
her knees apart, caressing her as Rose had taught him until, suddenly, he was deep inside her, with her tight vagina
clasping hard.

The girl stiffened under him and moaned, "Ow! *Ma-cambo!* You *hurt* me!" and then her voice faded to a crooning sob as he moved, arousing both their bodies as Rose had taught him.

If Rory was untutored in the dandy's game of gentle se-duction, he was more than adequate as a lover, and young Sheba could have been introduced to sex by a clumsier partner. She failed, of course, to climax the first time, but Rory was a man of lusty appetites. As they continued to make love the sun came out and Sheba suddenly smiled as she stared up at the dappled blue sky, her legs around his waist, aware at last what it meant to be a woman. She sobbed with mingled fear and pleasure as her first orgasm engulfed them both, and, when he stopped for a moment, sated, she held him tight between her thighs and purred, "Did I do right, Cap'n?"

He laughed down at her smiling brown face and said, "You're the best I've yet had, wee monkey."

"Can I be yo' woman now, Cap'n? Will you let me stay an' keep yo' house an' never send me back to Madame Rose?"

A wave of sanity swept over Rory as he suddenly real-ized what he was getting into. He looked away as he said, "We'll see, Sheba, but for now this thing between us must be our wee secret, you ken?"

"Ain' I gwine be yo' woman, Cap'n? You said, when you got on top of me—"

"Och, I know what I said, for a stiff prick has no consci-ence. But if you want me not to send you back to Rose, you'll promise to be quiet about our, uh, warm feelings. Ay, and mind your manners when the others are about."

She relaxed her hold on him, the numb hurt creeping into her voice as she murmured, "You want me to go on as just your house nigger, like before?"

He ran a work-roughened hand over her small right breast and kissed it, soothing, "Och, it's the *head* house nigger you'll be, Sheba, when white folks come to call."

"And when we're alone?"

He kissed her tear-wet eyelids and soothed, "Och, you know what it will be like when we're alone, for are we not alone right now?"

She brightened slightly and murmured shyly, "Do I have to call you Cap'n when nobody else can hear?"

Rory hesitated before he answered stiffly, "Well, lass, it's a captain I am, you have to understand."

Sheba closed her eyes, stroked his back with her languid palm, and sighed, "Yes, Cap'n, I understand. I understand ever'thing . . . now."

EIGHT

James Edward Oglethorpe would have a county named after him, but he would never return to Georgia.

Beset by political and financial problems in England, the benign Utopian would retire from public life with the rank of general and a modest pension from his king to spend his declining years on a comfortable English estate where people did as they were told—when it was for their own good.

For a bare three years, Georgia remained a proprietary colony, ruled from England by stockholders who never saw much profit on the books. The small buffer zone seemed viable enough in those days, for the colony founded on Oglethorpe's original dream of a refuge for honest small merchants and freeholding yeomen managed to hold its own. The Spanish empire, beset by the misrule and court intrigues that would end in freedom for Latin America, seemed content to settle for the status quo along the Florida border. Yes, the colony was thriving just as its planners had hoped—but at each meeting of the stockholders in London, the ledger books showed red. Most of the produce of the small farms was consumed locally by the growing population. Georgia's lumber and naval stores were not enough to show a profit in London, and food was not the only local product that seldom even crossed the Atlantic.

Efram Starr & Sons were refitting coastal vessels from the other colonies at a tidy profit. They'd paid off their loans to the creditors in London and were dealing directly with a money-lending Yankee rascal named Hancock, in Boston.

Isaac Pardus and his son, Drummer Aaron, were expanding their small local trade in metal tools and copies of English furniture. Their overseer, Coffee, had even shown them how to reduce the bog-iron ore of the coastal swamps, and they'd built a small but efficient blast furnace. But again, the products were locally consumed.

Donald MacUlrich had cleared some land on his military grant and was growing dyestuffs for his growing trade in sailcloth and rough clothing for the hard-working small farmers. The sailcloth went to coastal schooners and the

West Indies. The smocks and coveralls never showed on the London books as profit.

Angus MacQueen had nominally married a Cherokee squaw of good family and was carving out a petty fiefdom above the fall line, paying neither tax nor allegiance to the German Georges, while Rose Donovan had become the proprietress of the Red Swan Tavern on the Frederica road. Her establishment was outside the purview of Savannah's petty regulations about the prices and conditions of a lawful tavern, while not so far away that many a young macaroon could not reach it when town life grew wearisome.

Of all the once impoverished colonists, none had made more of himself than Captain Rory Martin. With Sheba catering to his physical comforts, the Starrs buying naval stores as fast as MacPhie's crew could produce them, and everyone from Angus MacQueen to Rose Donovan buying the corn liquor he produced as a side line, Rory was no longer riding on a pony. He'd bought a fine Virginia walking horse and a real wig of French manufacture. He was unable to own more land under Oglethorpe's nit-picking regulations, but he had started lending silver at interest to poor yeomen, who paid in kind with corn for his stills, hemp for the rope-walk he was building, and rice to feed his growing army of retainers.

Coffee had been wrong about it taking a year to build Indigo Hall. It had taken nine months, and the imposing mansion, while still a hollow shell for want of interior luxuries, was the showplace of the colony. New arrivals rode out in carriages or pony carts from Savannah to stare in awe at the Grecian temple rising among the Georgia pines near Indigo River. The once-shallow tidal creek had been dredged deeper since Rory had swum that day with Sheba, and if the water was no longer fit for killifish, Indigo Landing was a good place for a free trader in his schooner to put in, for he'd need have little fear of tiresome duty forms to fill out.

Other settlers prospered as Oglethorpe had hoped they would. A Swiss was making hunting rifles, while the Lombardi brothers from the Italian Piedmont had switched from making trade beads for the Indians to blowing bottles and producing a fine fanlight for Indigo Hall. The newly arrived Sephardic Spinoza family had opened a jewelry shop in partnership with Angus MacQueen's Savannah pearl salesman, Ewen Mackintosh, while the oldest Spinoza son, David, paid court to Sarah Pardus in a macaroon manner that would have shocked his once-despised ancestors in the Lisbon ghetto.

In truth, had James Oglethorpe returned to see how his debtors and misfits had made out, he'd have been astounded at his own success. But since none of this prosperity showed on the ledgers in London, the Proprietors of Georgia, disappointed in their investment, began to sell their stock to the Crown. Meanwhile, pressures were brought to bear in Parliament.

The first sweeping change was passed in 1750, when the production of iron, glass, felt hats, and other manufactured goods was forbidden in all thirteen of the American colonies. Henceforth, the Americans were to produce raw materials for the factories in England. Goods manufactured in England would be exchanged for staple American supplies, and a sensible transatlantic trade would thrive.

To quiet the howl of indignation from the ingrates in the colonies, Parliament removed all restrictions on the local manufacture or importation of spirits. Up in Boston, the father of the Hancock who would one day sign a most distressing document said, "God save the King!" and built another rum distillery. But in Georgia, Isaac Pardus allowed his little blast furnace to go to weeds and told Coffee to use pig iron from the Mother Country from now on. And the Lombardi brothers moved their glass foundry up among the Cherokee, settled in with Indian wives, and started to produce glass beads again.

The few Proprietors who still took any interest in Georgia were barraged with letters of complaint and desperation. It was one thing for a small property-holder to manage with a shop or smithy attached to his few quarter sections of tidewater land, and another thing entirely to live only slightly better than a peasant on the staples he could grow on a tiny military grant.

The land laws were relaxed, and axes rang as new croplands were cleared along the tidewater and beyond the fall line, where Toma-Chi-Chi had been promised no white man's farms would ever grow. Rory Martin claimed everything between Indigo River and the east-west road to the fall line. A small holder who'd settled on a quarter section of it was given a handful of silver, and, when he refused to be reasonable, was burned out by the turpentine crew, who calmly claimed that the wind had shifted as they were burning underbrush from Captain Martin's land.

But the expanded plantations were not enough. The Georgia planters were unable to compete with those in the Carolinas, whose chattel slaves were harvesting bumper crops of rice, tobacco, and indigo with no nonsense about indenture papers and the rights of Englishmen. The experiment had been a noble one, but a colony of yeomen wasn't possible under the conditions imposed by nature and the mercantile laws of Britain. The Proprietors of Georgia, anxious to show a few figures in the black column as they sold out their stocks and mortgages, removed the last restrictions on rum and the importation of Negro slaves.

The institution of chattel slavery was now the law of the land in all thirteen colonies, and the people of Georgia— the white ones—enjoyed the same rights as any other freeborn Englishman.

They'd come in chains and terror from Cape Verde to Benguela. Frightened, bewildered Fanti, Ashanti, Yoruba, and Mandingo. Clever Ibo, not quick-witted enough to escape the raiding Slattee hired by the Portuguese slavers. Indignant seagoing Kru-men, snatched from their fishing canoes by pale-faced men in whaleboats from the big black ships with canvas wings. They came from Goree, Gambia, Biafra, and Benin, or from the larger slaving ports at Bonny, Anamaboe, and Old Calabar.

They came with the men in chains and the frightened women and children huddled together in the fetid darkness of the lower hold. They were loaded aboard in shipments of three to five hundred on the larger vessels, but fifty could be squeezed below the hatch by an enterprising captain with a fishing smack and no fear of the wide Atlantic. It took as long as twelve weeks to load a slaver anchored off the African shore, and many slaves went mad or died of neglect before the palms of home were out of sight. Others died on the six-to-ten-week middle passage, seasick, starved, lying on shelves in their own filth with less space than a dead white man could expect in his coffin.

Temporary plank decks were placed like layers of a cake in the slavers' holds. Generous captains allowed three feet between decks, greedy ones as little as eighteen inches. The slaves lay between these platforms of raw lumber, each touching his neighbor; on the smaller vessels, they lay on their sides, "spooned" in one another's laps. And so they remained, a month or more at a time. At the end of the voyage they were sometimes dragged from the hold, permanently crippled if not permanently insane.

Even though as many as a third of them died on the way, the profits made the risk worthwhile. A slave could be bought on the African coast for eleven or twelve pounds' worth of rum and trade goods. They sold on the docks in the Americas for an average price of thirty or forty pounds. A captain who threw a third of his unwilling passengers to the following sharks stood to double his money. In fact, he could lose two-thirds of his human cargo before he started losing money. The average "wastage" of the middle passage was a fifth of the men, women, or children loaded aboard; the casualty list among slaves, had one been kept, would have been considered moderately severe by a hard-fighting infantry regiment in a war of average losses.

The captains were as varied as the tribal backgrounds of the people they loaded aboard. There were pious New England skippers who conducted Sunday services on the middle passage and prayed for the healthen souls of their passengers. There were jolly roughnecks who allowed the slaves to sing on deck or threw them overboard in chains, depending on the way things went. A young man named John Paul Jones would serve one voyage as first mate on a slaver, quit in sick disgust, and be ashamed of the experience for the rest of his adventurous life.

Others, while disgusted by the stench and the cries of human misery, would stick it out and found shipping empires in Boston, Liverpool, or Newport. Still others gloried in the grisly trade and, in time, became little more than sadistic beasts, unprofitable to their employers and unrestrained in their cruelty to the slaves who shipped aboard their vessels.

Most steered a middle course, being neither particularly humane nor outrageous in their cruelty. The successful slaver was a man who, in other eras, would have made a reliable prison guard, or perhaps a professional executioner. It was easier on a man's conscience to forget that the slaves were human, and a good slaver managed to feel about his charges the way the western cowboy was to feel, a few generations later, about the cattle he was driving up the Chisholm Trail: if a bawling dogie kept going the right way, you ignored it; if it strayed, you flicked it with a whip or rope-end; if it got too sick to travel or turned ornery, you killed it and kept going.

They called it the triangular trade. A ship might set out from Boston with a cargo of rum and salt cod. It would follow the northern westerlies to Liverpool, unload the New England cargo, and buy a load of calico and cheap hardware from the industrial north of England, saving a bit of the rum.

The next leg of the voyage would be to West Africa, where the rum and cheap gimcracks from England would be traded to tribal leaders for slaves. The slaves would then be ferried west on the southern trade winds to the West Indies or to the southeast coast of North America, where the sometime slaver made a profit on them. There he loaded up with sugar, rice, tobacco, indigo, and other staples, to be coasted up to Boston where, with a profit made on each leg of the triangle, the ship was once again loaded with Boston rum and salt cod for transport to England.

Crews might be changed. The ships themselves were insured, and their owners kept them moving under hard-driving masters until, inevitably, they sprung a seam, lost rudder or mast, or simply fell apart in mid-passage, sometimes with a cargo of trade goods aboard, sometimes with a cargo of living flesh chained below the water line.

Over a period of many years, as many as six to eight million Negroes were probably lost on the middle passage in the transatlantic slave trade. The numbers killed in the tribal wars, stirred up by the traders to feed the trade, caused twenty times as many deaths as the triangular trade itself. Whole sections of West Africa were depopulated, and the ethnic makeup of the so-called Dark Continent permanently changed.

But Africa was vibrant with life, and in time most of the scars would heal. The screams of the dying, the roar of cheap trade muskets, and the throb of the nation drums would fade from human memory, if not from tribal record, in the lush green rebirth of West Africa; but the short-sighed policies of colonial governments, coupled with human greed, would change both North and South America forever.

In no part of the world, on any leg of the triangular trade, would any place or people be as changed as in, or suffer more than in, the new Royal Colony of Georgia.

Rose Donovan drove her sulky through the pines with a firm hand on the reins, but the coach whip remained in its socket on the varnished outside of the single forward seat. Behind her, facing backward on a low plank seat between the rolling yellow wheels, her Negro "boy" rode with his feet nearly dragging, ready to leap up at a moment's notice to attend to the hitching of the horse and to help his mistress from her two-wheeled vehicle. The fact that he was thirty-seven years old and over six feet tall had not prevented Rose from designating him a carriage boy. Had he been a man of her own race, she'd have called him her lad.

Rose was dressed in a low-cut gown of watered silk. A high white French wig with artificial birds apparently building a nest in it was pinned to her rolled-up brown hair. Many other landed women of the colony wore wide-brimmed carriage hats to protect their fair skins from the harsh Georgia sunlight, but the years of summer tanning had left Rose with a complexion that could only be dealt with by the concealment of white-lead base and perfumed rice-powder.

Fashion also called for corset and stays of stiff whalebone, but, as in other matters, Rose was a free thinker, and in God's truth it had been a hot summer. The pines on either side of the road filtered the afternoon sun a bit, but she was sweating heavily with nothing at all between her skin and the expensive imported dress that had been designed for a more elegant outing.

The pines thinned as she approached Indigo Hall. Off to her left, through the trees, a gang of Negroes were heaving stumps out of the sandy loam with chains and long pine levers. Rose nodded in approval at the muscular sepia bodies moving as one in the dappled sunlight. Rory had taken her advice and bought his first gaggle of slaves by mail order, from Virginia. Raw Negroes off a triangular slaver could be bought on the dock for as little as twenty pounds with whip marks or thirty-five in good condition, but raw slaves took months to break in, while plantation-bred Virginia niggers were ready to go right to work and could be had for as little as sixty guineas.

Ahead, the Great House Rory was building loomed through the thinning trees. Rose frowned as she drove toward it. Had it somehow been turned around on its foundations? She'd been here often enough in the past few months to know that those monstrous Greco-Roman pillars and tall fanlighted doorways faced the other way, overlooking the landing on the other side of the building!

She was still frowning as she drove up the circular gravel drive to what seemed to be the front entrance, reined in, and waited while her groom leaped up and ran around to steady the horse's head for her. Another Negro who'd been seated on the veranda steps ran over to hold a white-gloved hand out to Rose, saying, "Cap'n Rory on the south veranda, Mistress Rose. He say I's to fetch you to him, direct you get here."

Rose allowed Rory's Negro to help her down from the tippy little carriage and asked, as he led her up the wide brick steps, how the big house had apparently been turned on its axis. The Negro smiled and said, "It's the same on both sides, ma'am. Cap'n Rory say it warn't right folks should drive up to his back door, comin' from Savannah instead of the water, so he had that Coffee build him a back the same as the front."

"Och, that's a mad way to build a house! Where's the service entrance and the summer kitchen?"

The Negro pointed toward the unseen Atlantic, to their left beyond the trees, and said, "On the downwind end of the house, ma'am. You see that high brick wall joinin' the corner of the veranda, there? Well, it hides the summer kitchen, servants' quarters, and sech. Miss Sheba got herself a kitchen garth ahint that wall, and, do you cross it, there's her kitchen, and ahint that, the house servants' quarters. He got the field hands back ahint the forty acres of truck garden they jest cleared past them pines."

"He still has a lot of trees around his homestead, if you ask me. I've cleared the scrub away from my tavern. Trees attract bugs, and there's enough of them for anyone in Georgia."

The Negro didn't answer. He'd been trained in Virginia never to argue with white folks, and it was not his problem if Cap'n Rory wanted shade at the expense of a few bugs. His new master was nicer to him than the dealer he'd been bred by, and, did Cap'n Rory have a few white-trash notions, that fact was offset by the better food and kinder treatment his new servants were getting.

The slave ran ahead to open the front door, which was the main entrance facing north. Rose followed him into the cavernous central hall and stared up at the gaping maw of the unbuilt main staircase. "How do you get up to the top floors?" she asked the Negro. He explained, "They's stairs on either side, along the end chimney shafts, ma'am."

"That Coffee of the Jew's must be running himself ragged these days, between overseeing for his sick master and building this big pile for Captain Martin."

"Yessum. Old Coffee rides all over on that dapple pony Cap'n Rory gave him."

Rose, who'd began to acquire a well-deserved reputation as a woman who minded her shillings and pence, said, "*Gave* him?" and the Negro answered, "Yessum, Cap'n Rory a right free-handed gentleman! He *pay* Coffee, too! I seen him give that sassy Ashanti a golden guinea piece one day, and does he send Miss Sheba in to town for trifles, he let her keep the change. Miss Sheba got lace curtains in her quarters and real silk ribbon bows for her hair. *Our* master is *quality*!"

"Damned Scotchmen never have known how to hang on to their money!" Rose muttered as she followed the slave out through a mirror image of the north entrance and onto the identical south veranda overlooking the water.

Rory got to his feet as Rose came out of the house. He'd been seated in a wicker chair with a brandy snifter in his hand and Sheba at his feet, the black girl's legs dangling over the edge of the veranda. The so-called housekeeper slid off the veranda and landed on her feet on the close-cropped lawn leading down to the water. She smoothed her rumpled skirts as she turned around, head bowed. Rose cast an appraising glance over the girl she'd leased to Rory. The dress, while made of simple linsey-woolsey, was dyed with indigo and was a cut above the clothing usually worn by slaves, or even by a yeoman's wife. The scarlet ribbons she wore on either side of her woolly head were silk, too. Rose smiled and said, "Good morrow, Sheba. You're looking well these days."

The Negress didn't look up as she murmured, "Please, Cap'n Rory, I got to tend to my kitchen help. That sassy Ibo gal burns the gumbo, does I leave her alone too long."

Rory nodded, and Sheba literally ran down the front of the veranda to vanish around a corner of the house. Rose chuckled and said, "I see she's starting to show, Rory. How far along have you gotten her, four or five months?"

Rory waved his guest to the one seat and said, "She's just putting on a bit of weight. She cooks for the whole house, you know, and I fear she's been sampling her own labors overmuch."

Rose sat down and laughed. "Och, you're among friends, Rory *Og*. You've knocked her up and that's the truth of it."

She saw the flush on his high cheekbones and twitted, "You can tell me, lad. What's it like with a nigger? I've been curious, but I have my reputation to uphold, and it's said they get sassy once they've rutted with us. Is it true they have bigger cunts? As an auld student of myself, you're in a position to make comparisons in such matters."

"Damnit, Rose, I didn't ask you out here to talk about twat! You know about my dealings with Efram Starr and the other chandlers along the docks, don't you?"

"Of course—you've been selling him naval stores on consignment."

"Ay, and not liking it overmuch. I've been trying to get better terms from the others, but they're thick as thieves, and while others are out tapping pine, the merchants in Savannah control the prices! More important, they control the flow of silver."

He raised the hand with the glass in it, swept it around the general view, and added, "No matter how hard we work out here, I can't seem to get ahead in my finances. I've had to put off work on this house, and MacPhie is pressing me for back wages. I owe that damned Jew for tools and hardware, and that skinflint, Starr, won't advance me a bob on a barrel of tar before it's been sold."

"Och, credit's no problem for a man with land, Rory. I thought Isaac Pardus was your friend. Why can't he wait for his silver like the rest of us? Why, I have more of my silver standing out than I'll ever see at one time in this life. Stop giving ponies away to niggers and squeeze them as owes *you,* if you're short of pocket silver."

"It's not pocket silver I want, damnit. It's an account in a London bank. That's why I need your help. I've been over to see poor Isaac, and, while he'd help me if he knew who I was, the wee man's too ill to function. He sits about reading his damned Jewish books and telling me his snot-nosed son, wee Aaron, is in charge."

"Wee Aaron your drummer boy?"

"Wee Aaron the master of Pardus Plantation. No large holders are required to serve in the trained band since the royal governor arrived with his detachment of regulars. Aaron's bought himself a macaroni sword, and there's no talking sense to the jumped-up little bastard since he turned fifteen. He says my scheme could backfire, and, as man of the family, he'll not adventure with his father's silver!"

Rose frowned up at him and asked, "Just what is this grand adventure you have in mind, Rory *Og*?"

"Efram Starr and the other chandlers have me over a barrel for silver. I mean to turn the tables on them, but I need the cash or credit to hold out at least a year without their trade."

"Och, they'll just buy the naval stores from other men clearing pine, Rory *Og*."

"Not if I time it right. It's not just my timber holdings that give me the edge, you ken. It's the stills, the cooperage, and the skilled tappers I have, both slave and free. I'm the only man here can supply naval stores in bulk on short notice. My plan is to hold back, piling up my tar and paint and spars in my own warehouses till I have Efram Starr by the balls."

"Och, what would that wee chandler do with a year's supply of naval stores?"

"Get rich, if I let him. Did you notice those trees marked with the king's broad arrow as you drove down from the main road just now?"

"You mean those bigger pines with the three cuts in their bark? I seem to remember passing some. What of it?"

"A timber-cruiser from the royal navy just spent the weekend with me here. He thought I might be upset with him for reserving so many of my best trees for the navy's mast supply, but I entertained him as best I could in this unfinished shack and, over brandy, we got to talking."

"Get to the point. I know the royal navy's been buying up ship's timbers on this side of the water, damnit. Do you think you're the only one here who's ever entertained a sailor?"

"Och, if you know so much, Rose, tell me where the new navy yard's to be built!"

The woman's eyes narrowed thoughtfully. "A royal yard, here in Georgia?"

"Just a wee one, down the coast, where worn frigates can put in for repair behind a fortified island. But you know how lavish the royal captains are with tar and fresh timbers. I've already an option on a virgin growth of live oak, and I have a couple of my tenants growing hemp already. I asked the naval timber-cruiser what he thought about using

Spanish moss for oakum, and he didn't see why it wouldn't seal a seam, soaked in plenty of turp-thinned tar. So, you see—"

"You could make a killing, if it's true, but where do I fit in?"

"I need more credit. Not silver, mind you, just the ability to draw on long terms from London instead of living from hand to mouth with devil a growin' season to breathe in."

"Och, what can *I* do about that, Rory? I'm a tavern-keeper in the same fix as yourself. What security can I offer for a letter of credit, my bonny great ass?"

"I happen to know your favors are no longer for sale to anyone, Rose. You've a few special friends you entertain of an evening when their wives are unwell, or perhaps just wearisome to a macaroon who likes a change of pace."

"Och, the gossip in Savannah is the only entertainment they have since the new threater burned down. Why this sudden interest in my virtue, Rory *Og*? Have you decided to make an honest woman of me?"

"Look, Rose. I know you've made friends with Cedric Howard, the younger son of—"

"You're mad! Ask the son of a belted earl to write a letter of credit for an Irish whore, as decent a whore as she may be?"

"I don't want him to write it for you. I want him to write it for *me*. I've met the man at cockfights and wagered a few shillings with him on the horses, you see. I've taken the man's measure and I know he's the one member of the gentry who'd do it—if you approached him right."

"Och, what would you have me say? Please help a High-land gillie establish credit in the City and I'll take it in the ass, your lordship?"

"As the younger son of an earl, he's addressed the same as the elder son of a baronet, and I don't care how you do it, Rose. He drinks and womanizes. I know you well enough to know you can do it."

"Maybe I can, then, but what do I get out of it, Rory? You've been a cold, standoffish man to me, for a jumped-up gillie asking such favors."

"I've just foreclosed on a quarter-section not far from your tavern. The land is yours as a gift if you'll do me this one small favor."

"Why don't you ask wee Cedric yourself, if it's such a small favor?"

"Och, the Sassunach's a macaroni dandy, as you well know. If he were to get on his high horse and turn me down, face to face, my honor as a gentleman would be publicly impugned, and I'd have to call out the silly wee twit."

"Are you afraid wee Cedric would win a duel with the likes of you?"

"Of course not, but I want the man as a friend, not as a litch to be avenged by his brother's bravos. If you eased into it gently, Rose, some evening when you're got him drunk and feeling expansive . . ."

"I know how to do it, Rory. I'm not yet sure I want to."

"Och, I'm offering a quarter-section of cleared land! You know your free trade in rum has fallen off, now that it's down from Boston legal. You have to think of your future, Rose. I tell you, land is the only thing that matters these days. With land and a bit of credit, there's no end to where a foxy lad or lass can go."

"Ay, there's some truth in that, though since gossip flows both ways, I know why you want to have the upper hand on Chandler Starr. It's no secret he's discouraged you from paying court to his daughter, and—"

"Wee *Martha*? Och, you're mad, Rose!"

"Am I, now? What other reason have you for mooning about down there in your lace and bright red broadcloth coat when Himself and his son are away on the docks?"

Rory kept his face impassive as he considered her words. The visits had been noticed, but the gossips hadn't tumbled to his feelings about Gloria. The suspicions of Rose and the worthless macaroons she entertained could still be twisted to advantage. Aloud, he said, "Well, the lass is not bad-looking, and there's something to be said for courting a woman of good family."

"Och, if you marry wee skinny Martha she'll bear you sons who sit down to piss! You're a terrible snob since you started wearing shoes, you ken. I remember when you were not too proud to roll in the hay with a woman of your own kind."

Rory flushed and said, "Getting back to young Cedric Howard and the letter of credit, Rose—"

"The devil take the wee Englishman and his scrawny

shanks. I'll do it for the land, and, well, a few other considerations, then."

Rory had an idea what the bawd had in mind, but, in truth, it might be piquant to spend an hour in bed with someone so different from the dusky lass he'd been pleasuring of late. Rose still disgusted him with her coarse mouth and sluttish manners, but he remembered her broader, paler hips and the thick triangle of dark hair below her pale white belly; Rose was very unlike the nearly hairless Sheba.

Rose licked her painted lips and rose from the chair. He remembered how she kissed, and the softer lips and pointed pink tongue of his younger, firmer serving wench. He nodded, smiling down at Rose as he felt his palms grown moist. Reaching out, he took a shoulder in each hand and said, "I haven't shown you about upstairs."

"Och, it's too hot for that, though I thank thee, sir, for the suggestion. I'll need a deed to that new holding before I jolly Cedric for you. Ay, and I'll want to take Sheba back with me this afternoon."

"Sheba?" He dropped his hands from her shoulders. "You sold me her indenture with those others I bought, Rose."

"Ay, you can keep the team of bucks I leased you. I've no use for more men at the Swan, but Sheba's been broken in, and broken in *well,* if I remember rightly. The silver you gave me for her papers will be my commission for getting Lord Howard's son write to his father's bankers in London."

Rory drew back from her and growled, "You *are* a slut!"

But Rose just laughed and said, "Compliments will get you nowhere. The girl will be better off with me, Rory. She's a pretty wee thing, and once you've cut into the loaf, what do a few more slices matter?"

She knew the stony expression in his eyes and quickly added, "Och, I'll be taking a worry off your mind, you fool! The girl's in a family way, thanks to not knowing her proper trade. Do you want her to bear you a half-black bastard, you fool?"

He didn't answer and she said, "You've been thinking about that, haven't you? I know you, Rory MacMartin, better than you know your ownself. You'd never own up to Sheba's bairn, and by the looks of things, she'll be having it before many months. I'll take her off your hands and we'll give out some traveler at the tavern did it, should the bairn turn out white enough to raise questions."

"God*damn*it, Rose! This is getting pretty thick, even for the likes of you!"

"The likes of *us,* don't you mean? Och, stop standing there with a scowl and your foolish new gentleman's code of honor. We've known one another too long, Rory *Og*. We both know you're going to do it!"

He didn't answer. He didn't have to. They both knew she was right.

NINE

For a man who'd just had the tables turned on him, Efram Starr was calm enough as he stared at Rory across the warm tar-scented gloom of his rear office. Gloria and her husband were off somewhere in the family carriage. The two men were alone, save for little Martha out front behind the counter. Despite the heat, Rory had dressed in his crimson broadcloth riding coat, and his neck was raw and sweaty under the collar of Flemish lace he wore. Had he known Gloria wouldn't be there to take in his new glory, Rory might have worn his usual silk kerchief.

Efram Starr smiled at the younger man's powdered face and goat's-hair periwig and observed, "You drive a hard bargain, young sir."

Rory shurgged and said, "I learned from a master, sir. It's not as if I'm asking silver, you ken. I know to the shilling how far I can push you in these matters."

"Ay, but you've tripled the price on me, whether we're talking about credit or not."

" 'Pon my word, sir, you set the prices low enough when the shoe was on the other foot. We both know you'll double your money dealing with the royal navy, and—"

"Damn it, Martin, it takes forever to collect from the Goddamned admiralty!"

"I know, sir. That's why they pay the highest prices. I've a hundred trees on my land I daren't cut down before His Majesty is ready for them, but in the end, he'll pay better than any shipyard I know of."

"Mayhap. And mayhap those trees will still be standing when the two of us are in the ground. Those damned broad arrows are a bother. The navy's reserved mast trees from here to the woods of New Hampshire. They'll never build that many ships in a thousand years."

"Getting back to the stores they've ordered from you right now, sir," Rory cut in, "I've eight hundred barrels of tar and nearly five hundred hogsheads of paint, both black and buff, for trim."

"Ay, I know about the blacking you bought on time.

How did you manage the royal buff for the gunport.planking?"

Rory didn't answer. His deal with young Pardus for bog-iron pigment might not be legal under the new mercantile laws, and, if it was, some trade secrets were best kept to oneself.

Starr said, "Suppose I doubled the old price and paid half in pieces of eight on delivery?"

"I said threefold and I meant threefold, sir. I can wait for the silver, you see."

"I know. I saw the furnishings for your new place when they unloaded them from the barque *Corgie.* How in blue blazes did you ever get credit in the City, son? Why, damn me, I've five times your worth on paper, and—"

"Friends in high places." Rory smiled thinly.

"I know. My son says you and Cedric Howard snubbed him on the Frederica road the other day."

"Och, I waved my crop at Nathan. Sir Cedric has curt ways about him when he's thinking of other matters than a passing stranger."

"*Sir* Cedric, is it? I thought he was a younger son."

"Well, he likes to be called that, and it does no harm this side of the water. We were talking about the naval stores you'll be needing to fill that contract with the admiralty."

The older man, who usually enjoyed a good haggle, said, "Done. You'll wait until the Navy pays me and—"

"Five percent interest," Rory insisted.

Efram Starr said, "Three and let's have done with it. I'll have Martha draw up the papers for us this evening."

"Wee Martha? Don't you mean your son or his wife, Gloria?"

Starr's voice was frosty as he snapped, "You worry about your business and let me worry about mine, young sir. If you can't read the script on the new contract, don't sign it."

Rory frowned at the older man and said quietly, "You're a worried man, and it's not money, sir. I know better than to ask what it is, but if you need help with anything but silver—"

"It's nothing you can do anything about, Rory, but I thank you for the thought." He looked away and added softly, "Nothing I can do about it, either."

Efram Starr refused to explain further, but he didn't have to. Rory's own relations with the chandler's son had warmed at least to the point where the thinly veiled invitations to a duel had ceased, but Rory still considered Nathan a worthless malcontent, and he knew, from going over receipts and his contract with the firm, that the old man, his daughter-in-law, Gloria, and now Martha, did all the office work at Efram Starr & Sons.

The other son, Joseph, was still reading law at Oxford and might or might not turn out to be useful one day. The only thing Nathan seemed to be good at was losing his father's silver at the weekly horse races just outside of town.

His business with the chandler taken care of for the moment, Rory got to his feet, bowed slightly, and said, "Your servant, sir," as he let himself out. The older man didn't answer. He moved a liver-spotted hand in what might have been a wave of dismissal, and Rory left him with his worries in the gloomy back office.

It was lighter out front. Martha Starr was perched on a high clerk's stool, writing in a ledger with a goose quill, her tongue between her teeth. She wore her own hair—it was piled up to keep it off her perspiring neck and shoulders—and Rory wondered, as he had in the past, just what color you'd call the girl's hair. Spider-web would be too gray, while a fallen leaf had more color. Her complexion was an odd shade, too. Save for when she blushed, Martha had no particular color to her pale skin. It was too warm to be the skin of a litch, but too bloodless for good health. He wondered idly if she suffered from the ague. She'd always seemed sprightly enough, but so did Isaac Pardus when his swamp fever left him and he was between spells of chills and fever.

Martha felt his gaze and turned, suddenly turning pink from the seam of her off-the-shoulder lemon linen bodice to the roots of her mousy hair. Rory smiled and said, "Your servant, mum," in the bantering macaroon tone he always found himself using around the girl.

Martha licked her lips and said, "Gloria and Nathan are down at the market, looking at some Negroes that just arrived."

" 'Pon my word, mum, you'll find few niggers off the *Gypsy Lass* that can write a fine legal hand."

"Oh, Captain Martin, we want a serving wench for the house. My brother feels it's not right that Gloria and I should work here days and keep house in the evening."

"For once I agree with Nathan, mum, though I doubt they'll find a maid worth having off the *Gypsy Lass*. I understand the brig's thirty-eight days out of Old Calabar. Gaggle of naked niggers with tribal markings and devil a word of English. It'll be field hands the *Gypsy Lass* has to offer."

"Nathan says you have some plantation-bred serving maids over at Indigo Hall, but that they're very dear. Would you mind telling me how much a decent house nigger costs these days?"

"Och, I mind your brother could pick one up for as little as sixty guineas if he wrote to Fairfax, or what's that other planter . . . um, Washington? Yes, I'd say the Washingtons would give as good a price as any. I happen to know they're strapped for silver. The younger brother's had to hire himself out as a surveyor on the Virginia frontier. I could contact them for you, if you like."

"Oh, heavens, Nathan and my father conduct such matters, Captain Martin! The firm is Starr and *sons*, not *daughters*."

"Pity." Rory smiled.

To keep him from making another of his caustic remarks about poor Nathan, Martha asked, "Are you going to the wedding of Sarah Pardus, Captain?"

"Yes, her father's a friend of mine, as you know."

"I don't know the Pardus girl, but I've passed her on the street. She's very pretty, but we've never been introduced, of course."

"Would you like to know her, then? You're both about the same age, and I think you'd like Sarah. I know she has few friends among the young women of Savannah."

"That's understandable, since she's not a Christian. Is the wedding to be a Jewish one, do you suppose?"

"One would imagine so. David Spinoza, the silversmith's son, is of the same faith. I don't know the lad, except for muster days, but he's a willing enough militiaman, and I've no care about his personal beliefs, as long as he keeps his musket clean and powder dry."

Martha laughed and said, "It will be Savannah's first Jewish wedding, then. What do you think it will be like? Do you think they'll sacrifice a goat, as Reverend Langley says they might?"

" 'Pon my word, I've no idea, mum. As long as I don't

have to be the goat or the groom, it's not a matter to frush me overmuch."

This time they both laughed, and, casting a quick glance at the door he'd come out of, Martha murmured, "I *would* like to know Sarah, if only out of curiosity. We read so much of the Children of Israel in the Good Book, but when they live just across town, we don't seem to be able to make friends with them. Don't you find that strange, Captain Martin?"

"I've never thought about it. I have Spinoza crafting some candlesticks for me. Perhaps when the young people are settled down over the shop, I'll ask Sarah if she'd like to attend on you."

The girl's pale face looked crestfallen as she asked, "Do you mean *after* the wedding? I thought, perhaps, since other Christian folk are going—"

Her plea was interrupted by the return of her brother and Gloria Starr. They'd been bickering on the way in, and Gloria was saying, "Honestly, Nathan, if you think I'd give house-room to a girl with filed teeth and a ring through her nose—" and then she saw that they had company and brightened, saying, "Good morrow, Captain Rory. Has Martha been pestering you again?"

Rory frowned as the younger woman flushed. "We were just passing the time of day, Gloria."

Gloria smiled knowingly, and Rory suddenly realized she was jealous of the little mousy Martha. Nathan, oblivious as always to other people's feelings, smiled at Rory and said, "I just had a look at those new niggers. Rum lot if you ask me. Half of 'em sick and the rest sullen and savage as wild cattle. One seemed a likely lass, but Gloria here is doubtless right." He chuckled, patted his wife possessively on the rump, and added, "I say, it would put me off my feed to be served by a cannibal maid with pointed fangs, what?"

Gloria asked, "What brings you here on such a miserable hot day, Captain?"

"I had a spot of business with your father-in-law, in the back."

"I see, and Martha caught you and started bending your ear before you could get away, eh?" She turned to the young girl and chided, "Can't you feel the thunder in the air, Martha? The captain has a hard ride ahead of him if he's not to get soaked before he reaches home."

Martha opened her mouth to protest, but nothing came out. She looked beseechingly at Rory, then lowered her eyes and sat there on the high stool, the picture of embarrassed dejection.

Rory would never know why he did it, but he smiled and said, " 'Pon my word, Mistress Gloria, it was my own idea to speak to Mistress Martha."

Gloria looked startled, as Rory had hoped she would. He nodded and added in a formal tone, "I was waiting until the two of you got back before I asked, of course, but I was of a mind to ask Mistress Martha if she'd like to attend a wedding ball at the Pardus Plantation the day after tomorrow."

In the corner, Martha Starr gasped and looked up. Nathan Starr frowned and asked, "You wish to squire my sister to that Jewish gathering?"

"With your permission, of course. I assure you most of the crowd will be Christian, and, of course, Mistress Gloria can chaperone us, if you like."

"I'll be *damned* if I will!" gasped Gloria, flouncing out of the room. Nathan blinked and muttered, " 'Pon my word, I don't know what to say, sir."

"Say *yes*, then, brother!" Martha pleaded, and the confused Nathan, pleased to be consulted on anything, said, "I see no reason why you can't go, attended by a Christian gentleman. Father will have to be asked, too, of course."

The girl jumped off the stool. "Wait right here!" she said to Rory as she dashed into the back, crying, "Father! Father! I want to talk to you!"

Nathan frowned and said, "I don't know what's come over her. I didn't think she knew the Jewish wench."

"Lady," said Rory flatly.

"I beg your pardon?"

"I said 'lady,' not 'wench.' Her father and I served against the Seminole together."

Nathan shrugged and said, "Quite. One forgets the Jew's an ensign in the guard, and from what I hear, a chap of good character, whatever his odd beliefs. You say other Christians will be present?"

"Yes. The men of my company, and some who served in the past with Ensign Pardus. I meant what I said about a chaperone, though I can assure you—"

"Oh, I wouldn't think of it, ah, Rory. Both of us are gentlemen, what?"

Martha came back, dancing on tiptoe. "I can go! I can go! Father said I can go!"

Rory wondered what he'd started and why he felt so pleased with himself as he bowed with a flourish of his lace-trimmed cuff and said, "I'll be pleased to call for you at sunset the day after tomorrow then, mum. We'll take my covered four-wheeler, in case the weather should turn inclement."

"A dress! I must have a new dress!" bubbled Martha, clutching at her brother's sleeve to insist, "You'd not have me meet those people in Gloria's hand-me-downs, would you, gentle brother?"

Nathan smiled indulgently and said, "I'll advance you a guinea, if you promise to keep it between ourselves," but the girl had her palm out and was babbling about the Frenchwoman down the street even before her brother had pressed the gold coin in her hand. Without another word, she was out the door and running down to the seamstress.

Nathan shook his head and marveled, " 'Pon my word, I've never seen her so excited. I mean, it's not as if this were her first ball, and she was pleased enough to wear a cut-down gown of Gloria's to the masque for the new royal governor."

"Och, no doubt she feels old enough to have her own fine clothes now," said Rory, wondering what it might be like to be alone in a dark covered wagon with a woman, any woman, whose flesh was wrapped in the perfumed taffeta the ravishing Gloria had worn.

He exchanged a few more banalities with Nathan and turned to go. Nathan walked out to the hitching post with him, cast a quick glance both ways, and murmured, "Um, Rory, you were at the races the other day—"

"Ay. I told you not to bet on that roan with the white blaze. You can never trust a horse with white hair around one eye."

"I know. The lesson cost me ten guineas, and this nonsense with little Martha caught me at a bad time."

"Would you like another loan, then?"

"Oh, just some silver to tide me over until my allowance. That damned Rose has been pressing me for my chits at the Red Swan, and—"

"Och, a man has to drink in weather like this, sir. I've a couple of guineas in gold on me, if you think it will carry you until we have a talk with Rose. I've told her you're good for it, but you know how tight-fisted she's become of late."

Nathan looked surprised and stammered, "I say, Rory, this is awfully decent of you, considering how I once mis-judged you!"

"Och, what's a few past differances between gentlemen?" said Rory, reaching into his coat pocket for the purse he carried there these days.

With any luck, the Sassunach bastard would drink him-self to death and leave a very beautiful widow.

Rory reined in and sat his horse in disapproval as he gazed out over the forty acres of indigo. The crop was chest high and the field was spangled with yellow blossoms as the herb went to flower. Honey bees hummed lazily in the muggy afternoon heat. A white man in a straw hat and a loose-fitting linen smock came over to the road with a sickle in one hand, and as he approached he removed the hat with the other. He held it against his chest and bowed, saying, "Good morrow, Captain Martin, sir. What think you of my fine crop for your press?"

Rory's voice was cold as he answered, "I think you've let it go to *flower,* you fool! Och, didn't I tell you the *juice* is what we want from the 'digo? Look at those yellow blooms out there, Rogers! You're letting the dyestuff go to useless flowers and nectar for the damned auld bees!"

"I've been cutting on the far side, sir. The old woman's poorly and the children help as best they can, but—"

"What's that toy in your hand, man? You need a *scythe* to cut forty acres of 'digo. The stuff will be straw before you've harvested the half of it!"

"We're doing the best we can, sir, but the rain brought the crop in so sudden, and with the old woman down with fever—"

Rory nodded. "Och, I know you mean well, Rogers, but I'm going to have to help you with this crop if either of us are to make a bob on it."

The smallholder smiled nervously and said, "Help me, Captain Martin?"

"Ay, I'll send a crew of niggers with scythes from Indigo Hall, and they'll cut it and bale it in a day. I can see 'digo is too much for a family farm, Yeoman Rogers. If you'll let me advise, you'll do better with corn and sweet potatoes in the future."

"Sir, there's little money in eating crops this side of the water."

"Och, sure there is. I'll take this 'digo off your hands before it's completely spoiled; then we'll work out a new contract and you can supply my kitchen with corn, taters, okra, squash, and such. If you plant a few acres in each, they'll ripen in turn and you and your childer' can keep ahead of your chores."

Rogers looked uncertain and murmured, "I owe you already for the tobacco the hornworms got. This 'digo figured to get us out of debt."

"Och, what are you frushed about, man? Have I been pressing you for the tax and seed money I advanced you and your family?"

"No sir, you've been a fine Christian gentleman and that's a fact, but a man likes to think he's his own master, and—"

"I'll tell you what I'm going to do." Rory smiled. "I'm going to wipe out your debt in honor of your poor sick woman. I'll send my niggers over to harvest this crop and we'll call it square."

Rogers gaped in pleasure and stammered, "The 'digo as it stands in the field and I'm free of all debts and duties, sir?"

"Ay, your wife needs you in the cabin while her fever's with her, man. If you want, I'll lend you a nigger wench to sit by her and tend to the cabin and your young ones till she's better."

"Oh, Jesus, that'd be the saving of her life, Captain Martin! But how will we ever repay you?"

"We'll talk about it later, when you're on your feet again. I'm taking the liberty of sending over some proper tools, too. If you're to grow truck for my table and the hungry servants I've been adding over at Indigo Hall, you'll need a two-handed scythe and some decent hoes to work with."

"I don't know how to thank you, sir."

Rory nodded briefly and made as if to ride on, but Rogers called out, "Captain, sir?" and he reined in, smiling patiently.

Rogers said, "I've only a few rows of garden truck over by the cabin, and our pig ran off three nights ago."

"You'll need credit at the market until your next crop is up, then." It was a statement, not a question.

Rogers tugged at his forelock unhappily and answered, "I only need a bit of hominy grits and a barrel of salt pork, Captain, but there's the seeds to buy and the hire of a team to plough and——"

"I understand. Tell the merchants to bill me for what you need and we'll work it out when things get better."

"You'll want half the next crop in payment then, sir?"

Rory hesitated. Rogers was a hard worker and a man who knew his place. Expansively, he said, "Och, a third should cover any new debts you run up with me, if your old woman doesn't ruin us both with jewelry and other female notions." A thought struck him and he asked, "How old is that daughter of yours, Rogers?"

"Going on twelve, sir."

"Ay, and she's going to be a bonny woman, too. When you go to market, charge some ribbon bows for both your woman and the lass to my account, and tell them it's a present from the two of us."

"I'll do that, Captain, and God bless you as a proper English gentleman!"

Rory waved his crop and rode off, pleased with the new deal he'd just made. It took so little to win the simple folk's loyalty and good will.

The importation of Negroes had thrown business into confusion at first as the colonists had readjusted to the sweeping changes of the new laws, but a man with his wits about him had been able to see how things were going to go: those marginal artisans and tradesmen without the silver to buy slaves or land would be ruined, but there'd be employment as overseers for some, and the others could either go back to Europe or out to the frontier, where a white smith or carpenter could still find work for his hands.

Those planters and prosperous merchants with money to invest would find their silver more wisely spent on slaves and the newly unrestricted purchase of land. Smallholders like Rogers or his old master, Thatcher, would manage to exist by growing cheap food for the bigger planters, who, naturally, would concentrate on cash staples like tobacco, rice, and indigo to be sold at greater profit on the world market. It was all very well to have a kitchen garth for fresh salad greens and seasoning herbs, but a man with over a quarter-section and as few as four or five slaves would be a fool to waste space and labor on cheap corn and taters!

Rory's next stop was at MacUlrich's, where his old clansman, no longer interested in weaving cheap cloth for shillings a day, was overseeing the indigo presses and vats Rory had invested in with him.

Donald MacUlrich now styled himself "Aldrich," though he still couldn't read or sign more than his new name to a bill of sale.

Rory sat his horse upwind from the vats, for retting indigo produced a dreadful smell. Aldrich came over on foot, but he was wearing the breeches and boots of a man who no longer worked with his own hands. He waved the riding crop he carried at the team of Ibo straining at the windlass of the indigo press and said, "It's starting to come in a wee bit dry, Rory, but the press the Jew's nigger built us works well enough for the noo."

Rory nodded, staring at the large wooden machine. The principle was simple enough. Coffee Pardus had designed an ingenious set of hardwood rollers geared to an upright windlass turned by four men as they walked in an endless circle around it. Other Negroes fed wilted stalks of indigo into the rollers at one end; they came out the other, mangled and crushed to a thick green pulp, to plop into the long wooden vats that ran like a string of pig troughs across the Aldrich work yard. Other Negroes stirred the spinach-green mess with big wooden paddles or scooped the surplus from one vat to another, exposing as much surface as possible to the sun and wind.

The deep blue dye that formed the only true fast-blue of the era was not visible as such in the raw juices of the East Indian herb called indigo. As it ran down the roller chute and into the vats, it was the color of pale urine. Only time and the endless weary stirring of the big blue-tinged paddles would complete the mysterious chemistry discovered by some long-forgotten genius on the Indian subcontinent. Neither Rory nor anyone else knew how it happened, for oxygen would not be discovered by Priestley for years to come, but the chemical change took place no less certainly for their ignorance.

As the paddles churned the floating vegetable mass, tiny grains of commercial indigo settled to the bottom of the vats as a blue-black sludge. It took tons of the plant to produce ounces of saleable dyestuff, but from time to time, a slave would scrape a scoop along the bottom of a vat, carefully lift a few spoonsful of the evil-looking sludge from the bottom, and spread it out on a metal tray to dry in the sun. When the sludge was dried to the consistency of modeling clay, another skilled workman formed it into small black cubes to be dried further in an oven of loosely piled brick and earth near the storage sheds. The work was tedious and exhausting in the hot Georgia sun, and one man, the day before, had thrown some clay into the vats to add bulk to the slowly accumulating sludge. Aldrich had caught him, and it was because of the incident that Rory had dropped by.

He asked the other Highlander about the wily Negro, and Aldrich said, "Och, he's over in the trees, if you've a mind to look at him."

Rory remained seated on his walking horse and asked what his business partner was doing to him.

"I've found the whipping of a nigger does little to change them, you ken," Aldrich said. "They've hides like bullocks and you only spoil them for resale by marking them with the cat."

"I know, but what have you done with the Ibo who played short measure with our 'digo?"

"Och, I have him tied down over there. They hate to be bound more than they do to be whipped. I had the others stretch him out and pin him to the dirt, spreadeagled."

"That doesn't sound like a great punishment for ruining a vat."

"It does when you've tied the nigger over an ant pile."

Rory frowned and spurred his horse around Aldrich and the roller press as, behind him, the other man called, "I mean to let him up this evening. I've no doubt he'll behave from now on."

Rory rode on, ducking under a low branch as he spotted the still, dark form spread out on his back in the clearing ahead. His horse shied and Rory steadied him, twisting in the saddle for a better look as his nervous mount danced on the ant-covered ground.

Rory gagged as he saw what the punishment had done to the slave tied over the nest of stinging red harvester ants. His body was crawling with the vicious little pests, and Rory didn't need to dismount to know Aldrich had gone too far.

He whirled his horse, rode back to the others at an angry canter, and snapped, "You've killed him, you fool! You owe me thirty-five guineas!"

Aldrich look up, puzzled, and stammered, "Och, I only wanted to teach yon nigger a lesson, Rory!"

"Ay, you taught him. You taught him not to breathe, too."

"I only meant to make him an example, you ken. Is he really dead, then?"

"Dead and half eaten, as you'd have known if you'd looked."

"Och, I'll pay you for him, Rory. You don't suppose there'll be trouble about this thing, do you?"

"I don't know. I've never been party to killing a nigger before."

Aldrich was for burying the slave quietly, but Rory knew the secret could not be kept with the dead man's comrades knowing of it and owing few favors to any white man.

He found Judge Crawford at the Red Swan, as he'd known he would. Rose had announced a cockfight for that evening in the pit out back, weather permitting, and His Honor was a devotee of the blood sports.

Judge Crawford was a Lowland Scot, but since Rory was now nominally a member of the Protestant Kirk, the beefy middle-aged Crawford had elected to overlook past transgressions of his generous young friend, Captain Martin. Rory, in turn, had been careful to lose the last few times they'd played whist together in the back room of the tavern. The judge held quite a few of Rory's unpaid IOU's, for his latest draft on the London bank was somewhere out on the wide Atlantic, and while his credit as a gentleman was good, Rory had learned the value of owing some men as well as having others in debt to him.

Rory found his genial friend at supper, for Rose served simple fare in generous portions, and Crawford was a man of lusty appetites. He joined the judge at the board, but didn't broach the subject of the Negro just then. Manslaughter was hardly a fit topic for two gentlemen sharing a cold joint and a bit of port.

Others were drifting in now, and the low-beamed room hummed to the merits of the game cocks to be pitted against each other later in the evening. Judge Crawford asked Rory's opinion on the entries, and since there was no way to fix a cockfight, Rory opined that Yeoman Baxter's white leghorn-cross looked good to him.

Crawford dabbed at his greasy lips with a lace kerchief

and asked, "Do you really think so? That big red brute of Wilkinson's outweighs the wee Italian bird by a pound."

"Ay, but Wilkinson's made a pet of the red cock, sir. He's fed it far too well, and the leghorn-cross is older and uglier. He's not a meat breed, like the red. Leghorns are only good for eggs, soup, and fighting. They're all gristle and bone, you see."

"Well, you've an eye for flesh, be it female, horse, or nigger. I've a mind to wager a few quid on your choice, if you don't think I'd change the odds to your disadvantage."

"Och, the red is the favorite, sir. I'll just hold back on this first fight and let you take those lads who judge a cock by his fine feathers."

"I say, that's decent of you, sir, but I insist on your having a piece of the action. Suppose we go shares on the Baxter bird and see if we can recoup on that speckled bird we were both so wrong about last week."

The indentured maid called Sheba came in with a tray of drinks, saw Rory, and passed by with lowered eyes. Judge Crawford grinned and murmured, "Did you see the belly on that one, Rory? I'd say some fine young macaroon's gotten her with a half-breed bastard, eh what?"

Rory looked down at his port and said, "No doubt, sir."

"I've never rutted with a Negress, have you? I had a Cherokee girl one time. Some of them are quite decent-looking, you know, and I confess she gave me a rollicking good time once I was past the smell, but I don't know if I could get it up with a Negress. I mean, dash it all, it would be rather like beastiality, don't you agree?"

"Some lads seem to find them more attractive than their own hand, I suppose."

Rose Donovan called out from the back doorway, "The fights are about to start, fine gentlemen. Take your glasses with you, if you like."

Judge Crawford got up, wheezing slightly as he said, "Let's join them, shall we?" and Rory followed. He managed to avoid Sheba's eyes this time as their paths crossed near the center of the crowded room.

Outside, Rose's servants had set up chairs around the boards of the scooped-out cock-pit. The first two owners were already in the pit, holding their birds teasingly as the dim-witted fighters glared at each other. Baxter, the smock-clad bumpkin who owned the white leghorn-cross, was breathing on its ruffled feathers and the cock was trying to wriggle free, its comb blood red as it eyed the enemy in the other trainer's hands.

The visitors took seats, shouting bets back and forth in good humor as they settled down to await the outcome of the first scheduled battle. Rory deferentially chose a spot on the older man's left, biding his time as the ceremonies began.

The first fight was short and one-sided. As Rory had predicted, the white leghorn-cross tore across the pit the moment he was released and hit the heavier red cock in a blur of flying feathers and steel-clad spurs. Wilkinson's red could do little but run from the fierce Italian bird, dripping blood and clucking in fear and agony until Yeoman Wilkinson, with a grimace of distaste, scooped it from the hardpacked dirt and wrung its neck with a practiced hand.

Someone shouted, "I say, it didn't go to the final scratch!" but the spoilsport was ignored as the others waved fingers to one another to signify bets won or lost. No gentleman stood up and no money would change hands, for they all knew one another and their economy thrived on exchanged debts.

Judge Crawford beamed and said, "I say, we made out well on that one, didn't we?"

Rory murmured, "Bet on the West Indiaman in the one that's coming up, sir. Och, I almost forgot, Donald Aldrich asked me a legal opinion today, and since I know you read law at Oxford—"

"Cambridge, but no matter. The West Indiaman, you say?" He held up two fingers at a man across the pit, and the periwigged gentleman from the governor's staff nodded agreement to the two-guinea bet when Crawford called out, "O'Brian's bird!"

Then he settled back as the next two men entered the pit, and asked Rory, "What did Aldrich want to know about the law, son?"

"He seems to have a dead nigger on his hands, sir. It was what you might call an industrial accident."

"Really? How did the nigger die?"

"He, um, had to be punished for adulterating merchandise."

"Oh, I say, that's definitely an offense under the mercantile laws."

"That's what Aldrich told him, sir. You know how hard

it is to make them understand our standards, though, and when the man persisted, Aldrich punished him."

"Quite rightly, too. An apprentice who adulterates or steals can be branded for the first offense—but stay, the fight's about to begin!"

The two men sat in silence as the bird they'd picked rolled over and over with its enemy on the blood-flecked dirt. This fight was much better than the first, as both birds fought viciously with beaks and steel-shod spurs. Judge Crawford sat forward in his chair, eyes glinting with pleasure as the cock he'd bet on crowed and trod on its fallen foe, sinking beak and spurs into the other, semi-conscious cock.

"I say, I do believe it's over!" the judge exclaimed. "That last strike went home to the brain, don't you think!"

Rory nodded and waited until the trainers had picked their birds up, blown on and kissed them to steady them up, then placed the two semi-conscious fighters back on the ground with their beaks on the scratch line in the center of the pit. As the men stepped back, one bird simply fell over on its side, fluttering a wing feebly. The bird they'd bet on strutted up and down the scratch line, head cocked to one side, as the West Indiaman's one yellow eye glared at the helpless enemy. Then, with a sudden determination, it sprang on the downed bird with both feet, dug in its claws, and proceeded to peck at its helpless oponent's open eye. Crawford nodded complacently to the man he'd beaten, who was seated directly across the ring.

As the trainers retrieved their birds and a young Negro boy swept the dirt with a twig broom, Rory said, "You were giving me an opinion on this dead nigger, sir."

"Oh? Quite! You say Aldrich killed the beggar?"

"Yes sir. It was an accident."

"Hmm. I'd have to know whether the servant was indentured or simply chattel."

"As a matter of fact, sir, the nigger was one of my slaves. I lent him to Aldrich, and I owned him free and clear."

"Umm, you mean as livestock."

"Yes sir. I bought him from a stud farm in Virginia."

Crawford frowned. "We do have a problem then. I'd know what the law was had Aldrich killed an *indentured* man. It's quite forbidden under English Common Law, you know."

"I know, but the nigger'd been bought as chattel property, and it's not as if he'd been English!"

"Oh, quite so. Nevertheless, he is dead. I'm certain there has to be *some* regulation on the matter."

"Och, there's no disputing an injury's been committed, sir. I loaned the man in good faith to Alrich, and I'm out what I paid for the slave."

"*Servant,* Rory. Servant, or Negro, or nigger, if you like, but there are niceties to be preserved in law, and 'slave' is such an ugly word. Do you understand my meaning?"

"Yes sir. How about chattel servant?"

"That has a nice ring to it. One can hardly write slave into the legal codes, after all."

"I understand, sir. Suppose I told Aldrich I forgave him for the damage he'd done my property? Would that square us under the law?"

The third cockfight had begun, and an unskilled trainer had launched his bird too early and too high. The cock flew across and out of the pit, confused and squawking as it bounced off the board rail, fluttering its wings and flashing the steel spurs on its flailing legs. Rory saw that it was about to gaff Judge Crawford's shin and lashed out with his own foot, kicking it like a feathered football along the circle of seats. Another man laughed and kicked the injured bird into the pit, where it landed, limply, at its trainer's feet. The trainer tugged his forelock, mumbled, "Your pardons, fine gentlemen," and since the bird was obviously unfit now for anything but soup, he stamped on its head.

Judge Crawford held a toe out critically and said, "Hmm, I have a few spots of blood on my boot, but I thank you for your quick thinking, Rory. The damned mad bird might well have marred the leather!"

"Cold water will take the blood off, sir."

"God strike me, young sir, do you take me for a man who's never ridden to hounds? I don't mind a few spots of blood on me boot, as long as the finish is sound. But, to get back to your trouble with Aldrich, have you decided to take him to law on the matter?"

"Aldrich? Of course not, sir. He's offered to pay me the price of the dead nigger, and gentlemen don't sue one another, even when they're *not* old friends!"

"Well, I could quibble with you on that point, but I do allow that you colonists take one another to law less often than I recall from the old country. If you're not pressing charges against Aldrich, I fail to see what the problem is, son."

"We were concerned there might be an inquiry into the nigger's death, sir."

"I fail to see by whom. Harsh masters have been indicted for the death of an apprentice, but in those cases the victim was a British subject. Do you have any idea who your dead chap's sovereign is?"

"You mean the nigger's king?" Rory laughed. "The king of Dahomey, or perhaps Old Calabar?" he suggested.

Judge Crawford nodded wisely. "There you are, then. You've agreed not to press a property tort against Aldrich, and, save he intends to move to Africa, there's no liege lord to charge him with manslaughter, so—"

"Then niggers have no rights at all under English Common Law?"

"I fail to see how they could, not being Englishmen, even if one assumes they're human."

"I can tell Aldrich to forget it, then?"

" 'Pon my word, I don't care what you tell him, Rory! The next fight's about to begin, and this chit-chat about fine points of law has completely thrown my wagers to the winds! God strike me, I don't know the *names* of the next two birds!"

"The only one you need to know is Mohawk, sir," Rory soothed. "He's that red-and-black fowl young Thompson's holding up over there."

"Mohawk, you say? You think he's a fair scrapper?"

"Yes sir. Young Thompson's one of my tenants and I've watched him handle the bird. He fights them over at his place—without the steel gaffs, of course. Mohawk's the best bird he has."

Judge Crawford frowned and held one finger up, shouting, "Mohawk!" until another man caught his eye and nodded.

Rory himself had to get back to his worried friend, Donald, with the good news that they could bury the nigger and forget him. He excused himself to the older man and rose from his low chair with an idle remark about a lady. The one thing no gentleman questioned another closely about was his attentions to members of the fair sex.

Rory walked around the corner of the tavern to reach the hitching rail out by the Frederica road. It was quite dark now, and in the light of the torches illuminating the cock-pit he cast a long dark shadow ahead of himself as he walked away from the noisy crowd. He started to reach into his pocket for a ha'penny, but then realized that the lad Rose had watching the horses was a nigger, and as such hardly expected a tip. Rory tripped over a creeper vine and cursed the slovenly Rose for her untidy grounds-keeping. One would think she'd buy a few male niggers to pick up about the place. The three or four wee grooms she had out here were too overworked to hack the lush growth of Georgia back to a respectable distance.

In the black shadow of the tavern's end wall, a familiar voice said, "Please, Cap'n Rory! I been waitin' and waitin' for a word with you, sir!"

Rory kept walking as he snapped, "Not now, Sheba. I haven't time. Don't you have work to do inside for your mistress?"

"*Please*, Cap'n! It's about the baby. It's about *our* baby!"

Rory stopped, turned to face the dim form of the pregnant bondsmaid, and snapped, "That's enough of that kind of talk, girl! You get yourself inside and we'll forget your insolence this once."

"Please, Cap'n . . . oh, for God's sake, Rory darlin', don't you *care* what happens to me and your chile?"

Rory cared. He felt sick inside and his hands wanted to reach out and comfort the girl who'd done so much for the numb hurt of the lonely boy he'd once been, but he made his voice as cold as steel as he said, "Now listen to me, Sheba. Donald Aldrich killed a nigger this day for getting out of line. I mean, he killed the buck just for annoying him, not for accusing him of fathering a bastard."

"Please, Cap'n, that Madame Rose makes me do bad things. Last night some gentlemen wanted to see a naked nigger wif a belly and she made me take my clothes off and climb up on a table!"

"You've only five or six years left on your indenture, Sheba. Mayhap, when you're free—"

"They stuck a corncob up me, Cap'n! They stuck a corncob up me an' laughed when I started to cry!"

"Well, you just behave yourself and I'll have a word with your mistress. I'm sure they were only having fun with you."

"*Please* take me with you, Cap'n. I know you don' love me no more, but I'll stay in the quarters an' never bother you till the baby comes."

But Rory wasn't listening. He was walking out to the hitching rail where he'd left his horse, and Sheba knew, as she heard the angry crack of his riding crop against his boot, that it would be unwise to follow.

TEN

The weather was kind on the evening chosen for Sarah Pardus' wedding. The young bride was radiant in her gown of white satin overlaid with Flemish lace and the seed pearls sent as a gift from Angus MacQueen from his trading post in the Cherokee nation. Angus Mohr himself, of course, had come down from the hills to attend; he was dressed in a magnificent beaded buckskin suit and escorted by Indians in turbans and cunningly quilled tunics. The groom, David Spinoza, was tall and almost as handsome as Sarah thought he was. As a member of the trained band, young David wore his full-dress militia uniform. After some heated discussion with the Talmudic scholars of the small Sephardic community, David had convinced them his white wig was a perfectly acceptable substitute for the traditional Jewish skullcap more usually worn on such occasions. With some difficulty, his elders had convinced Corporal Spinoza to wear the traditional shawl during the actual exchanges of vows.

The *chuppah* had been erected in the garden by Coffee and his Negro apprentices under the watchful eye of the bride's father. The floral canopy was woven from magnolia and cape jasmine blossoms, and it smelled, as Isaac observed, "like the gates of paradise."

Few of the wedding guests understood the ceremony. Lawyer Margolis officiated in his capacity as occasional rabbi to the Savannah congregation. As they watched from the steps of the black veranda, Martha Starr kept asking Rory questions, but he was hazy even about the Protestant ceremonies he now attended occasionally for social and political reasons.

Margolis, a political animal in his own right, was aware of how few of the wedding party were of the bride's and groom's faith, and at the risk of shocking the elders he conducted all but a few essential phrases of the ceremony in English, rather than the Ladino spoken in private by the older Sephardim. As David lifted Sarah's veil, Martha whispered, "Oh, it's so beautiful, Rory! I'm so glad I could come!"

"Ay, it's not that different from a Highland wedding. I like that part where they break the glass under heel."

"What do you suppose it means, Rory?"

"I've no idea, but it has a fine final ring to it. Listen, the musicians are starting up!"

The string quartet hired for the occasion were English, so an old Yorkshire wedding madrigal filled the scented air of the garden as friends and family pressed forward to congratulate the bride and groom. Angus Mohr jumped on a table, naked blade in hand, and roared in Gaelic that he'd kill the man who refused to admit wee Sarah was the bonniest bride in Georgia. Nobody paid any attention to him.

Isaac, feeling well after his most recent bout with malaria, hopped over to the musicians and demanded a minuet. Then, as they switched to the dance tune, Isaac bowed low to his daughter. Tears were in his eyes as he asked, "Shall we lead off, Donna Spinoza?"

The minuet was a stately dance as performed in the governor's mansion. As danced in Isaac Pardus' garden by people less sure of the social graces and encouraged by free-flowing Madeira, it bore more than a slight resemblance to a frontier barn dance.

Over in one corner, two Cherokees, not wanting to be spoilsports, were prancing around in a tight circle, scalp knives flashing and an occasional cry ringing out. On the other side of the picket fence around the garden, one of the Pardus Negroes, watching with happy but bewildered approval, began to tap out a Yoruba rhythm with his work-hardened fingers. Others took it up, for everyone on the plantation liked Mistress Sarah.

A red-faced Lancashire lad in a militia greatcoat went over to the hired string quartet, snatched a violin from a startled musician, and snorted, "You call that fiddle playing, damnit?" as he tucked the purloined instrument under his chin, ran the bow across the strings, and shouted, "Now, damnit, let's *dance!*"

Angus Mohr MacQueen howled the war cry of his clan as he snatched Rebecca Pardus up and whirled her across the grass in a wild North Country reel. The other musicians picked up the faster tempo as the Lancashire lad made the rosin fly, and over on the other side of the fence, the war beat of Yoruba mingled with the drum talk of Goree and a Maiden's Prance from Benguela. Watching from the shadows with his pregnant woman, Fiba—or, as the white folks called her, Phoebe—the tall Ashanti, Coffee, tried not to move his feet as he watched and listened, but after a time his fingertips were drumming on the porch rail of his cabin, and the wedding drums of Kumasi sang faintly.

If the bride was radiant and happy, little Martha Starr was delirious with joy. Her gallant escort, Captain Martin, whirled her over the grass in a sea of music and laughter. Other men wanted to dance with her, too, and when somebody trod on her hem and her new gown was ripped she didn't care. She'd never felt so pretty.

The party lasted past midnight, and it would have lasted longer had not the bridal couple been torn from the garden and thrust into a coach to rattle off, followed by hoots of good-natured laughter and a show of rice and flowers. By this time Martha was tipsy on Madeira and was looking for one of her slippers in the grass. Rory took her over to the veranda, sat her down, and told her to behave while he found it for her. She smiled up owlishly at him and said, "Goddamnit, I love you, Rory Martin."

Rory didn't answer as he turned away to peer at the trampled grass in the poor light of the flickering torches along the fence line. By the time he'd found her soiled satin slipper, the party was definitely breaking up. The Lancashire lad was still playing a reel, but nobody was up to more dancing. Those who hadn't left were sitting on scattered chairs at the edge of the veranda, or, like Angus Mohr, were simply sprawled in the grass. One of the big trader's Cherokees, dead drunk, was snoring against the sagging picket fence.

Isaac Pardus staggered over as Rory bent to put Martha's slipper on her grass-stained foot. Pardus beamed, grabbed a post to steady himself, and said, "It cost me forty acres of harvest, but, by God, it was worth it, don't you think?"

Martha rolled her head around, amused at the odd way it seemed to be attached to her neck, and announced, "It wash the granesh wedding there ever wash." Then she kicked off the slipper Rory had just put on, kicked the other one off after it, and shouted, "Wheeee!"

Isaac laughed and said, " 'Pon my word, mum. I do believe we're both drunk. Did your daughter just get married, too?"

"Rory and me don't hash no daughter, sir. We're not married yet."

Isaac grinned at the stricken look on Rory's face and asked, "Have the gossips overlooked something in Savannah, Captain?"

"Och, she's funning you, Isaac," Rory muttered.

"Not so." Martha frowned, suddenly feeling very queer as she held her stomach with both hands and gasped, "Oh, Rory, I think I'm going to be sick!"

He caught her head in both hands as she leaned forward, retching, and though he tried to turn her face to one side, they'd both been too late, and Martha threw up all over her skirt and bare feet.

Rory muttered, "Jesus!" as Isaac turned and called out, "Becky! Over here, dearest. We have a young lady who's not used to Madeira!"

Rebecca Pardus tore herself from the couple she'd been bidding good night and joined the two men staring helplessly down at the miserable girl. As a born mother who'd just lost half her reason for existing, Rebecca had been the right woman to call on. In a no-nonsense voice, she told Rory, "Carry her inside, you great oaf! We'll put her on my bed and get her out of those clothes before the stain sets!"

Rory bent over and picked the girl up; he was surprised at how light she was in his arms as he followed Rebecca across the veranda and into a dimly lit doorway. Rebecca called out, "Phoebe!" as she indicated to the embarrassed Rory the quilt-covered double bed in the candlelit room. As he leaned over to place the sick girl on the quilt Martha clung to his neck and whimpered, "Don't leave me, Rory. I feel so awful!"

Gently he disentangled himself and stepped back, muttering, "Och, I can't take her home like this!"

Rebecca started to undress Martha, swearing at the missing Negress she'd called to for help. She suddenly looked up at her husband and Rory and snapped, "Out, both of you! Can't you see the poor child has nothing but a petticoat under this gown?"

The two men beat a hasty retreat to the veranda, Isaac suddenly sobered by the emergency. Outside he fumbled for a cheroot as he asked Rory, "Isn't that Chandler Starr's daughter in there?"

"Ay, and I'm bringing her home drunk as a skunk. Och,

I should have watched her closer. The wee thing has no capacity."

"Well, you have us to back you if that snippy brother of hers calls you on compromising her honor. I take it you're engaged, of course?"

"Och, you must be daft! Engaged to that wee scrawny lass?"

"I thought she was pretty, but that's your problem, thank God. My Becky will have her right as rain in no time. She's had enough practice sobering Aaron up on muster nights."

"Ay, she brought up most of what she drank, and I know your wife's black coffee, to my sorrow. I didn't see Aaron here tonight, by the by. Is he off on business, then?"

Isaac looked down and didn't answer. The Negress, Phoebe, came toward them and Isaac waved her past, saying, "Inside! Your mistress needs you, girl."

Rory waited until Phoebe had gone inside before he insisted, "Is it true, then, about the words Aaron had with your daughter's new husband?"

"Oh, they're both so young, and this foolishness about Aaron wanting to deny the faith of his father . . . honestly, I don't know what their fight was about. You saw tonight that my new son-in-law is no religious fanatic."

"I told Aaron he was a wee bit young to speak of affairs of honor when he came to me asking for a second. It's my understanding young David laughed at Aaron when he challenged him, and now that Sarah's married to him . . . och, I'll have a word with Aaron when I see him."

"He's not sixteen, and we can't do a thing with him!" Isaac complained. "Everything's changed so since we came to this land."

"Ay, you've a fine new house and you've expanded your wee military grant to a plantation, Isaac. I'd say most changes have been for the better for both of us."

"I know, but this nonsense about my son wanting to attend the Anglican services, and even change the spelling of his name . . . I think that was what he and David quarreled about. David twitted him with a remark about wanting to be called Paradeen or some such nonsense. I mean, honestly, have you ever met any man of any faith with a silly name like Paradeen?"

"No. It sounds Irish. I knew a man named Caradeen

once. It means little friend in the Gaelic." He paused to consider and added, "I mind Paradeen would mean a man from a little park, if it meant a thing at all."

Phoebe came out with Martha's gown. Rory asked her where she was taking it and the Negress said, "Miz Becky say I's to wash it an' dry it wif my iron."

"Jesus, it's past twelve! How long will it take you, girl?"

"I s'pect a few hours, Cap'n. I dassn't git the iron too hot on my stove, lest I burn this fine dress!"

She hurried off on her errand as Rory swore softly. Out in the nearly empty garden, Angus MacQueen rolled over, got to his feet, and stared around in confusion until, spotting the two men in the shadows of the veranda, he came over, swaying slightly but reasonably sober. Rory filled him in on his dilemma and Angus laughed, saying, "You should have let her stay drunk, lad. I've never found much profit in sobering up a maid, but, on the other hand—"

"Watch it, Angus!"

"Och, I meant no harm, Rory. She's that pretty wee thing with the bonny smile I danced a measure with, isn't she? You've a good eye for them, Rory. Next to the bride, I'd say she was the belle of the ball this night."

Rory frowned in genuine puzzlement, and to change a subject that made him increasingly uncomfortable, asked Angus, "Have you had many niggers up above the fall line, Angus?"

"You mean have I slept with many or have I seen many, lad?"

"I mean have you *seen* them, damnit! There's been some running away of late, and it's said the niggers are running off to join the Indians."

Angus shook his head. "Creeks, maybe. Not Cherokees. Any nigger the Cherokees found would be sent back, or maybe sold in the Carolinas. Why do you ask?"

"It came up at a militia meeting. Someone there said a few runaways had managed to be taken in by wild Indians."

"Och, there's your answer then. Yon Creek might harbor a runaway, especially the Seminole Creek who hate us. You see, lad, the word you want is *wild*. Even peaceful Creek like Toma-Chi-Chi's band cling to their old ways and run half naked through the swamps. To a sulky Creek, a runaway nigger might seem another savage picked on by the white man. My Cherokees *admire* our ways and try as ever they can to act the way they think a white man would."

Angus waved at his sleeping friends along the fence as he added, "You can see they dress in clothes like us, and many are living in log houses now, up in the hills. They like to marry their daughters up with whites, and half the tribe's part white or pretending that they are. The two of you should come up on a visit one day and let me introduce you to some of those bonny half-breed squaws. Och, a man's not bedded a real woman till he's been with a blue-eyed squaw!"

"Becky would kill me!" Isaac muttered, but Rory brushed the invitation aside to insist, "What if you, Angus, were to take a nigger gal back above the fall line with you?"

"Me? Are you daft? I'm wed to a Cherokee princess up there in the hills! What in the devil would I want with a Negress—and even if I had one, where would I put her? My Sequwiwok is a jealous-hearted woman, lads, and that's the truth of it. I'd have two or three women, like a man of my station is entitled to up there, if my old woman didn't have this habit of waving tomahawks at such Cherokee lasses as smile on me."

Isaac asked, "Who are we talking about, Rory? I don't know any planter who's had a serving wench run off on him."

"One of the smallholders is missing a Negress," Rory lied. "I've forgotten his name, but next time I see him, I'll assure him she's not with the Indians."

"Not with the Cherokee," Angus amended. "If anyone took her in, it would be Seminole. If that's the case, though, your friend can forget her. She'll be in Spanish Florida by now."

Rory murmured, "Ay, I'll tell him to forget about her."

Rebecca Pardus came out and said, "The poor child's asking for you, Rory."

Rory went in to find Martha covered to her chin by the bedclothes. Her eyes were red-rimmed in the candlelight, and the room smelled of vomit and strong coffee. Martha's lip trembled as she looked up at Rory and said, "I seem to have disgraced you, Captain. I don't know what got into me!"

Rory smiled. "What got into you was Madeira. What

came out of you was Madeira, too. They're cleaning your gown, and your slippers are on the veranda."

"Oh, dear, what time is it?"

"It's one or two, but the moon is full and I'll see you safe home by three."

"Oh, my God! Three o'clock in the morning? I've never stayed up this late in my life!"

"Ay, we'd best keep a sharp eye out for cutty sarks, water-horses, and other things that go bump in the night."

"It's not funny, Captain! Gloria is waiting up for me, and what will we ever tell her?"

"Well, we might tell her the truth, if you've a mind to. What's frushing you, lass? Gloria's not one to carry evil tales to your father, is she?"

"Of course not, but I know what she'll be *thinking*. She knows how I— Oh, damn, damn, *damn*!"

She rolled over and buried herself under the covers, sobbing incoherently. Rory stepped over to the bed, put a comforting hand on her trembling shoulder, and said, "Och, get hold of yourself, lass. I know your sister-in-law well enough to set this wee trouble straight. If your family chides you, I'll take the blame from your shoulders. Gloria doesn't have to know you had a dram too much of the Creature and—"

"You fool!" she sobbed, peeking up with the linen half over her face as she added, "I'd rather tell Gloria the truth than leave her to think she knows what really happened!"

"Och, you're mad if you think she'd suspect us of anything like that, Martha! Why, she knows you're a maiden and I'd never— Och, you're mad as a hatter!"

"Am I really that ugly, then?"

"Ugly? Who said you were ugly, you wee daft girl?"

"A woman can tell when a man's looking through her instead of at her, Captain. I've seen how you look at Gloria and—"

"Now, that's enough of that, young woman! Your sister-in-law's a married woman, and it was yourself I took to Sarah's wedding this night!"

"Yes, but—"

"But me no buts, damnit! Away with your foolish jabbering about people looking through you. As soon as your gown is dry—"

"Do you really think I'm pretty?"

"I'll see what the niggers have done with your clothes."

When Rory left her there was a confused frown on his own face and a smug little smile on hers.

The master of Indigo Hall lay naked on the rumpled linen, staring up at the plaster ceiling with a puzzled frown on his sleep-drugged face. The morning light was coming through the jalousied French windows and the far wall was striped with bars of sunlight. Rory stared at the dust motes dancing in the narrow shafts of sunlight, wondering what had awakened him. Outside a mockingbird was singing, but it hadn't been that. He sat up and reached for the robe on a nearby chair, noticing with approval the depression in the other pillow on the bed.

That new girl, Mandy, knew her place. She'd gone back to the quarters as soon as she'd seen he was sated and asleep. He'd learned his lesson about nigger-wenching, and he'd used Mandy as he had the others—as a necessity, not a real woman. That damned Sheba and her foolish love words had left a bitter aftertaste. It was better if a man held back a bit, enjoying their flesh without committing himself. It was enough that he treated them decently and allowed a woman who had pleased him to laze about with fewer chores from time to time. It wasn't as if they expected the words or kisses a white woman demanded, damnit. Little Mandy was content to eat and dress better than the others and made no fool remarks about being his woman. Mandy knew what she was: she was his nigger, and a good one, too!

Now he heard again the noise that had awakened him. It was the low sound of human voices. Someone was talking out in the hall.

Frowning, Rory got to his feet, fastening the robe's sash. He went to the unlocked door and opened it to peer out at the five Negroes lounging on the floorboards just outside his room. All but one were seated on the pine planking, long, ungainly legs sprawled out in front of them as they leaned against the unpapered plaster of the unfinished hallway. One workman stood, breaking off his joshing to smile at the white man as Rory asked, "What's going on out here, Sam?"

The standing Negro, whose African name had been transmuted from Simba to the more familiar Sambo in Virginia, smiled nervously and said, "Please, Cap'n, that Coffee Pardus say we's to start paperin' this hall directly he rides over this mornin'."

"It's too early, damnit! You all wait down in the yard till Coffee gets here. I haven't had my breakfast yet!"

Sam motioned to the others as he said, "Yessuh, I mind Sukey has it most ready."

The other workmen got to their feet and slouched off down the hall. One of them said something in Ibo and two of the others laughed. Rory didn't know why the deep mellow laughter of his servants bothered him, but it did. He had thirty-seven men and eight women at Indigo Hall, not counting MacPhie and the whites indentured to him. None of them had ever been insolent to his face, but that laughter of theirs was oddly disquieting. It was hard to read a man's face when nature had fashioned his features in such a different mold from your own, and though they smiled every time he looked at them, there was a blankness in the eyes of all those smiling faces that made him wonder, sometimes, what they were really thinking.

Rory went back into the bedroom and shut the door. He'd have to see about a lock for that door. Coffee could no doubt attend to it. It was odd he'd never thought about it before, but a man had a right to a lock on his bedroom door. His house niggers were probably loyal enough, but there were those damned Indians wandering about with their baskets and furs and . . .

There was a discreet tap on the other side of the door and Rory flinched in surprise. Then he laughed at his own foolishness and reached out to open it for Sukey, the kitchen maid with his breakfast tray.

He pointed at the chair near the bed and ordered the slave girl to put it down there. Sukey was nervous as she slipped past him with the steaming teapot and the covered dish of ham and eggs. Rory eyed her intently as she bent to place it carefully on the woven reed seat of the bedside chair.

Like the other house niggers, Sukey had been trained and sold by Lawrence Washington in Virginia. House niggers from Virginia were expensive but the best that money could buy, if one insisted on quality and good manners. Like many bred in the hundred-and-fifty-year-old Virginia trade, Sukey had more than a noticeable trace of white blood in her. She was a pretty little thing with an Irish ass and skin no darker than most Indians'. Having put his breakfast down, Sukey turned, nervously smoothed the thin shift she wore, and asked, "Can I do anythin' else fo' you, Cap'n?"

Rory nodded absently, and, seeing the look in his eyes, the girl began to pull her shift up over her head.

"Och, I didn't mean *that*, lass!" he said, even as he saw how nicely formed his new maid's thighs were. Sukey hesitated, her face hidden in the tube of cloth as she stood there, naked from the navel down. Rory said, "Take it all the way off, then," and the girl finished slipping out of her shift, facing him with a shy smile, eyes downcast.

"Put your things over the door knob," he said, and he went over to have his breakfast as the slave girl obeyed. He sat on the bed and uncovered the ham and eggs, savoring their delicious odor. He tasted them and asked the unseen girl behind him, "Did you make my breakfast, Sukey?"

"No suh, Mandy done it. She say she know how to pleasure you jest right, Cap'n Rory."

"She told you how I like my breakfast, eh? What else did she tell you, girl?"

The naked slave by the door didn't answer. Rory didn't press her. The nigger gals probably compared notes in the quarters about him, but what of it? Obviously it saved time if others instructed a new and comely wench as to what her duties at Indigo Hall entailed.

Without turning his head, Rory patted the mattress and said, "You can sit down while I have my breakfast, Sukey."

The bed sagged as the slave girl came over and shyly crawled across the mattress to take her place, cross-legged, at her new master's side.

Rory sipped some tea and enjoyed his breakfast, savoring the mild erection occasioned by the awareness of the new girl's waiting flesh. It was early morning and a bit of jolly rutting was just the thing to wake a man and get his juices flowing. It was, umm, Wednesday, and he had a lot of things to do this day. There was the meeting with the banker's agent from London, and he had to see Efram Starr about his damned daughter.

He'd slowly grown accustomed to the idea that he was marrying Martha Starr in a few short months. He'd come a long way since he'd arrived in chains as a transported rebel, but there were still some damned Sassunach in the colony who felt he wasn't good enough for their highborn daughters, rich as he'd become.

That Palmer wench was bonny, and he fancied the ankle of Cynthia Davies, but unless he wanted to wait another few years, wee Martha was as high as he was likely to marry. She was related to an earl on her dead mother's side, after all, and it wasn't as if she were deformed. Everyone seemed to think she was rather attractive, as a matter of fact, and he knew she had a good mind. The damned London bankers were pressing him about his casual bookkeeping, and a wife who'd managed the complicated ledgers of a chandler should be able to put the books of Indigo Hall in order. He sometimes wondered, himself, just what he owned and how much he was worth. Like others newly risen to the gentry, Rory kept much of his business in his head. Crops and wagers changed ownership with a casual nod or perhaps a handshake, and if he meant to please his bankers, he'd have to see how much of it Martha could keep track of on paper, once she settled in.

He finished his tea, dabbed at his mouth with the napkin, and stood up to slip out of his robe. He turned, smiling down at the slave girl, and Sukey reached out shyly to take his erect penis in her soft fingers.

"Let me lie down, first," he said, and stretched out on the bed. Sukey knelt near the foot of it. She got on her hands and knees, her head level with his hips, and held his penis gently as she began to kiss its tip. Rory stretched luxuriously and locked his hands behind his neck, thrusting up into her mouth as he closed his eyes and imagined Gloria Starr's lush mouth doing that to him.

His breathing became faster as he wondered if, after they were married, he could teach little Martha to arouse him so skillfully.

He kept his eyes closed, imagining pale white flesh as the slave kissed her way up his abdomen and ran her tongue over a nipple as she eased herself onto his questing shaft. He stiffened and drove up hard, enjoying his secret fantasy as he murmured, " 'Pon my word, Mistress Martha, you do have a lovely wee cunt at that."

The slave girl began to pump up and down with obvious experience and he wondered idly how long it would take to teach Martha to do that. As his pleasure mounted, he opened his eyes and drank in the tawny beauty of Sukey's bouncing pear-shaped breasts. It was no use pretending she was Martha. When Martha wasn't about, he simply couldn't remember what she looked like.

He still felt detached when he realized an orgasm was welling up from deep in his groin, and he wondered what was wrong with him of late. Had he picked up a dose of the ague, or was he simply rutting too often and drinking too much?

He knew he was taking too long and putting too much effort into what would be no more than a flickering moment of pleasure. He suddenly pushed the slave girl off and swung his legs off the bed as she whimpered, "I's tryin' to do hit right, Cap'n!"

"Be still," he said, getting up and going over to his dressing table.

He returned to the bed with a powdered wig and a bottle of the French perfume worn by both sexes among the gentlefolk, and then ordered the slave girl to don the wig and lie with a pillow under her hips. As she stretched her sepia body across the white sheets, grinning up at him from under the ridiculous white periwig, Rory laughed and started to rub perfume over her warm, perspiring flesh. The Negress giggled and said, "That purely feels nice an' cool, Cap'n!" Then, as he ran a perfume-soaked hand between her thighs she gasped and whimpered, "Oh, Lordy, that burns! Please don't put no more on my pussy, Cap'n!"

"Shut up and spread your legs, damnit. It's not your pussy. It's *my* pussy. I paid good money for every inch of you, and, by God, I'll get my money's worth once I have you smelling like a white wench!"

Her vagina numbed, now, by the alcohol in the perfume, the slave girl opened her thighs invitingly and murmured, "It don' hurt no more, Cap'n. You jest do what you've a mind to."

Rory tossed the nearly empty bottle aside and said, "If you want to please me, shut up and don't say another word. I want you to just lie there and move your ass the way I tell you."

Then he climbed into the bed and mounted her, closing his eyes as he worked his half-limp penis into what he was trying, very hard, to picture as the pale body of Martha Starr. The picture refused to form, but the perfume and the feel of the wig against his cheek did make it seem he was making lackluster love to *some* damned white woman. He tried for Rose, but the firm young breasts and clean feel of the slave girl's unblemished flesh eliminated auld Rose, whose overuse of lead-based cosmetics and apparent ignorance of soap and water had left her with a rather reptilian complexion of late. Rory pictured the Palmer girl he'd danced with the other night and felt a slight tingle of mounting desire. Then, suddenly, he was not in bed with a slave girl. He was making love to the only woman he really wanted.

"Och, Gloria, Gloria, Gloria!" he moaned, thrusting savagely into the surrogate flesh crushed beneath his weight.

The willing Negress answered with hard upthrusting movements of her pelvis. Cap'n Rory was crazy, like all white men, but he purely jazzed good, and her own man, over to the quarters, was too tired to do right by her during the harvest time.

Rory had it now, as his fantasy jelled, and for a mayfly moment in time, he managed to imagine it would have been like this with his own Gloria, had fate willed differently. He kept his eyes shut tight, gasping love words into the delicate shell-like ear half buried in the powder-scented wig, and, since he spoke in Gaelic, the girl beneath him merely responded to his excited body as he poured out his love and hopeless dreams in words that sounded, to her, like meaningless gibberish.

At last he climaxed and, for a few seconds, it was right. It was what all this foppish courtliness and endless scheming was supposed to lead up to. Then, as he lay limp across the still gently moving slave, sanity returned, unbidden, as the treacherous cosmic jester it was.

"All right," he muttered to himself. "You'll not have Gloria on your wedding night. You'll be bedding her wee pale sister-in-law that you can't even picture as a naked woman. At least she'll be white, Goddamnit, and the children she'll give you will be bairns you won't have to get rid of as shameful secrets."

The woman under him felt the tears on her neck and, forgetting she'd been told to keep quiet, whispered, "Did I do it wrong, Cap'n?"

Rory rolled off her, patted her flat stomach fondly, as one might pat a good horse after a pleasant ride, and said, "You're a fine lay, lass. You'd best wash that fool French stink-pretty off before you go on about your chores. Put the wig back on its stand. Uh, you don't have nits, do you?"

The girl sat up, saying, "No sir, I combs my hair with larkspur lotion once a week, like the others tolt me."

Rory wasn't listening. He stared up at the ceiling, won-

dering why he felt so detached this day. He probably was
coming down with some fever. Indigo Hall was nearly finished, he was about to marry a lass from a good family,
and nobody ever laughed at the way he wore his sword
these days. Ay, he'd come a long way from the auld croft
in the Great Glen, and if he couldn't have Gloria in the
flesh, he had a white virgin about to play her role—and, in
truth, if he couldn't see her clearly in his mind's eye, he
might be able to see her, in the dark, as Gloria.

The slave girl murmured, "I's goin' now, Cap'n." But
Rory closed his eyes and muttered, "Not yet. Come here.
I'm not through with you yet."

BOOK TWO

THE
MASTER
OF
INDIGO HALL

ONE

It was called the Seven Years' War in Europe. In the British American colonies it would be remembered as the French and Indian War. The fighting began in 1756 over a squabble between Frederick the Great of Prussia and Maria Theresa of Austria, and it quickly became the true first world war, with England, Prussia, the German Principality, and a reluctant Spain on one side, and France, Austria, Russia, Sweden, and the Germans of Saxony on the other. Before it was over, the fighting would spread from India to the American frontier, and the Bourbons of Spain, congenital losers, would switch sides in time to go down to defeat with their ally, France. George II would die smelling victory.

In North America, Lawrence Washington's obscure young half-brother, George, made a name for himself defending the Virginia frontier against the victorious French and Indian guerrillas, who had wiped out the redcoat regulars under the ill-fated Braddock. On the southern frontiers there was little fighting, though Rory used the declaration of war to swiftly buy himself the new rank of colonel. The promotion came just in time, for the Negroes had begun to address almost any white man as "Cap'n," and it was distressing to be taken for a smallholder.

The first six years of the war brought boom times to Georgia. Screened from French-inspired Indian raids by the friendly Cherokees and sullenly neutral Creeks, the southern colonies found a ready market for their exports—munitions of war. The royal navy in a series of horrendous sea fights swept the enemy fleets from the oceans of the world and limped into friendly ports with shattered spars and gaping holes in their wooden hulls. American oak reframed the battered men-o'-war while masts of towering pine replaced those splintered by the Frenchmen's guns. New tar and paint were consumed at a great rate, along with hemp, oakum, and provisions for the hungry crews. Jack Tar lived on miserable fare, but the royal navy and army needed all the grain, salted fish or meat, and raw spirits it could get. The royal army clad its regulars in madder red, but the royal artillery, marines, navy, and the whole Prussian army wore indigo blue. Sudden fortunes were made by American colonists from the Grand Banks fisheries of New England to the sugar plantations of the West Indies. Few planters anywhere made more than Colonel Rory Martin of Indigo Hall, and his young wife, Martha, was hard pressed to keep track of the colonel's many enterprises.

The last of Rory's original timber holdings had been cleared and replanted to cash crops, mostly the profitable indigo. The gangs of new slaves, now delicately referred to as "our people," worked from dawn to first starlight to fill the Martin contracts and purchase orders as Rory, with restless energy, rode hard from holding to holding, driving poor white tenants to produce the crops he needed to feed his growing army of Negro harvesters and industrial workers. His indigo vats were overflowing. His stills and grist mills worked 'round the clock to feed the maw of war. The king's money, as always, was slow in coming, but in an economy based on credit, a royal voucher was as good as gold in Rory's London bank, and he, in turn, ordered fine furnishings and more gowns than Martha could have worn in any one lifetime—all on easy, high-interest terms.

It pleased Rory to lavish clothes and jewelry on wee Martha, despite her common-sense protestations. For one thing, it made up for the vague guilt he felt about his casual use of her unexciting, pale flesh, grown even less enticing to him since the birth of their first son, Donald Lochiel Martin. Another reason for spoiling his drab, adoring wife was the fact that his brother-in-law, Nathan, had been fool enough to seek a royal commission, and the pay of a navy second officer left him little with which to bedeck Gloria in a manner fitting to her station. Rory knew Martha delighted in passing some of her more ravishing gowns on to her beautiful sister-in-law, and it pleased him to meet Gloria at a government ball dressed in his own wife's finery. When Martha had asked shyly if she might offer Gloria an elaborate jeweled wig, he'd assented with an indulgent smile, and if Martha squealed with delight and declared him the most generous husband ever, Gloria, while truly grateful, wore the glorious wig to the masque with a strained expression in her beautiful eyes.

Martha conceived their eldest daughter, Flora MacDon—

ald Martin, on the night of the August masque, when, very
pleased at the way things had gone that evening, Rory had
the delighted Martha in several new and, for her, quite
shocking positions. She never knew, as she climaxed,
moaning, in her husband's arms, about the little game he
liked to play in the dark of the draped four-poster. It was
easy to pretend, since he'd ordered the same perfume for
his sister-in-law, that the woman moaning in pleasure with
her pale thighs around him had chestnut curls and eyes a
man could drown in. When Martha, red with embarrassment, agreed to the outrageous game her loving husband
called "the French position," it pleased him to imagine
Gloria's lusher lips and delicious pink tongue working fu-
riously on his fevered erection.

He knew it was a sickness, this awful, hurt longing for
the woman he could never have. Even when a letter from
Nathan reached them, informing Gloria that her miserable
little husband still lived, Rory tried to remember that
whether the Frenchmen put Nathan in the locker or not,
he'd be little better off than before. Gloria *liked* his wan
wee wife, and in a society where divorce was unheard of,
the woman he loved was forever out of his reach.

There were other surrogates for Gloria, for Martha,
while she was loving and willing, didn't arouse a man
whose heart belonged to a true beauty. The gallant Colonel
Martin was attractive to most women in the colony, and
among the simple folk morals were somewhat elastic. The
attentions of a booted gentleman were enough to turn
many a maid from the path of righteousness.

The taffy-blonde Lizzy Rogers lost her maidenhead behind a sand dune near the shore after a thrilling pillion-ride
with Rory on his great chestnut stud. The poor-white
fourteen-year-old dried her tears on his lovely lace-trimmed
kerchief, and if her father ever wondered how she'd come
by a few gold coins and a new silk petticoat, he never saw
fit to ask. When, a few months later, Lizzy married young
Luther Haycock, their generous patron sent a handsome
wedding gift, and when Lizzy's first child arrived, a healthy
eight-pound lass for all that she was a few months prema-
ture, Colonel Martin awed the simple folk with his most
princely attendance, along with his lady, the kindly Mistress Martha, at the child's humble baptism. The simple
folk never forgot how Martha comforted Lizzy Haycock

when, obviously overcome by the presence of her distinguished guests, the young mother became hysterical for a time.

A barefoot lass with chestnut hair was surprised but not displeased when one day Colonel Martin, inspecting the corn crop on her father's smallholding, suggested that they lie down a while in her parents' absence. Dad and Mum had gone to market in Savannah, and how was a simple maid to speak of bushels and pecks of corn, when all she'd ever done was hoe the weeds from around its thirsty roots?

Rory had her out in the cornfield, down in the dry clods between the waving rows of tassled cornstalks, and, in God's truth, if the man she entertained there seemed confused and called her Gloria, his skilled lovemaking and generous parting gift left her more than satisfied.

Rory rode up above the fall line, inspecting the frontier in his capacity as a militia Colonel, and while his host, MacQueen, had not lied about the beauty of the Cherokee squaws, there was little of the one woman he wanted in the tawny features and smoke-scented hair of the vigorous Indian girls he dallied with.

Variety helped. After running his fevered hands over the sepia skin and exotic tribal markings of a newly arrived Fanti virgin, Rory even found his wife's paler, smoother skin a novelty as he threw her down one afternoon and drove his penis into Martha's protesting rectum. He wound up the session in a more conventional position, as an indulgence to Martha's excited lovemaking. Her husband's moody, sometimes perverse passions still thrilled her as much as they had that glorious wedding night she still treasured in every detail. The poor dear had been so terribly drunk, and so terribly anxious to please her timid flesh with hours of tender lovemaking, and wasn't it their own sweet secret how, sometimes, he still cried a bit after they'd made love?

They'd been married nearly ten years now, and Martha couldn't believe she was a married woman with four children when, in 1762, after everyone thought General Wolfe's capture of Quebec had as good as ended the war, the Bourbon King of Spain, in some grotesque display of loyalty to the Bourbon House of France, suddenly switched sides. With Spanish Florida now in the enemy camp, the war came suddenly to the Georgia frontier.

If Martha Martin was terrified that something might happen to her gallant husband, she was pleased to preside as hostess to the redcoats quartered at Indigo Hall. They were officers, naturally. Common soldiers of His Majesty's Regulars were quartered with the simple folk as they filed ashore from the transports moored in the Savannah roads. Rory ordered a new uniform and his wife entertained their guests in the lavish manner Georgia planters were becoming famous for.

The young officers had healthy appetites, and the Martins' bills mounted as Martha purchased Madeira, port, and other luxuries in wholesale amounts. Their poor whites furnished most of the staples, but, not to be outdone by the governor's lady, Martha ordered refined sugar, imported East India tea, and expensive Havana cigars in place of the Virginia cheroots her husband and the other local planters had been smoking. Young officers from fine English homes expected, of course, to sleep on fine linens, and when some of the lusty young men insisted on companionship, Martha let them work the delicate matter out with her husband and the shockingly willing slave girls.

In truth, some of the young men had boorish manners, no doubt because they were away from home and trying to put on a brave show with the enemy only a few days' march to the south, but it vexed Martha more than courtesy permitted her to say when hooting, boisterous redcoats fenced in the hallways and left sword slashes in the wallpaper. The one who'd slid down the spiral bannister with his spurs on had done considerable damage, too, and there'd simply been no reason at all for riding that silly horse through one entrance and out the other; the animal had marred the floors terribly with its steel-shod hooves.

Rory was annoyed in his own right. It wasn't just the vandalism and mistreatment of his people. The Negress that one boor had stabbed in his drunkenness had been paid for by the regimental provisioner, and the lesser damages could easily be repaired after the quartering was over. Soldiers were soldiers, and Rory understood the graveyard humor of the breed, but their attitude toward his own Georgia militia was not a matter to be dismissed as youthful hijinks.

Perhaps it was because, in the Mother Country, the once-important English yeomanry had been reduced to humble rustics who bowed and tugged their forelocks when members of the fox-hunting gentry trampled their crops, and sometimes their children, under proud, flashing hooves. Or perhaps it was simple jealousy of the colonial militia, who'd been a bit of an embarrassment to His Majesty's Regulars during the fighting on the northwest frontier. It was true that the regulars had taken Quebec in a bloody set-piece battle worthy of European troops, but the history of this particular war recorded most unsettling episodes, like the ambush of Braddock at Fort Duquesne; there where a raw-boned, red-headed lout of a Virginia farmer had rallied his indigo-blue-and-buff militiamen and covered the retreat of the bewildered, shot-up redcoats. It was all very well for the Americans to say young George Washington had saved the day, but, damnit, he'd simply been lucky.

There'd been the bloody repulse at Ticonderoga, when the French had littered the green grass of Champlain's shore with bodies in madder red and white and the darker uniforms of the decimated Black Watch.

The damned jumped-up American colonists were most annoying when they harped on that business about the St. Francis Indians. It was hardly the job of regular infantry to muck about in a tangled jungle of birch and spruce after small packs of bloody Algonquin armed by the damned Frogs, and if the raiding Indians picked off a frontier cabin or two, that was to be expected in a war. Those New England Rangers dressed in ridiculous green and buckskin by a militiaman called Bobbie Rogers had, perhaps, done some small service to their king by marching overland a few hundred miles through untracked wilderness to fall on the main Algonquin town and trading post at St. Francis, Canada, but to hear the Americans tell it, one would think the burning of an Indian camp and the rescue of a few rustic New England captives had been another 1066!

The country militia in England, no longer longbowmen but little more than sheriffs' posses, wore simple smocks and perhaps a cockade on muster days. The damned colonials either mucked about in Indian clothes or dressed, at their own expense, like real soldiers. The regulars took some small comfort in the fact that there was neither a central plan nor rationality to the various militia uniforms.

The red coats of the regulars were not the macaroni show many civilians imagined. In the deadly confusion of eighteenth-century warfare, it was vital to keep one's slow-firing troops in closed ranks amid the heavy fog of gun-smoke that soon enveloped any European battlefield. An infantryman who strayed from his line was helpless while he took the full minute a hastily trained conscript needed to reload his musket. The bright red of his comrades' great-coats, visible even in heavy gunsmoke, made it easier for a man who'd fallen out of line to grope his way back in, and when another body of men suddenly loomed like a fog-bound ship in the gray pall ahead, it was equally vital to know at a glance whether they wore the red of England or the white of France.

The damned colonists, on the other hand, dressed in every color of the rainbow. Forbidden the madder red of the regulars, militiamen were outfitted in blue and buff, maroon and buff, green and orange, navy and white, or any other combination that suited their colonel's fancy.

They were ridiculous, of course, with those in the lower ranks insisting on wearing their own hair and their officers resplendent in powdered wigs and lace like proper English macaroons. A British regimental surgeon, amused by the proudly marching, albeit out-of-step, militia, had composed an amusing little ditty about the jumped-up colonists.

It went,

> Yankee Doodle went to town, riding on a pony,
> Stuck a feather in his hat,
> And called it macaroni!

Colonel Rory Martin of the Georgia militia did not find this amusing. He understood that New Englanders were sometimes called Yankees. It meant Johnny in New York Dutch, or perhaps, as some suggested, it was an Indian word meaning "long knife," but, whatever its etymology, he failed to see how it applied to himself.

Other Georgians were equally annoyed by the British regulars as they lingered in and around the colonial capital of Savannah, for the redcoats' good-humored disdain spread to anyone who was not a member of their own particular regiment. A Huguenot or Salzburg German found himself taunted by the same rough soldiers as he passed the drilling green. A soberly dressed Low Church merchant or a dandy young Anglican in satin breeches might have the lady he escorted whistled at on the same occasion. Spinoza the silversmith was twitted with being a Jew. A young militia officer who styled himself Paradeen was jeered at as a pup of a macaroon as he rode by on his splendid horse. United in their resentment of the roughnecks from England, the men of Georgia—at least, the white men of Georgia—were coming to think of themselves as a breed apart, a *noble* breed, if it pleased His Majesty. A man who owned land was already uplifted by the contrast of his own skin with that of the sweating Negroes in the fields, and he could hold his own at the game of macaroni with any damned English officer, who was probably in debt to his tailor in any case.

So if Yankee Doodle stuck a feather in his hat, why not trim that same hat in gilt lace? Thus foppish costumes blossomed peach, plum, and rose among the planters, and even smallholders took to powdering their hair and wearing brass buckles on their shoes. Challenges were issued, and several ugly deaths occurred on the dueling field across the river. It was time to do something to keep the soldiers busy before things got completely out of hand.

The British brigadier seemed confident in his resplendent blue silk sash and gilt-trimmed scarlet full dress, but as Rory stared morosely down at the map on the governor's desk, he had serious misgivings. Martha and the children were safe enough in the wing of the house that he'd reserved as their private quarters—at least they were safe as long as he was there to glare at the redcoats occasionally—but a long campaign on the Florida front would leave them at the mercy of those drunken Sassunach, for the planned patrol would leave most of the redcoats in the capital, where they would eat everyone out of house and home.

The brigadier tapped his riding crop on the map to gain the attention of regulars and militiamen in the room. "Our guns made little impression on that damned Spanish fort at St. Augustine," he said. "That soft coral rock the walls are made of swallows cannonballs like pudding. Our ships have pulled back to starve the Dons out with their blockade."

A Georgian murmured, "Beg pardon, sir, but you can't starve Augustine out from the sea. Even a white man can live off the country hereabouts. The Florida woods are filled with deer. The creeks are filled with fish. There's wild fruit, and I'm sure the Dons know you can cook cattail roots or make a passable flour from the pollen heads, while their Seminoles can smuggle everything from rum to tobacco through from the landward side."

The brigadier said, "Quite so, but Augustine is not our affair. It's the Navy's worry." He ran the tip of his crop across the map and explained, "The royal marines have a beachhead over here on the bay of Pensacola. You can see how it puts one jaw of a pincers strategy on the Floridas, can't you?"

Rory saw that the brigadier was looking his way, so he answered, "I'll be damned if I can, sir. If I read the scale of this map aright, it's a goodly four hundred miles or so between Pensacola on the Gulf and Augustine on the Atlantic. The Dons and their Indians have thousands of square miles to maneuver in down there."

"My point exactly, Colonel Martin. Our base at Pensacola seems pointless unless we establish overland communications from this coast. How long do you imagine it would take to drive a corduroy road through the wilderness from here?"

"A hundred years, with luck. That's not an English forest you're talking about, sir. That's nearly five hundred miles of unexplored swamp, pine barrens, live-oak groves, and God knows what else!"

"Indians, too," another militiaman said. "The Creek are friendly, or at any rate not openly hostile at the moment, but we'd be asking for trouble if we cut across their lands above the Gulf."

The brigadier smiled. "Come now, what are a few Indians to a strong force of regulars with a good screen of experienced local militia?"

"How many men are we talking about, sir?" Rory asked.

"Oh, I'd say a company of my men on the first patrol. We have to run a survey through before we actually start work on the road and—"

"A company? Two hundred men or so?"

"Well, you'll have your own six hundred, Colonel."

"Ay, that's maybe eight hundred, starting out, and we can reckon on losing a third along the way to desertion and fever. The Tuscaloosa alone number nearly a thousand, and that Creek chief they call their Black Warrior has at least a hundred muskets from the Indian traders."

Someone murmured, "That's the runaway slave who made himself a chief among the Creek," but the brigadier cut short the discussion of the Creek by saying, "We're counting on the Creek remaining friendly to King George.

Our only concern is with the Dons and their Seminole allies. How soon can your men march, Colonel Martin?"

"How soon do you want 'em?" growled Rory, his acquired English mannerisms falling away as he saw that these idiots meant business.

The brigadier smiled and said, "Good. It should only take Captain Fenwyk's company a few days to make ready, and we'll just see what lies between here and Pensacola, eh?"

Rory said flatly, "I can tell you what lies there. Four or five hundred miles of hell, as the crow flies, only none of us are crows, so I mind it'll be more like seven hundred miles of hell."

The meeting broke up and Rory strode out of the mansion, his brows knit and his head in a whirl. He had so many things to attend to before it would be safe to leave Indigo Hall in Martha's care.

She and the children would need protection from the troops quartered with them. His Negroes could be sent for safe-keeping to some of his friends too far out to have redcoats blustering through their homes and outbuildings. His father-in-law, Efram, could attend to that shipment of indigo, and Martha, he knew, would see that the due bills reached the Royal Exchequer via the next convoy. With any luck the Sassunach would take their own sweet time about moving out, for their wars were fought at a leisurely pace, but it was a matter of pride that his own men be made ready to march at a minute's notice.

A dapper figure fell in at Rory's left as he walked toward the Negro lad holding the reins of his horse. Rory saw it was young Aaron Pardus, or Paradeen these days, and paused to see what his new ensign wanted. He asked, "How is your father, Aaron?" as he tried not to smile at the macaroni picture the young officer made in his emerald green, orange-faced, silver-buttoned coat.

"My father is alive, sir," Aaron said. "I can hope for little more these days. Forgive me, but I must presume on our long friendship on a matter of honor."

"Och, you want to fight a duel with me, lad?"

"It's not amusing, sir. The man I called out is a damned loud-mouthed Englishman named Fenwyk!"

"Captain Fenwyk of the royal dragoons? Och, we're marching into the swamps with him in a day or so."

"Forgive me, sir, you're wrong. One of us will remain

here in Savannah, as a litch. I'd like you to second me, if you would."

"Has the Englishman accepted your challenge?"

"He has. I gave him little choice when I tossed a glass of Madeira in his face at the Red Swan just now."

"Och, it's just this afternoon you did it, eh? Perhaps it's not too late to get you out of it, lad." He saw the hurt look in the young man's eyes and quickly added, "It's not that I don't reckon you man enough to stand up to a captain of dragoons, Ensign Paradeen, but with all of us about to march out for the king—"

"I'll have no satisfaction but his full apology or an exchange of fire, sir. If you won't second me—"

"Foosh! Who said I'd refuse the son of an old comrade? You might tell me what it's all about, though."

Paradeen lowered his eyes as he explained, "You know, of course, that my family is of the Hebrew faith?"

"Ay, I've long suspected as much, though I understand you're High Kirk your ownsel'."

"Exactly, and that damned Fenwyk just called me a Jew."

"Och, at the risk of my own life, young sir, I fail to see what the insult was."

"There was more than that to his remarks, Colonel. I could see he'd been drinking. That old whore, Rose, has been quartering him with plenty to drink, and, I daresay, other comforts of home. Nevertheless, I kept a most civil tongue when I explained my position as the Anglican son of a Hebrew gentleman."

"He laughed, I'd imagine?"

"He not only laughed, he brought the women of my family into it. He said my mother was a fat Jewish slut and that my sister, Sarah—"

"Och, say no more, lad. Go home and perpare yoursel'. I'll see to the arrangements and call on you when the time and place have been set."

"I say, Colonel, this is awfully decent of you."

"Go home and make sure you stay sober. Be careful what you eat, for it's better to be shot with an empty belly. I'd be a fool to tell you to try and sleep, but rest as much as you can, and for God's sake, don't tell your mother!"

Rory found Judge Crawford at the Crown and Anchor and explained the situation. Crawford agreed to be young

Paradeen's other second and suggested himself as the go-between. He knew Captain Fenwyk from his visits to the Red Swan and said that while he had a low opinion of the dragoon's social graces, the man was over thirty and reputed to be a deadly marksman. It was the duty of the seconds to make every effort to bring about a bloodless settlement, and in this case the matter was imperative. The war needed Captain Fenwyk and, with Isaac Pardus a near vegetable, Pardus Plantation needed its only male heir.

Leaving Judge Crawford to worry about the pending affair of honor, Rory rode over to Efram Starr's chandlery. The boom in trade had brought a few small changes to the establishment of the tight-fisted Liverpudlian. A young English clerk now managed the counter in the front office, but the books were still entrusted only to family, and in the back room Rory found Gloria hard at work with quill and inkhorn.

He asked for his father-in-law and, when Gloria said he'd be back soon, Rory took a seat and announced casually that he'd been called to the colors with his militiamen. Gloria nodded and said she'd heard. The least she could have done, he thought, was *look* at him when she wished him good fortune at the front!

He sat there glaring at her cameo profile in the dim illumination of the musty office while she scratched meaningless figures in her Goddamned book. Rory had become quite good at glaring. Though nearly thirty-five now, he still looked young for his station when his face was in repose. But a single glare at one of the children, a servant, or a member of the simple folk was usually all it took to make the miscreant stop in his or her tracks and wait to be told just what the hawk-eyed Colonel Martin wanted him or her to do.

Gloria Starr was one of the few people his awful glare failed to impress. If anything, she acted as if she found it amusing. The years had been kind to the woman he loved. She'd borne no children to her weak-chinned husband, and her figure, a bit fuller now than it had been the first time he'd undressed her with his eyes, had, if anything, improved with age, like a fine wine.

He sat there drumming on the chair arm as he listened to the scratch of her quill and the ticking of the Swiss clock on the wall beyond her chestnut curls. Finally he cleared his throat and asked, "Any word from Nathan?"

"He's been promoted to first officer aboard the *Pegasus*. Did you really want to know?"

"What? Och, of course I wanted to know. Martha was asking of her brother only last night at supper. His squadron's off Pondicherry now, isn't it?"

"Madras. Clive has lifted the siege of Pondicherry as the war winds down in India. Nathan writes we may let Frenchy keep a few trading posts on the India coast to balance the Portugee. Clive's John Company has ninety percent of India under British control, and we can't be greedy about a few last chips to deal with at the peace conference."

Rory couldn't care less about the endless machinations of the European diplomats in London, Paris, and Vienna, but the woman was talking to him. That was something. She'd been cold the last few years, as if she bore him a grudge for the way their lives had turned out since first he'd seen her, the day he'd carried a log on his tired shoulder.

He asked, "Does Nathan reckon it's nearly over, then? I'd like to have him tell as much to the redcoats here. They've been driving Martha wild with their shouting and all-night brawls out at Indigo Hall."

"I know; we met at market the other day. Your children seem enchanted with the soldiers, however."

"Och, you know how soldiers are with childer'. Some of the lads are family men and it pleasures them to spoil a child they'll never have to discipline their ownsel's. One of them let wee Donald ride his charger yesterday. I thought Martha would have a fit."

Gloria's voice seemed a trifle strained as she asked, "What was it you wanted with Efram, Rory? He seems to be delayed, and as you can see, I'm very busy."

"I'm busy too!" he snapped, flushing in hurt anger as he added, "I'll be gone for months, and I'll want the old man to tend to my business interests while I'm away at the war."

"I'm sure Martha's capable of minding every penny for you. She's her father's daughter, after all."

He got to his feet and said, "I'll be back when there's someone here with a civil tongue, then!" and stormed out.

Behind him, Gloria looked up with misty eyes and softly called out, "Rory!" but he didn't hear her, and, in truth, she wasn't sure she'd wanted him to. She stared down at the blurred figures on the ledger page and suddenly

stabbed down savagely with her quill. The pen splintered
and spread an ugly blotch of wet ink on the neatly kept
ledger book's left page. Gloria put the ruined quill aside
and reached for the sand shaker to dry the mess she'd
made, murmuring, "Now, whatever made me do that?" as
she started cleaning up the spoiled column of figures.

Outside, Rory found Coffee Pardus waiting for him near
his tethered horse. The tall Ashanti stood with straw hat in
hand and a worried expression on his dark face. Rory nodded at him and Coffee said, "Please, sir, it's about the duel
Master Aaron's got himself into."

"Damnit, I told the lad to keep it to himself! How many
of you niggers know about it, Coffee?"

"All of us, I reckon, sir. There were black folks watching
when Master Aaron threw the wine in that officer's face.
Master Aaron done right, Colonel. That Captain Fenwyk is
trash, and he had no call to mean-mouth Miz Sarah like
that."

"All right, it's just as well it gets around. Mayhap the
governor will put a stop to it before someone gets hurt.
How does it concern you, Coffee? These matters only concern white folk, and as few of *them* as possible."

"Please, Colonel, you mind how Master Isaac gave me
back my papers a few years back?"

"Of course. Your indenture ran out in '54, the same as
mine."

"Yes sir, only I served my whole seven years with Master Pardus. Not that I'm complaining, mind. Half the men I
came with on the ship are still serving. Some white folks
have a hard time finding old indenture papers, and they
can get mean when a nigger pesters them about it."

"That's not your concern, Coffee. Master Isaac is an
honest man, and if you ask me, he treated you handsomely.
You've got the five-acre garth and cabin he gave you, and
as a freedman, you've done quite well, considering."

"Yes sir, I'm paid well enough for the blacksmith work
and such. My oldest boy's learning to shoe a horse right
well, and with my books and such, I'm content with my
lot."

"I should think so. How many of you free niggers are
there, anyway? Not more than a hundred, I'll wager. I understand your concern for your former master's son, but I
still fail to see the point of this conversation."

"I rode out to tend on Master Isaac a few days back,

Colonel. He's looking poorly, and when I spoke to him, he acted like he didn't know me."

"I know. He's very ill these days. What did you want with him, Coffee?"

"A letter, sir. When they set me free, they just tore the old 'dentures up. I need a letter of manumission for the files at the mansion, sir. Only, when I rode out to see Master Isaac—"

"Och, he's too sick to bother with paperwork, Coffee. Couldn't young Aaron write a few lines for you? What do you need with manumission papers, anyway? Everyone knows you're a free nigger."

"Please, sir, everyone don't. I shod a horse for a white gentleman last week, and when I asked for my pay, he hit me with his crop."

"The bastard! Och, you should have struck him back!"

"Please, Colonel, would you have struck a white man, had you been me?"

"Hmm, I see what you mean. I fail to see how manumission papers might help, though. A nigger is a nigger, free or bound."

"Yes sir, I'm not worried about a few licks now and again. It's my woman, Phoebe, and our three children. You see, should some white man ever claim them, or me, as strayed servants—"

"Och, that's mad, Coffee. I tell you, everyone knows Isaac Pardus gave the wench to you when your indenture ran out. If you mind the name of the white man who struck you, I'll have a word with him about it, if you like."

"Please, Colonel, what I'd like is a letter, signed by a white master, layin' all these facts out for everyone to read if they've a mind to."

"Very well, I'll mention it to young Aaron. I'm sure he means to honor his father's wishes, and when he has the time—"

"The time is what frets me, Colonel. He's *said* he'd draw up the right sort of letter for me, but, with all this running around to militia meetings and now this duel . . ."

"You have my word on it, Coffee. I'll ask my wife to draw up a legal document and then I'll ask your former master's son to sign it."

"That's kind of you, sir, but what if Master Aaron should get shot in the morning?"

"I doubt it'll come to more than a harmless exchange of

high fire, but should the worse come to pass . . . well, *I* know you're a free man, Coffee. Judge Crawford is a friend of mine. I'll ask him how to manage something like a legal deposition that'll hold water if the need should ever arise."

Coffee heaved a sigh of relief and said, "God bless you, Colonel Martin!"

Embarrassed by the Negro's gratitude, Rory almost offered his hand to the man before he recovered and blustered, "It's settled, then. And, by the way, we may need your skills out at Indigo Hall in a while. Those damned redcoats have near gutted the main hall, and I'm afraid to look in the wing they're quartered in. Does that oldest boy of yours know anything of carpentry?"

"Yes sir, Juba's goin' on nine and he has Ashanti hands."

"Bring him along and I'll pay him a bob a day while the two of you clean up after the soldiers. I'll have some of my people helping, of course. As foreman, you'll get six shillings a day, if that suits you. We'll probably have our house back in six months or so."

Six bob a day was a generous wage, but Coffee noticed, wryly, that the white man hadn't waited for him to accept. Like the others, Colonel Martin took it for granted that he'd obey, free man or not.

Rory waved goodbye as he mounted his chestnut stud and rode off. Coffee watched him leave with mixed emotions. They said Colonel Martin was decent to folks for a white man, but there was something wrong here.

Less than a dozen years ago, Ashanti and Scot had arrived in this land in chains. Now, having signed the same indentures, both of them were free. The white man rode with sword and lace-trimmed hat. He lived in a Great House built by black hands and Ashanti skill, while other Negroes slaved hours a day to make him ever wealthier and more respected. If half of what they said about him was true, Colonel Martin had black women pleasuring him too, and that poor white Rogers hadn't said a word when his daughter had born a bastard child.

Meanwhile, as a free man himself, Coffee slept with one fat old woman on a cornshuck pallet. He dressed in cheap "Negro cloth" and lowered his head when passing white folks on the road. He fed his family on hominy grits and such greens as Phoebe gathered from their small plot of land, and did they get a little silver hidden in the log chinks, the tax man came around to claim it or it went for the supplies a poor artisan with no credit had to keep on hand. He'd stopped buying books, for they cost more than they were worth to a man whose dreams had been pushed aside by the endless struggle to survive. It was easier to forget dreams than to wait too long for them to come true. It was easier to shuffle and talk like the others when the white folks spoke to you, for white folks were suspicious of a nigger who talked better than they did, and a friendless man had no need for enemies, even white-trash enemies. It was easier to . . .

Coffee crushed the hat between his hands as he stared down at them, cursing their color as he groaned, "God-damnit, I'm a *person*! My father sat on his own stool!"

Nobody answered. Nobody had an answer. Coffee sighed, put the battered straw hat on his head, and started home. A little white girl was coming down the street, and when she saw the tall Negro, she hesitated.

Coffee doffed his hat and laughed. "Good morrow, Miz Hanna! Don' you know yo' ol' frien', Coffee?"

The child smiled back, relieved. It was only old Coffee. Papa had said he was a good nigger, and Papa never lied.

The chosen ground was a flat, deserted island near the Carolina shore of the sluggish Savannah River. The morning mists hung heavy over the water in the cool dawn, and the willows on the island seemed to wait like twisted gray ghouls for the blood that might be shed to feed them. The island was notorious among the gentry and a place of suspicious terror to small boys among the simple folk. It was said that skulls and bones were to be seen amid the willow roots and rank Bermuda-grass of the island, though in truth not one of the young men who'd died out there had been left behind by his seconds when they'd rowed away.

Rory stood with young Aaron at one end of the small flat clearing on the island. Judge Crawford and the others were blurred figures in the mist a bare hundred paces away. While Crawford tried to reason with the other side, Rory murmured last instructions to the hot-headed young fool he stood by. Aaron was dressed in moleskin breeches and a simple linen shirt. It was against the code for a man to fight in uniform, and he had accepted Rory's suggestion that a ball that passed through silk lace and jeweled buttons made a nasty wound. As they waited for Crawford to bring Captain Fenwyk's final answer, he told the boy, "Mind you stand sideways to present a smaller target, and for God's sake, hold until the bastard is in your sight!"

"Do you think I should fire high on the first exchange, Colonel? It's not as if I really wanted to kill the man, you know."

"Then what the hell are you doing out here this morning?" Rory snapped, adding, "Listen to me, lad. I know Fenwyk's reputation. He's going to try to do you on the first exchange. He's a bigger target, which works to your favor, and from the little I could see of him, coming out in the boat, he's had a few drams of Dutch courage, which gives you another edge."

"I see. I'll try to wound him right off, then."

"You'll do no such thing if I'm not to attend your funeral, you mad wee thing! This is a serious matter you've brought us out here on, Aaron. Your macaroni gentleman's code is just fine between a drawing room and the dueling ground. Once you take the gun in your hand, you've shaken hands with the devil, and it's him or you, the devil take the hindmost!"

He saw he was frightening the younger man, and that was all to the good. He said, "Now, I know you can shoot, for I taught you myself while your mother wasn't looking. This next part is the hardest. Are you listening to me, lad?"

Aaron licked his lips and nodded. Rory said, "Any man can hit a target when his hand is calm and nobody's pointing a gun back at him. I want you to pretend we're at the target butts, Aaron. When you get the signal, you're not to think of the weapon in Fenwyk's hand. It doesn't matter whether he fires first or not, however mad that may sound to you. All that matters is that you take aim and fire as if we were back in the woods that day when I first let you fire my Highland Dragon. Do you remember that day, lad?"

"Of course. Back when I was your drummer boy."

"Ay. Now put your mind a few months further on, when you started hitting nine times out of ten and I promised you the gold sovereign for making it ten out of ten. You remember that, Aaron?"

The boy nodded and said, "I remember the look on your face when I took your coin, too, Colonel."

"Ay, it hurts a Scotsman to part with gold. You're to keep your mind on that moment, lad. That's not a man out there in yon mist. It's the last of ten gourds hanging on a tree, and you'll not get the sovereign unless you shatter it square!"

Judge Crawford came back, shaking his head, and said, "Fenwyk refuses to withdraw. Will you want to inspect the weapons, Colonel?"

The two older men left Aaron alone as they walked over to join the surgeon and the other seconds in the middle of the field. The judge murmured, "The others refused to go along with your suggestion of light powder and plenty of wadding, Colonel. I'm afraid we're in for a killing matter."

The surgeon was holding the cased brace of Parkers. Rory drew both from the rosewood case, tested the balance absently, then placed them back in the green felt with practiced sleight of hand so that nobody present could be certain which pistol was which. He stepped back, nodded curtly to the officer in civilian clothes representing the lonely young man at the other end of the field, and said, "Your man's the challenger, but we'll give you first choice."

The dragoon's second smiled thinly and said, "It's kind of you, sir, but I must insist that Ensign Paradeen have his choice of weapons."

Rory reached out again and lifted a Parker from the case. It was the one with the better balance, but they'd wanted it this way.

Fenwyk's second hefted the other pistol and asked, "How do you want to set the distance—French or English?"

"Och, let's hand them the damned guns and have it over with."

"Very well, each man is to hold his weapon at safe. Then, on Judge Crawford's word, present and fire. How many exchanges do you suggest?"

"As many as they want, within reason," Rory said. "I'd say, if they're both on their feet after the third exchange, neither of them is really serious."

Fenwyk's second smiled and said, "You express my thoughts exactly, sir. Shall we get on with it, then?"

"Ay, the sun will be up in an hour."

He walked back to where he had left Aaron and handed the boy the weapon, saying, "Hold it loose until Crawford gives the signal, lad. Then bring it down, wrist relaxed, and squeeze, not yank, as you bear on your target."

"Do I get a gold sovereign if I hit the gourd this time?"

"Och, you'll buy us all a drink. I . . . have to leave you now, Aaron. Remember, it's only a target out there in the mist!"

Rory walked away and Aaron Paradeen felt suddenly very small and lonely as he held his weapon up against his shoulder, staring down the field at the dim gray outline of the other young man with a gun. He realized he was standing wrong and nervously shifted his feet to present a slimmer outline to his opponent. There was a bright orange flash from the center of the dim outline he was facing, and something ticked at Aaron's shirt front as he heard Rory scream, "*Fire*, Aaron!"

Aaron's arm came down in a dreamlike sweep as he responded, not thinking, to his superior's military command. A detached part of his own mind seemed to mutter, "My word, he fired on me before the signal!" and then there was something out there in the mists and centered on the small brass bead of his gunsight, so Aaron squeezed the trigger as his father's friend had taught him. The Parker slammed back in his palm and Aaron let it ride up to safe present as, somewhere, someone was shouting, "Goddamn you, Fenwyk! That was a rotten trick!"

Aaron stood there, enveloped in smoke and trying to make out what had happened. Rory ran to him and grabbed his shoulders, asking,

"Art hit, lad?"

"I don't think so. What . . . what happened?"

"The sonofabitch fired before the signal! I think you got him, though!"

As the smoke drifted off through willows, they could see Fenwyk's seconds bending over a still form in the wet grass. Someone shouted, "Surgeon, over here! He's still alive!"

Rory heaved a great sigh and said, "You'll have to try harder for your prize, drummer boy!"

"My God!" Aaron had suddenly realized what had plucked at his shirt front. "The blackguard tried to murder me!"

"Ay, but he didn't invite you to tea. Wait here and let me see if they want to go on with it."

He strode grimly across to the seconds hovering around the fallen man, a challenge of his own ready, for Fenwyk, in violating the code, was no longer entitled to any further exchange of fire he might demand.

Then, as he could see the condition of the dragoon captain, he relaxed and said, "I'd say this had gone far enough, don't you gentlemen agree?"

One of the opposing seconds got to his feet, bowed slightly to Rory, and said, "My regiment's apologies, Colonel Martin. The coward tried to murder your man. Neither Lieutenant Wilson nor I wish to be associated with the drunken scoundrel!"

"I understand, sir, but we'd best try to get him back to his quarters alive. How does it look to you, Surgeon Matthews?"

Dr. Matthews looked up. "He'll live a day or so, in considerable discomfort. Your man's ball took him just under the ribs. I can't tell if it hulled his stomach wall or not, but it hardly matters now."

Rory grimaced, feeling a wry pity for the unconscious Norfolk man. He'd watched men die with mortified gunshot wounds in their abdomens. Infection would do Fenwyk if Aaron's ball hadn't hit a vital organ. Old Rose was going to have her hands full, keeping a screaming man in his sweat-soaked sheets until he passed on to his just reward.

Rory said, "I'll get the other pistol. I trust you officers will explain this matter to your own colonel's satisfaction?"

The second who'd apologized said, "There's nothing to explain, sir. The man disgraced his fellow officers and, with your permission, his resignation will be dated a day before this distressing affair took place."

"Ay, mum's the word, then. As far as we're concerned, young Paradeen simply shot a boor who attacked him."

"I say, that's awfully decent of you, Colonel."

"Och, it's the least we can do, seeing we'll all be marching on the Dons in a few days, eh?"

TWO

The old clan loyalties were seldom mentioned anymore, but Donald MacUlrich, now known as Aldrich, was godfather to the Martins' oldest boy, Donald Lochiel, and had attended the christenings of wee Simon and the two girls, Flora and Cluny. Martha liked and trusted Aldrich; he was big, not too bright, and glared almost as ferociously as Rory himself. More important, he'd dropped out of the militia some time back, and thus was the obvious choice to manage Indigo Hall in its master's absence.

The night before Rory's stripped-down militia patrol was to march out with the British survey team was one Martha would long cherish, for her gallant husband, now that his affairs were in as much order as he'd been able to arrange on such short notice, outdid himself as a lover. She couldn't know it, but Rory was feeling guilty about the way he'd neglected the poor thing, and, jaded after breaking in a new and very black Ibo wench with breasts like watermelons, he found his wife's fragile body a refreshing change. Martha's joy in her husband's lovemaking was the giving joy of a woman deliriously in love, and it mattered less what he did to her than that he took pleasure in her body. She wished he liked more conventional ways of making love—Martha had never got used to the unromantic notion of crouching before Rory like an animal—but what did a few moments' humiliation matter when she could arouse him to such passion? Now he had eased her onto her back again, and she tried to move her pelvis up to meet his thrusts. But Rory was not satisfied, and he pulled her legs up over his shoulders until she thought she must cry out at the awkwardness, the pain . . . ever since the last child, it hurt her to distraction when he thrust so hard, so deep. She tried to lower her knees slightly to ease the discomfort, but her husband growled, "No! I'm coming!" and Martha relaxed, content to feel the warm flowing of his love inside her.

After a while his movements slowed, and for a long delicious time she lay there, contorted but content as he breathed against her shoulder. She said, "That was lovely. Did I please you, darling?"

"Och, do you have to open your mouth and spoil it?"

She stiffened, hurt, and Rory sighed and said, "I'm sorry, lass, but I've told you I like it when you don't say anything for a time."

"You mean we should just lie in one another's arms, in a sort of reverie?"

He said, "Ay, something like that," and rolled off her, allowing Martha's cramped legs to fall back straight onto the mattress. He lay on his back, staring up into the darkness, and when Martha ran a shy hand over his cheek, she felt the wetness of his tears.

She soothed, "There, there, I'm sorry this night must end, too, my darling, but the war can't last much longer, and you'll come back to me, I know."

"Ay, I probably shall."

"I'm missing you already. Have you any idea how long you'll be away?"

"I don't know. It depends on the terrain, and the Creek."

"I was talking to Gloria the other day and she says she heard it will be several months at the least."

"Oh, what else did Gloria have to say?"

"Not much, really. There's been no word from Nathan, but he's half a world away. I suppose I shouldn't complain about your leaving in the morning, considering Gloria's not seen her husband for over three years."

"Ay, no doubt Nathan has a hard-on too!"

"Oh, Rory, what an awful way to talk about my brother and his wife!"

"It was yourself brought them into our bed, auld woman."

"You're teasing, aren't you?" she asked; then, a short time later, she repeated, "Aren't you?"

"Ay. Suck it a bit for me, will you, lass? We don't know when we'll be doing this again and—"

"Rory, you simply must wash it first, after the naughty places it's just been. I'll fetch you a wet towel, if you like."

"Don't bother. Let's just lie here, quietly, I mean."

Martha tried, but after a while she snuggled closer and asked, "Rory, are you still awake?"

"I am now. What is it, auld woman?"

"I was wondering about soldiers in the field. Is it true

what they say about men who've been without a woman for a time?"

"You mean do we bugger one another? Och, there's lots of talk and joshing along those lines. I've never seen it my ownself, though."

"I meant that thing men, and some women, do with their hands."

"You mean jacking off? What's got into you, lass? Didn't I satisfy you just now?"

"I was just wondering about it. Gloria says nine out of ten people do it, and the tenth one's a liar."

Rory felt a strange wave of shock run up his spine as he asked cautiously, "Did she, now? What else has our sister-in-law to say about playing with herself?"

"Oh, she just does it while Nathan is away. I fear I complained, once, when you had been up above the fall line for a long time. She suggested I satisfy myself, but she didn't tell me how."

A startling picture flashed before his eyes as they stared at the ceiling, and he could see, vividly, a pale dainty hand in a cleft triangle of chestnut hair. He groaned and muttered, "What a waste!" as Martha asked shyly, "Will you teach me how to do it, Rory? I miss you so when you're away."

He laughed gruffly, and said, "Och, there's nothing to it. You know how I play with your crack, lass."

"Yes, but it's not the same when I do it myself. I tried, that time you were away, and I just felt silly."

He took her fingers in his own, amused to have a new secret game, and placed Martha's hand in position on the faintly visible darkness between her thighs, moving the woman's cupped fingers as if they were some clumsy tool. It was rather like planing a bit of lumber, when you thought about it. Martha murmured, "Oh, it's better when you help!" and he moved her hand faster, thinking what a daft wee thing she was.

Martha said, "Oh, I see what Gloria meant!" and his own flesh responded to the picture her words evoked. He began to pretend it was Gloria's hand on Gloria's body as he imagined what it must be like for that voluptuous body of hers, alone in her bed this very minute! It was early yet. Was Gloria doing this very thing this very minute, breathing hard as she longed for a man inside her?

Martha sighed, "Oh, I think something's happening!" and he grabbed her by the hair, helping her masturbate with his free hand while he forced her face toward his groin as, kneeling beside her, he demanded, "Suck it!"

"I can't! Rory, it's—" and then he'd shoved it against her protesting lips and, moaning with mingled passion and disgust, she suddenly opened her mouth and accepted his furious erection. Once she had, her inhibitions vanished and she mouthed him feverishly as her climax approached. Rory took his hand from hers and, free to move, got a knee on either side of her shoulders, took her head in his hands, and forced himself deeper and deeper into her now gagging mouth. He felt her retching as he went too far, but the convulsions around his glans were driving him wild, and as he felt his ejaculation coming, he drove his penis down her throat.

Martha's body thrashed under him in terror until, abashed by his own savagery, Rory withdrew. With a ghastly gargle his wife vomited over his naked abdomen and genitals. He rolled off, trying to help her by raising her head as she gagged and vomited a second time on the rumpled sheets. He pleaded, "Och, lass, I'm *sorry*! I don't know what made me do it!"

Martha retched, gasped, and inhaled a long, tortured breath.

"Are you all right, dearest? It was mad I must have gone and as Mary the Mother of God is my witness, I never meant to hurt you!"

"It's all right, it's all right, you just choked me a little, my darling."

"You forgive me, then?" he murmured, sick with guilt as he held her soiled face and acrid-smelling hair against his heaving chest.

She kissed his sweat-soaked chest, licking like a playful kitten, as she ran a hand between them and felt for his genitals, purring, "I'll show you I've forgiven you, darling."

It was madness—what other woman would have submitted to his violence, willingly or otherwise, and then turned to him lovingly and asked for more? But even as he wondered at her, he realized that in all the nights he had spent with his wife, this was the first time he had thought of her as Martha.

* * *

Rory's dress militia uniform was resplendent with real gold buttons and gilt-braid epaulets, a gold-washed silver gorget, and a broad over-the-shoulder silk officer's sash—which, in theory, could serve as an emergency sling for a wounded officer as well as identification in battle.

But Rory was no stranger to campaigning in the woods and swamps of the southeastern coastal plain, so he dressed, the next morning, in thick snake-proof boots, loose linen pantaloons and shirt, and a buckskin Cherokee shirt with his rank insignia worked in dyed porcupine quills. In deferece to his appalled fellow officers of the royal regulars, he slipped the blue silk sash on over the fringed jacket and wore his cockaded lace-trimmed hat. An officer's sword was a silly encumbrance in the trackless wilderness to the southwest of Savannah, but he fastened it to his saddle, and it could ride as far as the horse lasted. Neither the sword nor the horse were his best.

He breakfasted with Martha, the children, and Donald Aldrich. His clansman listened to last instructions and the children, delighted to be allowed at table with their awesome father, listened quietly to the grownups' mysterious conversation. Mama had said she'd send them to eat with Aunt Sukey on the other veranda if they pestered.

Rory was calmly pleased with the children as he discussed the affairs of Indigo Hall with Captain Aldrich. Donald Lochiel—or Locky, as he like to be called—was a handsome lad of nine with his mother's pale coloring and a hint of his father's more rugged bone structure.

Flora MacDonald Martin, named after the heroine who'd saved Bonnie Prince Charlie from the Sassunach by disguising him for a time as her serving maid, had inherited her black hair and blue eyes from some remote Pict, or perhaps from one of the small fey folk of the Hebrides, as had her younger brother, Simon Fraser Martin, named for another martyr of the '45.

The youngest child, blonde Cluny, had been named, in expectation of another son, after the drawn and quartered chief of Clan MacPherson. When she'd been born a female, Martha, in one of her rare but stubborn displays of self-determination, had insisted Cluny was as good a name for a girl as any other if her husband must persist in this Celtic vein. Rory had given in when Martha had had the tantrum over his suggestion that the new girl be named Jeanie-Calma MacLeod Martin for an obscure heroine of the

Highlands who had apparently refused, after mass rape, to tell the Sassunach where someone or other was hiding.

Rory enjoyed his breakfast and was unusually reluctant to leave that morning, but he had things to attend to before the survey patrol marched out, so, patting Martha's pale hand, he walked to the veranda steps where one slave was holding his horse and another a silver stirrup cup. Young Locky dashed after his father, tugged on the fringe of Rory's Cherokee jacket, and asked, "May I ride down to the road with you, Athair?"

"Och, what's this? Who's been teaching you the Gaelic, laddy buck?"

"Uncle Donald. He told me Athair means father where you and Himself grew up."

Rory accepted the stirrup cup from his Negro with a nod, drained it with one gulp, and, handing it back, said, "Get up in the saddle, Locky. I'll walk auld Ned to the road and you can walk back with young Silas, here."

Locky climbed up, the groom named Silas helping him, and sat proudly atop what was, truly, not a very grand horse. Rory took the bridle reins and, with the groom following at a discreet distance, he walked the horse along the gravel path leading out to the road. The way was dusty and brightly sunlit now, for all the pines had been cut down since Rory had first came to Indigo Hall. He had been thinking of an avenue of live oak, but an old Highland superstition had made him hold off until after he came back from the war, alive or a litch.

Half turning to the boy on the horse, Rory asked, "Did I ever tell you about the beech trees of Achnacarry, laddy buck?"

"No, Athair, but you told us about Cuchulain helping Queen Skatha of the Picts fight the dark men of Rome at Graham's Dyke."

"Och, that's another story, and, in truth, a misty tale from the long ago. The beech trees of Achnacarry are a story recent, true, and sad. You see, Donald Lochiel was in the midst of planting an avenue of trees to lead up to his *Dun-tighearna* when Prince Charlie landed from the French ship and—"

"Lochiel was the king of Scotland you named me after. Right, Athair?"

"Och, well, not quite a king, but close enough."

Rory's habit of naming people after friends and enemies

was a source of amusement to his friends and a shocking habit to some English neighbors, who found a slave named "George of Hanover" not at all amusing. If his children, ignoring their mother's wishes, had been named after Highland martyrs, it was only fitting that his niggers be named Cumberland, Wade, Campbell, or, like the groom behind them, Silas Thatcher Blackamoor.

Locky asked, "What about the trees, Athair?" and Rory said, "They were ready to plant when the pipes of war called the laird away. The gillies had heeled them into a ditch to keep their roots moist as they dug the holes for them along the avenue to the great house."

"Then what happened?"

"Culloden happened, and Lochiel never returned. The heeled trees struck root, neglected as the Sassunach ravaged the Highlands, and I understand they grow that way this day, poor crippled twisted trees, crowded and stunted into a foolish leaning hedge that means nothing where it stands."

"Why hasn't someone cut them down then, Athair?"

"Och, Locky, it's the only remembrance Achnacarry has of a gallant chief and a lad who was born to be king. You'll understand such things when you're older, laddy buck."

They continued on in silence for a time. Then Locky asked, "Athair, is it true I'm not allowed to hit a nigger?"

"What? Och, why would you want to do such a thing, lad?"

"Aunt Sukey says I'm not allowed to hit False Argyll. I told her she was just an old coon and that I'd hit him if I wanted to, but she said it was wrong and that she'd tell on me."

Rory frowned, trying to remember whom he'd named False Argyll. Och, he'd been pretty drunk when Sukey'd had that bairn, but he remembered how relieved he'd been when it turned out as black as its mother. Had he ever really had auld Sukey? God, she'd gotten fat.

Aloud, he told the pouting boy, "It's not manly to hit our people unless they've done something wrong, laddy buck. What has False Argyll done to displease you so?"

"I don't know. I just don't like him. He's my age, but he's a 'fraidy cat. When I ask him to fight, he just runs to Aunt Sukey and cries."

"Well, when I come back, we'll see about getting you another nigger page from the quarters. There's no use trying to raise you with your future bodyservant if you don't like him."

"Bitty coon cries like a girl when I want to play Cuchulain and the giants."

"Ay, he's a soft wee thing, for a . . . what's that you call him, a *coon*? That's a new one on me. I don't see how a nigger resembles a raccoon, but—"

"Oh, Athair, it's from *barracoon!* The niggers made it up themselves. They call the new green slaves barracoon because they've just come from those Portugee stations in Africa. The Portugee call—"

"I know what a barracoon is, laddy buck. To get back to this game of yours, though, I want you to promise you'll not be beating our people for no reason while I'm gone. Och, you're the man of the house with me away, and it's time you learned to handle a nigger as well as a pony."

By this time they'd reached the county road and Rory stopped, helped Locky down from the horse, and kissed him lightly at the hairline before he murmured, *"Soirbheachadh, Mac beg,"* and swung himself up into the saddle.

Locky and the groom waved goodbye as he rode off at a canter, not looking back. Silas Thatcher Blackamoor licked his lips and suggested, "We'd best git back to the house, Marse Locky."

Locky looked down at the gravel road, bent to pick up a good-sized pebble, and announced, "I'm Cuchulain of the Chariots and you, you're a *giant!*"

The slave backed away, protesting, "I wish you wouldn't stone me, Marse Locky!" but a human being makes a delightful toy for a nine-year-old with a lively imagination, and Locky threw, hitting Silas in the forearm as the slave threw up his hands to protect his face.

Locky scooped up a handful of pebbles and followed the groom, who retreated warily, afraid to actually run away from the small boy he'd been charged with escorting; Locky followed, pelting him with small but stinging missiles. Silas winced as a pebble penetrated his guard and bounced off his forehead. He said, "Yo' daddy said not to hit us, Marse Locky!" but the boy laughed and answered, "Shoot, I'm not hitting you. I'm throwing rocks at you!"

Gloria was not at the Starr chandlery when Rory dropped by on his way to the muster green. This was just as well, since Rory wasn't sure he could look her in the eye after the previous night's fantasies. He nodded to the clerk behind the counter and went back to speak with his father-in-law about a few last business details.

He found Efram hard at work on the books and marveled at the spiderlike patience of the old man. It was a glorious day outside and there was going to be a parade, but Efram sat there scratching out figures with the wing plume of a goose.

They discussed the money owed by the royal navy for both indigo and naval stores, and Rory managed, gruffly, to ask the chandler to keep an eye on Martha and the children. Efram grunted and said, "It's my daughter and grandchildren you're talking about, Rory. Did you really expect me to boil them in oil?"

"Och, it's those redcoats out there, and Martha so . . . so . . ."

"Pretty?"

"Ay," he lied, remembering that the woman's father probably did think the wan thing was attractive. Efram said, "I'll see none of them get carried away with their games of gallantry. I'm terribly busy, but—"

"You should get more help, Efram. There's too much here for you and Gloria to manage by yourselves."

"And where, may I ask, am I to hire a trustworthy book-keeper? There's nothing to keep an ambitious young white man in Georgia these days, unless he has land and Negroes. Did you know Spinoza, the silversmith, just moved his family to Philadelphia?"

"Ay, I saw them off on the schooner. Your daughter and I became engaged at David and Sarah's wedding, remember?"

"Oh, yes, that's right. At any rate, Spinoza's not the only free artisan who's left. I've been after Joseph to come home for years, but he's heard, over there in England, how little attraction Georgia has these days for anyone but a planter."

Rory tried to picture the brother-in-law he'd never met, and, failing, said, "He's been reading for law a damned long time, hasn't he?"

"Oh, he's been a barrister in the City for some time, and he's married to a girl of good family. I've asked them to visit us, at the least. A man has the right to see his other grandchildren, after all, but the boy's ambitious, as I said, and this India business—"

"Young Joseph's a member of the John Company?"

"Not yet, but he's applied to Clive for a position with the East India Company. They're going to need hundreds of administrators out there, now that the other powers have been driven out. Joseph seems to think there's much more opportunity in India these days than these colonies can offer."

Efram scribbled a line in his ledger and added bitterly, "Look at what we produce here. Little more than raw materials for the mills of England. The Orient ships silk brocades, fine chinaware, and all that tea and those spices. Joseph writes he made a small plum on a cargo of cotton from Calcutta. Cotton's becoming very popular for shirting and undergarments in England, for it stays so white and washes so easily. Why the devil can't *we* grow cotton, damn it?"

"Och, some few have tried, out on the Sea Islands, but cotton's not the crop for Georgia. It's not as if we had millions of Hindu coolies, you ken. The growing and picking of the stuff is not the problem. We could raise it with a few more niggers, if there was only some way to clean it, but it takes forever to pick the seeds out of the lint, and there's more profitable work for our people's hands than a pound or two of carded cotton in exchange for a day's work."

"Well, no matter. Joseph will probably never come home in any case. It's a hell of a thing to raise a boy to a man and never see him again, you know. I pray that Nathan's coming home from the war, but there's something wrong with Gloria, and—"

"Gloria's *ill?*"

"Just barren, I suspect. It's odd that the grandsons I may have to leave this business to will bear another man's name. The Starrs were important people in Liverpool once."

"Och, your Joseph will doubtless give India a viceroy of the name. I have to go now, Efram. We're marching out at noon."

He got to his feet and the older man rose too. Efram suddenly held out a hand, and, as Rory took it awkwardly, he saw that his father-in-law's eyes were misty with tears. Efram held Rory's hand in both of his and said, "Go with God, son. You know I'm not a man for speeches, but, for God's sake, take care of yourself."

"Och, it's only a wee survey, auld man."

"Listen to me, damnit. I've never told you this before, but you've made my daughter happy and I wanted you to know, before you have to go, how grateful I am to you for it. I'll admit I had my misgivings about you, Scotchman, but . . . and I'll say it once and have done with it. You're one hell of a man, Rory Martin!"

Rory swallowed the lump in his throat and stammered, "Och, you're not so bad your ainsel', you auld goat!"

And then he left, wondering why he felt so queer, and was it *guilt* he felt? Och, what was there to feel guilty about? The man had *said* he'd been good to Martha, hadn't he?

The survey patrol marched out of Savannah with pennants fluttering and a sprightly tune on fife and drum. The two hundred redcoats had been placed under the command of newly breveted Captain Jukes, one of the seconds who'd disavowed the disgraced Captain Fenwyk, who still lingered, in agony, at Rose Donovan's tavern. The company was nominally dragoon, but because of the rough terrain they expected to encounter, the enlisted men had been dismounted to make the trek on foot. The officers, of course, rode.

The regulars stepped out smartly, bayonets flashing in the noonday sun, for the day was pleasantly balmy and a sea breeze cooled their wool-clad bodies. No private soldier carried more than sixty pounds of equipment, since it was to be a forced march most of the way.

The redcoats marched in ordered ranks and perfect step to the beat of the drum at the head of the column. The men were in good spirits, and there was no need for the staff sergeants marching out to the side of each platoon to use the heavy oak staves that gave them their title.

The picked company of rangers Rory had selected from his six-hundred-man regiment were in high spirits, too, albeit not nearly as elegant. Nor were all of them in step. Rory rode at the head of the column with the regular officers, a bit miffed because his militia rank of colonel barely made him the titular equal of the young brevet captain placed over him in command of the patrol. He'd never know it, but a few hundred miles to the north, an irate young Virginia militiaman had just been refused a commission as a regular officer after nearly seven years of hard campaigning on the northwest frontier. Historians of the future would be left to speculate on how differently things might have turned out had George Washington been accepted by the royal regulars.

A mounted aide rode up beside Captain Jukes and murmured something to him about the rag-tag militia rangers back between the advance redcoats and the baggage train bringing up the rear. Jukes laughed, turned in the saddle to wave at his fifer, and called out, "Mind the music and the *step*, Fifer Collins!" and the silver fife began to tootle "Yankee Doodle."

Rory didn't find the hint amusing, but he reined in and rode back to his own men, roaring at young Aaron Paradeen, "Goddamnit, Ensign, you're not just supposed to sit on your fucking horse looking macaroni! Keep your men in step with the drum!"

Aaron reined out of line, whirling his bay gelding as he started to repeat the order, but Rory glared down at the grinning rangers and began to cadence, "Hup, hoop, hreep, hore. Pick it *hup*, hoop, hreep, hore!" as the rangers stumbled, skipped, and managed to fall into some semblance of a marching body of soldiers.

Rory stayed back with them, dancing his mount and cursing men who slouched or lost their dress in line. An offending bayonet caught his eye and he roared, "Goddamn you, Holzmann! That's a musket, not a pitchfork! Hold it *right* or I'll shove it up your ass!"

The grinning Holzmann's blade snapped into place as his colonel shouted, "Ferraro, get that Goddamned hat on straight! Do you want those fucking redcoats laughing at us?" and in a little while the Georgia Rangers, homespun and buckskinned though they might be, were stepping smartly to the derisive strains of the hated "Yankee Doodle."

The column was coming on to the Pardus holding now, and Rory said, "Ensign Paradeen, attend on your parents and give them my best regards before you catch up with us. Take ten minutes if you think your mount is up to it."

Aaron saluted and galloped off at an angle, jumping his horse over a fence as he waved to the distant figures on the Pardus veranda.

Rory saw that his old friend, Isaac, was seated in an armchair with a quilt over his knees, his wife, Rebecca, standing at his side.

A young Negress stood in the yard, waving a small Union Jack as she smiled at the passing soldiers. Aaron had joined his parents on the veranda and had knelt at his father's side. Rory waited until his rangers drew abreast of the Pardus house and shouted, "Rangers, present . . . *harms!*" and two hundred bayonets flashed as one in the sun as the militiamen honored an old comrade. Rory removed his hat and snapped, "Rangers, eyes . . . *right!*" as he danced his horse and saluted the family on the veranda with doffed cockaded hat. And then they'd passed, and he replace his hat without looking back, snapping, "Eyes front, shoulder harms!" as the column marched on.

Up on the veranda, Isaac Pardus picked at the quilt with bony fingers and murmured, "That was handsome of them, wasn't it, Becky?"

"Murderers!" Rebecca sniffed. "That's all they are! I don't want my baby to go!"

Ensign Paradeen of the Georgia Rangers got to his feet and said, "Aw, Ma . . ."

"You can't stay home and take care of your poor father? You have to run off and fight Indians like a crazy person?"

"Ma, I'm an officer. It's my duty."

"Your duty is here with your family. You and your swords and crazy Gentile names. What kind of a name is Paradeen? Pardus wasn't good enough when your father led charges with it?"

"Ma, I've got to go," the boy insisted, turning back to his father to stammer, in halting Ladino, "Father, I want your blessing."

Isaac looked up, surprised, and spoke in English as he asked, "A Hebrew blessing, today, for a proud English officer?"

"Please, Father. I have to catch up with my men."

"So kneel and give me your hands, young macaroon. I'll see if I remember the old words."

Aaron Paradeen knelt before his father, his hands between the older man's, as, for a moment, a frightened boy returned to the faith of his fathers. And then he was up and running out to mount his horse, bidding goodbye with a wave as Isaac mused, "Such a long way we've come, and yet it's maybe not so far as I'd feared."

"He's going to marry a Gentile girl and my grandchildren won't be Jewish!" Rebecca sobbed, covering her face as she ran into the house.

Out on the road, Aaron caught up with the rangers, and

Rory, satisfied for the moment, rode ahead to the van of the column. As he fell in at Captain Jukes's side, they were approaching the small freehold Isaac had settled on Coffee Pardus when the Ashanti had worked out his indenture. Coffee and his family stood by the side of the road, and the tall Negro waved his straw hat at Rory. The white man nodded, feeling guilty. The matter of Coffee's letter of manumission had completely slipped his mind. They'd be sending back dispatches by Indian runner, however, so he'd mention the matter to Aaron as soon as he had the time.

They were making good time as they marched south on the old coast road blazed by James Oglethorpe back in the Thirties when he had fought the Dons for control of the coast. It seemed odd that yesterday's enemy had become first an ally against the French and now, suddenly, the old enemy again. Rory no longer thought it queer that he, a former Scottish Jacobite, should be fighting for the House of Hanover against Charles Edward Stuart's French allies, for Bonnie Prince Charlie was now a wine-sodden hulk in Paris, and the young axeman who'd worn chains for him was master of a growing English plantation.

They marched through a pine barren, a patch of sterile soil common along the Atlantic Coast where few other plants would grow, and then the country widened out again to fields of corn and indigo. So much of it had been cleared since last he'd marched south toward the Dons. He knew this next stretch well enough, for the Red Swan Tavern lay just ahead, and he still rode down for the cockfights and perhaps a bit of novelty in bed. His old aversion to whores had vanished over the years as he'd made the practical adjustment to sharing a woman's body—if the body was bonny and no tiresome attachment was involved. That game he'd played with the French girl and the Negress had been amusing. The contrast of their skins had intrigued him as they'd frolicked, three in a bed. If only novelty didn't wear off so quickly. Unless you felt something more than lust for a woman, the whole thing soon became little more than work. He wondered, as he'd wondered so often in the past, what it would be like with a woman you loved, really loved. It was an experience he'd never had and he sensed he was missing something.

Jukes was saying, "Yonder's the place we left Fenwyk. I wonder if we should see if he's dead yet?"

"Och, it'll take us an hour to get the men back in step if

we let them fall out by a tavern. I was thinking we'd give them their first route break a couple of miles ahead. With your permission of course, Captain."

"I think you're right, Colonel. Rum and doxies have ever been the ruin of soldiers. Fenwyk's wound hardly concerns us in any case. He's an outcast now, whether he recovers or not."

Rose Donovan and her whores came out to wave and jeer as the column passed by. A few paces farther on, a Negress stood holding the hand of a nine- or ten-year-old girl in a ragged shift. The girl's woolly hair was light brown and her skin was a paler, more golden shade than her mother's. The Negress pointed at Rory as she bent to say something to her child, and Rory realized with a start that the gaunt woman was Sheba.

He quickly looked away, but not before he'd seen how pretty the little girl was. Beside him, Jukes laughed and asked, "Did you see the nice-looking little half-breed back there? I'll bet in a year or so Old Rose will have her sucking cock with the best of them."

Then, noting the sick horror on Rory's face, he asked, "Is something wrong, Colonel? You look like you're coming down with the ague. Your face is white as a ghost's!"

"Och, I ate something for breakfast that hasn't set well, Captain. I mind it was the cheese. My wife imported some of that awful blue stuff the Frogs eat and—"

"You have to be careful with a long ride ahead of you. We can take a break sooner than planned, if you want to rest."

"I'm all right, I tell you. It was just a passing upset."

"I hope so. Have you ever felt it before?"

Rory rode a time in silence before he murmured, "Not for the past few years. I'm going to drop back and make sure my men are minding the step, since your fifer knows no other tune."

He fell out of the column, shooting a glare at the redcoat musician as the column continued on. No words were sung to the tweedle of the silver fife, but it seemed to jeer, as the words formed in his throbbing head, "Mind the music and the step . . . and with the girls be handy."

The Cherokee ran in a dogged mile-eating trot, his moccasins drumming softly on the forest duff as he hummed a monotonous tune to regulate his breathing. He didn't like

it, down here in the damp lowlands of the tidewater, but
the redcoats paid well for good runners who carried their
paper words. The runner's dispatch case rode lightly on his
back as he pressed on through the wilderness, and his feet
were dry again after working through the swamp that
morning. The coastal plain from the Gulf of Mexico to the
Jersey pine barrens has an odd geology a man on foot can
take advantage of. The ancient alluvial deposits, dead flat
to begin with, are slightly corrugated by long *cuestas* running roughly parallel with the coastline and by higher
mountain ridges above the fall line. The Cherokee had no
idea why the high ground between the swamps ran so con-
veniently, but he took advantage of the long dry sandy
patches to make up for time lost in fording the countless
creeks and the marshy areas between them. He was moving
under old red cedar now. That was good. Red cedar grew
slowly after moving back into abandoned fields. If any Muskegee had ever farmed the drier soil of this *cuesta,* it had
been a long time ago. It was important to avoid Muskegee.
The English said they were allies, but the Cherokee knew
better.

The dispatch pouch was from the survey patrol he'd left
many miles to the southeast. The redcoats and rangers had
followed the coast and cleared lands down to the upper end
of the Okefenokee and then swung west, into the unknown
country between the Atlantic and the other cleared land at
the mouth of the Mississippi. The Cherokee smiled as he
thought about the redcoats in their white wigs and silly
coats. Big Tomahawk and the other rangers had to keep
pulling them out of the mud, for they didn't know how to
walk where there were no roads. Big Tomahawk had told
him the redcoats were going to build a road someday. If
this were true, they were going the wrong way. Everyone
knew the best route between Savannah and Pensacola lay
over the corner of the Piedmont.

He jogged on, for the papers he carried were important.
The Cherokee knew, vaguely, that his pouch contained letters from the soldiers to their women at home and progress
reports on the trail they were blazing through the wilderness. One of the letters was addressed to the county record-
er in Savannah and concerned a free Negro named Coffee. Ensign Paradeen had told the runner to make sure it
went to the right place and had put a special mark on it so
the Cherokee could remember.

A mountain bird called from the trees ahead, and, since this land was not mountainous, the Cherokee dropped to one side and drew his big iron trade knife. He answered the call cautiously, and a man in the turban of his people appeared on the trail. It was the west-bound runner from Savannah.

The two Cherokee exchanged greetings and reports of conditions on the trail each man had covered up until then. The westbound runner said, "I must hurry. They told me the news I carry is important."

The eastbound runner nodded and said, "They are not far, brother. The white men walk like children. You will only spend one night alone on the trail, while I have maybe three ahead."

"Have you seen Muskegee sign where I am going?"

"No; have you?"

"Nothing. It must be true that the main body of that nation remains loyal to King George. The Seminole outlaws are few and scattered."

The Indian runners exchanged a few more words, and then each continued on his way. The eastbound man with the letters from the patrol drove himself faster to make up the time spent in gossip. He considered himself a professional, and it shamed him to arrive late with the paper words.

He'd covered perhaps three miles when the first reed arrow hit him. The Cherokee knew what it was and kept running without looking back. He ran silently, though the arrow in his back burned and little stars were dancing in the air above the trail in front of him.

The Seminole bowman said nothing either as he nocked another reed arrow, drew it back, and released it smoothly at the running enemy. This time the shaft hit true and the Cherokee fell forward in a limp heap, feebly groping at the hilt of the trade knife on his belt. The Seminole's two companions broke cover on either side of the trail and a tomahawk flashed twice in the dappled sunlight.

Then the laughing warriors tore open the dispatch pouch and spent the next few minutes mutilating the dead runner and throwing his letters to the wind.

The westbound runner was more fortunate. Ambushed by other Seminole who knew as well as anyone where to expect a man to pass dry-shod through the swampy coastal plain, the Cherokee escaped with a minor arrow wound and outdistanced his pursuers in a grueling fifty-mile chase before staggering into the British encampment on the shore of the tea-brown Chattahoochee.

A ranger helped the injured man over to the spot where Rory and Captain Jukes were supervising the building of another raft. As the Indian sank down on one of the great cypress logs, Jukes opened the pouch, broke the seal on a dispatch from headquarters, and read a few lines before he muttered, "Sonofabitch!"

Rory asked, "What's wrong, man?" as the officer balled the dispatch in his fist, threw it on the ground, and kicked it into the river, repeating, "*Dirty* sonofabitch!"

"Goddamnit, what's happened back in Savannah?"

"The fucking war is over! *That's* what's happened! The fucking Frogs have sued for peace, the cowardly sonsof-bitches!"

"Och, you mean it's over after seven long years?"

"I mean I'll never get my rank made permanent now! I'm only a brevet captain, and this rotten turn of luck means I'll be sent home a half-pay fucking lieutenant!"

But if peace was a dirty word to Brevet Captain Jukes, the news was welcome to most of the others. The rangers, of course, had families waiting for them. The regulars, while enlisted for twelve-year terms, found peacetime boring but not unbearable since few men rose from the ranks in the King's Army, and close-order drill was less painful than the slightest wound in those pre-anesthetic days.

Other letters were passed around as the officers told the men not to bother with the rafts. The news had reached them a little more than halfway to Pensacola, and it would be easier to go back the way they had come than to push on through the unexplored wilderness north of the Gulf.

Rory read his own letter from home, sitting on the log beside the wounded Cherokee while one of his rangers cut open and cleaned out the superficial but splinter-infested injury.

Martha had written a love letter sprinkled with minor complaints about life at Indigo Hall. Widow Falkner, the children's three-day-a-week tutor, had refused to come out to Indigo Hall from Savannah after complaining of some pranks the children had played on her horse. As a parting thrust, Widow Falkner had suggested that they be boarded at a religious school run by armed Jesuits. Martha wondered, in her letter, if this had been meant in jest, as she knew Widow Falkner was High Kirk.

One of the Negro children had been struck by a diamondback while cultivating indigo, but was expected to live. The hornworms were in the kitchen garth again, but some of the smaller Negro children were hand-picking them off the vegetables. Little Cluny had had to be punished when she'd persisted in sneaking out to pick the big green caterpillars with the little servants. (At four, Cluny simply couldn't understand that, while it was permissible to play with a Negro child, it was unthinkable to work with one.) Donald Aldrich had opined that they had far too many Negro children on the plantation and had suggested selling off at least half of them so their mothers would be free to attend to chores without distraction. It was a well-known fact that Negro children over six were efficient in medium-sized work gangs under a firm but fair drive-nigger. Martha would wait, however, till her "darling husband" came home before allowing any of the surplus stock to be disposed of.

Rory read on listlessly. One of the quartered redcoats had shoved a comrade through a glass door and Aldrich had boxed another's ears for invading the family wing with rum on his breath and a loaded pistol. He'd been looking, he said, for something Martha spelled, phonetically, as Peas Uffish. Donald Aldrich had explained, after thrashing the young officer rather more severely than Martha had felt was necessary, that Peas Uffish was an Indian dish, something like Succotash. Why the redcoat had thought *she* could furnish him with Peas Uffish was a mystery.

Rory shook his head wearily. Did everything have to be so infernally banal? Beside him, the Cherokee hissed softly as the ranger ignited the gunpowder he'd packed in the wound. The ranger soothed, "I'll just smear a little pine tar on you now and you'll be right as rain, lad."

Rory stood up, grimacing at the smell of burning flesh as he folded his letter to finish later, and walked away. A ranger spotted him and came over, saluting, to ask, "Permission to start back alone, sir. The war is over and I just got word my intended went to a promenade with another man."

"Permission denied, Private Fox. We're all going home together so there'll be too many of us for Mister Seminole to pester. Your duel can wait the few hours extra. Where's the sergeant of the guard?"

"Out checking on the pickets, sir. Your orders were to have the sentries well out from the inner circle of the camp."

"I know what my orders were, damnit. Tell the sergeant I want to see him if you stumble over him."

He saw that the younger man was terribly troubled and, clapping a rough hand to the ranger's buckskin-covered shoulder, said, "Och, don't let it frush you, lad. All women are whores except your mother, and she, of course, is a saint."

"I'm going to kill that sonofabitch, sir."

"Ay, of course you are, but meanwhile I'll have no dashing off in every direction. That's just what Mister Seminole is hoping for. Ask yon Cherokee if you don't mind my words!"

Leaving the young ranger to his dreams of revenge, Rory moved on, watching the others laugh and roughhouse as they finished letters from home and discussed the new peace. Rory felt older, wiser, and, somehow detached from it all as he strolled around the camp. He overheard two redcoats talking about the new government they seemed to credit with the English victory. Prime Minister Pitt hadn't been all that bad. The colonists to the north had renamed Fort Duquesne Pittsburgh after Billy Pitt, and his policies had taken Canada for auld George II. The new young German George who had mounted the throne . . . when? two or three years ago? . . . had been handed this peace by Pitt and his father. It seemed an ungracious way of starting his reign, but they did say young George III spoke English, so perhaps the new administration would make a bit more sense.

Rory found Aaron Paradeen seated on a cypress stump, staring out over the river with a letter from home hanging limply from the fingers of the hand between his braced knees. Something about the set of the younger man's shoulders made Rory choose his words carefully as he walked over and squatted beside Aaron, asking, "Do you want to talk about it, lad?"

Aaron's voice was bleak as he murmured, "I knew it was

going to happen. The day we marched past my father's house, something made me behave rather foolishly, but now I'm glad, in a way."

"Your father's ague is worse, then?"

"My father is dead. This letter's from Lawyer Margolis. He says my father died the night we marched away. My mother's insane with grief, of course, but Papa went peacefully, in his sleep. They buried him on his own land. It's not the way it's usually done among his people, but Papa wanted it that way."

"Ay, it's better for a gentleman to own the land he lies in."

Neither man spoke for a time; then Rory took out a cheroot, lit it with his pocket tinderbox to occupy his hands for a time, and said, "Isaac Pardus was a *man*, you ken. I could say more, but we both knew him and, ay, he was a man."

"He told me once how frightened he'd been of you and big Angus at first. He told a funny story about that charge against the Creek, the one he was cited by the governor for leading. He said what really happened was—"

"Och, what happened was what it says on the citation, lad. You know how your father always joked and made light of everything."

"I know. He was always smiling when Sarah and me were little, but . . . do you know anything about religion, sir?"

"Me? Och, I've never understood life. What do I know about the Laird?"

"I think I vexed Papa when I started going to the Anglican services, but he never chided me for it. Ma screamed and tore her dress, but Papa took everything that ever happened as a joke. He told me once that laughter was the secret, but he never said secret of what."

Rory puffed on his cheroot, staring across the river through his smoke at the wall of trees on the other side. Someday, he knew, he'd be buried on his own land himself, Laird willing and the bankers not ending up with Indigo Hall. The thought gave him no comfort. He knew it was the proper end to a gentle life, but, Jesus, wasn't there *more* to it all than that?

He saw that Aaron would be all right and got to his feet, silently patting the young ensign on the back before walking back the way he'd come. The men were quieter now, and he'd have to think about getting them ready for the return march. The damned war had ended in banality, too. There'd been no great charge, no bugles or banners, no flashing of gallant blades. Just a tired Indian, wounded and filthy with trail dust, bringing some wilted scraps of paper, and now . . . now it was time to go home and put his affairs in order.

The Cherokee was still seated on the thick cypress log, drinking a tin cup of broth. Rory walked over to him, braced a booted heel on the log, and smiled down at the Indian, asking, "How's the back, chief?"

The Cherokee shrugged and sipped more broth before he answered, "I have been wounded before. My people do not burn each other with gunpowder, but it does not hurt much now."

"I have a friend who lives up in the hills with your tribe. His name's Angus MacQueen. Do you know him?"

"Yes. He is a good man when he has not been drinking. Some long-hunters came down the great valley and tried to cheat us with bad powder and corn liquor. Your friend drove them away. He gives good value when he trades with us."

"Ay, that would be Angus Mohr," sighed Rory, thinking of the time he'd visited MacQueen's trading post above the fall line. The cabin had smelled of sour mash and green hides. When the glamor wore off, a trader's life was as mundane as a planter's.

He pointed across the river with the cheroot and asked the Indian, "Have you any idea what lies out yonder, chief?"

"More woods like these. Beyond the Muskegee, there are Natchez."

"Och, it's the *land* I'm interested in. What sort of land lies yonder, to the west?"

"Woods. Woods, canebrake, and cypress swamp, all the way to the Big Muddy River."

"Ay, and beyond the Mississippi?"

"More woods, more canebrake. More cypress swamp. I do not know the people. They are called Chitimacha. Beyond them are the Atakapa and Caddo. They are not our enemies, but they are not our friends. My people seldom trade that far."

"You mean the swamps just go on and on forever?"

"No. Beyond the Atakapa, the Tonkawa grow corn in

creekbeds, but the land between is too dry for trees. Beyond the Tonkawa are the Kiowa and Comanche from the north. They have many ponies and live by hunting buffalo. Most of the buffalo on this side of the Big Muddy River have been killed by the long-hunters, but there are many left out on the Sea of Grass."

"Sea of Grass, you call it? What is this sea of grass, a great meadow?"

"It is the Sea of Grass. It is many of your miles across and the Comanche say they own it all, but the Lakota and Pawnee say they lie."

"Ay, *that's* a thing I can understand. Tell me, if you can, what's on the far shore of this sea of grass you speak of?"

The Cherokee frowned and said, "I don't know anyone who's been there. An Osage told me once that there were shining mountains far to the sunset. He said they were much higher than our own green hills, and covered with snow in summer near their tops. He said there was yellow iron in the streams and many, many beaver. He even said he'd heard of stranger lands, beyond the Shining Mountains, but you know how Osage lie."

"Ay, the Hebrides folk told of Avalon and St. Brendan's Isle and the High Brazil, somewhere in the mists beyond the reach of a fishing *currach*. It's odd how men always place the fey lands in the sunset, isn't it?"

"I don't understand your words. *My* people say the spirits hide in the *north*. Why are you asking me so much of the sunset lands? Do you want to go there?"

"Och, in God's own truth, I don't know. I'll see that you're given some silver for that wound, lad. Make yoursel' at ease and if any man here tells you to do anything, tell 'em I said you were to rest."

He started to make another nervous sweep around the camp, but the other officers had everything under control. There was nothing for him to do but write Martha that he was coming home.

Rory turned and stared back across the river. The sun was a low red ball above the brooding treetops on the far shore. He wondered what would happen if he simply rafted to the other side and just . . . kept going?

"Och," he muttered. "The Indians would do you long before you reached the Shining Mountains or any other redskin fairyland, man. Your place is with your family at Indigo Hall, where, Laird willing, you'll be buried."

The whole camp, ranger and redcoat, stiffened in sudden surprise as Colonel Martin suddenly threw back his head and gave a long, wolflike scream. Then they shrugged and went back to their conversations and chores. The big colonel just did things like that at times.

THREE

It took six weeks to get the redcoats out of Indigo Hall, and the damage they'd done was awe-inspiring. Some would remain quartered in Savannah permanently now, for the new young king intended to rule with a firmer hand than had the two previous German Georges, and a small standing army of regulars on the North American continent should end these infernal Indian troubles inspired by agents of His Majesty's European enemies. Most, of course, would be stationed near the northwest frontier and in the newly conquered Canadian provinces. The one regiment left to guard Georgia and the new English colony of Florida was housed in the small capital city, where their sometimes boisterous behavior caused little annoyance to any gentlefolk.

One sultry afternoon with the promise of thunder in the air, Mr. Hiram Quiggs, late of Fairfax County, Virginia, sat in a wicker chair on the south veranda of Indigo Hall sipping a tall, cool rum punch as he watched a coastal lugger take on indigo down at the landing, and wondered if the northbound skipper would take him aboard on credit.

Mr. Quiggs was the tutor Martha had hired by mail from the Old Dominion, and the rather prim young man was appalled by what he'd gotten himself into.

Somewhere in the house, his employers were entertaining in-laws. Another wing rang with the sound of hammer and saw as the freeman, Coffee Pardus, oversaw the repairs of the damage done during their short stay by the officers and gentlemen of the royal army.

The Martin children he'd been hired to instruct in the three R's and in etiquette were nowhere to be seen. Quiggs could only hope they were with their parents, or, even better, had run away.

He took another sip and stared morosely down the slope toward the landing. It wasn't just the children. The whole damned colony was a madhouse, inhabited by slovenly women and foppish boors who seemed to think shoe buckles and a tailor's sword made a silk purse out of a sow's ear. Compared to the Virginia tidewater, this newer colony was an obscene joke. Why, these Georgians actually called their darkies *nigger*, or even, perish the thought, *slave*.

Chattel slavery had been established in Virginia as early as 1620, and since that time a few rules had been formulated concerning the institution. No gentleman from Virginia ever called one of his people anything more insulting than "darkie," or, if the Negro were free, "a gentleman of color." All free men were gentlemen in the Old Dominion—at least to their faces. It saved so much tiresome bickering over honor and all the other rubbish these Georgians spent so much time fighting duels about. The old established first families of Virginia knew who they were; they didn't care for the opinions of lesser mortals, black or white.

These Georgians, on the other hand, seemed uneasy in their periwigs and lace, and one had to watch what one said to them. Even the landless whites in this mad land seemed to think they were entitled to call out any man on a fancied insult, and the teamsters, in particular, had gained a fearsome reputation for dueling with their long rawhide whips. It was said that these so-called "crackers" could put your eye out with a single flick of those long, cracking teamsters' whips. Few gentlemen responded formally to such a challenge, of course, but the crackers took this as cowardice, and the language they used against a man who refused to fight them was said to blister paint.

The plantations, from what he'd seen of them, were scattered, unkempt, and poorly managed. A gaggle of children and chickens usually ran wild with the yellow cur-dogs and razorback hogs that these people seldom seemed to bother to control. Save for the scandalously high prices their produce had brought in the past few years, the whole lot of unwashed, illiterate boors would doubtless have gone bankrupt by now.

A shy voice called out, "Mister man?" and Quiggs turned his head to catch little Cluny peering around a veranda post at him. He smiled at the child. She was going to be a heartbreaker in a few years, if only he could teach her some courtly manners. The child came fully into view and asked shyly, "Will you tell me a story?"

The tutor sighed and said, "Do you know the one about Cinderella?"

"Pooh, I like the stories Athair tells better. Do you know

the one about Lugh o' the Lang Arm and Queen Mab's Brown Cow?"

"Ummm, I'm afraid I don't, Miss Cluny."

"Och, I'll tell it to you, then. You see, Queen Mab was a fey woman, as well as a queen, so she had this great brown cow that gave the Water of Life instead of milk, and anyway, one day Lugh o' the Lang Arm said he'd raid Mab's herd, as a favor, you see, to the Wee Folk of Glendubh who'd given him his magic sword and golden hoop."

"God give me strength!" sighed Hiram Quiggs, closing his eyes as Cluny crawled into his lap.

In the parlor of the undamaged wing, Efram Starr was telling another story as Rory paced up and down before the unlit fireplace, puffing nervously on his cheroot as Martha and Gloria chatted in the next room.

The older man was saying, "You can't spend your hard silver on these luxuries, Rory. You know there's a financial panic in London. Merchants are being ruined as if it were a plague going 'round, and—"

"Och, it's just the usual let-down business has after every war, auld man. The new government just needs time to get things running smoothly again."

"The new government is headed by a stubborn, willful boy and a gang of his libertine friends. Did you know Lord Germain was thrown out of the army for cowardice, or that the Earl of Sandwich spends so much time at the gaming tables that he lives on meat and cheese tucked between two slices of bread? And as for Frederick North and those other members of the Hellfire Club—"

"Och, none of the German Georges has been noted for the brains God gave a sheep, Efram. At least this one speaks English, and no doubt the panic will pass as always."

"Goddamnit, the Royal Exchequer's simply not paying its due bills! Do you have any idea how much of your wealth is tied up in unpaid vouchers that pouting young king's friends seem to have forgotten? Nathan's last letter home complains that half the officers in his squadron have had to send home for money. The armed forces are overexpanded, and the king does nothing but order men and ships about the globe as if they were his personal toys. The Whigs in Parliament are furious, but they're helpless. The Hanovers always were a stubborn lot, but *this* George takes the cake!"

"Well, I'll just plant more land in cash crops and weather this wee depression out. As long as my credit's good in the City, I—"

"Damnit, listen to me! You've piled up debts already that your grandsons will receive as heirlooms. This place and your other holdings have to be managed scientifically, perhaps under the new Norfolk system. You've heard of it, of course?"

"Norfolk system, you say? We're in Georgia, not Norfolk. What can those half-Dutch fenlanders teach an American planter like me?"

"Crop rotation, land plaster, and the reading of market reports—before you waste seed on crops with no buyers! The world economy is changing, Rory. The old cottage industries are giving way to new central mills, and agriculture must keep up if it's to survive."

"You talk like an auld woman, or a child afraid of the dark. How can farming change? Your braw new mills need raw materials, don't they? There's no science in planting, Efram. You put the seed in the ground and wait for the stuff to grow. It's not like planning one of those canals or opening a coal measure in the Midlands, back in the Mother Country."

"For God's sake, at least let me help you get your books in order. Martha's done her best, but she gives in too willingly to your foolish spending. You take that silver service you just ordered with your own crest, now—"

"Och, we had to have new silver. The redcoats stole our best service while I was off to the wars."

"Perhaps, but the crest is foolish. If you want to keep part of your wealth tied up in plate, you really should be sure it's quickly convertible. Who the devil is going to buy a silver service with a Highland shield and axe-bearing savages on it?"

"That's the arms of my sept. With the auld chief dead and his line extinct—"

"That's not the point! These grand airs are expensive, and you just don't have the cash!"

"The London silversmith will wait. He gets his interest, doesn't he?"

"All right, what about that silk brocade you're having pasted on the wall over there in the other wing? What's the matter with *wallpaper*? God knows *it's* dear enough!"

"Och, the governor has real silk on *his* walls. Would you

have folk think I was no better than a public official of tight-fisted Georgie?"

"All right, all right, forget the house. Aldrich tells me you have excess slaves, and there's a ready market for them in the ricelands to the south. One or two good auctions could almost pay for the improvements you've been making."

Rory frowned. "I need the men I have for the 'digo. As a matter of fact, I could use a dozen more, if I'm to expand my plantings."

"Yes, but what about some of the half-grown bucks? The rice fields use a lot of stoop labor, and a child's short legs are more efficient at that work. You've far too many women, too."

"Och, I'd hate to see any wee nigger in those fever-ridden ricelands, Efram. As for the women, they keep my bucks content."

"Perhaps, but scientifically managed plantations have one doe to four bucks. One woman can easily service any four average men, if you don't want them rutting all the time and sapping their strength. One or two nights a week is all a healthy man needs with a woman, and at a ratio of four to one, it leaves the Negress two or three nights of rest, too. I'd say it was more than generous."

"Och, I'd say it was Presbyterian! A man works better when his mind's not frushed about his woman, Efram. Believe me, I know. As for the bairns, they belong with their mothers until they're big enough to sell or put to work. My mind is set on that. I'll expand a bit and get more crops out for the bastards in London to owe us for, but I'm not ready to sell any of my people to the rice planters just now."

"And what about the money you owe to *other* bastards in London?"

"Och, what about it? We live in interesting new times! Hargreaves' spinning jenny is putting the Flemings out of work, and those mad new steam pumps are changing the scenery of the mining country. Whole syndicates of moneylenders are speculating in new lands, running canals over mountains. . . . Ay, it's the dawn of a new age and a new way of doing business. I owe the bankers, the king owes me, and, since his ministers control the banks, the debt just goes 'round and 'round."

"You'll be ruined, Rory. Believe me, I've been there."

"Not as long as I keep what's owed me greater than

what I owe. The royal vouchers may be so much paper, but a man can always borrow on what's due him. As long as my crops expand as fast as or faster than the interest on my debts—"

"It's insane! That's no way for sensible men to conduct *any* business!"

"Ay, but in a world of madmen, what does it matter? The set of mind you call madness has raised me to my present station, Efram. Where have your carefully kept figures taken you? Och, you've yet to be paid by the government your ownself."

"I know, but I've the silver to wait this bad time out."

"And I've the land and niggers, so it's no worse off I am."

In another wing of the house, Flora Martin stood in a doorway watching the Negro boy hammer nails into the floor. Athair had told her Juba was the son and apprentice of that freeman, Coffee. Flora watched him for a time before she asked, "What are you doing, boy?"

Juba glanced up. The white girl who'd spoken to him was about a year younger than he was. She wore a frilled white shift and her straight black hair had been tied into a ponytail because of the heat. Her eyes were exactly the color of the sky, and Juba couldn't read the meaning on her fishbelly face. He licked his lips and explained, in a neutral tone, "I'm puttin' in a new subfloor. When the rough planking's down, my pa is gonna lay parquet holly and oak over it."

"I see. Where did you ever get so many nails? You've been pounding for just hours."

"My pa and me made 'em. You gits a length of strap-iron, one of you holds it steady on the anvil, and the other cuts a slice off with a cold chisel. My pa cuts the nails. I just hold the strap."

Flora nodded and watched quietly as Juba pounded in a few more of the square blunt nails. The Negro boy was very thin, and the work had beaded his bare upper body with droplets of sweat. Flora waited until he'd stopped to reach for another nail before she said, "I'll have Aunt Sukey bring you some lemonade. You look very hot and thirsty."

Juba frowned and said, "I don't think you better, ma'am. Pa says I'm not to ask for favors when we're out on a job."

The idea that a Negro might *ask* for anything hadn't occurred to young Flora. She was a warm and generous child, but, as the daughter of Colonel Martin of Indigo Hall, she was accustomed to *telling* the niggers when she wanted something done. She felt truly sorry for the poor sweaty little buck, and, if she wanted him to have lemonade, he'd *have* lemonade. He had no more to say about it than her pony when she thought of offering him a carrot.

"I'll tell Aunt Sukey make you a pitcher," she said firmly, leaving Juba to his nailing for the moment.

The Negro boy shrugged and went on with his task. If pa had told him not to ask favors, he'd also told him not to argue with white folks, and the blue-eyed gal's suggestion seemed friendly. He had no idea what lemonade was, but it sounded good. He'd sucked a lemon once. He'd filched it in the market when he'd gone down with ma to watch them unload the West Indiaman that time. The memory made his lips pucker, for he was truly hot and thirsty.

Two other white children found him working alone in the empty room, attracted by the sound of Juba's hammer. One was a boy about his own age. The other was smaller and had the same dark hair and blue eyes as the friendly gal.

Donald Lochiel Martin said, "I want to play militia and Injuns, boy. Put down that hammer and come outside with us. We need you to be the Injun."

Juba replied, "I can't. Pa says I have to lay this flooring."

"Your pa says *what?*" Locky gasped. "You just lay down that hammer and *look* at me, boy!"

Juba kept the hammer in his hand but looked up wearily as Locky snapped, "All right, nigger. What do you see?"

"Nothin' much. I see two of you. Blue-eyes yo' brother?"

"Damnit, you see a *white man,* nigger! Don't you know you're supposed to stand up at attention when a white man talks to you?"

Juba said, "Hey, look, I ain't no slave. My pa's a free-man. He tol' me Ensign Paradeen sent a letter to the mansion provin' it."

"I don't give shit about no letter, nigger. You're still *black,* ain't you?"

Juba looked thoughtfully at his own sweat-beaded forearm and nodded, saying, "I reckon I am. My granddaddy was an Ashanti chief with a golden chair and my ma—"

"Fuck your ma and your granddaddy too! You gonna come outside an' be our Injun or ain't you?"

"I reckon I ain't. I take my orders from my pa. You want me to play with you, go ask him. He's down the hall with the carpenters he's trainin' for Colonel Martin."

Locky stared down at the Negro boy in genuine surprise. He'd never had a *grown* nigger defy him. There was something very wrong with this uppity boy. Locky frowned, as he'd seen his father do, and said in an ominous tone, "I bet I can whip you. Do you want to fight?"

Juba said, "No," and drove another nail with a single blow, his heart beating wildly as he wished, very hard, that these white boys would go bother somebody else.

Locky hesitated, eyeing the fists and forearms of the kneeling black boy. This one wasn't False Argyll, who cried like a girl when you twisted his arm. This one, for some mad reason, didn't seem to be afraid of him.

Turning to his younger brother, Locky suggested, "I'll pin his arms and you stomp him, Simon."

Simon Fraser Martin shook his head and said, "That's no fair. Two on one is nigger fun, Locky. Do you want to fight him, you just do it right."

"Shoot, are you taking a nigger's side agin your own brother?"

"I ain't taking nobody's side. This here boy's working for Athair, and I see no cause to pester him. Come on, let's go outside and take a swim in the creek. It's hot and smelly up here."

Locky scowled at Juba and jeered, "Yeah, it's all stunk up with *nigger*. What's yo' name, boy?"

"Juba Pardus. What's yours?"

"I'm Locky Martin an' I ain't forgetting you, you uppity coon!"

The two white boys left, and Juba went back to work, hitting a nail too hard and ruining it. Flora Martin came back smiling with a brimming pitcher of lemonade. She stopped a few feet from the kneeling young Negro and asked, "Whatever is the matter with you, boy? Have you been *crying?*"

Juba sniffed and wiped the back of his hammer hand across his face, stammering, "I never cry, ma'am. I jest hot, I reckon."

Flora bent over and placed the pitcher and a tin cup on the rough planks at his side, saying, "Well, you just rest a bit and drink some of this lemonade. Aunt Sukey made it with real white sugar."

Juba nodded and picked up the cup, dipping it in the funny piss-colored liquid the white girl had brought him. He tasted gingerly, then took a deep gulp as Flora said knowingly, "There, isn't it *good?*"

Juba nodded, not trusting himself to speak with the odd lump the cool drink seemed to have made in his throat. Flora said, "Well, I'd best be off so's you can get back to your chores. You just leave the pitcher over on yon sill when you've finished with it, boy. If you need anything else, go down to the kitchen an' tell Aunt Sukey I said you can have it."

Then she left, unaware of the tears in Juba's troubled eyes. She had other errands of mercy to attend to. One of her new kittens was sick, and she had to get the poor little thing to take some milk.

The gossip about Rose Donovan and Captain Fenwyk was outrageously amusing, but the gossips spoke in whispers, for Rose's new husband was a notorious duelist and had a terrible temper to go with his deadly reputation.

The surly dragoon, nursed 'round the clock by Rose and the other doxies of the Red Swan, had survived the pistol ball left in him by Aaron Paradeen. Since much of his recovery could be attributed to more rum than he'd ever be able to pay for, and out of bleary-eyed gratitude to his angel of mercy, Fenwyk had proposed in a moment of delirium. When he'd come to his senses again, he'd made a pragmatic adjustment. He'd become a cashiered, disgraced ex-soldier, and he was three thousand miles from home with devil a war in sight. Rose, albeit a bit long in the tooth and a barren slut besides, was a wealthy woman with a tolerant view of his continued drinking and an occasional game of three in a bed. Many a man had married with less to show for it, and, with her new-found respectability, Rose was a woman transformed.

She bought herself a dozen wigs and a closetful of gowns, and, if she wasn't invited to the best homes in Savannah, she was invited to enough reasonably respectable ones to make her decide to build a new and grander home a short ride from from her whorehouse.

The amusing antics of jumped-up Rose afforded some

distraction for the worried planters and merchants of the colony, but, in truth, things were in an awful mess.

The Union Jack now flew from the Mississippi to the Ganges, but the young king and his schoolboy chums were unable to cope with the birth pangs of modern capitalism. A pudgy youth of limited imagination and a superficial education, George III had been told by his mother on her deathbed, "George, be a king!" and, to the best of his ability, he would try. Born a few hundred years earlier, he might have been adequate, for he possessed the same courage as his bloody-minded, brighter brother, the Duke of Cumberland.

King George was not incapable of generosity. He gained the undying gratitude of the Highlands when he repealed the infamous Disarmament Act and allowed the Scots to flaunt their tartan kilts and play their pipes once more. He was kind to children and respectful to the ladies of his court, but he possessed a will too strong for his intellect and believed he ruled by divine right and the grace of God. Points of English constitutional law bored him, and the toadies and yes-men with whom he attempted to govern were either as inept as their king or, as in the cases of Sandwich and North, viciously corrupt.

In truth, the problems faced by the growing British Empire might have taxed the wisest men of that age, for the paperwork grew alarmingly and an army of clerks could scarce keep abreast of what was going on. While a young Lowlander named Watt worked to make the final improvements in the primitive steam engines that would bring in the age of coal and iron, an Englishman named Gresham was trying to make sense out of the confused currency of his time. British businessmen were driven to distraction by shillings and pence, pounds and guineas, florins, louis, farthings, and thallers. Money was issued in copper, brass, silver, gold, and paper of bewildering denominations and dubious value. The Spanish dollar, or piece of eight, became the most trusted coin in common use, for the simple folk could grasp the idea of two bits, four bits, six bits, and so on, but there were not enough Spanish dollars, or any other coins, in circulation. The expansion of the economy was conducted mostly in the cribbed hieroglyphics of the scribbling clerks, and the uneducated merchant or farmer was soon driven to the wall. Arkwright had invented the spinning frame and Cartwright's steam-powered looms were just over the horizon, but the adding machine and the cash register lay far in the future.

In the little Duchy of Hessia, a humble Jewish money-lender who did business under the sign of the Inn of the Red Shield would found the House of Rothschild simply because he was good at keeping figures in his head. Other men, less able, lost the labor of years to the slip of some tired clerk's finger. It was a time for quick wits, the cool nerve of a gambler, and, when all else failed, the killing instincts of a predator. The men who would build the British Empire wore cosmetics and perfumed their silk-clad bodies, but the survivors of the mad scramble for the loot of half the world would be callous cutthroats whom the pirates of an earlier day might have been well advised to steer clear of.

As the financial chaos of the post-war era continued, the rich got richer while the poor yeomanry of James Ogle-thorpe's dream were reduced to a living standard any well-kept slave would have wrinkled his nose at. Small farmers who managed to hold on to any land at all slaved from dawn to dusk to stay ahead of eviction and somehow feed their unwashed, barefoot children. A battered wool felt hat, handed down from father to son, became the badge of a white man who still owned land or had a steady job. Others, dispossessed and driven to begging or stealing (since there simply were no jobs for an illiterate white in Georgia), lurked on the edges of the settled lands, or, in desperation, pushed off into the wilderness and squatted on the land King George had reserved for the future. Those who survived the wilderness would be known one day as hillbillies. The others were dismissed, even by the Negroes, as white trash. Many of the newly created paupers would kill themselves, for more than one was of gentle birth but had been ruined by the runaway inflation and mad finances of George III's early reign.

Rory Martin, in a world of wolves and sheep, had not chosen to be among the shorn. Despite his nonchalant attitude toward his London creditors, there was a native cunning in his financial pyramiding. As long as he kept expanding his holdings, he stayed just ahead of the interest on his growing debts. Such unclaimed land as lay within his reach was purchased on credit from the government and cleared. Desired parcels of land held by lesser men were engulfed by the spreading amoeba of his estate through purchase, trickery, and, on occasion, harsher methods.

A small freeholder named Crocker had refused to sell at any price. Though considered trash, Yeoman Crocker was one of the original settlers and a canny man. He spent little and grew as much as his forty-acre grant would bear. He worked the land with his wife and children, and, through his persistence, he had become a thorn in Rory's side. The banker's agents surveying Indigo Hall for a renewal of the mortgage seemed displeased by the small square of cornfield cutting into the neatly mapped plantation, and despite offers of friendship and veiled threats, Crocker refused to be reasonable.

A verbal message was sent to Angus MacQueen up in the Cherokee country, and, prophetically, Angus Mohr arrived on a moonless night in a driving rain.

Their business meeting took place in a private room above the Red Swan. A single candle flickered in the neck of a rum bottle as Rory outlined his problem and evoked the old loyalties. Angus ran a thumbnail through the stubble on his jaw as he heard his old friend out. Then he shrugged and suggested, "Why don't I just have my tame Indians do the lot for you?"

Rory shook his head. "I'll not be party to a murder, damnit. Besides, the man has a family there with him."

"Ay, but you know how savage Indians can be, man. If my Cherokees, dressed as Creeks, of course—"

"That's not the way I want it done, Angus. I want the man's land, not his scalp."

"Ay, you always were a devious lad. What's your plan, then?"

"Well, I thought that if you and your Indians were to give the Crockers a good scare . . . I mean, the man's trash, and he has a heavy load of debts hanging over him—"

"You mean, burn him out? Run his livestock off and leave them sifting the ashes for a wee bit of silver to pay the merchants with?"

"Ay, that's just what I mean. His corn crop's half grown. A few on ponies riding through the stalks while the others burn the barn and outbuildings . . . but mind you, leave the house alone."

MacQueen shrugged and said, "It's a daft thing you're asking. We've too many old Indian fighters hereabouts, Rory. They'd never believe one man could hold off a Creek raiding party if they were serious enough to burn his barn. Barn burning is a hanging offense in this colony, Rory. No Indian would risk his neck to the hangman just to set a hayloft alight."

Rory stared into the candle flame and muttered, "I don't know what to do. I have to have a new mortgage and this white trash bastard seems out to ruin me."

"There you are, then. The braves who rode down from the Piedmont with me are camped less than an English mile from here, ready to go."

"I can't let you massacre them, damnit. I only want Crocker and his family frightened enough to sell out to me."

"Does yon Sassunach know you want his land?"

"Of course he does. I've all but begged on my knees for his damned forty acres."

"Ay, then you've no choice in the matter. Dead men tell no tales, but if he was to go with a singed shirttail to the governor, with a story about his mighty neighbor craving his land—"

"I see what you mean, Angus, but there has to be another way. I can't agree to more than a mock raid and a wee bit of property damage."

Angus laughed. "Och, who said you have to agree to any such thing, lad? You've told me you want the Sassunach and his kin off land you claim as your own. Why not leave it at that and let me worry about the wee details?"

"You'll give me your word there's to be no bloodshed?"

"Now, why would I do such a daft thing as that, Rory? You've told me what you want and we've agreed on a price. Go home to your bonny wife and bairns and let me see what my Indians and I can work out between our ainsel's, eh?"

"In other words, you bloody-minded bastard—"

"Foosh! Bite your tongue, me high and mighty Laird of Indigo Hall! Before you call an old comrade names, consider well who called him down from his peaceful ways among yon mountains."

"Listen, MacQueen, there has to be another way."

"Ay, and there well may be, for I'm an honest peaceful trader and my Cherokees are friendly lads at heart. It may be we can do it all the way you suggest. A bit of an All Hallows Eve with a few outhouses overturned and perhaps a hayrick or two set alight."

"You'll promise no more than that?"

"I will not. The man may fire on us. One of my Cherokees may have had a wee bit too much of the Creature. You've been on more than one raid, Rory. You know a man has to play the field as he finds it."

"I don't like it. I know you too well, MacQueen."

MacQueen shrugged and said, "Get someone else, then. I've a long ride back to the Piedmont, so I thank you for nothing, Rory *nan* Lochaber!"

Rory shook his head and said, "Listen, let's not be hasty. You're pressing me too hard, and a man needs time to think."

MacQueen snorted and took a sip of rum before answering, "Och, you've thought, all right, darling Rory. You've just lost your stomach for a man's work on a raider's night."

He saw that Rory wasn't about to answer, so, in a softer tone, Angus Mohr said, "We've agreed on the price. Go home and leave the details to me."

Rory shook his head. "I want it understood about the spilling of blood, Angus."

"Och, why frush your ainsel' about whose blood might be spilled? Damnit, man, for all we know it's my blood or the blood of my poor Cherokees we're after talking about!"

"Just tell me you won't kill anyone at the Crocker homestead if you can help it. Is that too much to ask?"

Angus Mohr nodded, but his eyes were glowing with the wolfish gleam of a born killer as he said, "Go home and say your prayers. Go to sleep with a clear conscience, Rory, for you've told me there's to be no bloodshed, and I've said I'll do my best."

Again Rory hesitated, and MacQueen got to his feet, saying, "It's settled, then, for I mean to be among the trees of the high country before the sun rises."

He left Rory to his own thoughts as the rain pattered against the diamond panes of the one small window and the candle flame flickered in time with the heavy breathing of the man alone in the room.

Rory took a healthy swig of rum, wiped the back of his hand across his mouth, and suddenly got to his feet, his mind in a desperate whirl. He went to the doorway, opened it, and called down the stairs, "Wait, Angus! I can't let you do it!"

There was no reply at first. Then, as he shouted a second

time, a Negress with a rush light peered up the narrow
stairs at him and called out, "Please, suh, that gen'man in
the buckskins jest done rode off in the night. Dast I ask
what you wants, suh?"

Rory sighed and said, "Have them make me a stirrup
cup of warm toddy. I'll be on my way directly."

He went back to the table, sat down, and stared for a
long time at the candle flame. Then he shrugged and muttered, "A'weel, I *tried* to stop them. Is it my fault if that
stubborn Sassunach, Crocker, wouldn't listen to reason?"

By the time he was halfway home, the rum Rory had
drunk to steel his heart had begun to wear off and in the
cool, sobering rain his conscience was starting to return.
He had dressed for the weather in a wide-brimmed slouch
hat and calf-length cape, but he knew he'd be soaked anyway by the time he got home. A hot bath and bed . . .
och, but would he sleep, knowing what a distant wolflike
howl in the distance would mean?

"Damnit, the Sassunach defied us to evict him!" Rory
muttered as the raindrops drummed on his hat brim. They
seemed to be trying to tell him something. It was madness
to ride at a canter in near pitch darkness on a muddy road,
so the chestnut stud was walking, head down, and shivering
from time to time. Rory knew he'd have to take the time to
see himself that the niggers rubbed him down with dry
straw before they put a blanket over him. Niggers had to
be watched or they did the damnedest things. That break-
down at the 'digo press had been occasioned by sheer stupidity, and if he ever found out which of them had put
those bricks in the cartload of 'digo . . . the idiots knew
they were judged by the weight of the bales they harvested.
Doubtless the poor coon had never thought what ten
pounds of bricks and an old wagon-wheel hub would do to
the hardwood rollers of the press. Niggers were stupid. It
had taken Aldrich's overseer three days to repair the press
while the 'digo had waited, unharvested, in the fields.

The sucking plops of the stud's big hooves in the mud
below seemed to mutter in a guttural, unknown tongue,
like the gibbering ghouls in the auld stories the childer'
loved so to hear at bedtime. Martha had chided him when
he'd told wee Cluny of the gory last fight of Cuchulain on
the Moor of Standing Stones, but they were the tales he'd
been raised on, and devil a hurt had it done *him,* had it?

The trouble with Martha and other Sassunach was that they didn't understand the messages in the auld tales. To the Sassunach, they were either charming fantasies of brownies, kelpies, and other wee people, or great bloody brawls of giants, ogres, water-horses and drunken Celtic warriors. To those generations of elders who'd handed them down from before the time of Jesus, they were messages with a moral.

The plodding hooves muttered, *"Gu h-olc, gu tinn, gu h-olc . . ."* and Rory shivered, for his shoulders were cold and he wished the muddy hooves would say something else. "Evil, am I?" he murmured. "I could tell you tales of evil, you poor sheep-brained beast of the bonny brown hide!"

As he'd tried to explain to Martha, there were two ways for a lad to survive in this world. When he met a giant, he had to be a trickster and outwit his opponent somehow. On the other hand, should he stumble over someone *weaker* than his ainsel', say a fairy with a treasure or an unarmed Campbell with a fine fat cow, a canny lad simply took what he wanted, as King Kenneth took Dalriada from the Picts. Yeoman Crocker was a friendless stranger who had something a stronger man wanted. It was simple as that.

The hooved plopped, *"Gu h'olc, droch, droch, droch . . ."* and the guilty rider insisted, "It's too late to call them off, for I know not where they are or when they'll strike."

Besides, the stranger bestriding his land had been offered a good price, which was more than the Taylor of the Black Axe had done when the grazing rights of Glengarry had been the question. The bankers in London cared nothing for Christian charity, and the old command to love thy neighbor put few shillings in any man's pocket.

"Maybe," he considered, "a few arrows in the door would convince them they'd do well to reconsider, for their cabin lies exposed to the west, and—"

A dark blur suddenly loomed ahead of them, and Rory's horse reared back as a harsh voice called out, "Halt! Stand and deliver!"

Rory steadied his mount as he peered through the rain at the ominous outline of the mounted highwayman, if that was what he was. Rory managed a light bantering tone as he asked, "Is that you, Jack? You've a wet idea of a joke, if you ask me."

The other replied, "This is no joke, sir. Your money or your life!"

Rory deliberately changed his tone to one of fear as he stammered, "I say, if you're serious, good fellow, I'd much rather deliver my purse. There's not much in it, only a few guineas in gold, but if you want it—"

"You'll toss it on the road and ride off," said the highwayman, the gloating relief in his voice unmistakable as Rory fumbled under his cloak, whining, "Please don't shoot. I have it right here." And then Rory's first saddle gun roared out in the night as he threw himself sideways from the saddle of his rearing horse.

He landed on one hip and rolled in the mud, a pistol in each hand. The highwayman had fired at the same time, and the two orange blossoms of flame had blinded Rory. He strove to regain his night vision as he lay prone on the wet road, squinting into the darkness. He heard his horse, or the other's, clopping away in the distance. He waited, unfired pistol ready, until, off to one side and level with his present position, he heard a low groan.

Rory slithered forward on his belly in the mud until the dark shadow in the far ditch resolved into a vaguely human form. He aimed the muzzle at the wounded man's head. Then, overcome by curiosity, he asked, "Is that you, Private Hanks?"

"Is that you, Colonel Martin? I thought I recognized that brogue!" The wounded man coughed and added, "I should have known you'd not deliver, eh? You really fooled me, ay, and you've done me, I fear."

"What drove you to this madness, lad? You were never cut out to play Rob Roy on a lonely road."

"Forgive me, Colonel. I was driven to it by the need to feed my family. They've foreclosed my grant and evicted us. Molly and the kids are waiting for me, sheltered like tinkers in Caldwell's tobacco-drying shed. I promised I'd come back with silver if ever I came back at all!"

Rory got to his feet, plasterd with mud, and moved warily over to the young ranger he'd shot, primed pistol ready, for two can play at the game of words in the dark. He knelt near the wounded man's side, tucking the discharged pistol away and placing the other pistol gently against the man's head as he felt over his wet buckskins with the free hand. He found the spot where the warm blood flowed and chided, "Och, I fear you've done yoursel', Hanks. Does your woman know you've taken up this new profession?"

"God, no! Do you think I'd saddle Molly with knowledge that could get her hanged?"

"Ay, it's just as well to keep a few secrets from the women. I'll say I met you this night and heard of your misfortune when I see about better shelter for your family, lad."

Hanks' grin was faintly visible in the darkness of the night as he gasped, "Oh, Jesus, you don't intend to turn me in then, Colonel?"

"What? And have one of my rangers hanged as a common felon? You just rest easy, lad. We're not that far from yon Red Swan, and mayhap someone heard our shots. Help may be on the way."

The downed highwayman coughed and murmured, in a husky voice, "I don't think anyone can help me now, but I forgive you, Colonel. You were always a gentleman and you did what you had to. I'll hold no grudge where I'm going, and that's the truth of it."

Rory's hands were finished with their bloody exploration and he mused, "You've taken a ball in the lights, but I've seen men live with greater wounds. Try not to breathe so hard, Hanks. It's the blood in your left light that's making you hack so."

Neither man spoke for a time as Rory listened to the falling rain. It was apparent the shots had been put down to distant thunder, if they'd been heard at all. Nobody knew what had happened, and at this hour, nobody was likely to be coming down the road.

Hanks whispered, "Are you telling me the truth or making it easy on me, Colonel? I feel so queer, and even if I should live—"

"Ay, a man who's lost his land has little to live for at that."

"It was the taxes as did us, Colonel. Two bad harvests and them damned papers they got me to sign. Then the county claimed I owed more than I'd reckoned, and the seed merchants was dunning me for more than the cutworms coulda ate, and . . . I dunno, it seems there's never a breathing spell for no man to get ahead in this world."

Rory lowered the hammer of his unfired flintlock and tucked it away as he muttered, "Lie still, lad. I don't like the sound of that breathing right now."

Then he noticed that Hanks wasn't breathing at all. He had started to rise, intending to ride for help with the litch, when it came to him how this chance adventure could be put to good use.

Rory worked swiftly. Using the dead man's battered felt hat as a pouch, he robbed the pauper of pistol, sheath knife, shoes, and worn-out stockings. He cut away Hanks's brass belt buckle with the man's own knife; then, grimacing, he carefully scalped the litch in the Creek manner.

Cherokee seldom scalped, unless they were getting a bounty on a Seminole from the royal governor. If Angus Mohr's Indians played their part with any imagination, they'd be using Creek arrows when they hit the Crocker homestead.

Finally Rory cut away a strip of buckskin from Hanks's jacket and bound the possessions in the hat into a neat bundle, suitable for convenient disposal at some distance. Then he went to look for his horse, repriming the discharged pistol as he walked, for these were desperate times and there was no telling how many other dispossessed farmers were out playing the auld Rob Roy.

He caught up with the chestnut stud a quarter of a mile down the road. The horse had calmed and was browsing by the roadside as Rory called to it and bade it stand. He climbed into the saddle, soaked to the skin and covered with mud, but most of the mud would wash off in the rain as he rode. He'd explain his appearance as the result of a simple fall in the darkness.

He'd been troubled that some busybody, knowing how badly he'd wanted the Crocker land, might put two and two together, no matter how well Angus played his part. But the litch back there had been an old comrade, and, if not a friend, at least no enemy. He'd have to make sure his generosity to the widow of the other white man murdered in the Creek raid on outlying settlers did not go unrecorded. Molly Hanks was not a bad-looking wench, as he recalled. He'd have to see that she and the childer' were taken in with at least a year's board at the Crown and Anchor. No doubt she'd be properly grateful.

FOUR

The massacre of the Crocker family, as well as the scalping of Private Hanks, so close to town, outraged and frightened the good people of Savannah. A company of rangers were sent out to track the murderous Creeks, and though they never caught up with the band who'd killed the yeoman and his wife and then carried off the children, the rangers did manage to bring back a few Creek hunters, who, after a proper trial by jury, were hanged as a public example and a warning that such murderous nonsense would not be tolerated, treaty or no.

The bodies still hung in chains from the end of Factor's Wharf when Nathan Starr returned from the war, retired on half pay—if and when the navy saw fit to send him his next cheque.

Rory and Martha attended the celebration at the Starr residence, and as the evening wore on, Rory proceeded to get coldly and deliberately drunk. He knew the sonofabitch had a right to hold Gloria on his knee like that, but, damn-it, he'd get little sleep this night, lying next to scrawny Martha as he pictured the woman he loved rutting with a sailor home from the sea!

Nathan was filled with stories of the war and the mad things the Hindu did with their dead on the banks of the fucking Ganges, but Rory excused himself as soon as he gracefully could to go out for a smoke on the veranda.

In far too short a time, he was joined there by the last person he could have wished to be with. His brother-in-law came out of the house with his own cheroot in hand, hooked his rump over the veranda rail, and said, "I've been wanting a word in private with you, Rory."

"Och, word away, then, Lieutenant."

Nathan's voice was bitter as he said, "Small comfort the rank of any half-pay officer's worth these days."

"Ay, I've not been paid for half the 'digo and other stores they owe me for. Will you be going back to work for your father, now?"

"That's what I wanted to talk to you about, Rory. The

war was not a total waste, for at least I learned to con a
ship in tropical waters these past few years."

"Ay, I hear it's tricky to work a ship through the dol-
drums and horse latitudes to the south of the civilized
world. I take it you're thinking of the merchant marine
now?" That was promising. The East Indiamen took as
long as two years on a round trip, and there was always the
chance he'd catch leprosy.

Nathan took a cautious puff of smoke, exhaled it, and
said, "I had more profitable sailing in mind. If only I could
lay my hands on a vessel, I'd be bound for the golden triangle."

"You mean to become a slaver?"

"Let's say I'd like to pick up some ivory."

"Ay, there's a need for black ivory down in the ricelands. I prefer salted niggers from the breeders up the
coast, mysel'."

"Plantation-bred are better," Nathan agreed, "but they're
infernally expensive! How much are you paying for a field
hand these days, if you don't mind my asking?"

"Och, I got a good one the other day for less than a
hundred guineas. Not a whip mark on him and—"

"I can buy a nigger in Old Calabar for eleven guineas in
trade goods," Nathan cut in, adding, "I can sell them as
low as forty on this side, and nearly triple the investment.
It takes, oh, less than five pounds to feed them enough to
bring them alive through the middle passage. The hermaph-
rodite brig I have in mind can be had for less than nine
hundred quid."

"Och, what have you been drinking? At that price she'll
be leaking like a Swiss cheese, ay, and the shipworms halfway up her mast!"

"She's a well-found vessel, I tell you. Seventy feet at her
keel and twenty-four across her beams. She'll carry five
thousand gallons of molasses or three hundred niggers on
the westbound leg of the triangle."

"That's a small vessel for such a cargo, man. How will
you pack them in, with a shoe horn?"

"You let me stand off the Calabar coast with my own
deck under me and I'll worry about trimming the hold.
Can I put you down for a quarter share, Rory?"

The other frowned, trying to calculate in his slightly befuddled head, and he mused, "Nine hundred pounds, you
say. That's—"

"I'll give you a quarter share for four hundred. I think I can get Aaron Paradeen and some others to put up the rest."

"Now *wait* just a wee bit, laddy buck!" Rory smiled a bit owlishy as he counted rapidly on the fingers of one hand with thumb and four digits. He shook his head and said, "Four hundred quid is no quarter of nine hundred."

"Hell, I have to take on trade goods and ship's stores, Rory. The crew I've in mind will work her for shares, but I can't just sail off in ballast!"

"Ay, but it's still a lot you're asking for a risky venture."

"I can promise to triple . . . all right, double your money on my first voyage. After that, of course, your profits will go up each time we turn the corner. It's the bargain of a lifetime, Rory."

"I'll sleep on it, then. Every time one of you Sassunach comes to me with another bargain, I wind up deeper in debt."

Gloria came out to join them, her chestnut curls outlined red in the candlelight from the window behind her. "So there you are, you two," she said.

She went to Nathan, slipped her hand through the crook of his arm, and chided, "Your first night home in three years and I find you out here talking business? That's hardly flattering, Nathan."

Rory made a strangled noise in his throat and turned away as Gloria asked, "I beg your pardon?"

He coughed and explained, "I got some tobacco down my throat. I'm all right now."

Gloria nodded knowingly. She understood all too well how the tall, gruff Rory felt, but, unlike her secret lover, Gloria dealt in fact, not fantasy. There was nothing either of them could do about this thing they seemed to feel for each other, and although she had dreamed idly of her brother-in-law's handsome face and brawny build as her own guilty fingers had relieved the tensions of a lonely bed, she now had a real man, if a less exciting one, to fill her hungry flesh.

Nathan patted her hand and said, "I'll join you in a bit, love. We're discussing my future at the moment."

"Your future? Don't you mean ours?" asked Gloria in a bantering tone, though her eyes were hurt as she drew her hand away and added, "I'll wait inside with Martha and your father."

As soon as they were alone again, Nathan chuckled and said, "Women. All they ever think of is attention."

Rory's eyes were glacial, but he kept his voice casual as he said, "I'd think you'd want more than a bit of attention, after three years."

"Oh, I imagine it's been lonely for Gloria, alone here with Father."

"Ay, and you were less alone? I trust the cabin boy was bonny?"

Nathan laughed and said, "Good heavens, that's the *captain's* privilege! Seriously, though, we spent a good deal of the time in port. The men, of course, had to make do with the whores we piped aboard—desertion and all that—but as an officer—"

"You'd have shore leave. What are the Hindu women like?"

"Oh, not so different from our own. They like to get on top and they tend to smell a bit odd, but there was this one little Bengali with a waist a man could hold in his hands with thumbs and fingertips touching, and a pair of tits . . . not half the size of Gloria's, but beautifully formed, with the damnedest nipples and . . ."

Rory stiffened, not daring to move a muscle for fear of grabbing Nathan by the throat as the simpering bastard gloated over his sexual adventures, comparing Gloria, casually, to the other women he'd had.

Enraged but curious, Rory forced himself to listen, snatching at stray facts to add to his fantasy of the only woman he'd ever really wanted . . . he'd never known about the mole just above her pubic hair, for instance. He groaned inwardly as Nathan boasted of a tattoo'd yellow-skinned wench he'd had dog style, of how he'd laughed at the dirty pictures on her back and noted how much deeper he could get into his own wife in this particular position. The oriental whore's buttocks, you see, were a bit boyish, and . . .

Rory suddenly snubbed out his smoke and announced, "I have to take Martha home. You know about the Indian troubles, and I want to ride by full moonlight."

"You'll go quarter shares with me on the brig?"

"Damnit, I said I'd sleep on it."

Rory knew, somehow, he'd not sleep on the venture, or much of anything else, this night.

Aaron Paradeen, in Rory's opinion, was a fool. To the rather desperate young planter, however, it seemed the only way to recoup his losses and save his plantation.

They were discussing the idea at the Crown and Anchor, near the waterfront, for though Captain Fenwyk seemed to have forgotten his duel with young Aaron, it was tempting fate to spend much time at the Red Swan these days, even when Fenwyk was sober.

Being gentlemen, they lunched, of course, in a private room overlooking the back garth. It was a balmy day, and the casement windows were open to catch the pleasantly scented breeze. Rory washed his roast beef down with a swallow of pale ale and said, "You're a planter, not a sailor, Aaron. There's no reason for you to ship out with my brother-in-law on yon slaver."

Aaron shrugged and said, "I've no choice, sir. You know what it cost me to settle my father's estate and send my mother up to be with Sarah and her husband in Philadelphia. My creditors are hounding me, and it's only through your good offices at the mansion that I haven't had my lands and chattels seized for back taxes."

"Ay, but second officer on the *Tuscarora* . . . och, what do you know of standing watch on any ship, lad?"

"Nathan says he needs trustworthy gentlemen to oversee the crew he's recruiting. Most are beached royal navy men, and though they know the ropes, they need a firm hand over them. My shipping with him means I'll have an eye on my own small investment, too. Nathan sold me a one-tenth share for the last of my silver *and* all my time for the next few months."

"Have you ever been aboard a slaver, Aaron?"

"No, I can't say as I have."

"I arrived aboard one. You'll need a strong stomach in rough weather, and I'm not talking about seasickness. What's to become of your plantation while you're away? The crops are half out of the ground."

"You remember those Irish brothers you had for a time, a few years back?"

"The Corrigans? Ay, Rose Donovan cheated me with their indentures, and I had to let them go. Sean is a drunkard. Seamus is a drunkard and a sonofabitch. Why do you ask?"

"I have Seamus overseeing the harvest for a share in it."

"Jesus! Why don't you just set fire to the whole place and have done with it? Seamus Corrigan is *trash!*"

"I know, but what can I do? I haven't the money to hire an experienced overseer. My people know what has to be done out there. All I need a white man for is to be in charge."

"I'd not call Corrigan a man, white or black. How many niggers have you now?"

"About twenty. No, twenty-one. Fourteen bucks and seven does. They have a few pickaninnies between them, of course. I don't remember exactly how many. I don't work the little ones."

Rory shook his head. "That's too big a gaggle for the likes of Corrigan. Do you mind my giving you a bit of advice, lad?"

"Have I ever, sir?"

"All right. I'll buy your crops in the field, as is, for a fifth their likely value harvested. That'll give you pocket money to work with until you can auction off your slaves and lock the house up tight. I'll give you free storage for your furnishings while you're away."

"What are you talking about? I've no intention of liquidating my holdings, Colonel!"

"Your holdings are your *land,* lad! With land, a good name, and a bit of pluck, a gentleman can stay ahead of the game. Furnishings and chattels don't mean anything as long as you keep your credit. I say sell off everything but the clods under your feet and use the proceeds to restore your credit. Then, when you come back from the Ivory Coast with a pocketful of silver and gold—"

"I haven't time. The *Tuscarora* weighs anchor with the neap tide, a day and a half from now."

"Give me power of attorney and I'll manage the sales for you while you're gone, then."

Aaron looked uncomfortable and said, "Rubin Margolis is my lawyer, Colonel Martin."

Rory nodded with a crooked grin and said, "Better the devil we know, eh? Never mind, my advice remains the same, lad. Remember that what counts is land and a good name. With land but no credit, you're as bad off as that poor Private Hanks whose widow and childer' are right upstairs as paupers, every one."

"I thought the Indians killed Hanks. What's this about his credit?"

Rory kept his gaze steady as he met Aaron's puzzled frown and explained, "Och, didn't you know what he was doing on that lonely road alone at night? His wife, Molly, tells me he was on his way to the Red Swan to ask for employment."

"A farmer and militiaman thought he could get a job in a whorehouse?"

"Och, you know auld Rose and your auld playmate, Fenwyk, have been buying up tax-delinquent lands. Fenwyk's a born bully boy, as you'll remember, but he can't evict a man with six or eight grown sons without a bit of help. They've been recruiting lackland gentlemen—or, to put it properly, unemployed men of any station, as long as they like a good brawl. The point I was trying to make was that Hanks was driven to desperate measures by holding land without the credit of a good name. My brother-in-law, contrariwise, has a good name without enough land to swing a cat in. That's what's driven him to the desperate measure of the *Tuscarora. Your* harebrained plans make no sense at all as you've just outlined them to me."

"Lawyer Margolis thought they made sense, sir. I should be back in a few months with—"

"Six. Never plan on less than six months to beat around the golden triangle, lad."

"Well, no matter. Whenever I do get back my plantation will be waiting as I left it, while I'll have the profits of my voyage and—"

"You'll have a *ruined* plantation, you mean! I tell you, Aaron, an absentee landlord is the ruin of his land and a fool with his own purse! Even with a *good* overseer it's a poor way to manage your holdings. With a drunken bit of trash like Corrigan in charge . . . och, you'd be better off leaving your niggers to run things on their own."

"Margolis says I can't do that. Unless there's a white man on the property, there's no preventing the roaming bands of trash from simply taking whatever they want, including my Negroes."

Rory took another sip of ale. "Ay, those roving pony boys are becoming a menace to everyone, black and white. That's why I still say you should liquidate everything that can be moved off your land and refurnish when you get back. That blacksmith, Coffee, could keep an eye on the house itself while you're away. The Ashanti's one of the few niggers who'd be likely to stand up to trash, and with nothing really worth taking in the boarded-up house—"

"Forgive me, sir, but I've already committed myself to Seamus Corrigan. He's counting on the job. I'll take you up on selling off my crop futures, for you know I need the money. As for old Coffee, he's not the man he used to be. I doubt if he'd stand up to a rabbit these days. There's something broken inside the man, like the mainspring of a clock."

"Oh? What's the matter with him? He's been doing repairs for my wife out at Indigo Hall. Martha never mentioned he looked ill. She seems to be pleased with the way he's been working."

"I don't think there's any sickness in his body, sir. It's more like something died deep inside his eyes. I mind when Sarah and I were little, Coffee used to read Papa's books to us. He had an atlas he'd bought with his own wages and he liked to point out Ashanti land to us on the map of Africa. He had this mad plan of returning there one day in his own great ship, as an admiral of some strange Ashanti navy. He built a marvelous model ship one time. Sarah and I used to love to play with it in the duck pond. . . ."

Aaron toyed with the half-eaten food on his plate and mused soberly, "It's odd how things turn out. Papa said once that there was no returning for any of us. Jew, Gentile, black, white, we're all exiles together in this string of colonies clinging to an unexplored continent. I asked Coffee about his ship about a month ago. He was shoeing my roan mare, and I was just passing time while I waited. I asked whatever had happened to his books and the little toy ship we'd played with as children."

"Och, the man's no fool, black as he is. He knows his nigger chiefs would just sell him again if ever he went back."

"That's more or less the way he put it. He said he'd sold the books, one at a time, to put a bit of tea and sugar on the table. He said he didn't have time for reading much these days."

"Does he still have the toy ship? I reckon my two youngest would like it, if it's as well made as you say."

"He doesn't have it anymore. He says he sold it to the young Davis boy, Henry. Henry and some friends launched it foolishly on a salt creek and the tide carried it off to the sea. It's a shame, too. I really liked that little ship."

"Ay, but you're a grown man now, and Coffee's outgrown his auld notions. You'll be down to the sea in a bigger ship, unless I can talk you out of your own mad dreams. I'm strapped for hard currency my ownsel', Aaron, but I'm sure we could work it out if you'd leave off this business with the *Tuscarora*. I know you, lad. You're not the stuff a slaver's made of."

Aaron's voice took on an edge as he answered, "I've been tested on the field of honor, Colonel."

"Och, it's not your courage I question, Aaron! We both know you're a fine Christian gentleman. That may be what I fear could limit you a wee bit off the Ivory Coast."

"Was that a veiled remark about my membership in the High Kirk, sir?"

"Of course not. Don't be so touchy when you sit at table with a friend, Goddamnit! I've never doubted you're a better Christian than myself, Ensign Paradeen. What I meant was that you may be too *much* a Christian gentleman. I know a bit about the trade you're going into, you ken. I mean it as a compliment to your dead father, but you're not cut out of the same cloth as my brother-in-law. Nathan Starr, and I'll say it to his face, is a man born to his chosen trade. Do you know what he said when I suggested three feet of headroom between the slave decks on the *Tuscarora*? He said I was ever a soft-hearted Celt."

Aaron laughed and said, "Papa said you'd never shown much kindness to Mister Seminole, but, admit it, Colonel, you do tend to pamper your servants a bit."

"I ride my stud with a gentle hand on the rein, too. But the horse knows we'll be going where *I* decide. My stud comes to me when I call. My niggers plant what I tell them to plant and reap when I tell them to reap. I've no need to rush about, frothing at the mouth, with a teamster's whip in my hand."

"What about that Yoruba buck who defied you last summer?"

"Och, what about him? He needed killing, so I killed him on the spot with a single shot. I've never been one for needless cruelty to man nor beast."

"You may be right, but it's a damned expensive way of keeping servants in line. I'll have to go along with Nathan that a rubdown with the cat or a dose of ipecac and mustard cures most of what ails them."

Aaron swallowed the last of his ale and dabbed at his

lips, adding, "I really have to be going. I've papers to be drawn up with Margolis, and I promised Nathan I'd help the first officer with the bill of lading. The mate's doubtless a good sailor, but he can't seem to read very well."

Rory walked the younger man to the door and watched as Aaron mounted his mare to ride the short distance to where the *Tuscarora* was moored, taking on stores. Rory was flushed from the meal and the ale, and he unbuttoned his waistcoat and fanned his damp shirtfront as he stood in the breeze, breathing the salt air from the southeast.

It was turning out to be a lazy summer's day, and bees were humming in the cape jasmine vine creeping up one side of the tavern entrance. Somewhere a nation drum was tapping out some fool nigger message. It was coming up on the Sabbath and the servants liked to have their all-night get-togethers on Saturday nights. He supposed it did no harm, provided they kept their pagan shindigs confined to the woodlot, away from the house. He didn't mind their all-night singing, but those damned drums could be annoying to a man sleeping off his own more civilized celebrations.

A humble voice at his elbow asked, "Will there be anything else I can do for you, Colonel Martin, sir?"

Rory shook his head. Then he had a sudden thought and asked, "Is the Widow Hanks upstairs with her childer', Goodman Tannenbaum?"

The taverner said, "The poor lad's widow is, sir. The childer' have gone down to watch them load the *Tuscarora* at the wharf."

"There's a toy shop in the neighborhood, isn't there?"

"Oh, yes, sir. Just around the corner, sir."

"Ay, I mind it now. I reckon I'll go upstairs and ask her what sort of play pretties her children might like."

"I'm sure she'll be most grateful, sir. She was telling my old woman how good you've been to her since her misfortune."

"Och, her late husband served under me against the very Creeks that killed him. I'll announce myself to the lady, Goodman Tannenbaum."

Rory climbed the narrow staircase built into one corner of the main room and knocked gently on the smallish oak door of the quarters he'd rented for Molly Hanks and her brats.

The woman let him in, her bodice half open and her

eyes red-rimmed from tears and the spirits Tannenbaum had told her could be added to her benefactor's account.

The big red-headed Molly was not as pretty as Rory had remembered her from the time he'd watched her kiss her ranger husband farewell the day they'd marched off for king and country. How could she have changed so in less than two short years? The new dress she had on was a gift from himself, but she wore it tight and she seemed no less slatternly than she had in her own poor garments.

He asked about the children and mentioned the toy shop 'round the corner as he stared down at the wide expanse of bare skin between her rather thick neck and overflowing bodice. Her upper chest was freckled by the sun, but her tits would be creamy white, he knew.

Molly took him to a windowseat tucked under the slanting pitch of the garret room's rough plaster ceiling. They sat side by side, his knee against hers as he chatted on in the meaningless conversation the game required. He was only dimly aware of what he was saying, but it hardly mattered, since she wasn't listening too intently. They both knew what he was leading up to, and they both knew she had no choice in the matter. Rory could not help but wonder, as his voice went on, soothing her fears about being all alone in the world, if it might not be simpler just to offer her a few bob and have done with it. What in hell was he *doing* here? Did he even *want* this great red cow of a woman?

Her gross peasant hand was resting on the back of his own, now. She'd put it there when, to emphasize his concern for her and the children, he'd placed a gentle hand on her leg, just above the knee. It wasn't clear whether her hand was restraining his or steering it as he moved his palm an inch higher on her plump white thighs. She was weeping now about her late husband's troubles and the fears of a friendless, lackland widow in a heartless land of strangers.

Rory put his free arm around her shoulders to comfort her as he soothed, "There, there, Moll, you're not as friendless as you reckon. Where came you from, in the Old Country?"

"The South Downs, sir. Near Tunbridge Wells, in Sussex."

She suddenly put both hands over her face and sobbed, "Oh, I miss the downlands so!"

Rory took advantage of her unguarded groin to move his hand into position for the final advance as he murmured, "I understand the chalk downs are bonny to ride over in the spring."

The stubby-fingered hand dropped back on his as she sniffed and explained, "It's not just the soft green hills of home or the gloaming light on the old church steeple of our village, sir. It's the family and friends we left behind!"

"Ay, we all need friends," he murmured, judging with a practiced eye the distance to the bed across the small room. They'd wrestle a bit in the window nook, of course. She'd make the usual protestations and he'd have the usual ready answers, and, if he kept the one hand around her shoulders and got under her great ass with the other forearm . . .

Molly was saying, "My father had near twenty acres of his own, but Robin had nothing but his strong arms when I ran off with him to the colonies. We thought we'd get rich over here, for the land was for the taking, and they told Robin if he joined the militia—"

"I know the tale Robin Hanks was told, Moll. It's a bit cramped in this window nook, don't you think?"

"Would you rather we sat on the bedstead, sir?"

"Ay, I reckon we'd be more comfortable."

Molly Hanks got up. Rory's hands lost their momentary advantage, but once he had her on yon bed . . .

The husky redhead walked over to the bedstead and sat down, her wide hips sinking deeply into the feather mattress as she shook her head and sighed, "Oh, if only I'd listened to my parents."

Rory stood over her, the light from the window behind him casting his shadow over her pink-and-henna form. The childer' would be hours at the wharf, but it might be wise to slip the oak bolt on the door before he sat down beside her. Women always asked about things like that at the damnedest times.

He pondered the best way to do it, since they'd lost a bit of spontaneity in maneuvering to a better battleground. To gain time without committing himself to the bedstead, he asked idly, "Do you ever hear from your people, Moll?"

"Oh, yes sir, my mother wrote me just last winter. She says my father's forgiven me, but alas, that's little comfort to me now."

Rory was a bit surprised himself, as he heard himself

saying, "The *Tuscarora*'s England-bound to pick up a cargo of trade goods and deliver some staples from Georgia. Her first port of call will be Liverpool, but she'll be putting into Southampton before she leaves for the Ivory Coast."

The woman on the bed gaped up at him, slack-jawed, and, as he read the undared hope in her watery eyes, he wondered at his own queer feelings as he smiled and said, "I could ask them to drop you and the childer' off there, Moll. This is no place for your sons to grow up, you know. A landless white man can still make a bob a day in the Old Country, or even up New England way, but—"

And then she was off the bed and kneeling on the floor with her arms around his legs, sobbing incoherent words of gratitude as he stood there, feeling an odd tenderness he didn't understand. He ran a gentle fingertip along the part of her hair and murmured, "Och, pull yoursel' together, Moll."

Her tears were staining his moleskin breeches as she pressed her face against his upper thighs, sobbing, "How will we ever repay you, Colonel? I'd do anything to get back to my home and family, but I've nothing to offer you. Nothing! They took our land and all we possessed. I've nothing but the clothes on me back, and they were given me by you!"

He wondered if that had been meant as an invitation. The Laird knew the poor wench knew her station. If he were simply to command her to disrobe and service him, Rory knew without the slightest doubt that she'd do it with no word of protest.

He disengaged her clinging arms, knelt, and helped her to her feet and then back to the windowseat as he said, "You'll need a bit of silver to get you from Southampton to your old home, Moll. I'll ask Aaron Paradeen to look after you on the voyage and slip you a purse as he sees you off on England's shore."

Molly Hanks sat there, staring up at him with her hands in her lap and a reverent look of devotion in her eyes as she murmured, "You're the kindest, gentlest, most Christian man I've ever known, Colonel Martin. If we live to be a hundred, my children and I will never forget you!"

He went to the door, saying, "Och, it's nothing. Your man was my comrade," and then he left, moving lightly down the stairs and feeling somehow elated as he walked out into the fresher air. It was odd how much more enjoyable the game of gallantry became if a man allowed himself to mean it once in a while.

FIVE

By now there were perhaps fifty thousand free Negroes living in the thirteen English colonies, not counting the thousand or so "Cimarrons"—runaways living as semi-savages in the wilderness—or the growing tribe of fugitive slaves and breakaway Muskegee known as Seminoles, most of whom lived in the recently seized but still unsettled Crown Reserve of Florida.

The free Negroes of Georgia, mostly former indentured men like Coffee Pardus or slaves set free by generous masters for any of a dozen reasons, existed in an economic limbo somewhere between the so-called white trash and their enslaved African neighbors.

Rory Martin and other planters of his apparent wealth and power were the exception rather than the rule. Indigo Hall, as it expanded to keep ahead of the interest on Rory's debts, was one of the larger plantations in Georgia. The planter who just managed to keep up appearances with pewter table service, German silver shoe buckles, and perhaps twenty slaves was the norm. He, in turn, made up less than a quarter of the white agricultural community. Between the planter class and the white trash, there existed a great number of hard-scrabble smallholders who could barely afford a horse, let alone a slave. When a smallholder needed extra hands at harvest time, he usually went to a free Negro. White trash were seldom hired if it could be avoided, for a man who'd sunk to "nigger work," as working another man's crops was considered, had to be worthless.

Between harvests, the free black community had a hard time of it. Like the unlanded whites, the freemen hunted, fished, foraged for edible wild plants, and gathered wild pecans and the Spanish moss used as cheap mattress stuffing, which their womenfolk sold in the open-air markets. When all else failed, both pauper classes resorted to the petty crimes of outcasts everywhere.

Impoverished whites specialized in armed robbery and horse thievery. A white man, at least, could sometimes sell a horse if he had a glib story and had given himself a recent shave.

Free Negroes, already harassed by petty officials with suspicious questions about their manumission papers, went in more for edible plunder. The humiliating legends of the shiftless darkie in the henhouse or watermelon patch would grow out of the desperate measures a few men took to feed their families—filching ears from a white man's cornfield or stealing the occasional welcome stray from some farmer's livestock pen.

Southern women, black and white, of the pauper class became ingenious cooks who could make something reasonably edible out of cast-off scraps begged from the butchers and greengrocers along Market Street. Twisted-off turnip tops left on the floor near the greengrocer's scale became a substitute for spinach. Hog guts, turned inside out and scraped free of their fecal contents, made savory "chitlins" when fried in their own fat. The quality meat of the era was muscle flesh. Chicken hearts and gizzards were fed to milady's cat or thrown to a begging Negro child by an indulgent butcher. The tails, feet, or snouts of butchered livestock were too valuable to give away, but could be had for pennies. But an oxtail soup was a rare treat, for even pennies were terribly hard to come by in Governor Oglethorpe's spoiled dream of Utopia.

Such advantage as there was went to the free Negro, for while the poor white tended to be uneducated, unskilled, or simply unable to learn, many of the Negroes, like Coffee, had brought crafts learned in Africa to their new homeland.

Morocco leather, despite its name, was the product of a long-established method of tanning goat skins in black Africa. Other slaves brought to the colonies the famous bronzework of Benin; quite possibly Africans had been responsible for the invention of iron smelting itself. Most West African tribes carved wood with nearly the skill of their contemporaries in feudal Japan, and if their art was oddly disturbing to European eyes, nevertheless many Georgia mansions were decorated with inlaid parquet in Yoruba, Ibo, or Ashanti motifs.

The baskets of Georgia Negro craftsmanship, slave and free, were becoming an item of trade all up and down the coast, while many a young macaroon sported an amusing hardwood walking stick with an African godling's grotesque face leering from its ornate handle.

Most of Savannah's coopers were black, either freemen or skilled slaves hired out to the cooperage by their masters. The few whites employed in the trade were eventually forced out, for Negro labor, free or slave, was impossible to compete with.

Disgruntled white artisans complained that free Negroes drove them out of business with slipshod work and the ability to live on wages no white man could exist on, but this was only partly true. The black men took as much pride in their work as anyone; however, they did indeed receive miserable wages. Many times a free Negro found he'd worked for nothing. Under Georgia law, no Negro could appear in court as witness against a white person. This gave a certain advantage to an unscrupulous gentleman who needed a boat caulked or a roof repaired but lacked the funds to pay for more than the supplies.

Hence, men like Coffee Pardus became shrewder than many a poor white in their business dealings. Their world was even more precarious than that of the often desperate white tradesmen, and when they were hounded too far, many free Negroes became as hard as the system that oppressed them.

Despite the odds, some free blacks did achieve a degree of prosperity. There was a standing reward for runaway slaves, and Isaac Pardus' former bondservant, Jake, now calling himself Mr. Jeaco Jackson, had built a flourishing small business on such rewards. Freeman Jackson, moving across the blurred lines of slave and free-black society, could tell a white master when a fed-up young field hand was about to slip off to join the Seminoles. For only a percentage of the reward that a white slave-hunter would demand, Jackson and the two young thugs who lived with him would bring a runaway back—beaten, sodomized, and disabused of any further foolish notions about freedom in the Florida swamps.

Some former slaves even began to buy slaves of their own from planters surprised but short of ready cash. Most of these unusual purchases, to the credit of the black community, were of friends and relatives still held in bondage to the whites. (One black man, in another colony would scrimp and save the pennies his master let him earn on his own time to buy first his own manumission and then, over a period of many years, the freedom of his entire family of eight.) Other Negro entrepreneurs, less charitably, simply bought slaves for the same reasons white men did: it beat doing your own work. And even the whites were scandalized when a Negro shoemaker bought a pretty young woman, kept her until she became pregnant and possibly a nag, and then sold her and the baby at a profit.

Other whites were becoming concerned at the confusion in the social order. Georgia had been planned as a Utopian colony of sturdy English yeomen, and when that had failed to work, they'd settled for a vague imitation of the English feudal system, with the once-poor whites as country squires and the happy, singing darkies as the faithful, servile peasantry. But now it didn't seem to be working out that way. The rules of the game would have to be changed by the men who still held most of the chips.

Seamus Corrigan had never lived so well or felt so important in his hitherto unfortunate life. As overseer for the absent Aaron Paradeen, Seamus had been left in charge of the plantation with written instructions and a detailed plan to follow. He'd decided, first of all, that his quarters in Coffee's old cabin wing were inadequate for a gentleman of his station and, after forcing the lock, he had moved himself into the master bedroom of the main house.

His younger brother, Sean, had not been hired by Aaron, but he'd tagged along to keep Seamus company, for sure and there was no tellin' when them murderous niggers might attack their new master in the middle of the night, and, be-Jasus, young Paradeen had left a fine stock of the Creature for a man who put his faith in such small padlocks.

The two brothers were accustomed to living like pigs, but now there were nigger wenches to pick up after them, weren't there? And sure they'd leave the master's quarters as they found them, save for perhaps a few missing items a man was entitled to for guarding so much on so little pay.

Aaron's notes included a warning about molesting the servant girls. The plantation, since his father's time, had been run on Talmudic injunctions, and the Negroes working there had always been considered singularly fortunate. All of the original indentured men had been set free as their time had run out, but a few had stayed on as casually paid retainers. The thirty-odd "Paradeen people" consisted of three extended and intermarried families. Isaac had earned the undying gratitude of the slave he'd named Beelzebub by purchasing the man's wife and daughter off the same ship when the frantic Ibo had managed to explain that the three of them had been seized in the same Slattee raid.

Beelzebub's daughter was the first of Paradeen's slaves to be raped by one of the Corrigan brothers on Aaron Paradeen's bed. She'd been changing the linens for the new overseer when Seamus had decided he liked the way she moved her body and, suiting action to thought, he had simply thrown her down and started tearing off her clothes. The girl's anguished screams had brought Sean to the door, a bottle in his hand and a moronic smile on his curious face. When it began to look as if she really meant to refuse the honors offered by a gentleman of Galway, Seamus had yelled at his brother, "What are you just standing there for? Come over here and hold her fucking wrists!"

They'd taken turns, after beating her into submission, and the bruised, humiliated girl had then crawled off into an outbuilding. There her mother had found her and helped her find some clothes, advising her not to tell her father or her husband, for the menfolk might try to make trouble, and what could they do against a white man?

Left to their own devices, the hands on Paradeen Plantation were perfectly capable of carrying on unsupervised, for they liked their young master and knew, far better than either of the brothers Corrigan, what had to be done to keep the plantation humming. The stable boys performed their chores willingly and with skill. The livestock was fed and driven out to pasture whether orders had been received or not. Marse Aaron had explained before he left that the crops in the fields would be harvested by Colonel Martin's people, so there was only the weeding and keeping the birds away to worry about.

But Seamus Corrigan had gotten his hands on a teamster's whip. It was a cunningly braided eighteen-foot length of oiled black leather with a rawhide popper on the end. Seamus had learned to crack it, loudly, with what he fancied as considerable skill, though he knew better than to crack it, or even have it in sight, when one of the ponderous ox-drawn freight wagons rolled slowly by on the road out front. The leather-breeched crackers who drove the teams from plantation to waterfront were a bored breed with an odd sense of humor. One of their casual pastimes was to engage in cracking contests with anyone they saw with a whip in his hand. Sometimes they aimed at chosen targets, with a small wager on the side. At other times they simply popped the hat, or an ear, off a stranger's head, just to see what he might do about it.

There were few freight wagons passing at this time of the season, however, so a few days after he'd raped the first Negress, Seamus was walking along a corn row cracking to his heart's content. A fence lizard caught his eye as it sunned itself on a cornfield rail. The Irishman took careful aim and sent an overhand coil of greasy black braid at the tiny reptile. The popper exploded like a pistol shot where the lizard had been sunning itself, but, of course, the reptile had vanished into the morning glories at the first blur of movement.

Seamus walked on, popping tassles off corn stalks and taking a sip, from time to time, from the flask he carried slung from his shoulder. It was a pleasant day and not too warm for his nice new shirt. He'd exchanged the homespun linsey-woolsey smock he'd arrived in for a linen shirt he'd found in one of Aaron's closets. It wasn't as if he'd stolen it, for he intended to put it back, pounded clean as new by one of the nigger gals, before the master returned.

A redbird landed on another fence rail and eyed the strolling man warily. It took off in a flutter of scarlet feathers before Seamus could even take aim. The overseer took another slug from the flask, wiped the back of his whip hand across his mouth, and continued his tour of inspection.

Just ahead, a Negro was cultivating between the corn rows, head down as he watched his hoe cut the dry clods to the right size around the roots of the half-grown stalks. A sly look crossed Seamus Corrigan's face as he judged the distance, wound up, and let fly.

The eighteen-foot lash flew true and popped the nigger in the ass. A divot of thin cloth and blood exploded from the startled victim's left buttock as, with a howl of surprised pain, he leaped two feet in the air and fell forward, flattening five or six stalks as he landed on his own hoe, cutting one shin to the bone.

Seamus Corrigan howled too, albeit with laughter, as the injured man rolled over, clutching at his lacerated leg and staring up at him with wide-eyed confusion and fear.

"That'll teach you to shirk your chores, you good-for-nothing black bastard!" Seamus jeered.

The slave took one hand from his bleeding leg, stared at his bloody fingers, and groaned, "Please, Cap'n, I wasn't doin' nothin'!"

"That's why I hadda give you a lick. You wan't doin' nothin'. You ain't out here to do *nothin'*, boy. You're out here to *work*!"

"Honest to God, Cap'n, I *was* workin'. Workin' *hard*!"

"Be-Jasus, you'll work harder than that if you don't want to feel me wrath agin! Get up and get back to . . . to whatever it was ye was supposed to be after doin'."

"Please, Cap'n. I'm bleedin' fearful. Dast I go back to the quarters and git my woman to poltice it first?"

"Aw, Jasus, I never hurt ye that much, me bucko. Sure it's only a scratch and I'll have none of your nigger-shirking while *I'm* in charge of yez. Get back on your feet and back to work, I say, and I'll never be after saying it again!"

The slave got up, gritting his teeth, and managed a few gingerly swipes at the dirt with his bloodstained hoe, favoring his hurt leg as the blood ran down his shin. Satisfied for the moment, Seamus Corrigan moved on.

Sure, he'd come a long way from the auld black hut in Galway. He was an overseer, a man who made others do his bidding, instead of the poor potato-eater tugging his forelock when Himself, the landlord's agent, rode by.

By Jasus, he was as good as them Flannery micks who'd snubbed him only a month ago when he'd come, clean-shaved, to pay a call on their Bridget. *Aragh,* who did that Conan Flannery think he was with his forty acres and his auld lame mare? Sure and Flannery didn't even have a nigger to call his own, and they had to send their laundry to that nigger woman down by the creek. Seamus Corrigan wasn't good enough for the likes of their daughter, eh? Jasus, he was *too* good for the proud wee slut her in her brass-buckled shoes she only wore on church days!

He snapped the whip loudly, strutting in his gentleman's shirt until, a quarter of a mile from the house, he came on a small fenced enclosure. A Negro boy was on his knees with a wooden bucket, whitewashing the pickets with a crude paintbrush. Seamus popped his whip for attention and the boy turned his head with a puzzled smile.

The overseer asked, "What are ye doing? I never told

nobody to be out here wasting whitewash on . . . what the hell are you painting, boy?"

Juba Pardus said, "This is where they put old Marse Pardus in the ground, suh. My pa tol' me I's to keep it seemly."

Corrigan came closer, staring dubiously at the small square of granite in the fenced-in patch of neatly trimmed Bermuda-grass. He crossed himself and muttered, "A grave it is, is it? What's it doin' out here all by itself?"

"I don't know," said Juba, unaware of the dreadful scene Aaron had had with his mother over placing a grave anywhere on property inhabited by living relatives of the deceased. Juba could read a bit, but the carefully chiseled Hebrew letters on the stone meant nothing to him, and to the illiterate Corrigan it wouldn't have mattered what language they'd been inscribed in. He watched the Negro youth dab another brushful of whitewash on the vertical pickets; then he said, "*Aragh,* that's enough for the litch. I want you back in the fields where you belong."

Juba laughed and said, "I ain't one of your niggers, sir. I'm free, like my pa. I's Juba Pardus. My pa's the blacksmith, over yonder, by them tulip trees."

"Goddamnit, you just *sassed* me, boy!"

"Beg pardon, Cap'n, I don't allow as I did. You ast me a question and I done answered." He dabbed another stroke of whitewash and added softly, "I never sassed nobody."

The teamster's whip lashed through the air and, although aimed at Juba's slender hips, cracked against the paint bucket, showering the startled boy with whitewash as he scrambled backward in the weeds, shouting, "What you *doin'*? You *crazy*, white man?"

Seamus Corrigan roared, "Crazy I am, am I?" as he ran at the young Negro, winding up for another lash of his murderous whip.

But Juba was up and running as the whip cracked behind him. He never looked back until he was over another fence, swift as a deer, and heading for the safety of home.

Coffee Pardus looked up from his anvil with a frown as his son staggered, out of breath, through the open smithy entrance. Juba sank to his knees near the forge as he gasped, "Crazy man! Crazy white man wif a whip! He like to kilt me, over to Marse Isaac's grave!"

Coffee sighed. "I reckon it must have been one of the

white men Marse Aaron hired over there. What did you do to make him angry, boy?"

"Honest, Pa, I never done nothin'! I was jest tendin' the grave, yonder, like you done bid me. This fool white man come at me like a yaller dog with the runnin' fits and whupped at me wif a cracker's lash!"

"He wound you, son?"

"Shoot, I crawfished outten there too slick for him, but he like to turnt me into a white boy wif all this durned old paint!"

Coffee sighed and said, "Wash yourself off at the well and go take a walk in the woods. I'll deal with them if they come lookin' for you, son." He hammered at the wrought-iron gate bar he'd been making, but the iron had cooled down. He stuck it back in the forge and began to pump the bellows as he added thoughtfully, "You'd best take your little brothers and sisters with you. Mind you don't let them get bit by Br'er Cottonmouth if you've a mind to swim in the creek."

Juba said, "I ain't afeared of no crazy old white man, Pa. We'uns is *free*, ain't we?

"You just mind and do as I told you, boy. You take the other chilluns and git!"

The boy retreated sullenly, for he knew his father intended to shuffle and scrape when the white men came. Juba hated it when white men came to the smithy. It was hard to understand how his pa had come to be such a grinning fool nigger.

Once, Juba knew, his pa had been a warrior of King Karikari, and ma said that when they'd first met, pa had sassed the white men something fierce. She'd whipped her son once for saying his pa was afeared of the white man. Then she'd tried to explain, with tears in her eyes, how she'd watched her proud man die, a little each weary day, as his dreams had faded. Ma had said pa had cried one night after reading in the white man's shipping news how the African intertribal wars worked to the advantage of the white men in the long black ships. She'd said the pink scar in his knuckles was a reminder of the night he'd smashed his fist against the bricks of his forge, cursing mindlessly the greed and stupidity of his own Ashanti rulers. That was likely the time pa had sold the last of his books. He'd said one time, when Juba had asked about them, that books were only tempting doors to nowhere. Pa talked funny sometimes.

Coffee heated up the iron bar after his son had slipped away, and, placing it back on the anvil, he hammered out the split floral end he intended for the new wrought-iron gate. Many of the fine wrought-iron grilles and gates of Savannah were his work, and he sometimes wondered idly how long his work would live after him. Would anyone someday admire that balcony he'd made for Mistress Nelson's bedroom in a magical protective pattern of Kumasi? And if they *were* told the cunning ironwork had been wrought by Kofi of Ashanti-land, would it really matter? What did anything matter, when you thought about it? Everything ended, in time, the same way. A man's body went to rot and ruin in the twinkle of a star. The work he left behind lasted little longer, for even the highest mountain was finally carried down to the sea by the gentle rains of Forever.

A man was coming down the road. Coffee worked on, aware of the other's approach, but hoping to prolong this short moment in eternity as long as possible. He hammered at the cherry-red iron, licking his lips as his mind formed the right answers to the humiliating questions the white man would be asking.

A low voice murmured, "*Jambo,* Kofi," and the smith looked up with a relieved smile. It was Caado, called Beelzebub by the white men. The stocky Ibo's face was deadly calm as he said, "Paradeen's overseer raped my daughter. The two of them held her down and took turns with her. I have come to you for advice."

Coffee put the bar of iron back in the coals and stood with his back to the outraged father, staring down into the shimmering red glow as he pumped the bellows and murmured, "They are animals. One of them just tried to beat my son with a whip for no reason."

"In the old country, the Leopard Society would pay those men a visit. I know this to be true."

"I know this too, but the Leopard Men are far from this land, my Ibo brother. Perhaps that is why, in Georgia, the people behave so badly. Sometimes I wonder if the Leopard Society still follows the old ways where we came from. I find it hard to believe our old leaders would sell their own people for rum and calico to the Portugee if they knew that one night the Clawed Ones would pay them a visit to demand an explanation."

Beelzebub said, "At night I still hear the nation drums, and they say an Obeah woman lives at Oakwall Plantation."

"This, I hear, is true. Do you really think the powers of Mumbo Jumbo can help you, slave? I mean this as no insult, Ibo. But I have little faith in a juju doll or a pinch of goofer dust left for the man who violated your child to find. The white men do not believe in our gods. Obeah powers seem to work best on those who know their meaning."

"I was hoping to evoke the Leopard Society. The Obeah woman may know of some Leopard Men here in Georgia."

Coffee laughed bitterly. "Another nigger dream? No Clawed Ones can help you here, Ibo. If any of our people sold by the Slattee ever did belong to the Leopard Society, I can tell you where you'll find them now. You'll find them grooming a white man's horse with fingers that once curled proudly around the steel claws of Those Who Make Things Proper."

"If I could only reach them with my wrong—"

"You know who you'll reach if you keep running about with your story? You'll reach Jeaco Jackson or one of the other informers, and the white men will hang you before you've had revenge!"

The Ibo grimaced and said, "I can't kill those two white men! They'll know who did it!"

"I know. Your choice is simple. You can take up arms and kill until they kill you, or you can pretend it never happened."

"By the gods of my nation, it *did* happen! What would *you* do in my place, Ashanti?"

"I don't know. My woman is fat and old. The matter has never come up, thank the Sacred Golden Stool."

"Yes, but what if when your daughters grow up—"

"My daughters are yet small. Don't try to make your quarrel with the white men mine, Ibo. I have enough trouble with the fishbelly-faced bastards as it is."

Beelzebub didn't answer for a time. When he did, his voice was that of a beaten man as he murmured, "You are wise. I thought you'd know what to do."

"What can any of us do, brother?" Coffee asked softly. "In the end, what does it matter?"

SIX

Jeaco Jackson couldn't be invited to the governor's mansion. Indeed, neither the governor nor any other official appointed by the Crown was present when the informal meeting was held at the Red Swan.

Judge Crawford, who had been elected to the colonial legislature, was the highest-ranking gentleman present. Jeaco Jackson, in his sky-blue satin suit, lace collar and cuffs, and snow-white periwig was the funniest impersonation of a gentleman Rory Martin had ever seen, and many of the young Georgia gallants tried, very hard, to look ridiculous.

The other white planters who crowded into the back room of the tavern tended to take the self-important young man in periwig and tribal markings a bit more seriously. If the growing army of slaves was a powder keg under them, many felt that the free Negroes, plotting God only knew what amongst themselves, constituted the very dangerous fuse.

Whether decent men or thoughtless brutes, the planter class of the colony knew they were in an ugly quagmire that they had no more chance of escaping than their hapless Negroes. In an economy gone mad, solving one problem only seemed to leave a greater one staring at you. Frightened, divided among themselves on nearly every issue, the landed gentry and important merchants of Georgia needed free labor one month and loathed it as an unreliable and dangerous innovation the next. The choices were to buy more slaves at inflated prices—slaves to be fed and clothed even when there was nothing to occupy their idle hands—or suffer extra help to barely exist in the shanty towns of mudflat and swamp. Efram Starr had ridden out to the Red Swan with Rory, and was of the opinion that every freeman should be required to leave the colony on receiving manumission. He was willing, he insisted, to pay a living wage to any man, but he could hardly compete with other merchants whose help worked for cast-off clothes and pennies, while, if he gave his clerks the going Georgia rates, the ones with any gumption simply quit and ran off to the North where a white man was still worth three or four shillings a day.

Another chandler now insisted, with heat, that there were not enough white artisans in all of Georgia to outfit a coastal brig properly. The niggers he employed as piece-workers turned a belaying pin or walked a ship's hawser as well as anyone, and the finished product would sell for not a penny more if wrought by white hands.

Rory lounged in a corner, waiting to see what the point of the meeting was before committing himself. He hadn't wanted to come out here to the Red Swan. Old Rose's hair-trigger-tempered husband was seated across from him, and, besides the matter of the affair on the dueling ground, there was no telling how much Rose had told her man about . . . everything.

Despite his being a cashiered officer, Fenwyk still styled himself Captain, and without opposition—at least to his face. It had been the sage Lawyer Margolis who'd resolved the problem with Talmudic logic by suggesting that since the Negroes called nearly every white man "Captain," Fen-wyk's puffed-up opinion of himself could be the other gen-tlemen's private joke.

There was the matter of the girl, too. He'd heard that Sheba had died of drink, the yellowjack, or both. The mu-latto daughter they'd produced between them was still alive and working, somewhere, here at the Red Swan. She'd been named Jezebel, he'd learned, and she was about twelve, or a little older than Locky. He didn't know whether Rose had her serving as a bar maid or . . . some-thing else. He didn't know how a gentleman asked about such things gracefully. He could hardly see himself going over to Captain Fenwyk and whispering, "I say, sir, I have a black bastard daughter working in your wife's whore-house. Couldst tell me if the wench is serving grog, cunt, or both?"

One of the planters had produced a small black figurine modeled crudely from pine pitch and human hair. The Ne-gro informer, Jackson, was discoursing on it, explaining, "That a juju doll, gen'mens! Obeah woman make it with someone's hair, nail parings, or maybe night soil mixed in the tar."

The planter said, "I found one of my children playing with it. What the devil does it mean?"

Jeaco was a natural actor, so, even though he knew the

tar baby was probably a toy fashioned for one of the worried man's slave ninnies, he rolled his eyes under the goat's-hair wig perched over his dark features and warned, "Suppose the Obeah woman put some part of yourself inside the juju doll, sir. Then, when your child git tired of playing wif it and maybe throw it in the fire or drop it down a well—"

"Sympathetic magic." Lawyer Margolis, a reader of ancient lore, nodded. He noted the blank looks around him and added, "The Moors had simular ideas in Iberia. The Moors were African, you know. This so-called juju thing is a childish superstition, albeit vicious in intent. The idea—as, um, Mister Jackson puts it—is that Planter Nolan's wife, himself, or possibly the overseer should die at the hands of the innocent Nolan children." He sniffed and observed further, " 'Pon my word, it would be a rather delicious revenge for a disgruntled nigger. That is, of course, if it worked."

Jeaco said, "I've heard of it working on white folks, sirs. Down Haiti way and over to New Orleans they say the white folks fears Obeah near as much as the nigger folk."

Someone in the crowd laughed and said, "Hell, those Papist French think they've eaten Christ's flesh and drunk His blood. Besides, the Creoles are half nigger themselves. No doubt you could, um, juju a rum-soaked French planter, but I for one say it's a lot of nigger nonsense!"

There was a murmur of agreement, but Margolis held up a hand for silence and pontificated, "It's not the question of whether juju *works* that we have before us, gentlemen. It's the matter of *intent*. I can tell you from sad personal experience that some of the free Negro women have been attempting to corrupt our own womenfolk with, um, what would you describe it as, Mister Jackson?"

Jeaco made his voice the voice of doom as he answered, "Juju, Vou-Doun, Obeah, Macambo, Mumbo Jumbo—it's all the same, gen'mens. The black folk from different tribes calls it by a hundred names. You white folks calls it witch-craft."

"And what about those drums they play all Saturday night?"

Jeaco hesitated, for he enjoyed the all-night festivals himself, and a gentleman of color did right well at a fertility rite, did he come with a jug of corn liquor and a brace of roasting hens.

Jeaco licked his lips and explained, "Some of the tappin's

just dance drummin'. Sometimes the bucks beat out the call of their nation drums. It's mostly in fun, over here in Georgia."

"We don't understand. Explain these so-called nation drums."

"Well, sirs, it's like say an Ibo wants to taunt some old boy from another tribe. He starts to tap out an Ibo war beat as a mock invite to a set-to. Only since they ain't allowed to fight over here, some Yoruba's likely to tap out something like, 'I can whup yo' ass and have yo' mama, too!' "

The worried Planter Nolan frowned and asked, "Do you mean our niggers can actually *talk* to one another on those drums?"

Jeaco's face went impassive as he realized he'd given away a secret. He'd assumed, hitherto, that the whites knew about drum talk. Could they really be that ignorant? It explained a thing that had puzzled him in the past when, on occasion, a distant drum had tapped out something like, 'New overseer at the Coleman Plantation likes to bugger young boys' or, 'Beware the white woman visiting the Palmers. She tells lies to get people whipped.' "

Grinning, Jeaco said, "It ain't exactly *talk*, sir. The drumbeats sort of . . . ah . . . they works like the militia bugle calls. That's it. They can lick out things like charge, retreat, assemble, and so on."

"Indeed?" Lawyer Margolis, who knew a bit about keeping some few secrets from the ethnic majority himself, frowned. "How, then, does one nigger tell another he's going to, um, have his mama?"

"It's just funnin', sir. Since I been here in Georgia I can't say as I's heard the Macambo beat or the rally taps of the Leopard Society. It's the womenfolks as plays at witchcraft, sirs."

"Leopard Society?" Margolis, who was really much better at cross-examination than the worried Jeaco had expected him to be, frowned again.

Jeaco started to lie, for there were secrets of his own race he wanted to keep to himself—not out of loyalty, but simply because it made his own position as informer and slave catcher more important to the fishbelly-faces if they remained in ignorance.

But Jeaco's nerve was wavering now as he found a score of white men staring at him, cold eyes unblinking. He smiled. What did it matter? He'd gone over to them, hadn't he? He took a deep breath and simply blurted, "It's a secret society that crosses all the tribal lines, gen'mens. You see, there's things a man goes to his chief about, like a man from the Fanti stealin' his yams or a Kru-man carryin' off one of his wives."

"We know about your endless tribal wars. Get to this Leopard Society nonsense."

"Well, gen'mens, the Leopard Men is picked from young warriors who has good reputations as men who knows what's right and fittin'."

"You mean they're versed in tribal laws and traditions?"

"Yes sir. Sometimes there's men who don't do right. They mess with other men's womenfolk when there ain't no war declared, or they beats a woman whose family is still fond of her, or they don't feed their pickaninnies enough and folks in their village start to whisper about 'em."

"Tackmen!" Rory suddenly blurted, from where he'd been half listening in his corner.

Margolis blinked and asked, "You know about this Leopard Society, Colonel Martin?"

Rory nodded and said, "Ay, they were called tackmen in the Highlands. They collected the tax for the King and the rent for the lairds, and, sometimes, when a crofter began to behave like an unworthy clansman, the tackmen came calling of a dark night."

"I thought the Highland chiefs had absolute powers."

"Och, there's things no chief could do to any clansman, however evil he'd become, for the chief is more than a land-laird, you ken. As head of the clan, and clan means children, the *Can-tighearna* was more like our father. A father can punish an unruly child. Driven far enough, a father can strike down a disobedient son. But what father has ever flayed a son alive, or nailed him, castrated, to the wall of a kirk?"

There was a horrified murmur and Margolis gasped, "Good God, is that what tackmen are sent to do?"

"Not often, but the auld stories keep people's minds on their auld virtues. Most of you here will remember how, after the '45, the Whigs put a price on Prince Charlie's head. It was a thousand pounds sterling, as I remember. A great fortune to any man, and beyond the dreams of any Highland crofter, to say nothing of the gillies and beggars who had to know where Charlie was hiding."

Captain Fenwyk chimed in, "The blighter got away, didn't he?" and Rory said, "Ay, after hiding for over a year in the Highlands with a Sassunach army searching under every heather bush for him. A man named MacPhie was known to have seen him, and he died with his lips sealed under the executioner's tortures. The Clan MacLeod hadn't even come out for the Stuarts, but a MacLeod boatman ferried Flora MacDonald and Prince Charlie over the sea to Skye, and the MacLeods and MacDonalds were enemies. Another MacLeod, a lass named Jeanie, was beaten, raped, and walled alive under a stone bridge to stay there, starving, with the traffic rumbling over her head because it was thought she could tell Cumberland where Charlie was hiding. Cluny MacPherson had sheltered him for a time in a cave and knew he'd escaped to Skye, but though they cut him open and slowly drew out his liver and lights, Cluny Calma spit in their faces and died with the secret sealed behind his smiling bloody lips. Not one Highlander of any station ever betrayed the hidden prince, though hundreds knew where he was and all of them were poor."

Margolis sniffed and said, "Very noble of them, I'll allow, but we were discussing this Leopard Society of the niggers'."

"Ay, that's why I mind it's like the tackmen. For I'll allow my people were no angels, and a hundred pounds sterling would tempt a saint. They acted from more than loyalty to the wee fool who'd run away at Culloden when his betters died like the men they were."

"You mean these, um, tackmen would have punished anyone who betrayed their so-called prince?"

"I mean they'd have been visited for violating the Highland law of hospitality. Charlie was a beaten man and a weakling and a', but he'd asked shelter and been granted it. That was what counted. They tell a tale of a clansman once who, discovering an overnight guest was connected with an enemy clan, murdered him in his bed."

"By George, I'll bet it was Macbeth!"

"No, though Macbeth's murder of Duncan under his own roof is what turned every Scot's hand against him. The man I'm speaking of was less fortunate than the False Macbeth. The tackmen of his own clan peeled him, an inch at a time, and sent his cock and balls to the enemy chief with an apology."

There were murmurs of protest in the crowded room

and Jeaco smiled and said, "Do Jesus, that sounds like Leopard Men, all right!"

A worried hum filled the room as another planter asked the informer, "Is that what this Leopard Society's about? You have to give us their names, Mr. Jackson. A thing like this has to be struck down root, branch, and limb. I'll not have my darkies terrorized by . . . um, what do these Leopard Men look like?"

"Nobody knows for sure, sir. They say they comes in masks and cloaks of leopard hide, with steel claws strapped to they hands, but to tell the truth, nobody has a lot to say when they been by. The folks they visits is left dead and tore up fierce."

Another murmur filled the room and a man on the far side of Rory said, "I had no idea the niggers were still mucking about with such dangerous notions. I confess my eldest daughter bought a fetish from an old nigger woman in the market, but she did it as a lark."

Other men had suddenly ominous thoughts about the love potions and lucky charms their bored womenfolk had bought from the Obeah mammies, and a young macaroon suddenly stared down, with an uneasy dawning wonder, at the grinning Negro face carved on his walking-stick handle. Those inlaid soup-bone teeth were devilishly pointed little things. He ran a thumb over the fangs of Mumbo Jumbo and wondered if he'd ever scratched his skin slightly while gesturing with the ugly thing. Then he laughed softly, for it was rather intriguing to own something that might have unsuspected evil powers. He already knew the interesting story he'd have to tell the next time someone asked him where he'd ever gotten such a monstrous thing.

Jeaco promised that he and his spies would try to make a list of suspected Leopard Men, and the conversation got back to what was to be done about the Negro freemen, be they witch doctors or simply jumped-up coons. Planter Nolan said, "I don't see what further laws we could present to the royal governor. They're forbidden to vote, even if they own land. They're not allowed to marry Indians or whites, and they can neither sue us nor bear witness against us. Save that they own their own labor, I fail to see how they're much different from our slaves."

Rory said, "I tend to agree. We can send them all back to Africa, banish them to other colonies, or simply revoke their manumissions and sell 'em to the highest bidder if you gentlemen are afraid to accept the status quo."

Margolis said, " 'Pon my word, that's a rather raw suggestion, Colonel Martin."

"Och, if you want a raw one, what do you all say we just slit their throats and have done with it!"

To the horror of the decent men in the room, more than one planter present shouted, "I second the motion!"

Margolis laughed nervously and said, "I presume the colonel uses the Jesuit method of devil's advocate to make his point. I daresay no man here really subscribes to jungle law!"

The merchant who'd seconded Rory's final solution asked, "Why not? They came from a jungle, didn't they?"

Jeaco Jackson edged toward Lawyer Margolis, suddenly very aware of his dark complexion and most uncomfortable in his fine satin suit. The sky-blue silk had cost a small fortune, but somehow Jeaco knew his finery hadn't helped a bit; more than one man present would still swat him like a fly if they caught him looking at a barefoot white-trash gal. It was hard to keep your head above water in this cruel white world.

Margolis was saying, "Now, now, we must remember we're all bound by English Common Law. A signed contract is a signed contract. I'd be very much opposed to negating any man's papers of manumission."

"Why, are you a nigger lover?" someone shouted, and the lawyer snapped, "No, I'm a man who believes in a gentleman's signed word! How many of you here hold IOU's signed by English merchants you'd not recognize if you found them in bed with your wives? What about the deeds to your lands? I warn you, gentlemen, all of us *live* on the sanctity of a written agreement."

"Ay, but a contract with a nigger?"

"A contract with the devil himself, sir! Let one man say, 'Oh, it's only a scrap of paper,' and, I warn you, every deed, mortgage, bill of lading, and the very ownership of your servants and livestock are in peril."

Margolis paused for effect before he added, "Your very marriage contracts are no more than signed and sealed legal documents. Start tearing up any such contracts and there'd be nothing to stop any man from violating your very wives!"

A planter laughed uncertainly and shouted, "By God, I'd kill them both!"

Margolis smiled thinly and asked, "Suppose he killed you first, in self-defense? It wouldn't be murder, you know. Void your legal contract with your wife and it's simply a matter of the stronger rutting with the weaker and every man for himself."

Rory was bored with the pointless discussion. He raised his voice above the roar of outraged husbands and shouted, "Och, we're all blathering like a bunch of washerwomen this night! I say we leave the free niggers alone for now and have a round of drinks."

Captain Fenwyk jumped up and shouted, "I second the motion, and the drinks are on the house!"

It was good to know Rose's husband was anxious to heal the old quarrel, thought Rory. Better to have a ready fighter with you than against you, and apparently the disgraced officer felt the same. Rose had married a man of more common sense than he'd been given credit for.

Their host went to the door and shouted something out into the taproom as the others droned on, more softly, about Jackson's infernal secret societies. Rory had attended some of the Macambo dances out behind the quarters at Indigo Hall. They were harmless enough in his eyes. They allowed the slaves to work off their frustrations, and while he'd watched from a dignified distance, more than once he'd noticed an intriguing wiggle on a nice black ass he'd not seen fit to dally with before.

Rory rubbed his tight-crotched breeches thoughtfully as he remembered that new doe from Maryland. She had a face like a frog and the shift she wore did nothing for her figure, but the other night, stripped down to an apron of fringed bark, and with her body oiled with sweat in the firelight as the drums directed her dancing feet. . . .

A small, frightened voice said, "Your punch, sir?" and Rory turned to stare down into the eyes of his daughter. They were gray, for God's sake, and there was something in the bones of her yellow face that reminded him of a toil-worn crofter woman in long-ago Lochaber. Stiffly Rory took the rum punch from the tray the child held out to him and, smiling with numb lips, he asked, "What's your name, lass?"

"Please, sir, my name is Jezebel. They calls me Jezzie."

And then she moved on with her tray of drinks, to serve

the others as she'd been ordered. Rory watched, the pewter punch cup clenched in his fist, as the first-born of his loins moved quietly through the crowd. Jezzie came to Jeaco Jackson and, uncertain of his status among the white men, simply held the tray in silence and waited for the man to make the next move.

Jeaco took a cup and said, "Do Jesus, chile, you gettin' big enough for a man to look at. How old you is now, Jezzie?"

"Twelve, sir," the girl said, edging back from the grinning toady. Jeaco laughed and said, "You got nice bitty tits fo' twelve, girl. You been broke in yet?"

Rory suddenly found himself roaring, "Hey, nigger! Leave the lass alone!" Then, aware of the others turning to stare, he quickly added, "She's got drinks to serve your betters, boy!"

Another planter jeered, "They don't service niggers here, Jackson." and the informer retreated to a corner, burning with humiliation and hate, but still smiling so hard his cheeks were hurting.

Another man, privileged by his more fortunate pigmentation, cast a thoughtful glance at the little barmaid and mused, " 'Pon my word, she is a pretty child. I wonder what Rose would ask for a night with her. God strike me, I'd swear she was a virgin, from her manner."

Rory made his way over to Captain Fenwyk and murmured, "How much do you want for that wench, Captain?"

Fenwyk blinked and said, "Oh, I suppose we could make it easy on your purse, Colonel. You'd have the privilege of deflowering her, but for——"

"Damn it, I don't want to bed her, I want to *buy* her!"

"You mean, outright?"

"Yes. My eldest daughter's bodyservant is a lazy, unruly Negress and I've been meaning to send her back to the quarters. Your Jezebel's not much older than my Flora, and she seems a quiet, obedient child. I'll give you fifty guineas for her. My daughter's birthday is coming on and I'd like to surprise her."

"Hmm. I don't know, sir. My wife seems to think we have a potential gold mine in Jezzie. That's why she's spoiled her a bit, I'd say."

"Seventy-five. My final offer, sir."

"Oh, well, I doubt Rose would let her go for less than a hundred."

"Done. Put it on my account and I'll take the Negress home with me now."

"We have papers to sign, sir."

"Have Margolis draw them up and send the bill of sale to Indigo Hall. I know you're a man I can trust, Captain Fenwyk."

Pleased at the compliment, Fenwyk grinned and called the slave girl over, pointing at Rory with his chin as he told Jezebel, "Colonel Martin just bought you, lass. You're to go with him and behave yourself as an obedient nigger, hear?"

The child stared at her father in fear and wonder as Rory pointed at the door and said, "My horse is waiting outside. Do you have any belongings to pack, girl?"

Jezebel stared down at the floor and murmured, "No sir, I don't have nothin'. I had me a cornhusk dolly once, but some chillun took it."

"Good. Follow me, then. My regards to your wife, Captain Fenwyk. I'll expect this one's deed by the end of the week."

He walked out through the dark, deserted taproom, aware of the frightened girl at his heels. They got outside and a Negro groom jumped up from where he'd been sitting on the stone step to untie the colonel's horse. The groom wondered what Jezzie was doing with the big white man, but he didn't ask either of them anything.

Rory took the reins and put a hand on the pommel as he turned to ask the little mulatto, "Hast ridden pillion before, lass?"

"Please, sir, I ain't never been on no horse."

Rory said, "I'll put you up, then," and reached down to put a hand on either of the girl's young hips. She flinched at his touch and a queer thrill ran up his arms as he lifted her, easily, to deposit her, seated sideways just behind his saddle's cantle. He climbed on awkwardly. The chestnut shied at its master's unaccustomed clumsiness, and Jezebel whimpered in fear as she threw both arms around Rory's waist. He steadied the horse and soothed, "Just hold on, if you like. I promise I won't let him throw you, lass."

They started homeward through the moonlight, the horse at a pacing walk instead of Rory's usual canter, and, after a time, Jezebel opened her eyes and marveled at how high above the shell road they were. Screwing up her courage, she asked, "Please, sir, where is we going?"

"Indigo Hall," said Rory stiffly. He already regretted his hasty decision. How in God's name was he going to keep this fool child and the other niggers from talking, and, Jesus, what if they let something slip in front of Martha or the children?

Cautiously he asked the girl behind him, "Do you know about Indigo Hall, Jezzie?"

"Yes sir, my mama tole me it was where you lived, Colonel Martin."

"Oh? And what else did she say about me? I want the truth, now, girl."

Innocently the child answered, "She said you was my papa, sir. She said that was why I wasn't as black as the others."

Rory rode a long time in silence before he said, "You mustn't say such things, lass."

"I know, sir. Mama said it was a secret."

"Ay, it is that. How many people know our secret, Jezzie?"

"Just me and Mama, sir, and Mama's daid. She said a secret was a thing you never told nobody, but I allowed as you knowed, so my tellin' you don't count, does it, sir?"

"No, I knew about it, Jezzie, but, you see, you're never to tell another living soul. Do you understand?"

"Yes sir. Mama allowed your white lady might git cross did she know 'bout Mama an' me. I reckon I'll never tell her, huh?"

"Och, you're a fine bright lass, Jezzie, but I don't like the name they gave you all that much. How would you like to be called Jeanie-Calma? That means Brave Jeanie. Are you a brave lass, Jeanie-Calma?"

"Please, sir, I'm mostly afeared."

"Are you frightened now?"

"No sir. You said you wouldn't drop me. Dast I ask why you're carryin' me to Indigo Hall, sir?"

"You're to be the playmate and bodyservant to my daughter, Miss Flora. Do you ken what a bodyservant is, Jeanie?"

"Yes sir. A nigger who only has to fetch and carry for one white person, sort of like they was a pet. Do I git to be my sister's pet, Colonel Martin?"

"Miss Flora is not your sister. She's white. You're never to tell her our little secret. Do you understand?"

"Yes, Colonel, I 'spect I does."

"Good. I'll tell you another secret, Jeanie. I knew, when I met your eyes back there at the tavern, that you were a bright lass with more than your share of the Hound's blood in you. I'd have never done this mad thing had not I thought, nay, *known* you'd be able to hold your tongue. You see, your mother and I—"

"Please, sir, is I part *dog*, too?"

"What?"

"I asked was I part dog? I knowed I was part nigger an' part white, but Mama never tole me about the dog part. You allowed I had hound's blood and—"

Rory threw back his head and laughed. Then he explained to the worried child, "It's not a real hound I was speaking of, lass. You see, on my side, we were called the Sons of the Hound, back in the Old Country."

"You mean you was in sumpin like the Leopard Society, sir? Mama said I had an uncle in the Leopard Society one time, but the Slattee kilt him. Did you-all have Leopard Men where the white folks come from, Colonel?"

"No, but I know a man who calls himself a Cat."

The rest of the ride to Indigo Hall was spent in explaining her secret heritage to Jeanie-Calma, though she hardly grasped much of it except that Clan Campbell were a lot like Slattee. Rory knew he was talking to himself and the moon as he recounted the old legends and grudges of the Great Glen, but he had to say something, and no man could take a half-breed child in his arms and sob, "Forgive me, daughter and kinswoman, for the terrible things I've done!"

By the time they rode slowly up the avenue of young live oaks leading to Indigo Hall, his unrecognized child had started to doze off and he'd lifted her around into his lap to hold her with her unwelcomely woolly head against his chest.

A door-nigger spotted them from the veranda and ran inside, calling out that the master was home from the meeting.

Rory reined in and said softly, "Wake up, lass, we're home."

Then he rode up to the front steps, tossed a bridle rein to the waiting groom, and lowered the child to the ground before dismounting. He took Jeanie-Calma by the upper arm as the young mulatto blinked up at the imposing candlelit entrance of Indigo Hall. As they mounted the steps together, the big white door opened and a white woman in a glorious gown came out to stare down at the nervous slave girl and ask; "My goodness, what have we here?"

Rory asked, "Is Flora still awake? I have a birthday present for her."

A few nights later, the nation drums were beating over on the Paradeen holding as Coffee Pardus finished the artistic creation he'd been working on in secrecy behind the barred door of his tool shed. The glow from his penny candle was feeble, but Coffee worked largely by feel, and it wasn't as if the things he'd made had to pass inspection by any eyes but a white man's. He bundled up his handiwork in a burlap sack just as someone tapped on the door. He wrapped the burlap in a length of rawhide thong and asked, "Who is it?"

His wife, Fiba, answered, "Mr. Jackson's about. I told him he was to tend you in the smithy, like you said."

Coffee got up and opened the door, asking, "Did Jeaco come alone?"

Fiba shook her head and said, "He carried that bad boy, Quaco, along wif him. They's both waitin' in the smithy for you."

"You put the children to bed like I told you?"

"Course I did. What's this all about, old man?"

"It's man talk, woman. You just go along and make sure the children don't stir from their pallets, hear?"

"You goin' over to that Macambo rite at the Paradeen place?"

"Shoot, woman, did I ever mess 'round with them dancing Obeah gals when I had enough woman right here?"

Fiba smiled, pleased at his all-too-rare tenderness, but insisted, "You be careful, hear?" as she went back to the cabin to keep the children out of their father's business with Mr. Jackson, whatever it might be.

Coffee went to his darkened smithy. He lit a dim rushlight stuck in the dead coals of the forge as he nodded to Jeaco and his bodyguard and placed the bundle on the brick rim of the boxlike soaking pit. Jeaco asked, "Did you git the silver I ast, Ashanti?" and Coffee said, "I got some; it's hid out back. You drive a hard bargain for a man with no more than a fairy tale to tell, Jeaco."

"Yeah, well, the white folks believes what I tells 'em, and

you drove a hard bargain up my ass one time, you horny
Ashanti bastard!"

"Is that why you've accused me of being a Leopard
Man, then? I didn't think you reckoned me for a rich
man."

"You rich enough, boy. I know you just got paid fo' that
gate grille over to the Coleman place. You gonna pay me fo'
the times you fucked me in my ass, Coffee. You gonna pay
me from now on, or I'll tell the white folks 'bout you!"

"Shoot, they ain't nothin' to tell, boy!"

"It's Mr. Jackson to you, nigger, and I got the white
folks pissin' they breeches 'bout the Leopard Society. Ain't
that right, Quaco?"

The bodyguard laughed and said, "That's right. Old
white boys been told 'bout them steel claws the Leopard
Society uses, and you is a blacksmith, too."

Jeaco laughed and asked, "How many leopard claws you
made so far, Coffee?"

Coffee's eyes were unreadable in the darkness as he
laughed and said, "Shoot, no more than a couple of pairs
or so."

"Yeah, well, I don't need to prove it, does I tell the
white folks I seen you out here wif the others on my list."

"You got others paying for this story, too? My, my, you
really are one bad nigger, Jeaco! You know there ain't no
Leopard Man in Georgia, don't you?"

"Just give me the money and maybe, this time, I won't
ask to shove my dick up yo' ass. That's sumpin else we
gonna talk about, nigger, some time when I ain't wearin'
my best breeches."

Coffee gave a defeated sigh and said, "I got the money
hid out back. White trash comes by here sometimes as ugly
as you two."

He didn't ask, but, as he'd hoped, the two blackmailers
followed him out behind the smithy and away from the
small cluster of log structures near the road. Jeaco tripped
over a root and complained, "Where you carryin' us, nigger? How come you keeps yo' silver so far out here in the
fields?"

"I told you. The pony boys are bad as you, and it ain't
like I can get a hearing at the mansion, does a white man
rob me."

"Well, where the hell it at, nigger?"

Coffee bent over, picked up an object he'd left ahead of

time in the rank weeds, and stood up, smiling grimly, as he replied, "It's right here, *N'Fisi!*" as the terrible blade of an Ashanti *panga* swung silver in the moonlight.

He'd aimed his first blow at the bodyguard, knowing he could get Jeaco at his leisure once the more dangerous fighter was out of the way. It was well he did so, for the night erupted in flame as Quaco fired from the hip with his illegal and concealed pistol. Something burned into Coffee's inside as the *panga* blade tinged through flesh and bone, beheading the man who'd shot him. Coffee hissed, "*Skee!*" as he swung at Jeaco and almost missed.

The blackmailer had started to run for it the moment he'd seen the awful sword blade, but the tip caught him across the back of the neck, severing the spinal cord and dropping the informer dead in his tracks.

Coffee staggered a few steps, gripping his injured side as blood oozed between his fingers. Then he took a deep breath and straightened proudly. An Ashanti warrior still on his feet was still, by God, a warrior.

Discarding the bloody *panga,* Coffee walked slowly back to the smithy, favoring his wounded side, and got the bundle he'd made up in advance. He carried it back to the field where he'd left the two dead men and, working with blood-slicked hands, stripped them and dressed both naked bodies in the leopard robes he'd made of deer skins spotted with lamp-black paint. He lashed the steel claws he'd made to their dead hands, the hardwood grips bound to their palms, the cruel curved blades jutting a full six inches between the fingers of their clenched fists. He dabbed blood from his own wound over each blade as a final artistic touch. Then he picked up the *panga* again and hacked them until it might look as if they'd died in their society robes.

Satisfied for the moment, Coffee put their clothes in the burlap sack, leaving the pistol where it was near the dead Quaco. He walked back to the smithy, lit the charcoal, and began to fan the flames under the burlap sack as he listened to the distant nation drums. The pistol shot had gone unnoticed over at the Saturday night festival. That was good. Everything was going according to plan.

A voice behind him asked, "What are you doin', Pa?" and Coffee said, without turning, "You go back to bed, Juba. I don't mean to say it again."

"I heard a gunshot, Pa. I heard a gunshot and, do Jesus, you're bleeding!"

Coffee grunted and said, "Come here and pump the bellows, son. Is your ma and the other children in the cabin like I told them?"

"Yes, Pa. You're bleedin' *bad*!"

"Take holt the bellows, then, and *help* me, boy!"

He waited until his son was fanning the forge white-hot under the giveaway clothes before he asked, "You mind, when you was little, how I used to tell you stories 'bout the way things was in Africa?"

"Sure, Pa. But you said them days was over and done wif forever."

"I know what I said, boy. Listen to me—you're half Ashanti. Your granddaddy was a Stooled One of Kumasi. I'm callin' on you now not as my pickaninny, but as one Ashanti *man* to another! You mind what I'm sayin', Juba?"

"Yes sir. You want me to burn these rags and jest *hesh*!"

"That's right, my son. When you've reduced them to ashes, I want you to go back to the others and keep them quiet. I want your word, as a man, you'll swear I was here all evening until I went out a short while, about an hour from now. You got that, Juba?"

"I swear by Mumbo Jumbo."

"That's a Congo god, Juba. You swear by the Golden Stool, hear?"

"Yes, Father, by the Golden Stool of our nation, I swear!"

Coffee suddenly grabbed his son and hugged him. Then he stepped away and murmured, "Get rid of that shirt. I got blood on it. If your ma asks what we're doin', tell her it's men's business and, does she ask again, give her a lick so's she'll know what we mean."

"Where you goin', Pa?"

"It's best you don't know. Farewell, Ashanti!"

And then Coffee was walking, walking through the moonlight and, Jesus, it was a long walk to the Paradeen place for a man with a pistol ball in his side.

He'd meant it when he'd told Beelzebub the matter of the brutal overseer was not his quarrel, but the white folk needed to be dazzled with rage when he told them his story, and besides, it would do no harm to kill two lions with one spear.

He reached the Paradeen Plantation and circled through the shadows until he found a Negro relieving himself away from the fire. He hissed and the man came over, smiling in recognition, and asked, "Hey, you come to jine the dancin', Coffee?"

Then he saw the dark stain running down the Ashanti's white pants, and his face went wooden as he waited, in silence, to be told what was happening. Coffee said, "Your woman is Obeah, isn't she, Cudjo?"

"Sure. You want a poltice for that hurt, brother?"

"No. It's just a scratch. I want you to do two things for me, though. First, I want you to get to the other family leaders and tell them to keep the drums beating and the young folk dancing no matter what they may hear. Where are the white men right now?"

"In the big house, yonder, drunk. They made some gals pleasure them earlier, but the gals slipped out to jine the Macambo when the fishbellies dozed off."

"Good. The second thing I want you to remember is that you never saw me and you don't know a thing about what's happened here this night. Jeaco's told the white folk a story, but none of you ever heard of the Leopard Society before. You understand, Cudjo?"

The other man gasped and stared down at the small bundle in the wounded man's free hand, asking, "Does the Leopard walk this night?"

"You just go on back to the fire and remember you don't know a thing. I want you to go *now*, Cudjo. And remember, I want everyone to have a fine time around the fire, hear?"

The other nodded and slipped away in silence. Coffee untied the bag and took out the gleaming steel claws he'd made from an old wagon spring. He had no need of the silly costume, and this pair of claws would be discarded when he was finished. The ones he'd left on the dead men would be assumed to have done their deadly work, though, in truth, they'd been hastily tempered in the oil trough.

Coffee went to the big house he'd built for the late Isaac Pardus and disrobed in a shadowed nook he knew from having notched its very logs. Naked, he slipped on the claws and went to a side door he knew was seldom used. It was locked, of course, but a curved steel blade made short work of the wooden latch he'd made for it, and the door opened silently as he slipped in, trailing blood with every step.

He found the younger brother sprawled on the bed in Miss Sarah's small room. The man was as naked as Coffee, and the Ashanti grimaced in distaste at the sight of his liquor-sodden body. Moving on the balls of his bare feet, Coffee went over to the bed and slashed the sleeping man across the throat, vaguely surprised at the jets of blood that spurted halfway to the ceiling before splashing down to cover the convulsed chest with a sheet of gore. Coffee ran the claws down the heaving abdomen as his victim gargled in his own blood. The four claws ripped the dying man's belly to sliced white tripe before he twisted them skillfully and ripped the genitals from the quivering groin.

Seamus Corrigan, attracted by the sounds in the next room, appeared in the doorway to ask blearily, "What's the matter? Are you sick, Sean?"

Then he saw the bloody black apparition looming over the mangled remains on the crimson sheets and screamed at the top of his lungs, "Jesus, Mary, and Joseph, it's the Boogie Man in the flesh!"

The black and crimson nightmare came at him, grinning like the devil incarnate and raising those awful claws. Seamus turned and ran as hard and as far as he could, crashing into the far door of the master bedroom with his naked chest and gibbering, "Help me! Mother of God, somebody help me!" as he fumbled at the door latch with hysterical fingers.

Four awful blades raked down his naked back as the overseer screamed in animal pain. Out by the fire, nearer the quarters, a dancing girl faltered in her step to the drums and asked, "Jesus! What was that?"

An older woman said, "You jest keep dancing, girl. You never heard nothin', you unnerstan'?"

The drum beat quickened in tempo as another elder shouted, "Hit the Yoruba taunt, Simbo! Maybe we can get us a drum fight goin' with Oakwall Plantation!"

The big log drum began to tap out, "Hey, I'm a mighty Yoruba spear man. All Ibo sleep with their mothers and the Fanti all eat shit!"

Somewhere in the night someone, or something, screamed like a woman dying in labor, but the grinning slaves around the Macambo fire clapped their hands and pretended not to hear. After a while, a distant water-drum growled, "Listen, everyone, Yoruba are only children who boast like the buzzing of a dung-eating fly in the ear of a mighty Ibo elephant! No Yoruba born of woman knows who the Ibo sleep with, for they vomit with fear when they

know they they have strayed within the sound of our
drums. Perhaps they heard such a lie from their own sisters
the last time they slept with them. For, truly, we admit the
Yoruba are not mother-fuckers. Their mothers are too
ugly."

The fun lasted all that night. None of the Paradeen
slaves saw fit to go over to the big house. What happened
in the big house was no nigger's affair.

A teamster whom Juba stopped on the road the next
morning carried into Savannah Coffee's tale of having
been attacked by Leopard Men. A posse rode out, stopping
first to see if the Corrigan brothers were all right. By the
time Coffee showed them the two still forms in mock leopard masks and robes, the white men were in an ugly mood.
They dragged the bodies behind their horses all the way
back to town, and the two litches hung on the waterfront
gallows bore little resemblance to human beings.

Jeaco and his sidekick had been identified, however, and
the heathen robes and murderous claws were used as evi-
dence in the trial that sentenced the informer's entire gang
to death by hanging.

Judge Crawford asked Rubin Margolis to defend them,
but the lawyer declined, saying he'd never trusted any of
Jackson's niggers in the first place.

SEVEN

It was a hot day, and Locky and Simon Martin were cooling off by dipping naked in a cove of the tidal creek. Their two bodyservants, General Wade and False Argyll, were watching wistfully from the reeds of the bank where they guarded their young masters' clothes. The air was warm, but the water was cold, so, after a time, the white boys crawled up on the flattened reeds to sun their goosebumps away. Locky pointed at his younger brother's penis and laughed, "Och, you've got a hard-on, Simon!"

Simon covered his lap with his hands and said, "Have not. It's cold from the water I am."

His older sibling laughed and said, "Shit, you wouldn't know what to do with a hard-on in any case. Do you know how to jack off, wee brother?"

Simon shook his head and asked, "What's jacking off?"

Locky laughed. "Well, for one thing, it purely beats pissing." He turned to one of the bodyservant boys and said, "Show Marse Simon how you jack off, General Wade."

General Wade looked uncertain, and Locky's voice took on an edge as he asked, "Didn't you hear me, coon? Open up them pants and beat your meat like I told you, hear?"

General Wade smiled sheepishy and opened the front flap of his knee breeches, pulling out his penis to fumble with it uncertainly. The two white boys watched in critical detachment until Simon said, "That's silly. What's supposed to happen?"

Locky said, "He can't show it hard. What's the matter, General Wade? You bashful or sumpin'?"

"Please, Marse Locky, I feel funny doin' this wif you-all watchin' me."

Locky turned to the other slave boy and ordered, "False Argyll, you'd best suck General Wade's peter till it rises. I want to show my little brother how a nigger comes."

False Argyll looked astounded. Then he whimpered, "Please, Marse Locky, don't make me do a thing like that!"

"What's the matter? You too proud to suck a nigger prick?"

"Please, sir, I jest can't."

Locky lay back on the reeds, stroking his own faint new pubic hairs, and said, "All right, you can come over here and suck *mine,* then."

"Aw, come on, Marse Locky."

"You want me to whup you again, nigger?"

"Please, Marse Locky, I *cain't* do that!"

"Sure you can—lest you want me to whup your black ass again!"

Simon made a wry face and said, "Leave him be, Locky. I don't see what all the fuss is about. I'll be damned if *I'd* take your old peter in *my* mouth!"

"Shoot, you're my brother. Besides, you still don't know what your pecker's good for." He flipped his own semi-erect penis and insisted, "Crawl over here and do it, False Argyll. Do I have to get up to *make* you, boy, you're purely gonna regret it!"

False Argyll was crying now, but he gingerly crawled over on his hands and knees, sobbing, "Please don't make me, Marse Locky. I swear I'm gonna puke, do you make me take it in my mouf!"

Locky said, "You puke on me and I'll learn you how nigger graveyards got started, boy!" Then he reached out, grabbed a handful of the young Negro's hair, and forced the boy's face down, hissing, "*Suck* it, damn you!"

False Argyll kissed the half-erect penis, retched, and then, as Locky twisted his hair, sobbed, "Don' hurt me!" and suddenly opened his mouth to receive his master's upthrust cock. Locky moved his head up and down, hissing, "That's it, you ever-lovin' black cocksucker. That's the way I like it. You stop and I'll whup you, hear?"

Simon and General Wade watched, revolted and fascinated at the same time. Locky grinned, breathing hard through his clenched teeth, and suggested, "Come over here and pull down his breeches, little brother. You can fuck him in the ass while I come in his mouth."

"You *crazy,* Locky? You think I'd put my peter in a shitty old asshole?"

Locky said, "You show him, General Wade. Come over here and show Marse Simon how to bugger!"

General Wade hesitated; then he grinned, got to his feet, and kicked off his breeches as False Argyll blubbered, his mouth filled with his master's flesh, "You jest leave my behind alone, General Wade!"

General Wade came over and unbuckled the other slave's breeches as False Argyll struggled to raise his head. Still holding him by the hair, Locky slammed a hard young fist against the side of his head and hissed, "You stop that, nigger! You just keep sucking like I told you!"

General Wade had the gagging boy's brown buttocks exposed now, but, as he tried to get into position the way he'd seen the dogs do it, he simply couldn't force his way in.

Locky raised False Argyll's head by its hair and told the other young bully, "You take my place, General Wade. I'll let him suck you whilst I cornhole him."

False Argyll was weeping now and pleading to be let alone. Unobserved by the others, Simon had found his clothes and started to dress. When Locky finally noticed that his little brother was buttoning his shirt, he asked, "Where you goin', Simon? Don't you want to come in this bitty black girl-baby?"

Simon said, "You three play that way all you like. I'm goin' back to the house."

"Hey, come on, I still ain't taught you to jack off!"

"You just jack your ownself off, Locky. I'd as leave eat shit."

Simon walked back toward the house, scuffing the ground with his silver-buckled shoes and frowning down at his own shadow as it preceded him up the slope. His big brother's obsessive bullying was beyond his understanding. Young Simon didn't know it, but he'd been born with his father's calm detachment in the face of possible danger; this was tempered by his mother's more generous disposition.

To Simon, an immediate threat was a problem to be dealt with promptly. Take that bully Nelson, who'd picked a fistfight at the Sunday-Go-to-Meeting-on-the-Green. A simple punch in the nose had discouraged Nelson's aggressive tendencies and, today, they were friends again. Simon couldn't understand why Locky was so anxious to avoid his own inevitable showdown with George Margolis. Sooner or later the two of them had to fight. Locky had passed that remark about the Margolis boy's religion, and it seemed only fair to answer George's offer to fight. Simon couldn't understand why his brother had hit False Argyll instead, or why he still avoided the pudgy George.

Simon's train of thought was interrupted by a low, dry buzzing sound and the boy froze in his tracks, searching the weeds on either side of the narrow foot-worn path between the swimming hole and the house. He spotted the mottled brown coil a few yards ahead and to his left, and slowly stepped back a pace, sweeping the summer-browned weeds with his eyes for a handy stick. The snake drummed its tail again as it rolled its coils sideways, its beady eyes unwinking as it kept its hissing little maw and flicking tongue pointed at the boy's vaguely comprehended form. Simon found an old sun-bleached pine branch with a nice solid knot on its thicker end and stooped down to grasp it, murmuring, "I'm sorry, Br'er Diamondback, but you're hunting your rats too close to the house, and I've a little sister who gets into everything hereabouts."

Simon advanced on the coiled serpent, unconscious of his own cool young courage, for, though Locky and the nigger boys screamed and carried on when they saw snakes, Simon attributed it to some obscure attempt at humor. Uncle Albion, from the quarters, had explained snakes' behavior to both of them last summer, and Simon knew he was much bigger than the buzzing reptile.

He raised the club, edging close enough to lash down without getting one of his stocking-covered shins within the snake's striking range. Then, as he got a better look at his intended victim, Simon laughed and lowered the pine knot to his side, saying, "Do Jesus, Mister *Rat* Snake, you're going to get your ownself *kilt*, buzzin' your fool tail in the weeds like that!"

Thanks to Uncle Albion, he knew now that the ugly reptile was a harmless rodent hunter with a strong resemblance to the deadly rattlesnake.

Simon kicked at the rat snake with his scuffed shoe, warning it, "You'd better *git*, auld scaly!" before continuing on up to the southeast veranda.

Mr. Quiggs was seated on the veranda with Flora, Cluny, and the new nigger gal, Jeanie.

Master Simon Fraser Martin of Indigo Hall had no great interest in the Greek alphabet, and, fortunately, he'd spotted Quiggs and the girls in time to slip sideways around the west wing of the house.

In his study in the west wing, Rory was going over the litter of papers that obscured the top of his writing table. Some puffed-up asshole of a London banker was threatening to take him to law, and another letter whined that a shipment of 'digo had arrived half spoiled by damp. What in God's name was a planter to do about a leaking ship's hold, damn their eyes?

Rory picked up a crudely written letter on foolscap and swore incredulously. It was actually a bill from that black bastard, Coffee Pardus! For God's sake, he'd been *sent* a wagonload of produce and a handful of Spanish dollars to ease his recovery after those mad Leopard Society niggers had attacked him, hadn't he?

Rory ran his eyes down the column of figures, noting Martha's check mark beside each item. He knew that if his wife had gone over the bill it was probably correct, but, damn, how could the repairs on Indigo Hall have mounted so at a mere few shillings a day?

At the bottom, under Coffee's signature, Martha had written, in her tiny spidery hand, "Most of the above Raw Materials. Can't he have a hundred pounds on account?"

Rory balled the bill up and threw it across the room, missing the unlit fireplace by a foot. What in hell would Coffee do with a hundred pounds? They were better off at the smithy with a few bob from time to time. Niggers couldn't manage money anyway, and if it got around there was a hundred quid in Coffee's cabin, the pony boys would ride by some night and likely kill the whole family searching for it.

The next letter was from the insurance underwriter, dunning him for another payment on the *Tuscarora.* Where in hell *was* that fucking Nathan and their fucking ship? The *Tuscarora* was overdue, and if he let the marine insurance lapse . . . but, damnit, where was he to get the money at this time of the year? The harvest stood a full two months in the future, and he'd already borrowed heavily on it. That asshole, Paradeen, had planted a third of his acreage in *corn*, for Christ's sake. Even converted to whiskey, corn was a bulky cargo for its price on the London market, and the damned Sassunach turned up their noses at bourbon in any case.

"Speaking of bourbon . . ." Rory muttered, and he got up to go to the sideboard, where he poured himself a stiff shot from the cut-glass decanter. He grimaced at the bite of raw corn liquor, though, in truth, he was coming to prefer it to the more expensive rum from Boston or even Holland gin.

A slender figure appeared in the French doors leading

out onto the north veranda, and Simon asked, "Athair? Could I ask you about something?"

Welcoming the diversion, Rory smiled down at his younger son and said, "Come in and ask away, then. What's on your mind, Simon?"

The boy said, "It's the niggers, Athair."

"Has one of them offended you, clansman?"

"No sir, I've just been wondering about them, is all. I don't understand why they are slaves and we're not."

Rory perched on a corner of his writing table as he sipped at his drink and said, "Och, it was the Laird's will, son. You know nobody's ever been able to make a slave of an Indian, and, as I've told you many a time, they had devil a time of it trying to make a slave of my ownself."

"I know, Athair. The Reverend Wapsham says they bear the mark of Cain and that it's only God's justice that they should be carriers of water and hewers of wood."

"There you are, then. It's only our Christian duty to take them from their savage shore and teach them to do an honest day's work when they'd as leave be eating one another."

"Yes, Athair, but do we have to be so *mean* to them?"

"Och, who's been mean to any of our people?" Rory's voice was carefully neutral as he asked, "Has Flora been mistreating the new bodyservant I gave her?"

"No sir. I think Flora and the new gal like each other. But you know Sister Flora's never mean to anybody."

"Ay, there you are, then. I'll allow Mr. Aldrich drives 'em a wee bit during the harvests, but you'll never see Uncle Donald whip a nigger unless he's been shirking."

"But why do they have to be whipped at all, Athair?"

"Why? Och, you're daft, lad! Don't you whip your pony when he takes a notion not to carry you the way you want to go?"

"Well, I give him a tap with my crop or the heel of my boot sometimes, but, Athair, my pony is an *animal!*"

"Ay, but don't you *like* your pony? Don't you pet it and give it a turnip now and again?"

"Of course, sir, but——"

"But me no buts, lad. You're talking like your mother, and I have a point to make. We agree you like your pony, and, no doubt, in the eyes of the Laird, your pony was given the right to frolic and eat grass and rut about with the mares to its heart's content. Agreed?"

"I guess so, sir."

"Ay, but the Laird made *us*, too, and with legs too short by far for man's ambition and a curious mind. So, too long ago to remember, some man caught a horse and, if you will, *enslaved* it. No doubt the horse would have it another way, but we have two choices. We can walk on our own wee legs or we can ride over hill and dale on a fine proud beast. Do you understand what I'm saying, lad?"

"I think so, but my pony has no human feelings, Athair."

"How can *we* ken what a pony feels, or a nigger either, for that matter? It's not our fault our world was made this way, Simon. In truth, if I'd been given the task, this earth of ours might be a gentler place."

He sipped at his corn liquor and chuckled as he added, "No doubt in seven days Himself overlooked the rights of a few butterflies. I'd have taken eight or ten, and made horses with no feelings at all, or fashioned the seeds of crops that harvested themselves."

"Och, Athair, you're funning me."

"Only to help you understand how things have to be, son. You've been spared the childhood of a crofter lad, but none of what you see about you was given to us by Christian charity and brotherly love."

He gulped the last of his drink, got up, went back to the sideboard for another, and said bitterly, "No, not a nail or a brick of this house, nor the very flesh of my body was ever given to me as an act of love. Right this very minute, I'm fighting off the moneylenders to hold what's mine by right of conquest, and, God strike me, I'll beat them at their own game yet."

He turned, glass in hand, to smile suddenly, wearily down at Simon and say, "Ay, you're too young to understand half of what I'm saying, lad. How does the old hymn go? 'Farther along, we'll understand why'?"

"I want to understand, Athair, but it seems so cruel."

"Ay, it's cruel. The bacon you had for breakfast was cruel, to the hog who died for your sins. The shoes we wear were ripped from the flesh of doubtless innocent creatures, or did you think leather came from a tree?"

"It's not the same, Athair!"

"It's only a matter of degree, son. Suppose, just suppose, we tried to live in Christian charity with every creature the Laird placed under us? Would you really like to go barefoot like white trash to spare the discomfort of a calf? Would you walk instead of ride because your pony would rather frolic in the meadow? When do you intend to give up bacon and eggs? The hogs and hens have their own reasons for existing, don't they? Ay, what about that side of beef in the pantry, Simon? Shall I tell the cook to serve you grits and greens in the future? Och, and leave us not forget the wee fish, for the hook is cruel, and doubtless the fish we ate yesterday had other plans for its ainsel'!"

"Its not the same" the boy insisted stubbornly.

Rory sipped his drink, and said, "Tell me how it's not the same, then, son."

Simon looked down at the parquet floor and said, "I know it's better to ride than walk, but if I had to ride on a black man's back, I'd as lief walk. I know my shoes are leather, but if I knew all leather was made of human skin, I'd as lief go barefoot. As for the eating of fish and flesh—"

"Och, away with ye, Simon. You're talking like a lass!"

"I just want to understand, Athair."

"Away, I say! I've work to attend to. If you want to understand why we have niggers at Indigo Hall, go out to the kitchen and tell the cook I said to let you sand the pots and pans. Ay, go out to the vats and tell Aldrich I said to let you turn the windlass on the crushing mills mayhap a full hour in the sun!"

Simon grinned and asked, *"Could* I, Athair? I asked Uncle Donald to let me press the 'digo one time, but he said it was forbidden to white hands!"

"Go! Go do whatever you like, for it's busy I am, and you're stubborn as an Ibo!"

Simon left, delighted with the new game his father had suggested, as Rory drained his glass and shook his head, muttering, "Too much of his mother in that one. He's turning out soft, and that's the truth of it!"

He wondered if Simon had been introduced to sex by one of the wenches yet. That was probably part of what was ailing the lad. Son Simon was almost at that age, now. Och, where had all the years flown? Ay, he'd have to speak to that new gal from the Carolinas. He hadn't gotten around to her himself, but she had a knowing look in her eye, and no doubt she'd be willing to break the lad in the right way. He'd have a word with her—once he was ahead of these fucking bills.

The *Tuscarora* rolled gently in the satin ground swells, becalmed in the horse latitudes. The noonday sun was a searing white ball in the cloudless Dutch blue sky, and the tar bubbled up between the white pine boards of the *Tuscarora's* baking topdecks. Her sun-bleached canvas hung as lifeless as great gray bats, listlessly shifting position as the two masts swung back and forth a few feet with each roll.

A rat scurried from a rope coil to the shade of a propped-open hatch cover, but no other living thing was visible topside to the albatross wheeling curiously above the becalmed vessel. The *Tuscarora's* wheel was lashed, the poop deserted. Aaron Paradeen knew the sails should be reefed lest a sudden squall catch her broadside when and if the calm broke, but he didn't know how the ropes worked. He didn't know where he was.

Aaron sat at Nathan's table in the master's cabin under the afterdeck, making another entry in the log with a dull quill despite his slowly fading vision. The heat was unbearable, even seated naked as he was. The stench from the open holds was either fading slightly or else his sense of smell was going, too.

Aaron's hand was sticky on the page as he wrote, slowly and listlessly, "Friday? Seventy-odd days out of Old Calabar and position unknown. . . . The last of the Negroes has died, I hope. I've been hearing her moan for the past few days in the forward hold, but there was no way I could get water through to her. The 'tween-decks are less than eighteen inches apart, and the rotting bodies have bloated, jamming the crawl spaces completely. I went to the forward hatch this morning and called down, but there was no answer. The rats seem to be kept below by the sunlight, and I've brought the remaining water butts back to the cabin. I intend to shove Mr. Murphy's litch over the side as soon as it gets a bit cooler. I find myself very weak this day and Mr. Murphy will keep, I trust, until evening."

Aaron laid the pen down and leaned back, idly flipping the filled pages of the log as he tried to remember if he'd left anything out. He knew he'd done a poor job of keeping it since Nathan Starr had first gone blind, but, damnit, there'd been so many days when nothing at all had happened. He was sure, if anyone ever read it, the log would contain enough information for them to piece it all together.

He read an early entry in Nathan's hand, saying, "Standing off Southhampton, bound for Old Calabar with 40 hogsheads Virginia tobacco. 100 barrels gunpowder in 10-pound Trade Kegs. 1,000 lbs. brown sugar, English dry goods, assorted textiles, calico, unbleached muslins, blue drill, assorted handkerchiefs, etc."

Aaron skipped down to "Brass kettles, tin buckets, one gross coils copper wire, 25 dozen trade muskets with lead pigs and Sussex flints."

Hadn't Sussex been where that English widow and her children had been let off? Aaron wondered idly why the South Downs knappers seemed to have a monopoly on gun flints. He wondered if the red-headed woman had gotten home all right with the silver dollars he'd given her. He read on, tracing Nathan's prim hand with a sweating finger, for his vision was blurred, but, damnit, he could still make out the pages. He had to make out the pages.

Nathan's entry droned on, as dry as the man himself. "Gentleman's boots and shoes, 100 pairs, large sizes. Ship's stores: 100 barrels salt beef, pork, mackerel. 100 barrels flour. 50 barrels kiln-dried corn meal. 2,000 lbs. refined sugar. 20 kegs salted butter. 40 kegs white lard. 25 boxes sperm candles. 1 box soap. 500 lbs. tea. 100 lbs. coffee. 1 dozen cutlasses, 1 dozen blunderbusses locked in master's cabin . . ."

Aaron snorted in annoyance and flipped pages until he came to "Off Old Calabar, Bight of Biafra, Negro villages of Old Town and New Town built on sand bars in Calabar River. Chief of New Town piped aboard to palaver re cargo. Chief called 'Joe Honesty' and speaks tolerable English. Demands 100 pieces of eight per Negro delivered in health and fat. Too much. Previous traders have spoiled Joe Honesty, but no other ships in river mouth, so doubtless price shall drop after adamant negotiations."

"God!" Aaron muttered. "Adamant negotiations they were, at that!"

He closed his eyes and pictured the firelight reflected in the waters of the river as the New Towners raided their Old Town neighbors. How the African night had echoed with the sounds of musket fire, the screams of women and children. Nathan had called it a tribal war, but hadn't the natives of the two island towns been of the same Ibo blood? It was probably true that the Old Towners would have done the same, given rum and muskets by Nathan's crew, but it had been horrible nonetheless. Nathan had insisted that only sound captives were to be taken aboard, so naturally the wounded had been slaughtered by the victorious Joe Honesty.

Nathan's comments on it read, "Off Old Calabar and loading. Fifty-seven men, thirteen women taken aboard at 60 dollars per man, 40 per woman. One woman killed self by pitching head first down the hatch into bilge. Joe Honesty promises to replace as soon as Slattee bring expected gaggle from interior, but scoundrel refuses to return money paid to him for litch."

The gaggle had come ten days later, Aaron mused, thinking back to his first sight of the bound men and laden women driven to the very beach by the rhino-hide whips of the Slattee and professional slave-catchers of various tribes. The women had carried supplies and tusks of ivory on their heads, for, though the men kept trying to escape or take a Slattee with them in last desperate fights, the women were for the most part cowed into submission by their inferior position in tribal custom. Joe Honesty had explained that the Ibo princess who'd killed herself to avoid slavery was some sort of freak.

Another high-ranking Ibo girl had fought Nathan tooth and nail in his cabin before submitting, in the end, to the master's lust. Aaron knew there was no entry about *her* in the log. The other crew members, himself included, had found the prettier Ibo girls anxious enough to please, and the crew's quarters, miserable as they might be, had been heaven for the few favored wenches who could leave the stinking misery of the hold.

Aaron found the entry Nathan had made the day they'd sailed from the steaming, drum-haunted African coast. In innocent bliss, he had written, "Standing off Bight of Biafra with light but healthy cargo 274 Negroes, heading west-norwest with fair offshore breeze, Savannah bound . . ."

The stink had been ghastly even before the *Tucarora* had weighed anchor, although Nathan had claimed the crew relieved themselves in the bilges of His Majesty's ships, too; it was something any sailor had to learn to live with, like worms in the biscuits or green slime on the bully beef.

In truth, the homeward leg had started well enough. A young lad who played the banjo had been brought topside to play for the cabin wenches as they'd danced, naked, on the moonlit deck. Aaron remembered his own bed partner fondly, though he wished he hadn't watched when they'd fed her litch to the trailing sharks.

The naked young man now got up and went to the taff-light, staring out through the wavery panes at the oily-looking green waters of the dead calm. Since the *Tuscarora* wasn't under way, there was no wake for them to follow now, but they were still there, the sonsofbitches. A trio of dark triangular fins cut cleanly through the still water, driven by tireless great tails and that endless, mindless hunger.

Aaron went back to the table and sat down, feeling dizzy from the slight exertion in this Godawful humid heat.

He leafed through the log and found the page where the truth first appeared. Nathan had written, "Joe Honesty has played us false, and I intend to deal harshly with him on the next voyage. One of the women from the interior has ophthalmia. I noted the film over her eyes when she was brought up on deck to be rinsed down and exercised. She was jettisoned, of course, so the claim against the underwrit-er may hold up in court. I greatly fear, however, that there may be other cases aboard. The Negroes make every at-tempt to hide any trace the disease, for they are a stubborn and unruly lot."

Aaron shook his head and muttered, "Ay, too ignorant to see the simple Christian charity in your heart, eh, Na-than? I *told* you to kill them quietly and slip them over the side with a weight tied to their feet, but did you listen? Did you ever listen? Didn't you think they had any feelings when you pitched that woman over the side, alive, to the sharks?"

Ah, well, Nathan had been treated much the same in the end. Aaron found the final entry Nathan Starr had made, after skipping entries dealing with the horrible financial losses they were incurring as the ophthalmia swept through the stinking confines of the jam-packed hold. Nathan had written, "God help us all, I'm going blind! The sickness has spread to the crew and both Bourke and Johnston are con-fined to their quarters, unable to see. As I shot the sun this past noon, I noticed it seemed unusually dim and thought, at first, that there was a high overcast above the masts. This night, I know the worst. I can barely make out this page, though Mr. Paradeen is holding the hurricane lamp above the log for me. Unless this attack of ophthalmia proves temporary . . ."

"That's all you could write, eh, Nathan?" sighed Aaron, turning to look for his own first entry as he muttered, "Jesus, for a man who couldn't write, you certainly screamed a lot!"

He tried to remember how many nights they'd had to listen to him, rolling his sightless eyes and begging for his God and his precious Gloria. Aaron remembered Gloria Starr as a decent, attractive woman, considering her age, but as he'd listened to her dying husband recount her charms, he'd truly begun to hate the damned woman.

He found his own entry, reading, "Captain Starr went over the side during the night, either by accident or design. Only Mr. Murphy and I still have our sight. The others, as well as the Negroes, are in a bad way."

He grimaced as he read his own words. How little they conveyed of the roaring pandemonium on those ghastly days and nights before the blind slaves, chained in twos below decks, had begun to grow listless from dehydration and neglect. Murphy had steered the ship, knowing little more of navigation than himself, while he'd tried, as best he could, to lower buckets of water down the hatch to screaming, sobbing men in chains. He'd ordered the buckets passed around, of course, but he'd soon noticed how quiet the far ends of the slave decks were getting, and in the end, he'd simply slammed the hatch cover down and tried not to listen to the survivors near enough to reach. It had been Murphy's suggestion that they ration the remaining water among themselves and the moaning white men in the forecastle. He hadn't seen fit to argue the point with his more experienced shipmate.

It had seemed a bit much, however, when he'd caught Murphy rolling Johnston over the rail, explaining, with a weary smile, that the two of them had to look after themselves.

Aaron smiled grimly as he found where he'd written, yesterday, "Mr. Murphy died this morning at dawn." There'd been no need to go into details. When he'd found himself staring into a rising sun the color and brightness of a silver coin, Aaron had known what he had to do.

Kevin Murphy had looked blankly at him when he'd come from the cabin with the loaded pistol. A blunderbuss might have been safer, but thanks to Colonel Martin, Aaron knew he was good enough with the gentleman's weapon. Murphy had asked softly, "Why have you armed yourself, Mr. Paradeen?" and Aaron had answered simply, "Because I have it. I'm beginning to go blind."

Then he'd fired, ignoring the other's protestations that they needed his good eyes to steer by. It was probably true that Murphy's eyes were as yet untouched by the plague, but Aaron Paradeen had no intention of being sent over the side with a jovial remark about sharks, and if he himself did not survive, neither would the callous Irishman.

He'd decided to wait for the litch to stop bleeding before he disposed of it, and, as the sun baked Murphy's blood black on the deck, he'd tended to put it off. Once Murphy was over the side, he'd be the only white man, dead or alive, aboard. He wondered how long he had, and how long a blind man could manage, alone on a drifting hulk in the middle of the Atlantic.

The *Tuscarora* would go to the bottom once the winds freshened again. Her square-rigged foremast and fore-and-aft mainmast were waiting for the gust that would turn her turtle. He'd probably never see the darkness on the horizon that foretold a squall line coming on fast, but, while he still had enough vision to get about, there was a chance he could make the sea work for her supper.

Aaron took a cutlass from the arms locker and went out on deck, wondering what the wheeling albatross up there thought of his nakedness and sunburned shoulders. He could just make out the big bird as a blur in a lead-colored sky, though he knew, from the feel of the sun on his shoulders, that there wasn't a cloud for a hundred miles.

He found a rope leading tautly up into the maze of rigging he'd never been able to get straight in his landsman's head. He cut it with a cutlass slash and nothing happened. He swore softly and cut another. A triangle of canvas sagged limply above the main sail, and Aaron decided the simple approach was to slash through all the masses of rope and belaying pins. He hacked away until, suddenly, the mainmast groaned and the top gaff slid slowly down, collapsing the main in a clumsy accordion fold of limp canvas.

The naked youth laughed wildly and waved his blade at the silent sea, shouting, "Try and turn us over now, you bitch!"

But the foremast still stretched its treacherous canvas wind-claws to the sky, as if the *Tuscarora* wanted to die with her sails still set and no man at the helm.

He came to where he'd left Murphy on the deck. Shiny green African flies were crawling over his dead face, humming metallic little songs as they feasted on the dried blood and the open eyes of the litch, its mouth open in a grotesque parody of a grin.

Aaron smiled back and said, "Good morrow, sir, and how are you today? I trust by your smile you've been chatting with my late father in the Great Beyond?"

Aaron went to the base of the foremast, probing at the mysterious tangle of lines with the point of his cutlass as he told the dead man in the scuppers, "Papa said it was all a joke, you know. I'm afraid I never understood him. He was always reading the Torah and the Talmud, you see, and I was never able to make much sense of it till now."

He slashed a rope and nothing happened. It was getting harder to see where he was aiming, and the ropes offered no resistance to the blade unless they were taut. Aaron muttered, "Papa was fond of quoting a Pharisee called Rabbi Hillel who'd ordered us to do nothing to any man we wouldn't want done to ourselves. I believe one of *your* boys said much the same thing a hundred years or so later, Mr. Murphy."

He cut through a line and somewhere above him a yard-arm groaned. Aaron nodded, slashed again with his cutlass, and mused, "I daresay we've been somewhat harshly dealt with by our gods—or possibly, it was Mumbo Jumbo—for our little lark along the African Coast, eh? How does it go in the Scriptures 'As ye sow, so shall ye reap'? I opened the hatch again a while ago, but we seem to have murdered every one of them, Mr. Murphy. Our papas should have warned us niggers were *others,* I daresay."

He hacked through another line, and the top gallant yard sagged crazily at one end. He shook his head, trying to see through the gauzy atmosphere between his eyes and the tangle of lines at the base of the mast. Then he croaked, "I've hardly any more vision left than yourself, Mr. Murphy. I'll just get the sails down and send you over to play with the sharks—unless, of course, you'd rather stay."

He cut another line, and something cracked like a pistol shot above him as he turned to the dead man and observed, "It *is* a joke when you think of it. You, me, those rotting niggers in the hold—we're all literally in the same boat.

Everyone on earth is in the same . . . damned . . . fucking boat!"

And then the main yardarm came crashing down on him in a chaos of tearing canvas and splintering wood, and Aaron's death, while gory, was mercifully swift.

A squall line would sweep across the *Tuscarora* two nights later, but, bare-poled and with only one hatch open, the derelict would survive until a Spanish West Indiaman overtook her two months later.

The log would be turned over to the British governor on Bermuda, but the ghastly cargo of skeletons would be shoveled into a three-mile depth of the all-forgiving sea.

EIGHT

Since Martha and the children insisted on coming with him, Rory drove over to the smithy in an open carriage, rather pleased with his matched team and the fine day it had turned out to be.

As he drove into Coffee's yard, Rory saw the fat Negress, Phoebe, with the children in the field where her man had fought the terrorists. He got down and tied the team's reins to a hitching post before helping his wife down. Martha was wearing a black silk dress and her own hair this afternoon, as a gesture to the other woman, however black she might be.

The girls were out of the carriage and running to join the darkies where they stood in a patch of new-mown hay. Locky and Simon held back to attend their mother as she walked across the flattened hay and tangled weeds, but little Cluny was dashing out in front, with Flora and her bodyservant, Jeanie-Calma, close behind. Rory had told the children not to bring their pet niggers, but Flora had insisted. She and Jeanie-Calma seemed inseparable these days, and in truth, although he scowled, Rory was pleased with how well his bastard daughter fit in at Indigo Hall.

He knew he had others, of course, both black and white, but there was something about Sheba's child that made him feel . . . what? Pride? Och, who could be proud of a nigger wench? He'd merely felt it was wrong to have the lass grow up a whore. Was there any shame in simple charity?

Cluny ran up to Fiba and her children and grinned up at them, saying, "Good morrow, I am Cluny MacPherson Martin of Indigo Hall. We've come to pay our respects to the dead nigger."

Flora caught up with her, grabbed Cluny's arm, and shook her, red-faced with confusion as she blurted, "You just *hesh*, you sassy miss!" Then she shook her head at the stone-faced Fiba and said, "I'm terribly sorry, Phoebe! My little sister never had a lick of sense."

A tall boy standing a few feet apart from his younger brothers and sisters said sullenly, "That's all right, ma'm. Pa was used to bein' calt a nigger."

Flora stared soberly down at what seemed to be a three-legged milking stool with its legs driven into the fresh-turned earth and murmured, "She shouldn't have said it anyway, Juba. Your father was a fine man, and we'll remember him fondly."

Jeanie-Calma stepped forward with a little nosegay of flowers she'd picked from the garth at Indigo Hall. She curtsied to Fiba in her nice new frock, and gestured with the flowers at the odd grave marker. "Dast I, ma'am?" she asked shyly.

Fiba nodded woodenly, and the mulatto placed the nosegay on the seat of the stool, running her fingers softly over the lovingly polished oak. The three legs were cypress heartwood, meant to last a lifetime in contact with the ground, but the seat was the bole of a live oak, and Juba had worn out three sharkskin sanding pads and used nigh a gallon of linseed oil before he'd been satisfied with its finish.

Cluny shook her blonde head and chided, "You ain't supposed to say ma'am to *her*, Jeanie!" but Flora shook her warningly and said, "Hesh, or I'll fetch you a lick with Athair and Mama watchin'!"

To cover her own embarrassment, Flora told Juba, "We were just shocked when we heard about your father, Juba. Athair, I mean my father, said Uncle Coffee had recovered tolerable from that gunshot wound."

Juba shrugged and said, "He was up and about at the end, but last night he allowed he had a stitch in his side where the pistol ball took him, and jest after supper, he said he felt poorly and went to lay himself down. We reckoned, for the longest time, he was jest asleep." The boy glanced over at the afternoon sun and added, "In a little while, he'll have been dead a whole day."

"We're all so sorry, Juba. What did the doctor say was the matter with him?"

"We never had no doctor, ma'am. Pa didn't pay no mind to Obeah, and that's only kind of doctoring we'uns ever gits."

Rory, along with Martha and the boys, joined them around Coffee's grave. He stared down for a time at the odd marker and murmured, "We came as soon as we heard, Juba. I have a bit of silver for you all. I know it's hard, lad, but you must bear up like a man."

Fiba suddenly turned and sank to her knees on the

weeds, her fat shoulders heaving in silence. Martha went over and stood at her side, one hand on a grief-wracked shoulder as she murmured, "There, there, my dear. I know how you must feel, for the terrible news of my brother's passing only reached us a week ago, and the two of us mourn together."

To Juba, it seemed that the white woman's comforting words were oddly chosen, since everyone knew Nathan Starr and Marse Paradeen had died while engaged aboard a slaver, but no doubt the fool white woman meant well. She'd always been nice to him when he'd helped Pa out at Indigo Hall.

Juba stepped over to Colonel Martin and took the small leather purse from his father's patron, hefting it with a puzzled frown as he murmured, "Please, sir, Pa allowed as how it was nigh five hundred guineas we'uns had coming."

"Och, do you think I carry all I own on my person like a Jew, lad? You'll get what's coming to you, in time. What sort of a grave marker do you call this thing, Juba? God strike me, it looks like a milking stool!"

Juba knew the man only asked to cover his embarrassment, but he explained, "It's an Ashanti headman's stool, Colonel Martin. My grandfather was allowed his own stool in the Old Country."

"It's a damned fine bit of craftsmanship, lad. How long did it take you to make it?"

"All night, sir. Pa had selected the wood and drawn me a picture. I mind he must have knowed."

"Jesus, you worked all night and dug his grave all by yourself, Juba? You're as hard a worker as your father ever was. You do him proud. But tell me, why didn't you go over to Paradeen Plantation for help? Surely you knew my own hands were harvesting and cleaning up for the auction over there?"

"Please, sir, I'd as leave stay clear of Marse Paradeen's holding. Lawyer Margolis tried to tell me Pa and us'uns was Paradeen niggers. He said we'd be sold at auction to satisfy Marse Paradeen's debts, and when I tolt him 'bout the papers Marse Paradeen sent to the mansion about Pa, he jest laughed and said we'd see about that by and by."

Rory nodded. "I remember asking Aaron Paradeen if he'd sent your father's manumission in, and, God strike me, he told me he had."

"Then they must be over there, ain't they, Colonel?"

Rory sighed and said, "I'm afraid not. I looked myself when Margolis and Judge Crawford were drawing up the auction papers. We simply couldn't find them, lad. Do you suppose your father misunderstood Marse Paradeen? I mind he did send something to the mansion, that time we were in the field together against the Dons. Had it been a ticket of manumission, I'm sure there'd be a record of it."

Juba gasped and said, "We's free niggers, Colonel! You *knows* we's free niggers! But that white lawyer man, he say—"

"Och, don't frush yoursel', Juba. I'll tell you what I'm going to do. I'm going to speak to Judge Crawford for you, and mayhap, he'll see it our way."

"God bless you, sir, but what if they lie about us, over to the mansion? I mind some creditor of Marse Paradeen took them papers outten the mansion and jest tore them up so's we'uns could be sold alongside the other niggers yonder!"

"Och, well, I'm the first to admit there are evil white men as well as evil blacks. You know, of course, how I was sold, my ownsel', not so many years back that I can't remember well enough."

"Pa tolt me 'bout that, sir. He said, one time, he'd come to Georgia with white slaves sold beside him. He said he'd never figured how all the white slaves wound up ownin' half the colony whilst the niggers did all the work."

Simon, who'd been listening at a discreet distance with the other children, piped up to ask, "Can't you bear witness for these people, Athair?" but Rory shushed him, saying, "Stay out of this, son. Young Pardus and I have serious business to talk about. Why don't you and Locky go back to the carriage and fetch the basket we carried over here for Uncle Coffee's grieving kin?"

As soon as the boys had left, bored and willing enough for any small diversion, Rory turned back to Juba, put a fatherly hand on his shoulder, and said, "I won't let anything bad happen to your family, son. I'll tell you what I'm going to do. I'm going to bid on the six of you myself."

Martha turned with a puzzled frown as Juba blurted, "*Bid* on us'uns? We ain't slaves! We'll run off to jine the Seminoles afore we'll be sold to anybody!"

"Och, you're not listening to me, lad! Wasn't I a friend to your late father? Dost think I'd harm a hair on the heads of my friend Coffee's kinfolk?"

"I reckon not, sir, but I jest don't cotton to bein' *bid* on!"

"Now, listen carefully, for it's all a hoax we'll play together on those greedy Sassunach. You know you need the protection of a powerful white man with the others trying to swindle you, don't you, Juba?"

"I 'spect so, sir."

"All right then. I'm going to Judge Crawford and have you all signed over to me. Then I'm moving you and your family to Indigo Hall. That way, none of Paradeen's creditors can get their greedy hands on you. You'll be safe and well cared for and freed of trying to feed your mother and the little ones who, God knows, are too small to work anywhere, save, mayhap, as weeders in the rice plantations."

"Do Jesus, Colonel! Don't let 'em sell us to no rice plantation!"

"I shan't. You have my word on it. You'll all live at Indigo Hall, and when there's no work for you to do for me and mine, I'll even let you sell your own time out to other planters for silver. How does that strike you, lad?"

Behind him, Martha murmured, "Rory, dear, for God's sake—"

But her husband silenced her with a wave of his hand as he said, "Take some time to think it over, Juba. The auction won't start for a day or so. Though, God strike me, I'll be hard pressed to buy you all away from the others unless I can get my low bid in first to a friendly judge."

"What about our homestead here, sir? I jest buried my *pa* in this here ground, and we worked so hard to build the smithy—"

"Hush ye, dinna frush ye, lad! I'll see if we can mayhap manage to buy this five acres away from the greedy creditors and—"

"But, please, sir, we'uns already *owns* it!"

"Ay, *I* ken that and *you* ken that, but there's no deed recorded at the mansion, save as part of the bankrupt Paradeen holdings."

Juba shook his head and said, "I don't understand what's happened hereabouts, Colonel. Yesterday we'uns was free niggers with our own land. Today you-all come here to tell us—"

"Och, it's past my own understanding, lad, for we live in a cruel and confusing world. You just let me do the worrying for you and your family, Juba. You know I was always fair to your father, wasn't I?"

"Yes sir, 'cept he said you owed him nigh five hundred pounds."

"We'll talk about that when you're all safe and sound over to Indigo Hall, lad. I may have to lay out quite a bit of silver to save you from the rice planters, but never fear, we'll just take it from my account with your late father, for I'm certain it will cover all the very complicated dealings we have before us."

"Rory!" said Martha in a tone he'd never heard her use before, "I want to go home now. These people are in mourning and I doubt that this is the time to talk business."

Rory took his hand from Juba's shoulder, saying lightly, "Ay. I see the lads have the basket from the carriage handy." He nodded at Simon, who'd carried the heavy basket while his brother supervised. "Give it to yon woman, son."

Simon looked uncertainly at the sobbing widow on her knees with her back turned to him. Then he went over and put it down at Fiba's side, murmuring, "I'm purely sorry, Aunt Phoebe."

Rory saw that Martha was marching to the carriage alone, her back stiff. He said, "Come, childer'. We'll talk about it after I see if I can trick the lawyers, Juba." Then he followed after his wife, wondering what had gotten into her.

Locky ran after him as Simon held out a hand to the Negro boy and said soberly, "My sympathy, sir," as he'd seen Athair do at another funeral. Juba took the pale hand gingerly and nodded, not knowing what he was supposed to say.

Cluny said, "We dasn't shake hands with them, Simon." But Flora shook her roughly and sent her after her parents. Flora knew her flesh was forbidden to a Negro's touch, but she went over to Fiba, still crouched in the grass with her smaller children huddled silently around her, and suddenly kissed her on the cheek, tears in her own eyes, as she whispered, " 'Bye now, Aunt Phoebe. You-all come and stay with us, you hear?"

At the carriage, Rory stared up at Martha, who'd climbed in by herself, and asked, "What's wrong, auld woman? You look like you've just seen a ghost!"

Martha's eyes were examining him as coldly as if he were a bug on a pin as she said flatly, "I think I did see a ghost. The ghost of the gallant man I thought I'd married. That was *rotten* of you, Rory!"

"Och, what did I do wrong, lass? Didn't you hear me tell yon niggers I'd look after them?"

"You're trying to swindle that poor ignorant black boy out of the five hundred you owe him! Worse than that, you'll steal his land, and his very freedom!"

Rory laughed and chided, "Och, who's *trying?* I reckon I *did* it! Don't frush yoursel' over business, lass. If you knew how hard it's been for me to keep you and the childer' living as gentlefolk—"

"Is that . . . that *child-molesting* what you call living like gentlefolk, Rory Martin? For God's sake, the man's not cold in his grave, and you're robbing his widow and orphans!"

Locky, near enough to hear, moved back as he caught the dangerous edge in his mother's voice. Mama seldom got angry, but when she did, she hit harder than Athair himself!

Rory stared at his angry wife in total confusion, for she'd never looked at him this way before. He pasted a smile across his face and stammered, "You just don't understand, lass."

"Perhaps I do," she said softly. "For the very first time."

"Och, what are you looking at me that way for?"

"I think I never really looked before. Do you know what you've become, Rory? A cold, cruel, ay, and *weak . . .* thing!"

Rory pulled himself up into the carriage and roared, "I'll not be spoken to that way in front of yon niggers and my sons, auld woman!"

Martha never flinched as she asked calmly, "Do you intend to strike me in front of the children, then? I thought no gentleman ever struck a woman with his *hand!*"

Rory slowly lowered his balled-up fist as Cluny skipped toward the carriage. Locky, with rare good sense, intercepted his little sister and led her back toward the other children as Martha asked dryly, "Are you going to use the carriage whip on me, Rory of Culloden Moor? What sort of a weapon did you use on Jeanie's mother, or was the poor Negress cowed by your royal wrath?"

"Jesus!" Rory gasped, the color draining from his face as

Martha smiled and said, "Oh, for heaven's sake, don't you think we womenfolk know *anything?*"

"Martha, lass, I swear before God—"

"Hush! It was unfair of me to twit you with wild oats sown before we were married. But you drew it out of me, Rory." Suddenly she laughed wryly. "Nothing I've just said will make you change your mind about those poor Negroes, will it?"

Rory went to unhitch the team, calling out, "You childer'! What are you dallying out there for?" as Martha murmured, half to herself, "No, I didn't think it would."

Gloria was working late in the chandlery. She was alone, for the clerks and warehousemen had been laid off during the slow months of winter on the North Atlantic. Few ships embarked or arrived on either side of Christmas. The West Indian Bermuda trade started falling off as early as late September, when the Carib Indian god, Hurricane, awoke from his summer sleep below the trade winds and started prowling up from the tropics. Despite the wonders wrought by modern machines, the world of finance still depended on the weather, the wind, and the stub of goose quill in Gloria's ink-stained fingers.

It was a warm evening, and she perched on the stool with every door propped open to catch any chance breeze. The hurricane lamp above her cast a small golden cone of light on her head and shoulders as well as on the dreary ledger she was working on. Rory stood for a time in the doorway, cherishing this moment of silent watching. He finally cleared his throat and warned, "It's not safe for a white woman to be sitting like that in a thin muslin shift with devil a barred door, much less a man, to protect her!"

Gloria looked up with a tired smile and, grateful for the excuse, put down her pen and straightened up, pressing her hands into the small of her back as she arched it wearily. "Oh, I must be getting old."

Rory's tone was wistful as he said, "Madeira, and some women, improve with age, lass. I meant what I said about these open doors just now. You've no idea how tempting you look from outside in that gauzy shift with the soft light gloaming in your hair."

"Oh, Rory, the Indians are all above the fall line or in the Floridas these days. That Leopard Society scare was ended when poor Coffee killed their mad leaders, and as for my hair, I noticed some gray strands in my brush too short a time ago."

"Och, my mother was gray at thirty. I mind an amusing piece just written by Dr. Franklin for the *Pennsylvania Gazette* about a woman having a bit of snow on the roof while there's many a fire left in the hearth."

"Oh, Rory, you and that old fraud should both have your mouths washed out with soap. What was it brought you by tonight? I'm afraid Efram is out of town on business. He rode over to Poplarville to see about some canvas. A man there has his slaves weaving on a new gangloom from England, but Efram wants to test the product before we commit ourselves. They're using hemp with a little imported linen, rather than the other way around."

Suddenly Gloria realized she was babbling, and stopped with a sheepish smile.

Rory asked where they stood now with their joint claim against the underwriters who'd insured the *Tuscarora,* and Gloria said, "It's stalled at Whitehall. Those awful Spaniards have put in an enormous salvage claim, and you know, of course, that the fools threw all the remains overboard without attempting a tally."

"How did the admiralty get into our insurance claims?"

"Because of the international aspects of the affair—the Dons taking our vessel into a British port under the merchant flag of Spain, I suppose. Efram insists the Home Secretary's people should handle that part of it, but you know how flummoxed the new Parliament is, divided as they are, and the king's friends do seldom a favor for a Whig like poor Efram."

"Ay, we'll be waiting a time for our insurance money, then, but when do we get the vessel back?"

"God knows. It's impounded until all claims are settled. As if they ever could be, with the cargo jettisoned as spoiled but neither weighed nor tallied. That poor Jewish lad just didn't know how to keep a proper log. We've no idea how many spoiled Negroes were thrown over by our own crew and how many by the salvagers. In fairness to the Dons, the Spanish captain couldn't read Nathan's log well enough to recognize that it was incomplete. I imagine they simply wanted to restore the *Tuscarora's* seaworthiness as quickly as possible and take her in as a salvage prize."

"Did they think to save the skeletons of such crew members as may have been aboard?"

"They saved one litch they assumed from the log was Aaron's. The skeleton was in the forward starboard scuppers, still wearing a white man's belt and shoe buckles. A Negro was apparently crushed by the falling yards when poor Aaron saved the vessel by derigging her before the next gale. The white man's bones were sent to Aaron's surviving kin in Philadelphia, and I believe he was buried near the Sephardic synagogue up there."

"Ay, the lad deserved a decent funeral after saving the *Tuscarora* for us. How did they know the bones found under the fallen yards were a nigger's?"

Gloria grimaced and said, "Because he'd died naked, of course. Really, Rory, do we have to discuss it? My own late husband was one of the men aboard that hell ship, you know!"

Rory came closer and put a light hand on her wrist as he asked soberly, "Do you really miss him, Gloria?"

She snatched her hand away automatically. Then she dropped her eyes, smiled slightly, and murmured, "We've always been able to see right through each other, haven't we, Rory?"

"Ay, and now you're free."

She didn't look at him as she answered, "You're not, and Martha is my friend. I mind we were better off talking about skeletons, my very old dear!"

Rory started to reach for her again, then dropped his hand to his sword hilt as he insisted, "There are some things a man has to say, Gloria. You've known how I felt about you since first I saw you, both of us scarce more than childer' and me in my great bare feet."

Gloria sighed and said, "Dear God, how long has it been? So much has happened since that day. So much to *you,* I mean. I'm very much as you found me, I fear. A little older, a little wiser, and still sitting here on this Goddamned stool with these Goddamned books!"

"Och, it's more beautiful you've grown each time I've seen you, lass, and . . . damnit, you know how it's become with Martha and me!"

"Stop it, dearest. I know about my little sister-in-law's momentary annoyance with you. She loves you, Rory. Right now, she's upset because she's seen the rust on her knight in shining armor. But she'll get over it. You'll see."

He suddenly took her shoulders in both hands and lifted her off her stool, crying, "I don't give a damn what Martha thinks of me! It's *you* I want! It's you, Oh Jesus, it's you I've *always* wanted!"

Gloria tried to twist free as she pleaded, "Please, Rory, we can't! It's not right! I'd never be able to face Martha again!"

"Och, what's right or wrong save what a man can grasp in this upside-down world God created for us in a moment of cruel levity? To hell with Martha! We'll run off to the Carolinas together! I'll carry you up to the Cherokee country and we'll live like Indians with my auld friend MacQueen!"

She laughed and braced her body away from his with two hands planted firmly on his chest. "You'd never give up Indigo Hall and the children. I know you too well, my gallant."

He started to protest and she shushed, "Not to *me*, Rory! Don't tell your macaroon lies to me! Can't you see how much alike we are? Can't you see why I've always admired you so?"

"Admired?" Rory blinked, smiling wistfully as he added, "I've oft seen *something* loving in those eyes, *ma cusla*, but I never thought it admiration!"

"Admiration, understanding, love, they're all just words, dearest. You see, Martha loves you for what she thinks you are, or for what she thought you were. I've always *known* what you were, for much of you is mirrored in me, deep inside."

"Och, what's this you're saying? It's a raw rough Lochaber man I've ever been, despite this wig and my wee toy sword. *You*, darling . . . och, you're a proud queenly beauty!"

"With ambitions that far outreached her luck," said Gloria wearily. She disengaged herself from his arms and moved a pace away, looking down with distaste at the littered writing desk as she mused, "I wanted so much when I came over here with poor Nathan, and as you see, I've gotten so little. Had I been born a man, or even had the toughness of that awful Rose Fenwyk of yours, by now I'd have *been* the queenly creature you think me."

"Come away with me then, and I'll cover you in Indian pearls!"

"Freshwater mussel pearls worth little more than wampum, Rory? You forget I keep the books for you and Efram. I ran away with one man already whose promises exceeded his future by miles! *Look* at me, Rory. I mean, really look at me as I *am*, a barren widow, no longer young, with the best years of my life tied up in this shabby little chandlery you see around you."

She closed the ledger, capped the inkhorn for the night, and added bitterly, "It's little enough, but I'll be damned if I'm going to give it up."

"Och, I'm certain Efram means to keep you on here, Gloria. After all, you're the widow of his elder son."

"Have you forgotten our brother-in-law Joseph, in India?"

Rory had, never having met Martha's younger brother, but he smiled reassuringly and said, "I doubt he'd be interested in robbing you of your widow's mite, lass. As an officer of the John Company, Joe Starr has his thousand square leagues of the Punjab to loot."

Gloria's voice was bitter as she asked, "What widow's mite? Nathan died in debt."

"Och, he was the son of a rich man, however much auld Efram plays the humble merchant for the tax assessor."

"You mean the son of a rich man too frightened by one spell in debtor's gaol to part with a copper coin he doesn't have to."

"Ay, Efram is a bit of a miser, but surely he's settled *something* on you, Gloria?"

She looked away as she answered, "Not a farthing, if you mean as part of Nathan's estate. You're going to hate this, though I'm certain you'd have made the same move had nature put you on my side of the chess board, but, yes, Efram *has* agreed to put me in his will, *now*."

"Och, there you are, then. What's there to hate about the soft hearted auld miser's taking on an extra heir he's not required to under law? God knows he's always been fond of you, lass."

"I know," said Gloria, "We're posting the banns as soon as my period of mourning is over."

Rory laughed at her grotesque joke, but said, "That's a jest to keep among friends, darling. You know how tongues wag in a wee town like Savannah, and though he's nearing seventy, you *are* living alone with a man these days."

"I know. Efram and I discussed the gossips before we decided it would cause less scandal to simply post the banns and have done with it!"

Rory shook his head, still smiling, albeit grimly. "Don't

talk that way, damnit. We've exchanged a few dirty stories over the years, lass, but this joke's not funny. It's only sick!"

She sighed and said, "It's not a joke. I'm going to marry Efram."

"The *hell* you are!" he roared, grabbing her again to shake her roughly, as one shakes a stubborn, naughty child. She stood limp and unresisting as her chestnut curls fell over her shoulders, and Rory shouted at her, "You've surely gone mad! What you suggest is not only incest—it's a slut and a whore you'd be making of yoursel'!"

"You're hurting me," Gloria said calmly when Rory had stopped whipping her head and shoulders back and forth and was merely holding her at arm's length, staring at her in anguish.

He licked his lips and muttered, "Jesus, I think she means it! You can't mean it, Gloria! I won't let you! The Kirk won't let you! It's against God and nature!"

"The minister was a bit sticky about it when Efram approached him. But they need a rectory window at First Christ, and according to Rubin Margolis, the law can be flexible on degrees of kinship. We're going to set a lot of tongues wagging, I'll allow, but what would you have me do, live on here as his kept woman, to be put out in the streets when he finally goes to meet his maker?"

"Och, Jesus, lass, you *haven't* been!"

"Does that shock you, Rory? Did you think the old man was a monk? Did you think I was a plaster saint? I've not had your advantages in *my* loveless marriage, dearest. Perhaps if I'd owned a harem of younger, more attractive slaves—"

Rory slapped her, hard, and she staggered back to the wall behind her, dazed, as he screamed with tear-filled eyes, "You *whore!* You fucking, nigger-loving whore!"

Gloria rubbed one hand over her bruised cheek, meeting his gaze with a mocking little smile as she said, with honey and venom in her tone, "I've never slept with a slave, my dear, but tell me, is it true they're far more passionate than us?"

"You—bitch!"

"How so, my gallant macaroon? Is curiosity about such matters the sole privilege of the strutting male? What did you think I'd occupied my mind with all the years I've spent alone in my bed?"

She laughed at the look on his face and added, "You couldn't fill all my fantasies, darling. You'd be surprised what pops into a bored woman's head at the strangest times, and, oh, Jesus *Christ* I've been bored!"

"You're not to marry Efram. I won't have it."

"Oh my, you *have* gotten used to ordering women about, haven't you? What do you intend to do, dearest, take your riding crop to me? I'm not poor Martha or one of your slave girls, you know. Go back and beat some Yoruba virgin into submission, Master Martin. I'll do as I damn well please!"

"Och, it pleases you to bed an auld bastard with the head of a vulture and the virility of a litch?"

"Ah, you'd be surprised at the virility of a man who's only serving one woman at a time." Then, as her own temper cooled, she shrugged. "What else could I have done? I'm a penniless widow on a strange and savage shore. Nathan's death left me with three choices. I could live on as a charity ward as long as a stingy old man indulged me. I could take up Rose Fenwyk's profession, no doubt at a slight discount because of wear, or I could simply face the inevitable and submit to Efram, with honorable intentions as my sole bargaining point."

"Jesus! You could have come to me!"

"Why? Because you're prettier? What would *you* have offered me, Colonel Martin? Marriage? Or a furnished room at the Crown and Anchor?"

"Goddamnit, Gloria, I never touched that widow I put up at yon Crown and Anchor!"

"You didn't? She must have been deformed. Everyone knows you kept her for a week or so before getting rid of her on the *Tuscarora*." She stared thoughtfully down at the floor between them as she mused, "I wonder if she ever got home, or if the Spaniards shoveled her bones over the side with the others'. Nathan was no more discreet about such matters than yourself, you know. Though, knowing Nathan, I'd imagine he had an Ibo wench in his cabin at the end."

Swallowing the bitter taste in his mouth, Rory said coldly, "I seem to hear the pot calling the kettle black overmuch this evening, woman. You know I detested Nathan, but by God, neither of us ever sold our bodies for an auld man's silver!"

"Perhaps because you were never asked. You forget how

well I know you, Rory. I'm sure, if there was silver in it for you, you'd rut with a 'gator or anything else that would pay you!"

Rory's memory gagged on the codfish smell of Rose Donovan's unwashed groin as he drew himself up and said, "That's a damned lie." Then, as sudden understanding came to him, Rory shook his head wearily and asked, "Och, what are we fighting for, lass? You know we're fated lovers. Now that you're free at last—"

"I'm free for the moment. You're married to my best friend. This talk is leading us nowhere, Rory."

"Damnit, Gloria, I *love* you!"

She closed her eyes for a moment before she nodded and said, "As I love you, but what of it? We're two of a kind, my darling. We'll curse our fate and dream of a better one, but in the end we'll always follow the main chance."

"It sounds so heartless, coming from you."

"I know. Martha said much the same about you when she wept out her story on my shoulder. You really are a bastard, my dear, as I, alas, am a slut."

He moved over to where she leaned against the wall, took her in his arms, and kissed her cool but unresisting lips. She stood there limp in his arms as he explored her mouth with his tongue, but as he put one hand on her breast, she twisted her face to one side and said, "Enough! It's not fair to either of us."

He groped at her, as clumsy as a boy, and she insisted, "Stop it. You're teasing both of us and we—"

"One night! For God's sake give me one night, darling!"

"Where? Out in the warehouse on a coil of rope? Go home, Rory. Go home and make up with your wife."

"Once, just once. Give me at least a real memory instead of the empty dreams I've made love to for so many years!"

She twisted one of his fingers painfully as she moved his hand away from her breast and said, "No. I mean it, Rory. If you persist in raping me, I swear I'll take you before the magistrates and have you hanged."

"Jesus, you've an odd way of jesting this night."

"If you think I don't mean it, try me. Your wife is my friend and you called me a whore. I want you inside me, Rory. I want you as much as I've ever wanted anything. But I value the little pride I have, too, so, away with you, and we'll forget any of this ever took place."

"God strike me, I'll give you anything you want! I'm not the miser you're planning to waste yoursel' on, damnit!"

Her voice was cold as she replied, "Are you offering to *pay* me?"

"Anything! Name it!"

"You can't afford the price of *this* whore, Rory. For, if whore I be, I vow I'm an expensive one."

"Ay, and I'm a rich man, so—"

"Marriage. That's my price, to any man!" She laughed a trifle wildly as she half shouted, "What do I hear for a slightly used white woman, sound of limb if a little long in the tooth? Do I hear a gold ring and respectability? What's that, sir? You bid a fine home and thriving business establishment, with the widow's mite of at least a third of your estate thrown in? I say, who has a better offer, for it's going once, going twice—" Then she hung down her head and murmured, "Gone. You'd best leave now, dearest."

Rory stood there, numb but for the hurt in his chest as he stared at her and asked wistfully, "Don't you feel anything for me, *Macrie*?"

She nodded. "I love you. I want you. But what of it?" She looked away and added, "Love cannot feed me—or you either, Rory Martin. Love wouldn't come cheap for the master of Indigo Hall."

NINE

Life at Indigo Hall settled into a time-swallowing pattern as the crops and children grew. Harsh little lines settled in around Martha's mouth. From time to time, she and her husband made love, but sex had become for Martha what it had always been for Rory, when she'd been the one who'd given herself completely. If his wife's lovemaking seemed more detached, they made up for it with bizarre experiments and curious positions, for, without love, sex had become just another appetite, calling for unusual new recipes to pique the tastes of the jaded.

As time passed, their intervals of frenzied hate-love occurred seldom, for Rory prowled the confines of his small colonial world like a caged jungle cat, and Martha discovered how a ladylike mixture of Madeira and corn liquor helped to get one through a lazy Georgia day.

The laziness at Indigo Hall was entirely the privilege of its white inhabitants, however, for as Georgia's colonists learned more of how slavery was practiced by their neighbors to the north, many of the indulgences accorded slaves by inexperienced masters were replaced by so-called "black codes" regulating everything from a Negro's religious activities to his sex life.

Some few masters, such as Rory, still allowed the nation drums to throb as late as midnight of a Saturday as a reward for industry and unquestioning obedience. And the rules concerning Obeah and the other cults were flexible, for the institution of slavery was still ruled by custom rather than statute law at this point. Some planters had converted their servants to a form of Christianity in which semi-educated Negro preachers taught the gospels as the white man wanted them understood by his darkies. Other whites, perhaps because they were better Christians at heart, preferred to leave their slaves unencumbered by theology. The Golden Rule was difficult to explain to a woman whose excess children were being sold away from her, and a marriage vow between slaves, however meaningless under law, could cause problems when a male was auctioned off to someone who had all the Negresses he needed.

To Rory and many of his fellow planters, it seemed much easier to leave the slaves in their blissful state of ignorance, and the orgies of a Macambo Saturday night rather neatly justified the belief that the savage Africans were better off under the firm but fair guidance of a wise white master.

The slaves worked fifteen- to eighteen-hour days in the harvest season; the rest of the year, labor from dawn to dusk was considered enough to keep them busy. It was sometimes difficult to think up enough work for them to do, but they had to be kept busy, for it was widely held that idle niggers constituted a vague menace.

Hence, roads were painstakingly paved with crushed seashells and live oaks were planted along them for shade. Fences were whitewashed over and over, until the outlines of the wood blurred under thick coatings of lime, and many a mock Greek temple of cypress and brick began to resemble the original marble models cribbed from Sir Christopher Wren's widely plagiarized drawings.

To keep her summer kitchen busy, Martha stationed a slave in Martin livery out at the gate on the high road. His instructions were to invite any passing stranger who looked like a gentleman to pause in his journey for a meal at Indigo Hall. When Rory complained about the added expense, she threw a drunken temper tantrum and tossed a costly imported vase through a window. He left, of course, for the Red Swan, and the matter was never discussed again; Indigo Hall continued to be noted as an outstanding example of Georgia hospitality.

When she wasn't lavishly entertaining total strangers, Martha simply drank, sitting on the cunningly placed shady south veranda and nursing her growing grudge against her husband and her doubts about her children.

The delivery of Cluny had been a difficult birth, and Martha was now secretly pleased about the tipped womb that the midwife said would mean the end of her childbearing. The children were almost as great a disappointment to the once idealistic Martha as her husband's tarnished armor. Young Cluny was going to be a beauty, but she was spoiled rotten and far too immodest for any well brought up young miss of her era. Although she'd been warned, scolded, and occasionally slapped by her mother, Cluny simply couldn't understand that white girls did not expose their bodies in front of the servants.

Cluny had little tolerance for the muggy heat of a Georgia summer, however, and, when not paddling about nude in the swimming hole, she lounged about her quarters, naked, with her bodyservant, Candy. Martha might have been even more concerned had she known that Cluny and her slave girl were already practiced Lesbians. Candy had introduced her mistress to passive cunnilingus at the age of nine.

Flora, to her own credit, seldom chastised her bodyservant and half-sister, Jeanie-Calma. It was considered unwise to teach any slave to read and write, but as the harassed Hiram Quiggs drummed a bit of classical education into the only Martin child who seemed the least bit interested, Jeanie too picked up a few things as she sat at Flora's feet. By the time she reached full puberty, Jeanie-Calma was possibly the only slave in Georgia who could conjugate a Latin verb. Martha's main concern with Flora was her beauty—or, rather, the lack of it. For though the damned mulatto wench her husband had sired on some half-witted Negress was turning out to be a head-turner, poor sweet Flora was either going through a gawky phase or was destined to remain a plain woman all her life.

As for Simon, he simply wouldn't behave as a young white gentleman was expected to. He'd inherited his father's restlessness, and his hands were as calloused as any artisan's or mechanic's. No matter how often he was chided for working with his hands—as if he'd been born a common white trash child!—Simon was forever taking things apart and putting them back together again to see how they worked. He and that unfortunate Ashanti youth, Juba, had dismantled the hall clock twice before they'd been satisfied that they understood its complex gearing. They'd taken apart every lock in the house and even done something to the indigo press that Rory had been surprised to admit was an improvement. Having robbed Juba of his birthright, Rory seemed to go out of his way to spoil the boy as a slave. The black drivers had been told Juba wasn't to be made to work the fields, and though Simon already had his own body servant in General Wade, he seemed to prefer the company of the often insolent Juba.

Juba, by now, had learned not to question the master about the missing manumission papers or the money owed to his late father. Shortly after arriving at Indigo Hall, he'd made the mistake of bringing it up while Colonel Martin was in one of his uglier moods. The boy had survived the beating with no more than a split lip and a loose front tooth, but the matter of the debt had been dropped, and the only signs that he remembered anything of his previous existence, were an occasional visit paid to his father's grave— and an occasional smoldering glance at the Colonel's back.

Martha's *greatest* concern was her darling Locky. She was sure he was going to be killed in a duel, for her handsome first-born's proud carriage and unblemished profile were enough to make anyone jealous, and as he grew to young manhood, Locky was the perfect picture of a dashing macaroon in his periwig and tight satin breeches.

His mother might have worried less about his death on the field of honor had she known the reputation he enjoyed, behind his back, among blacks as well as whites.

The white youths his own age held him in scarcely concealed contempt, for he'd backed down from more than one fight with George Margolis, and had even been forced to crawl, once, when slapped with a kerchief and asked to publicly repeat a remark about young gentlemen of the Hebrew faith. A smallholder's son named Higgins had forced another public apology from Locky after the latter had passed what he'd meant as a gallant remark to young Higgins' sister. Among those of his own pigmentation, Donald Lochiel Martin was learning to keep a civil tongue in his mouth and a polite smile on his lips.

To the Negroes, Locky was an unholy terror.

Backed by the willing False Argyll and the husky General Wade, all three mounted on fine horses, Locky roamed almost as far afield as his father, albeit in a far less gallant pursuit of distraction.

A human being is a dangerous toy to give any growing child, and Locky might have been spoiled with lesser ones. Having sampled most of the young Negresses at Indigo Hall before he was old enough to think of shaving, Locky and his two young thugs now indulged in vicious sexual jokes at the expense of any slave they might catch alone.

Young stable boys were introduced to the dubious pleasures of multiple sodomy. A ten-year-old girl was held down in a field between the rows of indigo, and as False Argyll raped her, Locky mounted his grinning bodyservant and occasional lover from the rear. When False Argyll pronounced the experience interesting, Locky took his place on the screaming child and presented his pale rump to General Wade as he ravaged the stripped-down virgin in the dust. The feel of the other's penis in his rectum was interesting but uncomfortable, so Locky ordered his slave to desist, and then watched as his companions ravaged the girl unconscious. Later that same afternoon, Locky killed one of Indigo Hall's geese while discovering that avisodomy was not a very good substitute for the real thing.

Occasionally an abused Negress would complain to her own overseer or master. The masters, in turn, occasionally mentioned Locky's youthful pranks to Rory.

As a man who held property sacred, Rory chastised the lad and, after a particularly revolting complaint about a small black child found hemorrhaging at Oakwall Plantation, Locky was actually struck and made to pay the veterinarian's fee from his own allowance.

Negroes unwise enough to tell on Marse Locky seldom did so twice. False Argyll and General Wade might pay them a visit on their ponies, masked and armed with teamsters' crackers. The one time they had actually killed an abused Negress with their boyish enthusiasm, Locky had chosen to remain at home—reading, he said, Shakespeare.

The early complaints dropped to sullen whispers and the discreet tapping of a talking drum warning, "Young Martin and his Slattee ride" as they searched for further adventure.

In 1769, the Tory Parliament passed the Townsend Acts, and all thirteen colonies cried, "Taxation without representation!" The new regulations forbade further manufacture of nails, glass, paper, and paint by colonists, and placed a sales tax on such small amounts as were allowed under rules of *ex post facto*. All legal documents were now to be notarized with a royal stamp, issued to regulate the confusion between royal judges and the often free-thinking magistrates elected by the local legislatures. A sales tax on East Indian tea was added as an afterthought to help pay for the quartering of regular troops sent over to protect the colonists who got themselves into difficulties with His Majesty's Indian subjects by encroaching on those lands set aside for them by the Crown. The tax on tea amounted to less than a penny on the Spanish dollar, but the cry of outrage from the colonists prompted the befuddled young king to repeal, the following year, all but the taxes on tea and legal documentation.

It wasn't enough. In Boston, an unsuccessful lawyer named Samuel Adams formed what he called a "comittee of corespondence" and began to write to other disgruntled colonials for their views on what was to be done about the matter.

In France a radical named Voltaire outraged polite society with his cynical political satires. Another Frenchman named Rousseau was writing utter nonsense about something he called "the natural rights of man," and, in Philadelphia, Benjamin Franklin was publishing translated copies at a nominal fee, and King George was so incensed that he fired Dr. Franklin from his position as royal lieutenant postmaster general. One copy of Rousseau would reach a young red-headed Virginia planter named Thomas Jefferson and impress the young slaveholder so much that he would one day borrow a few lines from it for a longer remembered document.

In Georgia, little note was taken of the riots and demonstrations in Boston, or of the activities of a young frontiersman named Boone, who, confronted with a Shawnee chief declaring "This land is mine!" would laconically state, "Not no more" as he shot the redskin and moved his people through the Cumberland Gap into the Crown Reserves beyond the mountain barrier.

The Georgia planters, as always, were having trouble getting their bills paid across three thousand miles of sea. Some, as quick and hard as Rory, survived as Britain's financial chaos worsened. Others, weaker or more trusting, went under.

Donald Aldrich, faced with debtors' prison after a series of unwise financial deals and a very unfortunate game of whist, sold his junior partnership in the indigo presses to Rory, while Rose Fenwyk and her husband got his land, household goods, and slaves. Donald said he was off to the Tennessee Valley in the Cherokee nation, along with Sam Higgins and some others invited to join Angus MacQueen in his mountain fiefdom. The Cherokee chiefs, some of whom were partly white now, had decided their only chance of surviving the western migrations, royal protection or no, lay in aping the white man's way sufficiently to be accepted as civilized British subjects. They were wrong, of course, but even MacQueen believed, at the time, that if his Cherokee friends and in-laws lived in houses, wore white man's clothing, and farmed their cornfields with Negro slaves of their own, they would no longer be classified among the "savages" said to be the only inhabitants of the fertile Great Valley.

To the south of the Cherokee nation, the so-called Creeks had elected white or half-breed chiefs and adopted many of the white settler's ways, including chattel slavery. Their unruly cousins, the Seminoles, still clung to their old ways and nursed their sullen emnity against Muskogee and white man alike, thus showing a prescience that the more naïve tribes lacked.

Over at Efram Starr & Sons, Gloria and her new husband survived the terrible business conditions as well as the scandal occasioned by their marriage. Martha, of course, still visited her father and new stepmother, formerly her sister-in-law, but Rory avoided Efram and his bride as much as possible. He'd hoped that the first few nights in bed with Gloria might kill the old goat, but as time passed and the chandler's health, if anything, improved, it became increasingly painful to go there, even on business, and, when business pressed, Rory generally visited them about as drunk as any gentleman can be without being in danger of falling off his horse. It was easier simply to stay away.

While not yet drinking as heavily as Martha, Rory felt that his life was becoming a pointless, wretched bore. He knew he was developing a paunch, and his once clean-cut features were becoming blurred with excess flesh as he ate and drank his way through a world that held no meaning.

For slaveowners, life in Georgia was one of laziness punctuated by short intervals of frenzied activity and financial panic. If it was hard to be a slave, it was slow destruction to be a master. As one who'd started out with a fundamental sense of decency and reason, Rory was still not as bad off as many another planter who'd let himself sink into the mire he attempted to hold his slaves down in.

Rory had his children to think of, such as they were, and, while she lived, he'd still have his dreams of Gloria. But his ways of compensating for those thwarted dreams were uglier now. Years of indulging any fancy a man might dream up in an idle moment had jaded and perverted him more than he realized. Once he'd kept a tally of the women he'd dallied with, both black and white, but, as he'd lost count, he'd lost much of his interest in normal sex. It was easier, given a cowed slave girl to indulge himself with, to lie back and let her do all the work, as Nathan Starr had explained East Indian women did.

Sometimes, sprawled nude in a hammock on a warm night with one girl fanning him as another sucked his semi-erection in feigned passion, Rory found himself wondering what in God's name he was *doing* there. Was that all there was, pricks and cunts, until they came for you with a shovel?

As a novelty to top his sole unsatisfactory experiment with homosexuality, Rory tried celibacy for a time, but that was boring too. It was easiest simply to masturbate.

This, too, proved to be work. One hot afternoon when Martha had taken the children to visit the Starrs, Rory stretched out on the bed upstairs. He tried to picture Gloria's widespread legs and arms, but grimaced as, unbidden, the scrawny, liver-spotted hand of Efram Starr crawled over his partner's flesh, as loathsome as a spider. He remembered he'd gotten good results in the past by imagining he'd been less gallant that afternoon with the widow Hanks. But, try as he would, his penis refused to rise, and his imagination could do nothing with the poor husky peasant girl he'd sent home to Sussex and, Jesus, good riddance!

Giving it up as a pointless exercise, Rory put his breeches back on and decided, "The hell with it. I'll ride over to the horse races at Oakwall."

But he didn't. He'd forgotten who had riders up that afternoon and, for the life of him, he couldn't seem to give a damn. He rode, instead, to the Crown and Anchor, where, as luck would have it, his ennui was relieved for the moment by his finding Angus MacQueen in town.

They took their pewter mugs to the back garden, sat down at a table under an arbor of scarlet runner, and proceeded to get drunk together as Angus explained his business in Savannah.

He'd been asked by friends of the king, Angus explained, to sound out as many old militiamen as he knew about their position on that distressing affair in Boston a few months before.

"They're calling it the Boston Massacre," scoffed Angus, adding, "Good God, only five or so of the poor longshoremen died in the wee brawl, and it's been settled in the courts, but to read that damned broadside of Revere's, you'd mind it was another Culloden!"

"Who's this Revere?" asked Rory, not really caring.

Angus said, "Och, a jumped-up silversmith they allowed into the Free Masons and it went to his head. Our party's making a list and, once Freddy North pins the king down to a warrant of fire and sword, young Paul Revere and them others will wish to God they'd tended to their trades instead of drinking with auld Sam Adams at the Green Dragon."

"I doubt it will come to death warrants, Angus. My own lad, Simon, had a copy of that broadside Rousseau wrote, but I made him burn it. It was harmless enough for a white lad to read, but let some nigger start frothing at the mouth about equality before God and, och, there's no telling what the poor coons would make of it."

"The Indians are divided. Some are with the Crown, of course. Others have friends among the settlers with views much like those Boston Yankees'."

"Well, I'm a wee bit divided my ainsel', Angus. God knows we owe few favors to the House of Hanover, and you'll have to admit wee Georgie is an asshole."

"Damnit, MacMartin, have you forgotten it was the *Whigs* in Parliament who sent Cumberland north to savage us back in '45?"

"Ay, the Whigs are assholes, too."

"All right then. Franklin, Adams, Hancock, and Warren are all of them Whigs. The Tories have offered to restore the auld chiefs to their lands and titles in exchange for their loyalty."

"Will darling Charlie be fighting for German Georgie, too? Och, we live in a mad world, Angus MacQueen."

"Nay, you know he's been exiled to Rome by King Louis as a gesture to King George. Flora MacDonald's come out for Hanover, though."

"Dame Flora still lives?"

"Ay, up in the Carolinas with her bra' husband and an infantry squad of Tory sons. And what of you and yours, Son of the Hound? Shall I put you down as loyal to the King?"

"Och, put me down as a man who's ready, now, to fight just about anybody for any reason they give. For I'm weary with fighting my auld woman, and a war, right now, would be welcome."

"Aha! You agree it's coming to another rising, then?"

"I hope so. The last rebellion was not to my taste. If

there's another, my sons and I will prefer to be on the winning side this time."

"Then you'll stand for the King?"

"Why not? Every man knows the German Georges always win."

Juba Pardus' plan was poorly thought out and, of course, reported to Rory at once by a slave girl seeking his favor. The master of Indigo Hall considered several ways of dealing with the matter, including a couple that might have crippled Coffee's son for life. In the end, he called in Simon as a consultant, for he knew his younger son was thicker with the Ashanti youth than he should have been, and, if anyone could talk sense to a nigger planning a mass runaway, Simon was the logical choice.

They were seated in Rory's study—Simon now, since he'd had his first shave, privileged to drink with his father like a man.

Rory explained, "The harebrained nigger plans to carry his whole family with him, on foot, to the Florida line."

Simon's voice was carefully neutral as he asked, "He plans to join up with the Seminoles, then?"

"Ay, we're going to have to do something about cleaning that lot out, once this trouble with the Whigs blows over. They keep enticing our niggers to run off to yon Florida swamps, as if there was anything but serpents and fever waiting for them there. What in God's name do you reckon put such madness in young Juba's head? Haven't I always treated the wee nigger decent?"

Simon knew his father's sensitivity on the subject of the swindle that Juba would never forget. So he sipped his drink and murmured, "I daresay he has some notion about wanting his freedom, Athair."

"Och, what does a nigger want with freedom? Was Juba's father better off after Pardus turned him loose? Jesus, poor auld Coffee built half the gates and grilles in Savannah, and he was never more than a day ahead of starvation."

"I know, Athair, he had trouble getting people to pay him."

"Don't twit me, lad," Rory snapped. "Everyone in Georgia is waiting to be paid by someone. *I* owe London and Philadelphia, Philadelphia and London owe *me*. The world runs on credit, Simon."

"Ay, sir, and the wheel as squeals the loudest gets the grease?"

Rory nodded soberly and agreed, "There you have it, son. That's why Juba and his kin have been better off under my wing, for what free niggers get more than a few dropped crumbs, however loud they might try to squeal?"

He poured himself another drink from the Waterford decanter and explained, "Nobody ever intended to cheat poor Coffee, and, had he lived, he'd have been paid sooner or later. You see, Simon, it was a simple act of nature."

"You mean that he died with everyone owing him, sir?"

"No, I mean that he was born black. You've seen me tearing my hair out at this very writing table over bills, bills, more bills, and threats to take a man to law. I ask you now, as one sensible man to another, who'll pay a free nigger, who can't sue, before he pays a white man who can? I liked auld Coffee, but he was a fool to leave the protection of the Pardus family."

Simon knew better, but he couldn't say so. He smiled and said, in mock agreement, "Ay, with any luck he'd have been sold to a rice planter when the estate was liquidated."

But Rory had become so used to the grotesque sophistry his fellow planters used to justify the unjustifiable that the boy's sarcasm was lost on him. He merely nodded and said, "Ay, Coffee was a stubborn willful fool, however good a worker. His damned son seems to be cut from the same cloth. What do you think we should do with him, Simon?"

Simon didn't imagine his father would consider paying the legally free Juba and letting him go, so he dropped his eyes and said, "I'll have a word with him, Athair. There's always a chance Queen Bess was telling false tales to get Juba in trouble. I happen to know Juba refused her favors at a gathering in the quarters a while back."

Rory looked relieved and said, "Och, that's different, then, for I know how they like to try and use us to get back at one another. Let's hope that's what it was, a false alarm, but you'll have a word of warning with him anyway, won't you, lad?"

"Yes sir. I'm certain it's just spite work, though."

Rory sipped his drink; then, piqued by curiosity about Juba and the slave girl he'd rutted with that very afternoon, Rory asked, "How does Juba get along with the nigger gals these days? He's a bit older than that damned False Argyll, and your brother tells me *that* fool buck prefers buggery!"

"Takes a bugger to ken a bugger," Simon murmured to himself as his father turned to pour another drink. Jesus, the old man was putting it away this night. How many drinks did that make? Athair must have a hollow leg!

Rory turned and repeated his question about Juba's sex life as Simon squirmed inwardly. He hated to lie to his own father, but Athair had such odd ideas, and a bull-like temper to go with them. Had he heard anything about Juba and Jeanie-Calma? Flora couldn't have told him, for Flora didn't know about her bodyservant's shy trysts with the tall-grown Juba, whose maintenance work about the house offered opportunities no field hand could hope for.

Cautiously Simon said, "I mind Juba's been too busy to be serious about any particular wench in the quarters, Athair."

"Ay, but we know he turned down Queen Bess, and, though I only know this from the servants, I understand auld Bessie moves her black ass like a tavern door when the fleet's in!"

"I daresay." Simon smiled, staring down into the amber depths of his own drink as he thought back to his own afternoon with Queen Bess in the corncrib. What could have possessed Bessie to carry Juba's plans to Athair? More important, had she told about Jeanie? Did she *know* about Jeanie's begging to be taken along? The young lovers would have to be warned that their plot had been uncovered. If only Juba had enough sense to lay low, like that African hare they told about in their bedtime stories over to the quarters. . . .

"Angus Mohr was telling me a tale of the trouble in Boston," Rory was saying. "Did you know one of those rascals who got shot throwing snowballs at the royal governor's guard was a nigger?"

Relieved to be off the sticky subject of his Negro friends, Simon nodded and said, "Ay, a 'gentleman of color' he was called in Revere's broadside. He may have been an Indian, though. They call anyone who's not pure white a colored man in Boston."

Ignoring the academic question of Longshoreman Attuck's ancestry, Rory gulped a good belt of corn liquor and sighed, "Ay, I can feel the auld harlot's siren song in the wind these days. We're in for a rising, and that's the truth of it, lad."

"Harlot, sir?"

"*War*, lad. The auldest whore of them all. You've been reading the broadsides both sides are putting out. Can't you hear the promises of the raddled whore she is? Och, Angus Mohr is puffed up with dreams of being a colonel of Cherokee rangers, once one side or the other offers it to him. Captain Fenwyk will decide he's had his fill of pimping, does the king offer his commission back, and, if I know the breed, he'll take his tarnished sword to offer the rebels should the redcoats turn him down!"

Stiffly Simon said, "I don't see how one can call the Whigs the rebels, Athair. It's the king's friends who've tried to *change* everything. Conservatives like Hancock and Warren are attempting to maintain the status quo."

"Och, damn the Whigs and damn the Tories too. Both sides, being human, are out for what they can get."

"Forgive me, Athair, but the troubles up north were started by the king's friends. The colonists have asked for no changes in English Common Law. It's German George with his divine rights that brought the mobs out last winter. We Englishmen have been ruled by laws, not men, since Cromwell dealt with the last king who thought he was above the Parliament."

Rory frowned and muttered, "First he calls us English and then he insults the House of Stuart! I'll have a word with Mr. Quiggs about this, for I fear he's done a damned poor job of educating you, Simon lad!"

"Hiram Quiggs is a Tory, in case you're worried, Athair."

"Hell, what have I to worry about? I have my commission, if it comes to actual fighting, and I mind I'll be able to afford two more for you and Locky. How auld are you, sixteen? Ay, that's auld enough for an ensign. I'll form Locky a company of his own to command, and you can be his ensign."

"Athair?"

"No, wait, you have to be twenty-one for a captaincy, and Locky's only eighteen. Och, well, the fighting may not start in earnest for a year or two, and by then——"

"Athair," Simon insisted, "Which *side* are we talking about?"

Rory blinked and said flatly, "Tory, of course. Do I look like a Goddamned Whig?"

"I'm neither, sir, but if it comes to fighting in my time, I intend to fight for Georgia."

"Ay, that's what I said, lad. Georgia and the Crown."

"Forgive me, Athair, but I've spoken to the younger men on the neighboring plantations. It wouldn't surprise me, when it came to a vote in the legislature, if Georgia didn't stand with the other colonies."

"Och, that's daft! We do all our business with London."

"*And* Philadelphia and Boston, Athair. Forgive me again, but the merchants in the north pay their bills a bit more promptly than our friends in the Old Country. George Margolis says it makes more sense to stick with customers who pay, if one has to risk losing either trade."

Rory drained the last of his latest heroic drink and turned back to the sideboard, muttering, "That's what you get when you name a Jew after a German king. A poor daft loon who thinks he understands what baffles his elders to distraction."

Before they could argue further, a Negro neither of them had ever seen burst through the French doors, wearing livery and carrying a sealed note. Obviously exhausted from a hard ride, he gasped, "I's to give this-here to Colonel Martin, suhs. Sumpin awful's done happened over to Marse Starr's!"

Rory snatched the note from the messenger and tore it open, his worried frown suddenly melting into a thin little smile as he muttered, "I'll be damned. . . . Your grandfather, Efram, just died of a stroke. You'd best ride over to Oakwall, where your mother's visiting, and, um, comfort her. I have to ride at once to stand by poor Gloria's side in her hour of grief."

Simon rose as his father headed for the door. The boy called after him, "Shall I stay at Oakwall with mother or carry her to Grandfather's place?"

"Stay with your mother and comfort her. It's too late for her and the girls to be riding into Savannah!"

And then he was gone. Simon heard his running footsteps as he headed for the stables. Simon went to the sideboard and poured himself a stiff drink. He didn't really like the taste, but he knew it helped Athair through a difficult decision, and this sudden death in the family, with both his parents distracted and away, was an opportunity that might never come again.

Turning to the liveried messenger, who still stood by the doorway in confusion, Simon said, "I want you to go out to the quarters and fetch me a lad named Juba. Tell him Marse Simon wants him directly, hear?"

"Yes sir," said the slave, relieved to know what he was doing and that the pale young man he faced was not, after all, the dreadful Marse Locky he'd heard of.

Simon went out to the great hall and climbed the stairs. He passed Cluny's door and listened a moment. Cluny and her bodyservant were giggling about something behind the locked door. He doubted that Cluny would be downstairs again this night.

Locky was out on some macaroon escapade of his own, and Mr. Quiggs was at the Red Swan, probably for the night if that story about the new French girl was true.

He came to Flora's door and knocked softly. The door opened and Jeanie-Calma smiled uncertainly at him, saying, "Yo' sister ain't dressed, Marse Simon."

He saw that the slave girl was in her nightgown and said flatly, "Get dressed, Jeanie. Put on that work dress of dark blue denim and pick out your stoutest well-broke shoes. You can take whatever can be packed in one kerchief but no more. Juba will have some silver and a brace of saddle guns. So get cracking."

Jeanie-Calma's eyes widened as her half-brother's words sank in. Behind her, Flora suddenly appeared, squinting sleepily into the light from the hall, and asked, "What are you two up to, Simon? I told you I'd have no back-stairs trifling with my Jeanie."

Simon took a deep breath and said, "Flora, I'm helping Jeanie and Juba run away this night. You can tell Athair when he gets back if you like, but, if you stir from this room in the next few hours I'll . . . I'll . . . damnit, girl, stay *put!*"

Flora, to Simon's surprise, remained quite calm as she told Jeanie, "My riding boots are better for walking through snake country, dear. He's right about a stout dark dress, but we'd best stag the skirt halfway to the knee. I'll fetch my shears and get to it directly."

Flora vanished inside her quarters as, down the bedroom corridor, Juba stuck a cautious head around a corner and hissed, "Marse Simon?"

"Down here, quickly!" said the white boy, opening the door to his sister's room as Juba joined him.

"I can't go in there!" Juba said.

Simon grabbed his arm and snapped, "Inside. That damned Cluny may come out!"

He shut the door behind him and the four young conspirators stared nervously at one another by the wan glow of Flora's bedside candlestick. Flora was sitting on the bed with Jeanie's darkest dress, hacking away the bottom six or eight inches of the dragging skirt with shaking hands.

When Juba asked Simon what was up, his friend said, "You talk too much, you fool Ashanti. The whole damned plantation knows you're aiming to run off to the Seminoles."

"Jesus! Who told your father?"

"Never mind that now. Your African gods must like you, boy. Both your master and your mistress are away and likely to remain so all this night. Our Goddamned brother's out baying at the moon somewhere with the only nigger I'd match against you in a fight, and—"

"Shoot, I ain't afeared of General Wade."

"Oh, shut up and *listen,* damnit! I'm going to have to say you stole them, but I doubt I'll miss my two best mounts before, oh, tomorrow afternoon, unless the stable hands report it to me. I've got a couple of guineas in silver, and I can let you have two pistols and a fowling piece. You'd best take a cutlass, too."

"Food and water," said Flora, glancing up from her rough hemwork as she added, "Cornmeal's too heavy for the light way it sticks to your ribs. I'll pretend I'm hungry, soon as I'm finished with this skirt, and I'll fetch some goober peas and a couple of hams from the pantry."

Juba nodded and said, "I'd best get back to Ma and the chilluns and tell them to be ready to move out."

Simon grabbed Juba's arm and said flatly, "You'll do no such thing, damnit! Old Phoebe's in no condition to walk a mile, and your little brothers and sisters will slow you down even if they run. I have two *horses* for you, damn it! Mounted and armed, with a full night's start on the slave-catchers, you and Jeanie here—"

"I ain't leavin' without my kin!" protested Juba, but Simon snapped, "Then you'll not leave at all, you fool nigger! Don't you *want* to be free? Was all that talk about setting up another smithy in the Seminole nation just a lot of foolish talk?"

"Jesus, you knows I does, Marse Simon, but my kinfolks—"

"Forget your Goddamned kinfolks! Your mother's a broken woman who's as content as she'll ever be in the quarters. She has no more business in an Indian camp than a rabbit in an eagle's nest."

"But my bitty brothers and sisters—"

"Leave them. They're better off with a mother and three square meals a day. When they're old enough to think for themselves, and if my father hasn't killed me for this fool trick, I'll tell them where they can find you and Jeanie."

Flora suddenly handed the dress to Jeanie-Calma and said, "There, it's finished. I'll fetch the vittles while you get dressed."

Simon said, "No. You're to stay here, Flora, and if Athair accuses us, you'll be able to say truthfully you never stirred from your bed. I want Jeanie to get ready right now, and the three of us will creep down and leave for the stables through the pantry. It'll take only a second to stop by my room for the weapons and . . . What are you waiting for, Jeanie? Get dressed!"

"Please, Marse Simon, I dasn't take my nightgown off with you-all watching!"

Simon turned, facing the door with his back to the girl as he muttered, "Jesus! She's aiming to run off and live like a Seminole squaw and she's afraid I'll see her ass!"

Jeanie-Calma swiftly stripped and donned the boots and dress as the two boys stared at the door panels. Flora got up and went to the mulatto girl with something in her hand. She said, "I want you to have this ring, dearest sister." Then she took the slave girl in her arms and kissed her, weeping softly. "Goodbye and good luck, Jeanie. I'm going to miss you."

"I'll miss you, too, ma'am."

Simon opened the door a crack, saw that the coast was clear, and hissed, "Now. Let's go!" as he led the lovers in a quiet dash for his own quarters. He thought about Flora's last words to Jeanie as he armed Juba to the teeth and broke open the jar he'd been saving part of his allowance in. So Flora knew about Athair and that nigger woman too, did she? He'd thought he was the only one who'd heard the story whispered among the slaves. He wondered if Locky knew Jeanie was a kinswoman, and if it would even matter to his brainless brother.

He led them down to the pantry and, as Juba filled a poke with food, Simon whispered instructions. "Now, listen. There's a riding moon, so you'll cover maybe thirty miles by morning. Try and make the pine barren just over the county line before you hole up for the day. I'll probably be riding with the posse, and I can be as arrogant as Locky if I have to. Knowing where you are, I can lead my riders just far enough to one side to avoid suspicion. For God's sake, don't pull a fool trick and hide anywhere *else*! You got that, Juba?"

Juba tied the end of the burlap poke and nodded, repeating, "Pine barren. Thirty miles and over the county line."

"Right. I'm going to suggest that you followed the old military road toward Frederica, and the fords and swamps may discourage us a mite after the first few days. You're to make inland for the fall line, but don't carry Jeanie above it into Cherokee country. Follow the *cuestas* south in the disputed hunting grounds between the Cherokee and Creek."

"We will, but how does I know when we're in Seminole country?"

"You won't. They will. I'd avoid everyone, Indian, white, or free nigger, as far south as you can go. Sooner or later, you're bound to find yourselves face to face with some damned Injun, and he'll likely have the drop on you. If he's Creek or Cherokee, you'll be sold to the slave hunters. If he's Seminole, he'll either kill you or invite you home for supper."

Juba muttered, "Jesus," and Simon nodded, saying, "You two are not exactly off for a Sunday-go-to-meeting. You can still back out."

Juba stared at Jeanie in the pantry gloom and asked, "Woman?"

Jeanie said, "You lead, I'll follow, husband."

Simon said, "The stable then," and led them out and across the dark garth to the barnyard. He halted them at the fence line and said, "Wait here. I'll send the stable hands on some fool errand."

The white youth left and the two young lovers held hands in the darkness, hardly daring to breathe. It seemed hours before Simon reappeared with two horses in tow and grinned, "There's an Obeah rite over to the quarters. Cromwell and John Knox won't be back for hours, now that I've given them permission to attend. Mind you ride off at a walk and don't run the horses till you've passed Oakwall."

Juba took the reins from him, suddenly crying, "You're a *stooled man,* Simon Martin!"

"Och, get your woman and black ass out of here before we all start blubbering like babes."

Jeanie-Calma touched her half-brother shyly on the sleeve and asked, "Dast I kiss your hand, Marse Simon?"

Simon suddenly took her in his arms, hugged her tightly, and kissed her cheek as he whispered, "Go with God, kinswoman."

TEN

The runaways were never recaptured, and, to Simon's and Flora's relief, Athair asked few questions and none of them were suspicious. Their impulsive act drew brother and sister closer together, and they would often congratulate each other on the cleverness with which they'd helped their friend and half-sister to escape. In truth, the horses and supplies had been a godsend, but no white could know about the discreet drum taps that had followed Juba and Jeanie all the way to the Okefenokee, pounding out repeated messages such as, "Two of our people ride south. The Leopard says to hide the signs of their passing. Two of our people ride south. The Leopard will visit anyone who betrays them to the white men!"

Nor would the young runaways understand, at first, how the Seminoles could be waiting for them with friendly smiles to conduct them through swamps no white man dared to enter. Later, they would meet the Ashanti-Seminole who'd translated the drum talk to his Indian friends. They would take Indian names and vanish from recorded history, to become part of the only North American tribe that remained undefeated, free, and self-governing on land of their own choosing.

Rory, in truth, was not as upset as he might have been about the loss of two horses and a pair of niggers. Martha might stop twitting him about his taking advantage of Juba, and it was just as well about Jeanie-Calma. He'd grown fond of the lass, but it was hard to keep secrets at Indigo Hall, and perhaps it was all for the best that she'd run away before his white children had guessed the truth.

The main thing on his mind, at the moment, was Gloria. The only woman he'd ever loved was free again, and, this time, a rich widow. He knew better than to risk another humiliation with the flowers on auld Efram's grave barely faded, but he couldn't keep from torturing himself with hope. Save for Martha, there was nothing to keep them apart now, and he knew Gloria's friendship with his wife had cooled of late.

It was hard for anyone to be friends with Martha, drunk

as she was day and night. Rory hadn't been to bed with her in months, for it was a cold way to spend an evening, and she'd taken to pointless accusations, suddenly staring owlishly at himself or one of the childer' and saying, "I know what you're thinking, damnit! Don't you dare look at me in that tone of voice."

The childer', confused and hurt, tried to defend themselves, asking what they'd done to offend her. Rory had given it up as useless, and merely took another sip from his own glass as he met her wild stare and wilder accusations. The auld woman was daft on the subject of niggers, and, though he seldom felt like bedding *anyone* these days, he couldn't go to the outhouse without her accusing him of having dallied along the way with some servant girl. Once, in front of the boys, she'd goaded him into saying, "Ay, ay, you're right! I fucked a half dozen of 'em all in the space of ten minutes, for it's a ravenous rutting beast I am!"

Locky had made the mistake of laughing and asking, "Did you fuck any horses along the way, Athair?" and Rory had knocked him semiconscious with a savage blow, roaring, "Dinna you talk like that in front of your elders, ye puling brat!"

Mostly, however, he simply avoided his wife. A man of simple appetites, however great a portion he demanded, Rory found it easier to sup at the Crown and Anchor, or, on the occasions when his more carnal appetites needed satisfaction, at the Red Swan.

Most of the doxies there were white these days. There was little novelty in any black whore to a man who owned women of their race outright. Rose's and Captain Fenwyk's stable now consisted mostly of indentured girls from Europe or the daughters of poor Georgia trash hoping to improve their stations. Some were quite young and most were bonny, for Rose knew there was little sense in having a brothel filled with plain women when potential customers had slaves at their beck and call; but, while that blonde fourteen-year-old named Suzan was very skilled at what Rose called French lessons, it was Gloria's lips around his shaft that Rory hungered for. Sometimes he found himself content to wager on the cockfights out back, or merely to sit at a tavern table and listen to them jaw about the troubles to the north.

As time passed, the political friction between the Mother Country and her colonies became more than ever the common topic of conversation. Men who'd never been heard to express a political opinion before were suddenly quoting Rousseau or echoing the dangerous rhetoric of that mad Virginia burgess, Patrick Henry. Others had suddenly taken to flinging the contents of their blackjacks in the faces of former friends while shouting such royalist slogans as *"Pro Rege et Patria!"*

Like everything else in Savannah, the Red Swan was getting to be a bore.

Normally given to strong opinions as well as strong spirits, the master of Indigo Hall found himself more confused than enlightened by the tedious arguments over the divine rights of Good King George versus Rousseau's rights of man. When, on one occasion, Lawyer Margolis began defending some tract he called "The Wealth of Nations" against Judge Palmer's dissertation on something he called "Imperial Mercantilism," Rory stormed out in a terrible rage and nearly killed his horse by riding wildly through the night. At dawn, returning sobriety found him miles from town and deliciously alone in a cool patch of unfamiliar pine woods.

After a momentary panic at the unfamiliarity of his surroundings, Rory wheeled about to get his bearings, and found that he was amused. Dismounting, he patted his lathered mount's neck and murmured, "Ay, now you've done us for fair, you poor daft beastie. You've carried us clean out of Georgia if I'm to be the judge."

Leading the tired horse by the reins, Rory followed the red clay path between the walls of pine on either side. The sun was just about to come up and the sky was a soft ceiling of mother-of-pearl. A gentle morning breeze whispered in the pine tops, but neither wind nor dawn shadow was strong enough to hint at direction. Rory had no way of knowing, as he followed the enchanted path between the trees, whether he was leading his weary horse north, south, east, or west.

It didn't really matter.

They came to a clearing, roughly an acre or so of uncropped meadow grass frosted by wildflowers. Rory unsaddled his mount, rubbed him down lightly with the sweat-soaked saddle blanket, and said, "There, now, push your auld face in yon greenery and speak no more of the way I misrode you, eh?"

He dropped the reins in the grass, knowing the trained

horse would not run off with the stout thongs dragging just
ahead of its forehooves. Then Rory carried the saddle to
the center of the clearing and dropped it in the grass. He
stomped the sod with his heel and, as he'd hoped, found
the drier clay in the unshaded center to be firm and, if he
were lucky, free of snakes and chiggers.

The horse, though abused, would be all right, he knew.
There was no clover in the rough pasturage and, without
more water than he could chew from the dew-moistened
grass, the young gelding couldn't bloat himself, despite the
heat in his weary bones.

Rory's own bones felt abused, and, still treasuring his
boyish delight at being lost in the woods for the first time
in years, the master of Indigo Hall unbuckled his sword-
belt, threw his hat in the long grass, and stretched himself
flat on his back with his head on the saddle. He had no
idea where he was, or what time it was, or what he was
going to do when he woke up.

"To hell wi' one and all," he chuckled, closing his eyes
against the growing light as he chewed a sweet grass stem
and allowed his weight to sink into the firm but yielding
sod. He'd sleep a while, he decided. He'd sleep as long as
he liked and then, when he awoke, he'd see about finding
his way back to . . .

"Where *do* we want to go?" He frowned, opening his
eyes again to stare up at the uncaring, unanswering sky.

Rory closed his eyes a second time and insisted, "Sleep
on it, lad. Och, we've wearied our mind with all this talk of
Whig and Tory, free trade and mercantilism, and that's a
fact."

After a time, the sun was shining red through his closed
eyelids, and Rory grimaced, reaching for his hat in the
nearby grass even as he realized he'd been sleeping. He
placed the hat over his face and opened his eyes, remembering how he'd played this game as a boy. It was better
with an old knit bonnet with a few holes worn through it so
that the sunlight made constellations of pinhole lights in the
dome of blackness over your face. The trouble with a fine
felt tricorn like this one was that there was only blackness,
ay, and the smell of hair powder and the waxed leather
sweatband.

He tried to go back to sleep. But he was cold sober now,
and the earth is only soft to the truly weary. Removing the
hat from his face, Rory sat up and looked around at the

wall of pine. The horse was dozing on three legs nearby. The slanting sunbeams told Rory his booted feet were pointed at the eastern quadrant of the compass. Despite his best efforts to remain lost for at least a while, the world-weary man was having his bearings thrust on him. He'd ridden from the Red Swan with the moon riding the tree-tops to his left, and, if the sea lay beyond yon pine tops to the southeast . . .

"Damnit!" a voice called out in the middle distance, as, somewhere, chains jingled. "Git that off ox outten them bushes afore he fouls the derned ole drag!"

Rory rolled to his knees and reached for his sword-belt as, echoing through the trees, he heard the pistol-crack of a drover's whip. The white-trash crackers were given to gro-tesque attempts at humor at times, and Rory was alone.

The master of Indigo Hall buckled his sword into place and got to his feet with the saddle in his left hand as he walked over to his dozing horse, trying to locate the distant ox-team by the sounds he heard, widely spaced and filtered by the pine trunks. There was another whip crack and a second voice yelled in fear or pain. It sounded as if the head teamster had flicked his helper with the tip of his fifteen-foot lash, but, to Rory's relief, the sounds seemed to be fading. The crew dragging logs through the woods had apparently passed onto another trace.

Rory went to his horse, clucking softly so as not to star-tle the weary animal before throwing the saddle blanket across its now dry back. He saddled the gelding but didn't mount, choosing, instead, to lead his horse on foot. It was still early, and the air in the shaded roadway was cool enough for walking the kinks out of one's legs.

Now that he knew more or less which way the coast road lay, Rory thought of moving away from it, farther into the woods, but he was being foolish, he knew. He wasn't hungry yet, but he would be soon, and besides, the crackers he'd heard were somewhere to the west. It was time to get back to civilization and start thinking about . . . what? Food and drink? There were roots and nuts and berries, as well as fish and game, all the way to the Shining Mountains, unless the Indians lied.

Rory led his tired horse toward the sea, frowning as he tried to understand this strange black mood that had come over him. What was the matter with him? What was he running away from?

It wasn't the coming struggle between Whig and Tory, he knew. In the first place, he'd seen enough of man and war to suspect that when the time for talk was over, very few indeed would carry "*Pro Rege et Patria*" or "*Liberty or Death*" to the point of shouldering a musket. And if there should be some sort of uprising, what of it? He had a royal commission and, should the governor call out the militia to restore order, it would be a fine opportunity to petition His Lordship for commissions for the lads. Many of the junior officers had been spouting Patrick Henry's nonsense of late, and it might seem prudent to the governor that young men of proven loyalty to the Crown hold the vital positions in the trained bands. Simon was a bit young for a lieutenant's sash, but Locky could take over that damned Margolis whelp's company now that Whigs had been barred from holding royal commissions, and . . .

Rory's eyes narrowed thoughtfully as he caught sight of a familiar landmark against the sky. It was an abandoned eagle's nest in a dead and wind-silvered forest giant he'd ordered his turpentine crews to leave alone. Something clicked in Rory's mind and, as if he'd just looked at a map, he knew where he was.

"Och, it's on my own land I've been wandering lost!" He grimaced, wondering, even as he tried to laugh, why the thought depressed him so.

Martha had never heard of Rousseau. The nit-picking arguments between the young king and his increasingly truculent subjects were a matter for the menfolk to fret about; yet, in her own tormented soul, Martha, too, wavered between sullen resignation and outright rebellion.

She was unaware of how grotesquely her growing distaste for the man she'd once loved echoed the pending revolt against a crown and flag her neighbors had been willing to fight and die for only a few short years before. Like the desperate men who met in secret all up and down the Atlantic coast, Martha wavered both in her remembered but dying love for Rory as well as in the growing hatred she felt for the stranger who'd betrayed a virgin's dreams of marriage to a knight in shining armor.

Some nights, with a few drinks and a cool sea breeze catching her in an unexpectedly sensuous mood, Martha would catch herself wanting Rory's arms around her—although, of late, he never came to her room. On more than one such occasion, she'd been forced to masturbate, pretending it was as it had been when they were younger and Rory had been off to the Indian wars.

But while a loving wife, despite the warnings of the Church, might ease the tension of an enforced separation that way, it was degrading to be forced into self-abuse because one's husband was rutting with some tart at the Red Swan, or even, dear God, breeding more mulatto bastards with the slaves!

It was easier simply to drink oneself to sleep—though even in her dreams Martha was tormented by mingled feelings of desire and disgust. The orgies her rum- and heat-stimulated mind created in her nightmares would have shocked Rory and the girls at the Red Swan.

Awake, on the rare occasions she managed to get Rory alone, Martha alternately argued, pleaded, and, increasingly, raged at her husband. His replies, when he bothered to attempt any, were very much like those of the equally baffled King George, who, when badgered by the confused demands of the American colonists, had taken to sputtering, "Damn me, what do they *want?*"

Like his king, Rory Martin felt neither guilt nor remorse for anything he'd done to his kith, kin, or slaves. And since his indiscreetly conceived daughter had run off to the Seminoles with that irregularly acquired Juba, Martha's jibes and drunken appeals to something she called Christian charity were less relevant than ever.

Hence, Rory seldom heard what she was saying, and Martha had to repeat herself on three occasions before it sank in that she was threatening to leave him.

It was hot and muggy the evening Rory actually caught the drift of what had become, of late, the meaningless whimperings of an animal in pain.

They'd dined after sunset, and Martha had followed Rory out onto the veranda, where he was now giving some instructions to St. George, the butler. Martha bumped a wicker table with her thigh, grabbed the top with both hands to steady herself, and repeated, "I'm leaving you, Rory. I'll not stay another night under the same roof with the man you've become."

He nodded and said, "I'm busy, lass. There've been gangs of pony boys riding the roads of a night, and I want St. George and the others to look sharp to the stock."

"Can't you hear me? I want a divorce!"

"Ay, the childer' are off to the masque at Oakwall and I've a wee business in the town, so—" His eyes narrowed and he suddenly asked, "*Who's* getting a bill of divorcement, Martha? I've heard no such talk in Savannah, but, och, the whole colony's gone mad and nothing would surprise me these days."

Martha let go of the table gingerly and managed to stand straight as she repeated, with drunken dignity, "We, I repeat, *we* are getting a divorce—or, rather, *I* am divorcing *you*, you nigger-stealing, tart-chasing . . . *Scotchman!*"

"Och, you're drunk as a lord, lass. Who do you take me for, the king or some bloody belted earl?"

The sarcasm, of course, lay in the fact that under the then-existent laws of Great Britain, it took an act of Parliament to dissolve any marriage sanctified by the Church of England, but Martha was in no mood to quibble over the fine points of English Common Law. She sniffed and said, "You've betrayed me a hundred times over, and everyone in Savannah knows it. Don't you think the other wives and I know what goes on at those so-called cockfights at the Red Swan? Don't you think the slaves talk about what goes on in the quarters?"

"Easy, now!" Rory warned, glancing in the direction St. George had last been seen in. The butler, however, had faded back from the veranda into the gathering darkness like a crawfish threatened by the looming outline of a moss-covered snapping turtle appearing unexpectedly near its mudbank cave. A wise crawfish seldom waited for Br'er Snapper to announce his intentions, and a wise slave made himself scarce when white folks were drinking and making free with words like "nigger," "tart," and "divorce."

Relieved to find they were alone, Rory soothed, "Och, you've been listening to malice, lass. Auld Rose has a few doxies at the Red Swan who may be no better than they ought, but you know me better than to think I'd trifle with such trash when—"

"Is that why you deflowered that new Bambara girl the other night, then? You didn't think I knew about that, did you?"

"What are you talking about? I haven't bought a Bambara in over a year, Martha. That last gaggle of field hands were Moptibozo, and the two wives Captain Hughes threw in were older than sin and twice as ugly."

Martha stared bleary-eyed at her husband and insisted,

"Don't change the subject. You may think I can't get a bill of divorcement at the governor's palace, where you and your friends have it all your own way, but *I* have friends, too, in *London*. You may have forgotten, but my brother is a very important official with the John Company."

"Martha, for God's sake, let's put you down somewhere before you fly into a lamp and singe your wings. What in the hell have you been drinking this night, turpentine?"

He reached out to take one arm, smiling indulgently, but Martha threw herself back, gasping, "Don't touch me, you damned—" and then, before she could finish the sentence, she was sitting on the bricks of the veranda with a surprised look on her face and a plump strand of her powdered hair over one eye.

Rory shoved the wicker table aside and bent to help her to her unsteady feet as Martha blew the hair aside like a child and asked, "Did you do that? How did you do that?"

Rory sighed and swept her up in both arms, carrying her in through the French doorway as she marveled, "For such a weakling, you've always been very strong, haven't you? Where are you taking me?"

"To bed, auld woman. You're in no condition to be staggering about on your feet."

"Maybe I'll fall down again and break my neck. Wouldn't you like that, Rory? Wouldn't you just love for me to fall down and break my neck? Then I'd be dead and you wouldn't have to put up with me any more. Wouldn't that be grand?"

"Ay," he muttered under his breath as he carried her across the foyer and started to mount the semicircular staircase. The stairwell was dimly illuminated by a single lamp on the hall table near the foot of the bannister. His own shadow, topheavy with Martha's awkwardly balanced form, preceded them up the red-carpeted risers like a blot of ink soaking into a blood stain, and he'd never noticed before how sinister were the little African mask designs that the long-dead Coffee had carved into the live-oak paneling as a decorative frieze.

Martha was saying, "If you threw me over the balustrade when we got to the top, I wouldn't have to divorce you, Rory. Why don't you do that, my brave husband? I'll go 'Wheeee!' all the way down, and then you'll be rid of me, and I'll be rid of *you*, you bastard!"

Rory shifted her weight as her suddenly outflung hand

nearly threw him off balance. "Take it easy, damnit!" he warned. "We've both put on a stone or two since first I carried you up these damned stairs, and it's the two of us you'll be sending to the bottom with broken necks!"

"You don't think I mean a word I'm saying, do you, Rory?"

"Och, here's the top and yonder lies your chambers, auld lass."

As he carried her along the nearly black hallway, she insisted, "It won't do you any good to put me to bed, Rory. As soon as *you* leave *I'm* going to leave, too."

"Don't be such a loon, lass. It's fair late and there's no place for you to be leaving for."

He kicked open the door to Martha's room and, by the light of the moonbeams filtering through her lace curtains, carried his drunken wife to her four-poster. He lowered her to the brocaded white counterpane as she shook her head weakly and said, "I don't want you. I don't ever want you inside me again."

Rory snorted and stepped back, saying, "Sleep it off, lass. You'll feel better in the morning and—"

"Rory?"

"Ay?"

"Why didn't you throw me down the stairs just now?"

"Och, you must be mad, auld woman!"

"No, I mean it, Rory, and I'm not as drunk as you might think. I've drunk just enough so that nothing seems to matter, and yet it does . . . it does. Do you know what I'm saying?"

"Ay, I've put away a few cups of the Creature in my own time, but there's no answer, lass. Sometimes, when you're too drunk to stand and too sober to pass out, it seems as if, just this once, you're about to discover something grand, but och, try and get some sleep, Martha."

"Don't leave me, Rory. I'll let you go in a minute, but I'm so confused, and I want to understand what's happened. I want to know what happened to you and me and why you're so cruel."

"Martha." He sighed, not knowing why he bothered to explain. "We live in a cruel world, and a man has to do right by his kith and kin."

"Then why can't you either love me or kill me, the way a *real* man would?"

"Och, you don't know what you're saying."

"I do, I do! I've been saying it and saying it and nobody *listens!*"

Rory saw, by the pale moonlight, that one of her thin white arms was reaching out toward him, the pale starfish of her hand swimming in a befuddled circle between the bedposts. He reached out and took her cold clammy fingers, sitting down on the edge of the bed at her side as he said, "It's not easy to listen to a scream, lass. I'm all ears right now, if you've aught sensible to say."

"I think it's very sensible that I go to London and file for a bill of divorcement. That way you can be free of me and I'll be well rid of you. Will you pay for my passage on the mail packet, or must I go to Gloria for the money?"

For a long moment, Rory didn't answer. He couldn't answer until he'd mulled her words over in his mind. Annoyed at his hesitation, Martha jeered, "What's the matter, art worried about your reputation as a mighty stallion? Art feared what the others at the Red Swan might say behind your back if word got out you couldn't keep your own wife abed?"

"Och, you're jabbering like a mad auld whore, Martha!"

"You'd have to give my dowry back, too, if the bench found you at fault!" she insisted, adding, in a hurt voice, "I rather imagine *that* would grieve you more than losing my somewhat shopworn body, wouldn't it, Rory dear?"

"Damnit, Martha, there's no way decent people can get a bill of divorcement in any English court of law, and you know it."

"I see you've been giving the matter as much thought as I, then, haven't you?" She sighed, starting to draw her hand away as she added, "That's why I wonder why you haven't murdered me. I've certainly considered killing *you* more than once."

Rory held her hand insistently as he frowned and asked, "Has living with me been all that bad, then?"

She shrugged. "Only the past year or so, and only then when I've been cold sober." She shuddered and tried to sit up as she murmured, "Speaking of which, I've a bottle up here someplace. Let me go, Rory."

He released her damp fingers but remained seated as he stared at her in the dim light, trying to understand what had come over the wee mad thing he'd married. Martha rolled across the rumpled bedcovers, groping about in the tabouret on the far side and knocking something over in the dark as she muttered, "If this isn't toilet water, it has to be rum."

"Listen, Martha, I think we'd better talk this out with sober heads."

"There's nothing to talk about anymore. I'm going away, far, far away and . . . ah, it's rum, after all."

Rory reached over to take the bottle from his wife, but Martha flinched sharply, spilling liquor over both of them as she jeered, " 'Peter, Peter, Pumpkin Eater, had a wife and couldn't keep her!' "

"You bitch!" he snapped, making another grab and only managing to catch the edge of her rum-soaked bodice in his groping hand. "You scratched me!" she gasped, as he felt the stitching give way in his strong fingers. Then, as her left breast was exposed, Martha fell back on the pillow, took a healthy swig from her bottle, and said, "Jesus, you don't have to tear my dress off if you want it all that bad!"

Rory snatched his hand away as if it had touched a hot stove as, sprawled across the bed, Martha insisted, "You can have me this one last time, but I warn you, I won't enjoy it."

Rory got to his feet, muttering something about having to see a man about a team of horses as Martha, oblivious to his words, asked, "Haven't I always done my duty to you as a wife, even after you killed our love?"

He shook his head hopelessly and murmured, "I suppose you've tried, lass. God knows, in the beginning, we both tried."

Martha fumbled with her torn bodice, gave up, and said, "You'll have to undress me tonight. I seem to be all thumbs. If I should fall asleep, no doubt you'll manage to finish without me."

Rory tiptoed to the door and was about to step out as he heard her first snore. He shook his head and turned to stare down at the small pale form on the oversized bed. He didn't like to leave her alone in this condition. There was no telling what she might do or say if she should wake up alone in the house, but the childer' were over at Oakwall for the night and the house niggers were afraid of Martha even when she was sober.

On the other hand, auld Rose had promised him the first night with that new German girl at the Red Swan, and while he seriously doubted that Brunhilde was the virgin

Rose claimed she was, the child had a pretty little bee-stung pout and a well-turned ankle, so . . .

Martha rolled over and sighed in her drunken stupor. Rory's lip curled in distaste as he remembered the last time he'd made love to her while she was drunk. It had satisfied any curiosity he might have had about necrophilia— although, dead drunk, a woman was obligingly oblivious to suggestions she would otherwise rebel against.

Absently Rory began to unbutton his shirt. He knew to the last feigned moan and maidenly withdrawal how Brunhilde was going to play her part at the Red Swan. On the other hand, he didn't want to leave Martha alone like this and, anyway, it might be a novelty to spend a night in bed with his own wife after all this time.

Rory lay in the darkness, wide awake, wondering what had awakened him. He reached out to pat Martha's naked rump.

He was alone in the bed.

Running his tongue over his fuzzy teeth, Rory sat up, staring out the window for some indication of the time. Martha was probably using the outhouse. No doubt that was what had jarred him awake. The moon was down and it was as black as midnight outside. He wondered if she had thought to take a lantern with her on her way out back. As drunk as she was, she could well . . .

"Get thee behind me!" he said aloud to the darkness, adding, "You're no thought of mine, you wee dark gibbering thing. Ay, it was her ownself brought up the subjects of death and divorcement, and never a Highland gentleman!"

But the thought crept again, unbidden, from the darker shadows of a mind oft at war with his heart. He *had* wished Martha dead more times than he could remember since Gloria had become a free woman; yet despite his disillusioned wife's bitter suspicions, he was no more inclined to cold-blooded murder than most unhappy husbands.

As Martha rightly knew, Rory Martin was capable of unthinking cruelty and delighted in driving a hard bargain to the point of criminal fraud. Yet, reared in a different culture, Martha had missed Rory's few essential decencies. Though seldom followed to the letter, Martha's English Protestant code extended the fundamental Christian charities to everyone, while Rory's primitive Highland code extended only to kith and kin; unless he had been taken into a Highlander's home, a stranger was entitled to little or nothing, but the members of one's household were to be defended to the death against all comers.

Rory had been genuinely shocked at Martha's suicidal suggestions earlier that evening. Now, as he lay alone in the darkness, waiting for her to return to bed, he allowed himself to toy with the idea as a bored cat might play with a toy mouse, only half intending to tear it open.

The idea was ridiculous, of course. The childer', the slaves, and half the people in Savannah knew Martha had become a drunken shrew and that he'd been avoiding her for months. Should anything happen to her, tongues would certainly wag, and while it might be difficult to prove anything, he certainly didn't relish a repetition of those agonizing weeks after Angus MacQueen's somewhat clumsy "Indian raid." Even if he were willing to brazen through the suspicious questions, he knew Gloria would never be party to such a dark deed. His Gloria was bright as well as fond of poor wee Martha and, och, at the rate she was going, Martha might drink herself to death under the surgeon's eyes.

A catbird called from the trumpet vines outside the window, and Rory frowned thoughtfully. He swung his legs off the bed, went to the window, and peered out through the curtains at the eastern sky. There was a streak of pearly rose above the pine tops toward Savannah; it was later than he'd thought. Where the devil was Martha? Had she fallen in, for God's sake?

Rory knew he was up for good, now. He'd always been an early riser when he was sober, and he didn't relish his rum-soaked wife's damp flesh next to his in the coolness of dawn. Pulling on his rumpled shirt, he went to the door, stepped out into the dark upstairs hallway, and called out, "Porter! Who's hall porter this morning?"

There was a patter of bare footsteps and a dimly visible form approached, calling out, "I's comin', Marse Rory, sir."

Rory said, "Put the kettle on and prepare me a bath in my own chambers, Boz. Did you see Mistress Martha when she stepped out back just now?"

The slave didn't answer.

Instantly, with the sixth sense of those born to be in charge, Rory was wide awake and attuned to his servant's discomfort. He snapped, "Out with it, Boz. What's happened?"

"I don' know, sir. Miz Martha tolt me not to let on."

"Let on *what*, you black bastard? Is there some argument about who's in command, hereabouts?"

"No sir, you is my master, Colonel, but Miz Martha's my mistress, an'—"

"Goddamn it, what's going on? I'm not going to ask again!"

Boz licked his lips and stammered, "She had me harness up her sulky an' put her trunk in the boot, sir. She said I wasn't to let on I knowed where she'd gone!"

"Follow me," said Rory, moving back into the bedroom and bending to scoop his clothing and boots from the floor as he asked, "How long ago did my wife drive off?"

" 'Bout half an hour, sir," Boz replied from the doorway, "Does you want me to help you with them boots, Colonel?"

"No. Run down to the stable and have them saddle my bay. I'll be right behind you. Did she take the Savannah road, Boz?"

"No sir, she drove north, on the coast road to Carolina."

"Shit!" Rory muttered, pulling on a boot as he considered what he knew about the current coastwise traffic. Then he nodded, stamped his heel to settle his foot in the boot, and muttered, "Ay, the mail packet from Charleston is due to cast off in a day or so. It's a long drive for a woman alone, and she's only an hour out on the road at the most."

Martha's head had started to clear in the cool rush of pine-scented air as she drove full gallop through the woods, but her stomach roiled as the bumpy clay ruts of the narrow lane bounced the light sulky back and forth on its two steel-rimmed wheels. Her hair was unpinned again and whipping across her face, and as the dappled gray pulled the sulky over a particularly horrendous bump, she felt something rip just above her waistline.

Reining her horse to a stop, Martha repinned her hair and investigated her poplin trail dress with a free right hand. The tear wasn't serious. She'd just put on a bit of weight since the last time she'd worn this outfit, that was all. There were plenty of nicer things to wear in the trunk the stable hands had loaded in the boot for her, and when she got to Charleston, she'd just buy a few more things on credit. So there, Colonel Martin!

Reaching down between her boot tips, Martha lifted the half-empty earthenware jug she'd fetched along for such emergencies and took a healthy swig before replacing it on the floorboards and clucking to the horse.

The sulky rolled forward a few short yards and then rolled back a pace as the horse reared. A rough male voice asked, "What's that you got for us'un in that jug, little lady?" and Martha saw that a shabby white man was holding the dappled gray by the bridle.

An unnerving laugh sounded off to her right, and Martha flinched as the second cracker popped his long rawhide lash a few inches from her terrified eyes. The one holding her horse yelled, "Cut that out, Rafe! You'll have this durned old horse aclimbin' my ass!"

The cracker with the whip laughed again, exposing a snaggled maw of rotten, tobacco-stained teeth as he approached Martha, pleading, "Jest let me crack her one good'n, Ben. It gits me all horny to hear gals yelp the way they does!"

"You jest come over here and take aholt this-here horse, damnit. We'll talk about who does what to wimmen after we see what's in her durned old wagon."

The one called Rafe ambled over to his comrade, dragging the whip in the forest duff behind him as he muttered, "I don't keer 'bout what's in her durned old wagon, damnit. I want to see what's in her skirts. I ain't had a woman since I don't know when and—"

"Shoot, a warm meal and a good fuck'd likely kill you, boy. Here, take holt as I let go and mind you keep her steady."

As the two ruffians fumbled near the head of her horse, Martha suddenly saw her only chance, and, not really thinking so much as simply reacting, she snatched the light buggy whip from its socket on the dash, slashed the dappled gray as hard as she could across the rump, and tried to drive between them.

It almost worked. The lout called Rafe was knocked aside as the pain-crazed horse lunged forward, but the older one called Ben hung on, and, though partially dragged off his feet, managed to stop Martha's sulky a second time by forcing the horse to its knees between the shafts. The dappled gray, panic-stricken, flailed at the dashboard with its rear hooves as Rafe, bounding to his own feet, threw an unaimed but powerful whiplash in the general direction of the noise, dust, and confusion.

The tip of his cracker tore a square inch out of Martha's right cheek and sent her, screaming in agony, over the far side of the sulky. She landed, spreadeagled, between the flailing hooves of her horse and the pendulum roll of the steel-clad wheel. In all the noise and confusion, neither Martha nor her two attackers were aware of the approaching hoofbeats until it was too late.

"*Chlann nan Con!*" screamed Rory as he bore down on the scene. This was not Colonel Martin of Indigo Hall, constrained by the Sassunach's confusing rules. This was Rory of the Broad Axe once again, face to face with life and death as a Lochaber lad had been raised to face them. Rory had taken in the scene at a glance and was moving in at a full gallop, sword in hand and a Highland war cry on his lips.

The cracker, Rafe, had been raised by a primitive code too. He dropped to one knee to get below the slash of the oncoming horseman and, at the same time, snapped out a coil of his long whip to entangle the legs of Rory's mount. Rory anticipated the horse's fall and, kicking free of his left stirrup, threw himself sideways from the saddle as Rafe leaped to his feet and ran backwards to jerk the bay down with the long whip. Rory landed on his own feet, ran forward with the momentum of his ride added to his own speed, and drove the blade of his rapier to the hilt into the screaming Rafe's lower abdomen, breaking off the tip on a spinal bone.

By this time, Ben, who'd been holding the dappled gray, had let go and was running for his life. Rory freed his hung-up blade by driving a boot heel into the dying Rafe's middle. Then he, too, was running, and gaining with every step.

Ben heard the pound of bootheels coming up behind him and screamed back, "I got me a dagger-knife here, mister! You jest better let me alone, you hear?"

Rory didn't answer. He was out of shape, he knew. He had to catch the bastard before the fresh energy of his rage cooled. He had a stitch in his side already and breathing seemed to be a waste of time, but damn it . . .

"I'll *cut* you, mister!" the cracker pleaded, not even looking back. "I'll cut you good, do you come any closer!"

Rory made a supreme effort, overtook the fleeing cracker, and slashed one tendon above a flashing barefoot heel with the broken tip of his sword. The cracker wailed like a child and fell in a ball, holding the injured ankle with both hands as he blubbered for mercy through the dirt and tangled beard on his face.

Rory took a deep strangled gasp of what seemed to be pure fire, shook his head to clear the pinwheeling stars from before his eyes, and, without a word, kicked Ben's face back to expose the dirt- and sweat-blackened throat for the one practiced slash it took to kill him. Then, holding his side with his free hand, Rory limped back to where he'd left Martha. She was sprawled in the road and covered with blood.

His own mount, having freed itself from the cracker's lash, had struggled to its feet and was standing nearby, albeit nervous and limping on one foreleg. Martha's dappled gray had also recovered its footing, and, pulling the sulky behind it, trotted a few yards into the trees before being stopped by saplings wedged between the wheels and running boards. Martha lay alone in the center of the clay road, a dust-covered, broken doll.

"I knew you'd come," she murmured as Rory dropped to one knee at her side and started to dab at her wounded cheek with his pocket kerchief. She tried to shake her head, gave it up, and said, "Don't move me, Rory. The wheel went over me more than once, and I'm all broken glass inside."

"Och, you'll be right as rain, lass. I'll fetch the surgeon and he'll no doubt have you up and about in no time."

"They were going to rob and rape me, but you made them stop, didn't you?"

"Ay, but if only you'd been *sensible,* lass. You knew these woods are filled with desperate men these days and—"

Martha laughed, caught her breath in a gasp, and sighed. "I knew you'd come. I remember thinking, just as that awful man hit me with the whip, I remember thinking, just wait until Rory comes . . . you'll be . . . so sorry then."

As Rory fumbled gently with the hooks on her trail dress, trying to discover the extent of her injuries, Martha shuddered and said, "I seem to be dying, Rory." Her tone was matter-of-fact, without self-pity.

He was of the opinion that she was right, but he smiled and shook his head, saying, "Just a few bruises and the wind knocked out of you, lass. If I can just get you back aboard the sulky without bending you——"

"Does it really matter, then?" she whispered. "I thought you'd be pleased with . . . with the chance I'm giving you."

Rory frowned in genuine confusion. "Chance? Och, what are you talking about, auld lass?"

She smiled faintly. "Have you forgotten our conversation already? You've been wishing me dead long enough, Rory. I've no doubt you'll find the advantage somewhere."

Rory didn't answer.

She explored one corner of her mouth with the tip of her tongue. "I'm almost numb now. It won't be much longer. May I tell you one more thing, Rory?"

"Ay," he sighed. "Say anything you like, for you always have."

Martha's eyes misted over as she whispered, "I love you, Rory MacMartin. Heaven help me, but I've always loved you, and you've always known it and taken advantage of it and——"

"Martha," he cut in in a strangled tone, "what do you *want* from me?"

"You might say you once loved me, just for a little while."

"Och, sweet Mary Mother of God——"

"Is it so hard, then, even as a lie?"

Rory looked away; then he touched her lightly on the chin, met her eyes, and said, "You know I love you, Martha."

It would have been comforting to think she'd heard him as she died, but Rory had seen enough of death in others' eyes to recognize it in those of his wife.

ELEVEN

The coroner's inquest was held at the governor's palace not because His Lordship suspected Colonel Martin of anything, but simply because English Common Law called for an inquest and, for once, His Lordship might be able to give a simple order without having those damned Whigs in the colonial legislature disputing his word.

Neither Whig nor Tory cared to claim the two crackers Rory had killed in the attack on his late wife. A few questions on the part of the high sheriff's possemen had quickly established the attackers as a pair of drifters from out of the county who'd been sacked from a logging camp for laziness and suspicion of theft. The story Colonel Martin told seemed simple and straightforward enough to the coroner's jury, and they accepted it without cross-examination.

Martha's death was recorded as murder most foul, while the killing of the two crackers was accepted, and commended, as justifiable homicide. Rory left the coroner's inquest and, shaking off the friendly hand of Lawyer Margolis, who'd suggested a drink at the Crown and Anchor, walked the few short blocks to the Church of Our Lady, one of the few Roman Catholic establishments in Savannah.

Rory found the young priest, Father Conan, polishing a brass candlestick near the altar. "Do you have the Gaelic, Athair?" he stammered to the Irishman.

As the younger man nodded with a puzzled smile, Rory dropped to one knee at his feet, made the sign of the cross, and said, in his native tongue, "Forgive me, Father, for I have sinned!"

In the same lilting tongue, Father Conan asked, "Is it a Catholic you are? I've never seen you at services, and there are not that many of us in Georgia, if you follow my drift."

"It's Church of England I'll be buried, Father, but I was raised in the old ways, in the glens. My people were Jacobites in the '45, and it was as a transported man I came to this land."

"I understand. From the fine wig and tailor's sword, I'd

say you thought it prudent to pray in High Kirk English, too."

Rory got to his feet, brushed off the dusty knee of his moleskin breeches, and, reverting to English, muttered, "Och, you can go to hell, too."

But Father Conan put a hand out as Rory started to turn and said, "Forgive me. We seldom have the opportunity to mock our lapsed brethren, and I'm afraid the temptation was too much. Why don't we start all over again? The confessional is over there, through that archway."

"Confessional?" Rory frowned. "In the glens our own chief's brother was our priest and confessor, Athair. We didn't crawl into a box with him like some damned Frenchman!"

Father Conan laughed. "I know a few things about saying a mass behind a hedgerow when our Sassunach brethren are taking an Orange Walk with torch and bayonet. I can hear your confession out here by the altar, if that's the way you want it."

As Rory knelt a second time, Father Conan fingered his rosary and asked, "Do you wish to keep your name to yourself, then?"

In Gaelic, Rory identified himself, and, as the young priest nodded in sympathy, having heard of the murder along with everyone else in Savannah, Rory plunged on in a sobbing torrent of words until, during a momentary break in his account of Martha's death, the priest asked, "But what are you *confessing*, my son? Is it absolution for the deaths of those murderous outlaws you fought in defense of your children's mother?"

"Why should I ask God to forgive a thing like that, Father?" Rory snapped. "They were scum too lowly to rank in God's scheme of things as high as a fine clean timber wolf. Besides, the coroner just told me I did the right thing."

"I agree as a man and as a priest of Mother Church. I doubt you'll have to answer overmuch for either of them. But what is it you've done that's brought you here? You said you had a *confession* to make!"

"I do, Father. I want to confess. I *have* to confess. I have so much on my mind, and I tried to make them understand, but I know they think I murdered my wife."

The young priest kept his voice carefully neutral as he asked, "*Did* you murder your wife, Rory MacMartin?"

"No, as God is my witness, it all happened just as I told

them over at the governor's palace. I know they think I
made it all up, but I swear to you, Athair, it happened just
as I said it did."

"Did any of the jurors say they thought you'd lied,
Rory?"

"No, they just sat there like the Sassunach owls they
think they are and nodded their heads at me as if they
swallowed every word."

Father Conan rolled his eyes up to the rafters of his
modest church as he tried to remember what they'd told
him at the seminary about this sort of problem. He placed
a hand on Rory's shoulder and asked gently, "Don't you
suppose it's possible, my son, that your Protestant friends
believed your account as I do? I mean to say, though I
hold Protestants in error on many accounts, that I doubt
they'd have acquitted you had they thought you were a liar
and a murderer."

"Och, that's because you don't know the way things are
in Georgia, Athair. The whole colony runs on lies and theft
and murders! Not a man on that jury would have dared to
accuse me of any crime had I handed him a confession
signed in my own blood!"

Father Conan nodded and looked away, murmuring, "I
am unfamiliar with political favors, having received so few
in my time, but if you'll forgive me, your conscience is not
bothering you about the deaths of those three people on the
Charleston road, Rory MacMartin."

"It is, Athair. I can't get the look in Martha's eyes out of
my mind and, just now, at the governor's palace, it seemed
they were all looking at me the same way."

"Accusingly?"

"Ay, that's the word I was groping for. My wife's last
words were love words, yet as the life faded from her face,
she seemed to be accusing me of some terrible thing I'd
done to her."

"I see, and what terrible thing do you suppose it might
have been, my son?"

Rory frowned and, meeting the priest's gaze with the
puzzled innocence of a child, said, "I don't know. I mean,
of course we had our angry words from time to time, but—"

"Are you glad she's dead?" the priest cut in.

Rory leaped to his feet and sputtered, "Och, Athair,
that's a *terrible* thing to ask a man!"

"I know. That was why I had to ask it. Your emotions

are not as unusual as you might think, my son, and, with God's help, I'll try to explain."

"Be off with your explaining!" Rory snapped, turning away and heading for the door as he added heatedly, "Och, I don't know why I ever came to a bead-mumbler in the first place! There's more salvation in a jar of the Creature than any man ever found in a book!"

In Gaelic, Father Conan called out softly, "I'll pray for you, anyway, Rory MacMartin."

Then, as the confused and angry man stomped out of the church, he sighed and turned back to his polishing. A Negro man came in from the rectory, carrying a broom and wearing a worried frown as he asked, "Was somebody yelling in here, Father?"

The priest nodded at the old man and said, "A tormented man with a terrible load of guilt, I'm afraid. He didn't stay long enough for me to find out what it was."

The black sexton shrugged and changed the subject to complain, "You hadn't ought to polish your own brass, Father. If you can't wait for me to get around to it, why don't you buy that boy I told you about the other day?"

"Buy a *slave*, for a *church*?"

"Why not, Father? They got slaves over to St. Joseph's Church."

Father Conan sighed, crossed himself, and murmured, "If they want to call it a church, I suppose they have a right to, but forgive me, Lord, I'm having a hard time getting used to the colonies."

TWELVE

The wedding could not take place until Gloria was satisfied that a decent period of mourning for Rory's late wife had elapsed.

Meanwhile, despite his pleadings, she remained adamant in her refusal to go to bed with him.

Gloria knew many tongues were going to wag in any case, and she'd known all along about the spies watching her bedroom windows. It might have been to discipline him, too, that she warned Rory that her own darkies were keeping an eye on *him*.

And so, as he waited for his dreams about Gloria to come true at last, Rory put his house in order. Indigo Hall was cleaned and redecorated, and its staff reorganized. Queen Bess had a wagging tongue and knew too much about her master's more unusual habits. Other house gals who wouldn't have dared speak of such matters to their new white mistress might, nevertheless, titter a few secrets to the black maids Gloria was bringing over from the Starr holdings. So the wenches who'd serviced him were sold aboard a northbound coastal brig, as were Boz, the night porter who knew too much about the back-stairs sports of Indigo Hall, and a sullen Kru stableboy who'd been heard repeating some of Tom Paine's tommyrot about equality.

The children, badly shaken by their mother's murder, accepted the idea of Gloria without demur, although young Cluny couldn't resist twitting, "I do so wish we could get Aunt Gloria to stay put, Athair, for first she was our aunt, and then she was our grandmother, and now you say she's to be our mother?" If the others found the situation a trifle grotesque, they never mentioned it. The children had known Gloria all their lives, and even the spoiled Locky liked her.

A few giggles might well have been exchanged among the neighbors, but Rory was known in the colony as a deadly swordsman with a famous temper, so the banns were posted on the church door with no comments passed in public. Whig and Tory alike appeared at the big church wedding, and when Colonel Martin led his bride down the church steps to the waiting coach and four, an honor guard of the King's American Rifles faced the Georgia trained band, their crossed bayonets forming a steel arbor for the newlyweds to pass under. Not a man there guessed that in less than eighteen months they'd cross bayonets again in a less joyous manner, but the mounting tension was starting to show around the corners of some mouths, and the vicar made a mental note, as he watched from the doorway, not to ask the governor for military honor guards until this current nonsense had been resolved.

At Gloria's suggestion, they'd agreed to spend the first few nights of their honeymoon at the Starr house, rather than at Indigo Hall. The children and the painters rather cluttered up the larger house, she'd insisted, and had added, a trifle archly, that after waiting twenty years, they might well want to be alone for a time.

Rory hadn't cared for the idea, for, if Martha's ghost still haunted Indigo Hall, Gloria had lived with not one but two previous husbands over at the Starr place! He went along with her whim, though, and after a dull and interminable wedding reception, followed by the dismissal for the night of Gloria's house niggers, he found himself as nervous as any virgin bridegroom.

Rory had waited years for this moment, and as Gloria led him to her pink-satin-covered bed, his heart was pounding like a trip hammer. He kicked the door shut with his heel and took her in his arms at the foot of the four-poster. Gloria melted in his arms, returning his kiss with soft passion, but when he started to lift her onto the bed, she shoved herself gently but firmly away and dimpled. "Wait, my darling. I have to put my wig on its stand and undress properly if either of your girls is ever to wear this wedding gown."

"Och, hang the gown, I'll buy you a dozen!"

"I know, Rory. I want you too, but you see, I'm all pinned in and laced up the back. Here, I'll turn around and you can help me with the back while I see if I can unpin this overskirt without stabbing myself to death."

"Gloria . . ." His voice was a groan. "Och, I've waited for this moment all these years, and you stand there fiddling . . ."

"You just stay here and take your own clothes off, then," she suggested, pulling away from another clumsy embrace as she added, "I'll go into the next room and make myself presentable."

Then, before he could stop her, Gloria had skipped around him, laughing, as she pulled off her powdered wig. She went into the small dressing room that opened off the master bedroom, and as Rory sat down to tug at his boots with nervous hands, he could hear her humming an old English madrigal above the silken rustle of clothing being removed and folded away. He'd barely gotten boots and shirt off when Gloria reappeared in the doorway, naked in the candlelight, smiling into his eyes.

Rory's breath caught in his throat at the sight of her, for she was, if anything, more beautiful than his imagination had envisioned. He felt his face flush, as she walked over and sat down beside him on the bed, asking, "What's keeping you, darling? Do you want me to snuff out the candle?"

By way of an answer, Rory leaped to his feet, tore off his moleskin breeches, and, tripping as he tried to kick them off, fell heavily across the bed. Laughing, Gloria rolled out of the way.

The humor of the situation escaped Rory as he pulled her body against his own, and then it was happening. The love goddess he'd waited all these years to possess was his, her warm, lush breasts crushed against his sweating chest as he parted her thighs with one knee and probed for her vagina with fingers clumsy from nervousness. Gloria sighed and returned his kiss with passion, running her tongue between his suddenly dry lips as he moved his pelvis into position between her widely welcoming limbs. Her throbbing, moist opening rose to meet his glans as, grasping the shaft of his penis, he attempted to enter in fact the body he'd so often entered in fantasy.

He ejaculated almost immediately and at once went limp as a wet dishrag.

Cursing against Gloria's encouraging kisses, Rory rubbed the wet tip of his traitorous member between his bride's vaginal lips, as she, in turn, drew her knees up to encourage entry. After a time of incoherent, frustrated panting on both their parts, Gloria moved her lips aside to soothe, against his cheek, "You're trying too hard, dearest. Why don't we snuff the candle and try again in a little while?"

"I'm all right!" he insisted, even as he felt his penis shrivel further in his fingers.

Gloria said, "We're both tired and overwrought, Rory.

Let me snuff the candle, and when we get our breath back, I'll get on top."

Rory tried to argue, but Gloria was as willful in bed as she'd ever been anywhere else, and so, disengaging herself, she slid across the counterpane to reach out with one long creamy arm to put the candle out. Then she urged Rory onto his own back and, as he insisted, "This has never happened before!" she ran cool fingertips over his moist flesh, soothing, "I know, dearest. We've had to wait so long . . . I know how to make it better."

Rory started to ask how she knew, but gagged mentally as he answered his own thoughts with a picture of Gloria caressing her two late husbands. She was fondling his genitals now, and if she did so with the skill of experience, what of it? It wasn't as if he'd expected her to be a blushing virgin, after all. He felt his flesh responding and whispered, "Kiss it, lass. Take it in your mouth and make it hard."

"Don't be vulgar, darling. You're already responding . . . see? Just be patient, my dearest."

Rory frowned up at the dark ceiling and asked, "Haven't you ever, uh, done it the French way? I mean, just as a change?"

Gloria stopped what she was doing and said, "I asked you not to talk that way, dearest. Nathan used to talk that way and I found it quite disgusting. I mean, it's hardly *my* fault if you're not up to serving me as a man is expected to serve his wife, is it?"

"*Who's* not a man?" he growled, rising on one elbow as Gloria firmly stroked his shaft.

She insisted, "Oh, do lie back and behave yourself, Rory. I want to do it just as much as you do, you silly darling."

Then, suiting action to words, his bride slid a firm thigh across his knees, moved into position, and sank onto his semi-erection with a contented sigh. She leaned forward, brushing Rory's chest with her swaying nipples as she moved experimentally, saying, "Oh, yes, I like the way it feels in me, darling!"

Rory moaned in pleasure and thrust his hips from the mattress as it came to him that, yes, this was really Gloria. After all these years of wanting her, she was here in his bed, welcoming him inside her.

And that, as it turned out, was the trouble.

The impotence of that first tense night never returned to plague them. And his new bride was, in truth, a wonderfully responsive sex partner. But that was *all* she was. In the flesh, Gloria was only a warm-blooded, passionate, but mortal woman. She'd been born with the normal appetites and physical possibilities of any other beautiful woman of her generation. Gloria was possessed of a truly stunning figure for a woman her age, but it was, after all, the figure of a middle-aged human being, not that of an acrobat. Gloria had little trouble reaching a climax, and while she was a good sport about experimenting with some new positions, her pain threshold, too, was normal. She was not, after all, either one of Rose Fenwyk's doxies or a frightened slave girl. She was gentle but adamant about what she called "beastly behavior" and refused to submit to either oral or anal advances.

By the third night in bed with Gloria, Rory was stimulating his erection by pretending, with his eyes closed, that Gloria was that Yoruba girl with the plucked pubic hair and delicate tribal markings on her budding breasts.

By the fourth night, he was pretending Gloria's rather tight vagina was Martha's willing rectum. The Yoruba girl he'd had that afternoon in the drying shed *had* been a virgin, after all, and no more willing than this damned wife of his to sympathize with a man's need for a change of pace.

And so, once Rory and his new bride returned to Indigo Hall, things were much the same as ever, after all. If Gloria made a more gracious hostess and a more presentable wife for Colonel Martin than had her sister-in-law, Rory, in turn, drank a bit more, took longer rides alone, and spoke less to his family as he tried to understand just what had happened.

He was bored and unhappy. That much he knew. The puzzle, to Rory, was *why*.

He had everything he'd ever dreamed of having. Once an illiterate boy in chains, he'd risen to a royal commission and the respect of the very Sassunach who'd taken him prisoner so many years before. He owed debts his grandchildren would doubtless be paying interest on, but in this he was no worse off than any other Georgia planter, and in every *other* way he was better off than most.

He had a thriving plantation, a gracious home, a fine family, loyal slaves, and, damnit, his horses and game cocks even won more often than they lost. What more could any man want? What more *was* there?

THIRTEEN

Georgia had sent no delegates to the first Continental Congress in '74. By the time the second congress could convene in '75 another country squire and militia officer named John Parker had brawled with Pitcairn's Regulars at Lexington, a village in Massachusetts.

The news took weeks to reach Savannah, and when it did, nothing seemed to change. The darkies worked the fields, sometimes singing mellow work songs, sometimes running off to join the Seminoles. Nothing else seemed worth getting excited about.

The militia drilled on the muster field as before, not quite certain whom they'd be sent to fight if and when the troubles reached this far to the south. Tory and Whig went armed these days, for the woods were filled with rough gangs claiming to fight for one side or the other in a struggle few Georgians understood.

News of other disturbances came down the coast by schooner, and about the time that the darkies were dusting the peach trees with lime and sulfur, the royal governor and his staff moved out to a British man-o'-war moored in the Savannah roads. Someone had thrown rocks through his bedroom window, and the news of Bunker Hill had upset His Lordship greatly.

In the taverns, Rory and his friends exchanged the latest market figures and gossip, dimly aware that two militia companies had exchanged fire as close as the Carolina Piedmont in a short, bitter fight the Whig side claimed to have won.

Over beyond the Cumberland Gap, Shawnee warriors loyal to the Great White Father in London had attacked Whig squatters led by the ruffian Daniel Boone. Angus MacQueen sent word that he needed powder and shot for his Cherokees, who were, he claimed, loyal to King George. Other Cherokees, however, were reported to be joyously helping Boone and his Kentucky boys against their old enemies, the Shawnee, while to confuse matters further the Creeks under their half-breed chief, MacIntosh, had declared for the king, and the Seminoles, as always, killed any white man, Whig or Tory, they could get a shot at.

Yet, as if preserved in amber, life in the Georgia tidewater seemed poised in time. That lazy summer, Gloria entertained as lavishly at Indigo Hall as Martha ever had, and the gossips conceded that the new mistress was not only prettier but a good deal less inclined to make caustic comments than Mistress Martha had been. The children still missed their murdered mother, but not at Gloria's expense, for she was less a stepmother than an old and understanding friend.

Rory, too, fell into the lazy routine of yet another summer, having resigned himself to the bitter fact that the Gloria he'd pined for all these years had simply never existed. His new wife, while sometimes an annoying stranger, was bonny enough, and at least she never yelled at him. But he realized, now, that he'd driven Martha to both strong drink and her last erratic behavior. The lesson made Rory a more considerate husband than he might have been to Gloria, and while he still rutted with the new slave girls from time to time, he took care not to be as obvious about it; knowing the way gossip flew in Savannah, he even took to avoiding the Red Swan completely.

Since the Red Swan was the local hotbed of the Whig cause, Rory was unaware of how close the war clouds were drifting until one evening when he was sitting on the veranda sipping a tall cool drink and Simon found him there and blurted, without preamble, "Athair, I've decided to join the army!"

Rory nodded approvingly. "Ay, I may be called out with my rangers myself if the trouble spreads much farther south. I'll see if I can buy you a commission as ensign in the King's American Rifles. Your elder brother's already my lieutenant in the militia and—"

"Athair, you don't understand. I'm joining the Continental Lines."

"Continental Lines? I've never heard of any such regiment."

"It's new, sir. Colonel Washington is forming up a force of regulars just outside of Boston at a place called Cambridge, and—"

"*Washington?* Have you been drinking, lad? Washington's a Goddamned *Whig!*"

"It's gone beyond Whig and Tory, Athair. It's us against them. Americans versus the English."

"Och, you're mad, Simon. You *are* English, on your poor wee mother's side. Let me tell you what they say about yon Washington, ay, and that lecherous auld devil, Franklin, too—"

"Athair, I know your views on the Continental Congress, but you don't understand what the fight is about."

"Och, Simon, Simon, have off with the rights of man, divine right of kings, and other puling phrases made up by men who've never faced cold steel in a foeman's hand. Stay here with me and let the fools fight it out, for it's all nonsense, Whig and Tory alike. Besides, the fighting's far from Georgia, and our only real worry this summer will be the 'digo. This damned dry heat is starting to wilt the crops in the fields, and if we don't get some decent northeast rain—"

"I'm off for the north with the evening tide, Athair. The lugger *Spanish Dancer* is putting out with a cargo of naval stores, and they've agreed to carry us as far as Philadelphia."

"I'll be damned if that's so, laddy buck! You'll board no wee rebel lugger with a squadron of royal navy standing just offshore! Whose mad idea was this? Have you been listening to that damned Jewish lad, George Margolis, again?"

"George is one of us, Athair. Seven, in all, have agreed to volunteer for Savannah's honor in the Continental Lines."

Rory snorted and took another sip of his drink. "Well, I've just *un*volunteered you, then, for no son of mine is about to run under the guns of a royal '74 in broad daylight, and that's the last I'll be hearing of it this day!"

Simon started to say something. Then he shrugged and turned away, murmuring, "If that's the way you want it, Athair."

He went back through the house to George Margolis, who was waiting on the front veranda. George asked, "Well, what did he say?" and Simon answered, "What did you expect him to say? *Your* father forbade you to join us and he's a *Whig,* for God's sake!"

George nodded and, glancing guiltily around, insisted, "Just the same, I'm going aboard *Spanish Dancer* this afternoon. What about you?"

"Och, did you think I'd stay here while you and the others got all the glory?"

Both boys laughed and started for the stables. George Margolis was whistling "Yankee Doodle," and if they swaggered more than they had any right to at this stage of their military careers, it was because both were very young and very frightened.

"It's madness, utter madness!" Lawyer Margolis was saying for perhaps the hundredth time since bursting out onto Rory's veranda with an anguished cry for help. The two fathers were on Factor's Wharf; they had just ridden hell for leather to Savannah in pursuit of the runaway boys. Four other fathers and an anxious widowed mother had gathered around the foot of the same gangplank as Rory argued with one Captain O'Brian, skipper of the schooner *Cherokee Rose*.

Rory assumed that Rubin Margolis thought it was mad for the boys to have boarded the *Spanish Dancer* a few minutes before, but Captain O'Brian thought it would be mad to cast off in pursuit of them now.

Waving a hand at the brown sails of the receding lugger, O'Brian explained, "They'll hug the shallows along the far shore and hope to play innocent, I'll vow, but I know the sonofabitch in command of the H.M.S. *Corgie*. He's a spanking new young twit of an officer, and he'll be spoiling for a fight."

One of the other fathers asked, "Why should a royal vessel fire on the *Spanish Dancer*, Captain? She's flying no colors, and she's known in these parts as a peaceful coastwise trader!"

O'Brian laughed. "Ay, that's the point of it. The *Spanish Dancer* is known. Her skipper's known to be a Whig and a smuggler. The odds are better than fifty-fifty that she'll be ordered to heave to for inspection as she comes under the *Corgie*'s guns."

Margolis asked, "Won't that solve our problem, then? If one of His Majesty's vessels stops the *Spanish Dancer* and we catch up before they release her——"

"Release her?" O'Brian barked. "You've not been listening, Lawyer Margolis. The H.M.S. *Corgie*'s commanded by a young whelp with a taste for prize money, and the crew of the *Spanish Dancer* are known to him as rebels. You see——"

Rory cut in, "Yon lugger's not waiting for us to *talk* about her half the night. Will you take us aboard, Captain O'Brian? I can pay well for a short merry chase, and—"

"I'd like to help you, ladies and gents, but I've grown fair accustomed to my skin."

Margolis started to argue with him, but Rory turned and asked, "Can any man here hold a vessel this size on a steady tack?"

Two men in the growing crowd nodded. Rory said, "Ay, and both sails can be manned from the deck by anyone with an ounce of brains. How many guns do you have aboard, Captain?"

"Guns?" O'Brian frowned. "I've a swivel gun fore and aft, just to keep the Indians at bay in desert coves. What the devil would you be wanting with *guns,* Colonel Martin?"

"We may have to fire a shot across the *Spanish Dancer*'s bow, if we can overhaul them before they reach the British fleet standing off the harbor bar."

"Don't be daft," the captain snorted. "Any skipper who puts out to sea without a royal pass is just begging to be seized as a prize by those royal navy rascals waiting just around the bend. My vessel stays where she is this night."

Rory sighed, drew his pistol, and said, "Get out of my way, Captain. I'm commandeering this schooner in the name of the Georgia militia. You can stay here if you like. I'll need your six crewmen to man the lines. These other gentlemen and I are in a hurry, so don't make me kill you."

"This is piracy!" gasped O'Brian, hastily getting out of Rory's way as the taller man strode up the gangplank. Just behind him, Rubin Margolis murmured, "He's right, you know. Georgia's not at war with anyone, Colonel Martin."

"Do you want to stay ashore, Margolis?"

"I didn't say that. I only said we were committing an act of piracy. Which side are we seizing this vessel for, anyway?"

"Our own side, of course," Rory growled. "I'll want you on the forward swivel gun, Margolis. You've ever been a fair shot on muster days."

"Who am I suppose to be shooting at, Colonel?" Margolis asked with desperate calm.

Rory's voice was dead flat as he replied, "Any sonofabitch I *tell* you to shoot at, of course!"

* * *

The sun was low in the west, gilding the normally tea-colored waters of the Savannah estuary a glaring orange as the commander of the H.M.S. *Corgie* tried to make out just what that dark blur against the sunset might be. He lowered the spyglass thoughtfully and, turning to his first officer, said, "I make her a small lugger ghosting just outside the reeds along the north shore and hoping for the best. Signal her to heave to for inspection. Oh, and while you're about it, have the gunner's mate unlimber the bow chasers."

"Ay-ay, sir. Shall we be wanting the broadside guns run out?"

"For a shallow draft lugger, Mr. Hames? Let's not get carried away with this nonsense, eh? I'm hoping, at best, for the interception of a few cases of contraband, seditious dispatches, or perhaps one of the rebels on our wanted list. There's not a vessel in Savannah harbor that would rate a broadside from a ship of the line!"

The lookout shouted from the masthead, "Another sail! Port astern!" and the young officer raised his glass with a puzzled frown. Squinting into the blinding glare, he managed to make out the two raked masts of a Baltimore-built coasting schooner. If either vessel flew colors, it was impossible to make them out in this light.

"Whoever she is, she's moving to overhaul the lugger, Mr. Hames. As you were, with the signal to heave to. I want one shot across her bow. If she doesn't put about at once, the second shot is to sweep her cockpit."

Mr. Hames, an older man with less important family connections in naval circles than his captain's, shot a nervous look out to sea; there the governor's flagship rode at anchor, clearly visible against the dark blue of the eastern horizon. Clearing his throat, Hames said, "They're not signaling from flag, sir."

His commander sniffed, "Of course they're not signaling. The commodore can't see what's going on over here. We're just a dark blur against the sunset from where he's riding, and as for the two little vessels between us and the shore, I doubt His Lordship knows they exist. I'm waiting for my orders to be carried out, Mr. Hames."

Hames nodded, went to the quarterdeck rail, and shouted forward, "Mr. Bridges, one warning shot from the

bow chasers across that lugger. Second shot to sweep cock-
pit aft the main."

Then he turned back to meet his amused young skipper's
stare with a wooden expression. The captain twitted, "Are
you afraid I don't know what I'm doing, Mr. Hames?"

."It had occurred to me, sir."

"Well, you're wrong. It's obvious the lugger is running
from the schooner. Hence, the people aboard one vessel are
for *us*, and those aboard the other are for *them*."

"That sounds reasonable, sir, but have you considered
that the rebels seem to be in control of the local colonial
government these days?"

"Of course I have. Why do you think we have His Lordship bobbing around out here instead of in his palace in
Savannah?"

"But sir, if the little lugger is running from Savannah
with another vessel in hot pursuit, might that not mean the
people aboard the first vessel are for His Majesty? I mean
to say, the Whigs have been hounding our people out of
their homes and—"

"You really have no imagination, Mr. Hames," the commander cut in with a smug smile, adding, "I'll admit I had
no way of being certain about the lugger when first we
spotted her out there against the sun. But her actions since
the schooner came into view have settled the matter once
and for all. She's a rebel."

"I'm afraid I don't understand, sir."

"No doubt that's why you're overage in grade, Mr.
Hames. I'll spell it out for you. Yon lugger is being chased
by another vessel, in full view of a British man-o'-war. If
she was on *our* side, she'd be headed our way as fast as her
little sails could carry her. Do I have to draw you a picture, for God's sake?"

Hames nodded, red-faced, and said, "You're right, sir.
Do you want chain or bar shot fired into her as the guns
bear?"

Tacking northeast, west of the British fleet offshore,
Rory and the hastily assembled rescue party aboard the
Cherokee Rose had the sun at their backs; hence, the lug
sails of the *Spanish Dancer* as well as the buff-and-black
hulls of the ominously looming British vessels were sharply
readable against a dark blue eastern sky.

A string of fluttering colors had risen to the yardarm of

the H.M.S. *Corgie,* and Rory asked the nearest crew member what they might mean. The sullen and unwilling deck hand answered, "Orders to heave to, Colonel. If that lugger tries to slip between the *Corgie* and that reed swamp to the north—"

There was a sudden blossom of smoke, pinkish salmon in the low sunlight, and as the dull report of a fired cannon rolled across the calm waters of the harbor, he added, "See what I mean?"

Rory felt the tilt of the deck shift under him and he ran back to the helm, asking the planter at the wheel, "Why are you changing course, Watson?"

"That Goddamned ship is firing on us! We've got to put about!"

Rory shoved him away, took the spokes of the wheel, and yelled loud enough for all to hear, "They're not firing at us. They're firing at our children! Have you got that swivel loaded, Lawyer Margolis?"

From the bow, only fifty feet away, Rubin Margolis called back, "Loaded and primed, Colonel, but it's only a half pounder. I hope you don't intend to shoot at anything larger than an Indian canoe!"

Before he answered, Rory put the helm hard over, swinging their bowsprit out to sea. Then he called to Margolis, "I'm cutting across the *Corgie*'s stern. Be ready to rake her when I give the order!"

A mutter of amazed protest swept the length of the schooner as Margolis ran aft, wig and shirtsleeves in disarray, to protest, "You can't be serious! Putting a half-pound ball into that monstrous hull would be like attacking an elephant with a pin!"

Rory said, "More like a mosquito taking a man's mind off what he originally had in mind, I hope. The *Corgie*'s sails are reefed, and she rides at anchor. Her crew can turn her on her keel by hauling on the anchor springs, but it's a slow weary business and—"

There was another puff of pinkish white, and this time, as the sound reached them across the water, a tall gout of water rose just a few yards from the stern transom of the lugger *Spanish Dancer.*

Rory snapped, "Ay, they're shooting to kill now! Man your post, Margolis. For you'll do as I say this minute, or you'll never see any of our sons alive again!"

"This is madness!" sobbed Rubin Margolis even as he

ran forward, a pudgy parody of a swashbuckling rebel privateer, with the bravery only the desperate can ever know.

The other planters, Whig and Tory, took their places for what every man aboard knew was a hopeless farce. More than one longed to turn back, but, afraid as any man might be of a British cannon, the fear of what his neighbors might say about him was stronger, and what might they say of a father cowardly enough to desert his own son?

A tiny puff of white blossomed near the top of the lugger's mainmast, and a man near Rory shouted, "One of those lunatic young whelps just fired a musket from the tops! If I find out it's my Algernon, I'll tan his hide!"

The H.M.S. *Corgie*'s bow chaser coughed again and another father groaned, "Oh, Jesus, they put a bar shot through the foresail! A third of the canvas is gone, and the *Spanish Dancer*'s losing way!"

Rory shouted back, "Ay, but she's near out of range and making for the shelter of yon point with nightfall coming on fast. Have you got your swivel bearing, Lawyer Margolis?"

"I have, God help us all, but what do you want me to aim for? That stern is like the side of a barn at this range!"

Rory glanced over at the black bulk of the H.M.S. *Corgie* as he took the schooner in at a forty-five-degree angle. Men aboard the *Corgie* were aware of their approach, of course, and the transom rail was lined with gaping crew members. One officer in a cocked hat was peering at them with a brass spyglass, and another man was waving a pair of signal flags at them. Rory asked a crewman of his own vessel what the royal signals were, and the worried merchant seaman answered, "They're ordering us to heave to and show our colors, sir."

"What kind of colors do we have to show them, then?"

"We've all kinds, sir. The *Cherokee Rose* makes a lot of ports up the coast. We generally fly the red ensign of the British merchant, save when putting into New England waters."

"What do you fly for the Yankees?"

"The pine tree, Colonel. That's the one the rebs surrounding Boston generally fly."

"You have one in the flag box?"

"Ay, sir, but we're right under the stern guns of a man-o'-war!"

"Run it up. That's an order. Can you hear me, Lawyer Margolis?"

"I hear, I hear! What do you want, you crazy bastard?"

"We've taken their attention off the lads for the moment. I'm going to see if I can't keep them busy a mite longer. When I give the command, fire up into those glass windows under the stern rail. We can't hurt them enough to matter, but I want a lot of broken glass and plenty of smoke, so—"

An orange-centered cotton ball materialized against the looming black bulk of the H.M.S. *Corgie*. Rory just had time to think, "The bastards didn't wait to see our colors!" and then the shock wave and a spinning bar shot reached the cockpit at about the same time.

The lethal bar shot was a yard-long twisted bar of wrought iron with a ball at each end. It flew like a boomerang, cutting a wide swath of destruction as it ploughed through rope, timber, or human flesh and bone.

The one that hit Rory took a four-foot length of planking out of the bulkhead before bouncing off the deck, cutting both Rory's legs off at the knee joints, and flying, screaming, over the far rail. Rory dropped on his bloody stumps, dully surprised, but still clinging to the wheel and holding the *Cherokee Rose* on course.

Rubin Margolis had fired his puny swivel gun as the second stern gun put another bar shot through the foresail over his head. Margolis hadn't been aiming. The swivel gun was a small cannon mounted in what looked like an oar lock and was primitive to aim, but with luck or the instinctive skill of a born duck hunter, the paunchy lawyer put a half-pound ball right between the eyes of the young British skipper, whose head then exploded in a frothy red cloud that rained blood, brains, and confusion all over the British quarterdeck.

The stern guns of the H.M.S. *Corgie* fired again, but only after a fatal delay that had allowed the little schooner time to scoot shoreward, out of range. By this time Margolis and the others had propped the dying Rory up in one corner of the blood-spattered cockpit, and as two men fought to stanch the bleeding, Margolis took Rory's hand and soothed, "We *did* it, Colonel! The lugger's out of sight beyond the point. We'll all be safe ashore in a few minutes."

Rory opened his eyes dully and murmured, "I hear singing, or is it shouting? Lots of people, shouting in the distance."

"That's from the shore, Colonel. Half the town is down at the waterfront to cheer us. Do you know what we just did, sir? We just fought Georgia's first naval battle, and, damn me, I do think we might say we *won!*"

Rory chuckled deep in his throat and said, "Och, at most we didn't lose, but in the end that's all any man can hope for. How bad are my legs, Margolis?"

Nobody answered.

After a time, Rory sighed and said, "As bad as that, eh? I thought I felt them go before it all went numb down there. Will you do me a favor, Lawyer Margolis?"

"Anything, Colonel."

"Get rid of my litch quietly, so that Indigo Hall won't be tainted as rebel property. I feel the life draining from my head, but if I'm still breathing when we reach the shore, you can cover my face and—"

"Don't be absurd, Colonel Martin. You've just become a hero to our cause. There's a guard of honor waiting for you ashore!"

"I've been a hero before. Listen to me, old friend, for I hear the keening of the gray piper in the wind, and it's the wisdom of a dying man I'm leaving you—"

"I'm listening, Rory. Tighten that left tourniquet, damn it!"

"It's all a great cruel joke, Margolis. Leave off the heroics and let the fools fight for the crumbs the Laird and the devil, between them, drop to the floor for us. I've fought as hard as any man for the cumbs I've gotten, and in the end, what do I have to show for it?"

"Come now, you're a respected planter with a fine family and loyal servants and—"

"Jesus, you're as great a fool as myself," sighed Rory. Those were the last words he would ever say, but as he closed the dead man's eyes with gentle fingers, Rubin Margolis was composing the dying speech they'd want to record for Georgia history.

Another man came over and, standing above Margolis, asked, "Is he?"

Margolis nodded, and the man said, "Funny, we thought he was a Tory. You know Lem Turnwall and the Nevens brothers, over to the crossing?"

"I know them. They're the lads who tarred and feathered that Tory minister and his wife last month, aren't they?"

"Ay, Turnwall's a caution when it comes to patriotism. Anyway, Lem and the other pony boys have been talking about the Martins over to Indigo Hall. I reckon, between young Simon running off to join the Continental Lines, and the colonel, here, fighting it out with a British man-o'-war, the pony boys won't be burning Indigo Hall out after all."

Margolis nodded, getting to his feet with a sardonic smile as he stared at the shouting crowd on the shore they were rapidly approaching. Then he glanced down at the mangled litch at his feet and, shaking his head, marveled, "I just don't understand it. Even when you kill them, men like Rory Martin manage to find the advantage in it somehow!"